HISPANIA

HISPANIA

Book I, The Middle Empire

CONN HALLINAN

Ballingarry Press

First Printing, 2023

PAPERBACK ISBN: 979-8-9874240-0-1
EBOOK ISBN: 979-8-9874240-1-8

1. Fiction—Historical. 2. Fiction—Ancient Rome. 3. Fiction—Roman Spain. 4. Fiction—Rome, Middle Empire period.

For information refer to: https://middleempireseries.wordpress.com/
or write to: ballingarrypress@gmail.com

To my father, Vincent Hallinan, who insisted I read Edward Gibbons' *The History of the Decline and Fall of the Roman Empire* when I was a high school sophomore.

Characters in Hispania, in order of their appearance

Marcus Favonius Facilis, centurion (Pilus Prior, 2nd Cohort, Legion XXX Ulpis Victrix)
Demaratus, signifer
Flavius Priscus, optio
Titus Flavius Domitianus, Flavius's cousin in the Praetorians
Postumus-Gallineus, prefect of the vigiles
Quintus Pompeius Falco, legate of Rome's vigiles
Sextilius Germanus, tesserarius VII Legion in Tarraco
Publius Felix, tribune VII Legion in Tarraco
Antonius Crispus, centurion Third Century, 10th Cohort VII Legion, Tarraco
Androdamas, clothing merchant
Telamon, clothing merchant's son
Domitius Celer, optio in charge of training in Tarraco
Coventina-Celto, Iberian woman in Tarraco
Gnaeus Antonius, centurion, Ist Cohort, VII Legion
Manius Petreius, tesseraius of the Ist Cohort, First Century
Vallerius Tullius, retired centurion in Tarraco
Timotheus, Greek doctor for the First Cohort
Julius Dasumi, wealthy merchant in Corduba

Aelia Dasumi, Julius's sister
Clodius Petreius, head of the Corduba merchant council
Sextus Aelius, tesserarius, Second Century, First Cohort
Cleomanes, Cretian archer officer
Tiberius Granius, merchant spokesman in Emerita
Cassius Cornelius, cavalry officer, Ala II Flavia Hispanorum
    Romanorum
Fabricius Tuscus, senior Magistrate from Norba
Arrius Granius, wealthy Decurion at Capera
Tiberius Porcius, Decurion ally of Arrius at Capera
Titus Valens, legate VII Legion at Legio
Quintus Junius, tribune, VII Legion at Legio
Manlius Valeranus, senior Optio in Legio
Cassius Dentatus, junior Optio in Legio
Spurius Annius, headquarters Tesserarius at Legio
Julia Aquillius, Marcus's sister
Tiberius Favonius, Marcus's brother
Mamercus Favonius, Marcus's brother
Sabina Aquillius, Marcus's niece
Lucius Aquillius, Julia's husband

Contents

Prologue

249 A.D.

It is 300 years since Julius Caesar conquered Gaul and made it one of Rome's wealthiest provinces, but once again the Empire's legions are fighting desperate battles in the dense forests of the north. Victories no longer signal the end of a war, but instead presaging future wars. The myriad tribes Rome once defeated so easily or manipulated have banded together in great confederations that contend almost as equals on the field of battle. While the Empire strains to hold back the floodtide of Goths and Franks pouring across the Rhine and the Danube, fierce Parthian horsemen press on Rome's eastern borders. Assailed from without by invasion, the Empire is shaken from within by inflation and political upheaval.

The year 249 AD is the heart of the "Middle Empire," that period between the conquests of Julius Caesar and the last stages of the empire. "Hispania" opens in the fourth year of the reign of the Emperor Philippus "The Arabian," who seized power following the murder of Emperor Gordian III, who in turn had become emperor following the murder of Maximinus. From the reign of Caracala (211-217 AD) to the Emperor Diocletian (284-305 AD), Rome will have 12 emperors. All but two die by violence, five by murder. Civil war becomes the norm. Rome is still immensely powerful, but a careful listener might hear the first whispers of decline and fall.

"Hispania," follows the lives of its three principal characters. Centurion Marcus Favonius, the younger son of a politically ambitious family, is fleeing the enmity of the Praetorian Guard that has marked him for assassination. Optio Flavius Priscus, Marcus's second in command, is a street fighter from the tough slums of Rome. Demaratus is the centurion's third in command, a former sailor from Athens, and a man with a keen sense of history and an outsider's view of the empire he serves.

Pursued by the Praetorians, the three flee to Hispania, only to be caught up in the complex politics of Rome's oldest and richest province.

As instability grows and trade declines, the Empire shifts from conquest to defending its borders, and the once all-powerful Roman economy begins to falter. For hundreds of years, Rome's economy had depended on the millions of slaves captured through war. But by the Middle Empire those days are a distant memory: The era of cheap slaves is over and, as slaves grow increasingly expensive, slavery's inefficiency and instability accelerate.

In 249 AD, Hispania was a land of vast mineral wealth, and Rome's oldest and richest province. It was here that the empire began. It is here that Rome first confronted an enemy as powerful as itself: Carthage. It was here that Caesar defeated Pompey in the civil war that ends the Republic. And it was here that the western empire makes its last stand.

Hispania was also home to one of the most interesting units

in the Roman Army, the VII Legion Hispania Gemina Pia, the legion that is the centerpiece for this book. The VII Legion, the oldest serving legion in the Roman Army, had an unerring knack for picking the winning side in a civil war.

I

In a momentary respite from the clinging Roman summer, a soft breeze stirred the curtains, flickering the shadows cast by the oil lamps. Marcus stirred as well, uncomfortable and restless in full armor. The breeze died, and the room grew still again. He had been sitting in a chair facing the double door to the street for more than three hours, occasionally rising at imagined sounds.

But they did not come.

He had expected the Praetorians hours ago, ever since his brother had sent word that things had gone badly in the latest political power struggle. The Emperor Philippus was rumored to be gathering forces to confront the usurper Gaius Quintus Decius, commander of the Pannonian legions somewhere to the north of Rome. Marcus's brothers and sister had a bad habit of backing the wrong side-in this case the previous Emperor, Gordian III—which these days could get one killed. A flood of resentment washed over him. He was minding his business, doing his duty, but because his family thought they knew a shortcut to power and wealth, he was going to die.

He calmed down and considered what he was about to do. He had carefully arranged the encounter with the Praetorians. They would arrive, pound on the door, demand entrance, smash their way through if he did not answer, and cut him down in his own house. He would not make it simple for them. The Praetorians were skilled at murder, their usual targets soft politicians or has-been warrior emperors. He would see how they fared against a real soldier, not a civilian offered up to the butchery of political intrigue.

He had donned his chain armor, greaves and senior centurion harness, with its decorations, torques and phalarae. He looked around his house. He had not seen it for three years, but he still felt affection for it, particularly his pillars. The front door had a tiny upper porch flanked by two pillars. It was the pillars that drew him to the house in the first place. Private houses simply did not have pillars, which is why the house stood out. They were not much as pillars went, just plaster over fill, but they tapered nicely from top to bottom, and were painted the same red as the broad stripe that covered the lower quarter of most Roman houses.

His friends and family kidded him about the affectation, calling it "Marcus's Pillars of Hercules," but he paid them no mind. He could afford the house on his centurion's pay.

He would miss the pillars.

But the pillars would serve him this night. They constricted the entrance to the door, which would prevent the squad of eight Praetorians—he expected nothing less than a full contubernium

—from using their superior numbers. He allowed himself a wolfish smile: they would find that assaulting a narrow front defended by a determined enemy could be an expensive undertaking. He would not go unaccompanied to the Elysian Fields.

Rome in August is an uncomfortable place even without full armor. The sweat poured off him, soaking his sandals and forming a small puddle under the chair. For a while he wore his helmet with its high, transverse crest, but the sweat from his forehead blurred his vision, so he took it off. Then put it back on. Then took it off.

The breeze off the Tiber stirred again, cooling him for a moment, allowing his mind to slip into another time and place.

The Legion XXX Ulpia Victrix had moved up toward the Rhenus in early summer, pushing back against the Franks who had overrun several forts northeast of Confluentes. Scores of homesteads and small towns scattered near the border of Northern Gaul had been attacked and burned. The Legion, based at Augusta Treverorum, had marched east to Tabernae, then turned north to Boudobrigo. Its orders were to punish the raiders and to retake the western border of the river.

Even though it was early summer, the weather had turned cold—in Marcus's experience Northern Gaul was always either wet or cold regardless of the season, and he was having quiet doubts about the worth of shedding blood over it. His tribune, a young Senate hopeful, issued him impossibly vague orders— the man had neither sense nor seasoning—and told him to "do his duty for the Empire." Marcus politely saluted. As the Pilus Prior, the first among the centurions of the 2nd Cohort, he was responsible for passing on the tribune's orders—such as they were—to the other centuries. He held a brief staff meeting with the other five centurions, and then deployed the cohort, spacing out the six centuries of 80 legionnaires apiece.

The tribune had requested cavalry, but they had not come and Marcus was not unhappy about it. He was no fan of either horses or cavalrymen, and thought both were mostly useless in the close forests of the north. Even though the men who rode them were no longer members of the wealthy equestrian class, they still thought of themselves as a cut above the infantry, which annoyed him.

The real reason he disliked cavalry, however, is that he disliked horses, a sentiment the animals returned at every opportunity. He had stopped counting how many times he had been thrown, bitten and stepped on by them, and he was irritated by anyone who rode well or liked the stupid creatures.

The cohort had passed through a burned-out villa in the early morning, its embers still hot. A scatter of bodies, all men, had lain in the inner atrium where the inhabitants had made a last stand. He ignored the bodies and moved the cohort into the forest beyond. The Franks could not have gotten far, particularly since they had taken the women and children with them.

He put out a screen of light auxiliary troops to warn against ambush.

They vanished into a forest that seemed to inhale the light. A ground mist clung to the dips and depressions in the woods. He had deployed two centuries in the front line, two behind those, and two bringing up the rear.

In order to cover a wider front, each century was formed in

three, rather than four, lines. The first line was strung out for some 150 feet, the second 10 feet behind them. Behind his second line was a mixed troop of archers and slingers. In order to keep in contact with the century to his left, he had placed himself between the two lines rather than in the front rank. He was particularly concerned about his left flank. The centurion who commanded the unit was a young, political appointee who had never seen war.

The troopers were quiet, moving gingerly through stands of dark pine, trying to keep their lines intact. He watched a Greek slinger load his weapon, swinging it back and forth. The man was slight—he looked more boy than man, but it was hard to tell with Greeks—and watchful. The man passed a comment to a Thracian slinger next to him and both slowed their pace, allowing the second line of legionnaires time to move ahead and give the two slingers a better field of vision. Marcus's second-in-command, Flavius, glared at the exchange, pointing his iron-tipped staff at them. Until the century closed with the enemy, silence was the rule.

The attack seemed to explode from the woods, smashing into the century on his left. A shouting clot of men swinging long swords and battle-axes had risen up out of the trees and mist and fallen on the century's front line. Marcus watched three troopers go down, disappearing into the undergrowth. His first thought was that he would flay those light auxiliary troops alive, then realized that they were probably already dead.

"Tighten up," growled his optio, and the soldiers automatically moved closer together, shields three feet apart.

Marcus's first instinct was to wheel his century and go to the aid of the century under attack, but he held his center in place. The attackers were making too much noise, and the assault could be a feint. The left century finally stiffened, although the Franks had made a dent in the front rank.

Then the main attack struck, directly in front of him. Silently a great mass of Franks smashed into the center of the century, driving it back. Swords and battle-axes rang against shields, and once the battle was joined, the attackers shouted, some biting their weapons and shields in battle madness. There was a moment when it looked as if the line would crack, but it held. The attack had come so quickly that many of his soldiers had not been able to hurl their heavy pila, using them instead as lances. Others dropped their spears and drew their swords. The century's front line gave ground slowly.

One enormous Frank, swinging what looked to Marcus like an iron tree trunk, broke through, cut down the signifer holding the century's standard, and came directly for Marcus. He gripped his shield, looking for an opening.

Out of the corner of his eye he saw the Greek step through the second line of legionnaires and whip his sling forward, already reaching for another lead missile. The German staggered from the blow, and Marcus quickly lunged forward, driving his gladis sword at the man's chest. It cut through the man's leather armor, slicing a deep wound on his left side, but the huge German roared, yanking the sword out of Marcus's hand, throwing him off balance.

Ignoring the sword wound, the man raised his enormous weapon to strike. Once again, the Greek slinger struck, and the German staggered.

Marcus looked desperately for his sword but couldn't find it in the chaos of battle and undergrowth. He snatched out his pugio, but if the sword had failed to stop the attacker, he couldn't see how his dagger would have much effect. It would not need to. A legionnaire from the second line drove his pilum into the German's chest and the man went down.

The front line was holding. Now his men were shouting, and a trumpeter was sounding the cornu. The initial shock had shaken the century, but discipline and training were reasserting themselves, and the Franks began giving ground. Suddenly they broke and ran.

"Hold," cried Marcus. He had seen this tactic before. The troopers would break formation to pursue, and a counterattack would catch them scattered and strung out.

He ran his eye down the lines. He had lost men, not a lot. The Franks had lost men too, but no more than a dozen. They had melted away as soon as it was clear the cohort was too powerful to overrun. He doubted they would renew the attack, but he signaled the centurion to his left to stay alert. Like most of the battles in the north, it was short, ugly, and indecisive.

He dropped the two leading centuries back and waved the others forward to pursue the Franks and try to recover the captives. His own men were already fashioning rude litters to move the dead and badly wounded to the rear. His optio, Flavius, came forward and reported on the causalities—three dead, two badly wounded, four others with minor injuries.

The optio was turning to re-organize the century when Marcus remembered the slinger. "Flavius, bring me that slinger, the Greek."

"Yes, sir," said Flavius, and strode to the rear. Soon the young Greek appeared. On closer inspection, the Greek was not so young, though his boyish looks and slim build gave him the appearance of youth. The man saluted and waited for Marcus to address him.

"Your name?" asked Marcus.

"Demaratus, sir," the man answered.

"Well, Demaratus, that was a fine piece of work you did with your sling. I would be on one of those litters were it not for you," said Marcus.

"My duty, sir, to my cohort and my century," the man replied.

"There is duty and there is being good at duty, which are not the same," said Marcus, smiling.

The Greek smiled back. "I haven't used a sling in many years, sir. I am glad I have regained my former skill."

"How do you come to be here, Demaratus?" Marcus asked.

"I am a sailor by trade, sir, a cargo master. But our ship was wrecked near Burdigala and I took a job with the auxiliaries for food and shelter. They said they needed slingers," he answered.

Marcus stared at the man a moment. "A cargo master? You can do figures and books?"

"Yes, sir. That was my primary job," said the Greek.

"Flavius," called out Marcus and waited until the optio reappeared.

"Optio, this is Demaratus. It turns out that not only can he wield a sling, he can do books. We are suddenly bereft in that department," said Marcus.

"Sir?" asked Flavius, and then caught himself. "Right. Yes, sir, we are. Lucius didn't make it."

The fact that Marcus and Flavius were so casual about the death of the signifer, Lucius Fannius, was a measure of how they felt about the man they had inherited when they took over the First Century. Lucius's incompetence with the unit's payroll and expenses was matched only by his ineptness as an officer. Marcus felt relief, not sorrow, at his death.

"We need a signifer who will stand fast, Demaratus, but also one who can do our books. Do you think you can handle that job?" asked Marcus.

"Yes, sir," said the Greek, saluting. "I am honored."

"Our optio will instruct you on your duties, Demaratus. I want all my officers for a staff meeting this evening," Marcus said, dismissing the two men and turning to a messenger from the centuries that had gone forward in pursuit of the Franks.

The Franks had slipped across the Rhenus taking their captives with them. The savage little battle in the forest had been a delaying action, and a successful one at that. The cohort stopped at the banks of the river. To cross it with anything less than a legion—indeed, several legions—would be suicide. Legions had crossed that river before and never returned.

The cohort pulled back, burned their dead and garrisoned some forts in the area.

Marcus saw an immediate improvement in the unit's books, and the Greek seemed to be fitting in fine. Flavius said there was some grumbling that the signifer position should have gone to a man from the regular ranks, rather than the auxiliaries, but as no one from the century could read, write and figure well enough to do the job, the grumbling gradually subsided.

Marcus was sitting in his tent constructing a letter to his niece Sabina, trying to give her a flavor of the battle but glossing over the details. Sabina was deeply curious about all things foreign and plied him with endless questions about Britain and Gaul, and strange food and the army. He was not sure he should encourage a young woman's interest in the army—she should be thinking about weaving—but Sabrina's curiosity was infectious and he enjoyed her company and the letters she regularly sent him. These were filled with gossip and startling insights about the family and current conditions in Rome. Sabina was a smart and a careful observer. Not much got by her.

As he was finishing the letter, a clerk brought by a sack of mail for the century, including a scroll with an army seal: orders from Rome.

Marcus turned the scroll over in his hand. It was unusual to receive orders directly. Normally they would go to the Principia, and headquarters would pass them down. He broke the seal and quickly read the short paragraph. He was being re-called to Rome for "reassignment." There were no explanation or details. A reprimand? He thought not, though he quickly reviewed his actions over the past several months. Nothing merited discipline; indeed, he had won two awards for valor.

He looked at the orders for a long time. There was no hint of anything amiss in his brother's most recent letter, although everyone knew Rome was complex and not a little dangerous.

But a reassignment was hardly cause for alarm. In the old days an officer stayed in his legion until he was mustered out, but the army was under a great deal of pressure just now. Invasions threatened Dacia, Greece, and the east, and his legion had just beaten back a raid from the north. Experienced officers were being moved around to train and command new troops. He assumed that the reassignment would put him into a green legion that needed experienced leadership.

But the feeling of uneasiness did not go away.

He sent a clerk to fetch Flavius and told him to prepare for the journey. On the spur of the moment he asked, "What do you think about taking our Greek, optio?"

Flavius shrugged. "It is no harder to travel with three than two, sir. He is fresh to the century, so I doubt he will be missed much until it comes to payday."

Marcus considered for a moment and then said, "We'll take him. Tell him we are traveling light."

"Yes, sir," saluted Flavius and left to warn Demaratus and start pulling together what the three men would need for the next three weeks.

Flavius had a deep foreboding about the orders. Rome was not a place one wanted to be right now. Since the death of Emperor Severus Alexander, there had been two emperors—both murdered—and a civil war. Rumor had it that the current emperor, Marcus Julius Philippus, known as "the Arabian," was marching the II Legion Parthica toward Beroea in the north to intercept Decias and the Pannonia legions. Flavius did not think the Arabian's chances were all that good.

He also knew that Marcus's family supported the previous Emperor, and choosing the wrong side these days was dangerous.

Flavius found Demaratus going over the century's rolls and told him to gather up what he would need.

"Short notice," remarked the signifer.

"Rush and wait, signifer, that's the way of the army," Flavius replied, and left to draw rations and what little equipment they would need for the journey south.

The three men had ridden south to Mogontiacum, where they chartered a small river craft to take them down river to where the Rhenus turned east. From the river's bend they rode southwest to pick up the Rhodanus River, which took them all the way to Massilia on the Mare Internum.

It was a rich, well-farmed country through which they passed, with sprawling manor houses and miles of tilled fields. Towns gave them regular shelter when the river put into ports. Otherwise, they slept on deck and ate the sailors' fare, which was considerably better than army food. It took them less than a week to reach Massila.

Flavius and Demaratus would have preferred to take a small coasting vessel to Rome's port at Ostia, but Marcus insisted on going the rest of the way by horse.

Flavius had served with Marcus for almost a decade and knew about the centurion's distaste of horses and his vulnerability to seasickness, and he figured that the choice to go by land was an indication that Marcus was more afraid of the sea than of horses.

But the choice of conveyance had little to do with the centurion's likes and dislikes. Marcus was no less aware than Flavius of the dangers Rome posed in these times. The disquiet he felt when he got his orders still troubled him. He needed to think and welcomed the week it would take them to reach the capital.

If Marcus was choosing horses over the sea, he did so with great care. Every day the three men would exchange their horses for fresh ones at an army depot. Hours were spent picking the "right" horse—which was invariably old and slow—for the centurion.

But even at a sedate pace, the miles rolled away. The three took the Via Dominata to Genua, where they picked up the Via Aemilia Scauria to Pisae. From Pisae the Via Aurelia Nova ran straight to Rome, passing the River Allia, where the three stopped to rest after crossing a bridge over the river. Near the road was an ancient monument commemorating the legionnaires who had fallen here in their failed attempt to stop the Northern Celts from sacking Rome. The inscription was almost obscured by 500 years of weathering.

Tracing the writing with his finger, Marcus remarked, "Rome endures."

"Aye," chimed in Flavius. "Now Rome rules the world, and where are the northern Celts?"

Demaratus said nothing.

Six days after they left Massilia, the three breasted the hills to the northwest of the capital. The huge city sprawled out before them, topped with the Capitoline Hill.

Demaratus was excited, Marcus preoccupied, and Flavius worried.

Flavius knew that Marcus would offer to house the two men, which, given what the optio was planning, would not be a good idea. Flavius had spoken with Demaratus at Cosa, ordering him not to accept an offer to stay with the centurion. If he did, Flavius said, there might be unpleasant consequences, which Flavius would explain after he had a chance to find out more about the situation into which they were headed. Demaratus had already figured out that their trip south was not just a reassignment, but that some sort of intrigue was afoot—and he nodded agreement. In any case, as Flavius was Marcus's second-in-command, the signifer had little choice.

When Marcus made his offer to host the two, Flavius begged off with the excuse that he had to stay with his family, although he had no intention of doing so. Even a social visit could put his relatives in danger. Demaratus said he had an aunt in Rome whom he had not seen since he was a child. Since the Greek had never mentioned he had a relative in Rome, Marcus gave him a quizzical look, but was preoccupied enough not to press the issue.

Flavius and Demaratus saw Marcus to his modest domus, with its odd-looking pillars, in the Campus Martius section of Rome, then made their way to the southwest quadrant of the city. On the way, Flavius told the Greek just enough about what was worrying him to keep him wary of idle conversation, but not enough to alarm the man.

Flavius got them rooms at a small inn near the Probi Bridge, just behind the immense Honrea Galbana warehouse. When Demaratus left to do some sightseeing, Flavius set out to look up his cousin, Titus Priscus Domitianus, an optio in the First Cohort of the Praetorian Guards.

Like virtually everyone in the regular army, Flavius had no love for the Praetorians, and resented their privileges in pay and shortened service requirements. While Flavius had to do 25 years in the army, a Praetorian's service was up after only 16 years. But he suppressed his resentment. He needed a favor and there was nothing to be gained by giving his cousin a bad time about being a Praetorian.

Taking a small bundle of fresh linen with him, he headed for the huge Caracala Baths to think things through and to look his best for what he knew would be a long day. Storing his clothes on a shelf in the dressing room and tipping an attendant to watch them—not that anyone would contemplate stealing an officer's clothes—he oiled his body and scraped off the dust and dirt with a bronze strigil. As he moved from a long soak in the hot baths to a plunge in the cold pool, a plan began to form.

In the end, the summons to Rome might come to nothing, but Flavius had not survived the challenges of Rome's tough, working class insulae by assuming that things would go his way. The optio had no illusions that he could fathom the convoluted politics of the Empire, but he understood power and violence. Rome was all about power and violence these days.

Marcus's family was addicted to power and that could be dangerous when emperors seem to come and go with the seasons. Marcus's family had been supporters of Gordian III, whose murder brought Philippus to power. With another usurper marching on Rome, the new Emperor might have decided to eliminate his enemies on the home front, and the Favonius family would likely be among them.

If Marcus was a marked man, so were he and the Greek. In these times the circle of death that followed the Praetorians' ire was wide, and growing wider. Saving Marcus's life was saving his own.

How he would manage this was a good deal trickier. What he was contemplating would try every social skill he had, and require a substantial quantity of good luck as well. He automatically said a brief prayer to Fortuna, promising her a substantial sacrifice if he was still alive in a week.

Somehow, he had to arrange for orders sending Marcus, Demaratus and himself to someplace other than Italia. But first he had to find out what the enemy was up to and how their forces were deployed. His cousin might be useful in this regard.

Leaving the baths dressed in his uniform and fresh linen, he set out for the huge Praetorian camp on the northeast edge of the city. Rome was spilling over with people; merchants hawking wares from carts, tabernas selling everything from wine to jewelry to pigeons. This was the Rome Flavius knew, the one he grew up in. Passersby shouted up at the residents of the crowded insulae that overhung both sides of the street. A middle-aged man prepared to read the Acta Senatus aloud to a crowd, while a young child—probably his daughter—held out a small bowl for donations. Slaves carried bundles of goods or shopped for their masters' food. Others marched by in chains, watched over by bored-looking legionnaires. One group of municipal slaves were prying up a manhole cover and preparing to clean the sewers. The smell of garlic, olive oil and fried meat, mingled with sweat and a faint odor of human waste, hung over the streets like an invisible tapestry.

With the Palatine Hill on his left, topped by its huge, sprawling palace and enormous temples, Flavius made his way through a traffic of ox carts, wheelbarrows and slaves carrying litters of the wealthy, until he reached the confluence of the Quirinal, Viminal and Esquiline hills and the walls of Praetorian camp loomed before him. The camp was enormous because the

Praetorian Legion was 9,000 men, almost twice as large as a normal legion.

The sentry at the gate glanced at his uniform and harness and asked his business.

"I am just back from Gaul and looking for my cousin, Titus Priscus Domitianus. He is an optio in the First Cohort. I thought someone here might know his whereabouts," Flavius said, looking properly respectful. Having to look respectful to a junior was galling, but with Praetorians, necessary.

The sentry gave him a once over, and waved him through.

Normally, the First Cohort would have been housed just inside the gate on his left, but Flavius was not certain which century Titus was assigned to, so he headed for the principia, the administrative heart of the legion. Again, he presented himself to the sentry and was waved inside to the tesserarius, the duty officer. He repeated his request to the harried tesserarius dressed in a resplendent uniform that must have cost half a year's wages. Well, regular army wages, Flavius thought.

But the tesserarius looked at the orders and bravery awards on Flavius' harness and saluted him. "Titus Priscus is with the fourth century, sir. You will find him in the middle barracks back the way you came," he said.

Flavius thanked him, pleased with the "sir." He was superior to a tesserarius, but who knew with Praetorians?

As he headed back toward the gate, his cousin emerged from the barracks.

"Titus," Flavius called out.

Flavius liked his cousin, though the two had not seen each

other for over six years. They had grown up together in the insulae and covered one another's backs on occasion. They embraced.

"Optio in the First Cohort. Well done, Titus, " said Flavius.

Titus was friendly, but guarded. He did not ask why Flavius was in Rome. "He knows," Flavius thought to himself, and for the first time since he arrived in the capital, a chill went through him.

"Come, cousin. Let me buy you lunch and we can drink to your promotion," said Flavius, putting his arm around Titus' shoulders. "You can catch me up on your family. Did that pretty sister of yours ever get married? I heard your brother was in Pannonia. What have you heard from him?"

Titus hesitated, then shrugged. "Sure. There is a decent place near the Castrensian Amphitheater."

The two passed the sentry—who snapped to attention this time—and talked and gossiped all the way to the small tavern. Flavius ordered bread, oil, cheese, and grilled fish. "Now we want Muria, not Garum," Flavius told the young slave, ordering the best fish sauce. "Bring us some Rhodian wine as well," he added, "not that thin, sour stuff from Baetica."

It took the better half of an amphora of good wine before Titus began to loosen up. After about a half-hour of gossip and reminiscences, Flavius decided to come to the point:

"Titus, my cousin, I need some help. You and I have always stood together. Remember when those Tillus twins tried to steal your father's leather working tools and we gave them a good thumping? They left us alone after that, right?"

It was Flavius who gave the Tillus twins a thumping. He was bigger and stronger than his cousin, although the years had filled in the latter. Praetorian food and easy living will do that to a man, he thought. The story would remind Titus that while the two did indeed support one another in the old days, it was Flavius who had played the role of protector. Titus owed him more than just the blood they shared as cousins.

"What did you have in mind?" asked Titus warily.

"What have you heard about my centurion?" asked Flavius. "Are we in trouble?"

By including himself in the situation, it would make it much more difficult for Titus to feign ignorance.

His cousin stared down at his cup for a good half minute, then looked up at Flavius. "I have heard a rumor that there is an order out to arrest the Favonius family," said Titus.

Flavius had a flash of anger, which he quickly suppressed. Titus could have sent word to him. But then, Titus had no idea where he was. The anger was unfair.

Both of them knew that an arrest order in the hands of the Praetorians was a death sentence. The story would be that the subject had resisted, attacked the arresting party, and had to be subdued. There would be no questions.

The two men were silent for a bit. "They will get me as well," commented Flavius.

Titus nodded. "What will you do?"

Flavius thought a moment. "Who is commanding the vigiles these days?" he asked.

"Quintius Pompeis," answered Titus. "Didn't you serve with him in Britannia?"

"Aye, we did. Marcus won a Corona Vallaris from him fighting the Ordovices near Viroconium."

Titus considered the matter for a moment. "But I am not sure what good he can do you," he said. "The vigiles is not the army."

"But Quintius Pompeis is a legate, and army or not, the vigiles is seven cohorts of a thousand men apiece," said Flavius.

Titus demurred. "Seven thousand police and firemen, not soldiers."

"True," Flavius agreed, "but Quintius Pompeius is rumored to be amassing enough sesterces to buy himself a senatorship and command of a legion."

"Well, making money is what the vigiles is about," said Titus.

Command of the vigiles, or the "watch," was a plum. Unexplained fires plagued areas of the city that did not "donate" to the vigiles. Generous bribes meant that the police actually focused on stopping crimes as opposed to enforcing the myriad of municipal codes that could make a businessman's life miserable.

"Well, it won't hurt to try to see if he can help, since I would rather not consider the alternative," said Flavius.

"Good point," said Titus. "I know his prefect. Postumus Gallineus. He is a cousin on my wife's side. Not a bad sort." He hesitated, then took the plunge. "You can use my name. But you need to move quickly."

Titus might have just signed his own death warrant, and the two of them knew it. "I couldn't have better blood than you, cousin. I won't forget this," said Flavius.

Flavius paid the bill and took leave of Titus. He knew where the headquarters of the vigiles was—he and Titus had spent some time there getting a proper thrashing for various infractions in their youth—and an optio uniform should get him in the door without scrutiny.

Postumus Gallienus had been a tribune under Quintius Pompeis when Marcus and Flavius had served with the legate in Britannia.

The vigiles sentry saluted him as he strode through and he went straight to the duty desk. "Is Prefect Gallienus in residence?" he asked.

The duty officer looked at his uniform and harness, and asked, "Who should I say wishes to see him?"

"Tell him an old comrade from Britannia wants a word with him," said Flavius, deciding not to use Titus' name unless it was essential. He was certain that Postumus would not remember him, but he had exchanged a few words with the man in the ceremony awarding Marcus the Corona Vallaris, so at least in theory he could say he was an old comrade.

The duty officer disappeared down the hall, then reappeared and beckoned Flavius to follow him, directing him to an office.

Postumus looked up, went blank, and then frowned. "Do we know one another?" he said somewhat coldly.

"We did, sir," replied Flavius. "You pinned this Corona Aurea on my harness after you awarded my centurion the Corona Vallaris for taking a hill fort from the Ordovices." Postumus had not actually pinned the award on him, but Flavius was banking on the fact that he wouldn't remember, and that, if he did, he would think it rude to deny the story to someone who had been awarded an Aurea for killing enemies and holding his ground.

"Of course," Postumus said after a moment's hesitation. "I remember the Corona Vallaris. I believe it was the only one awarded that year. The centurion's name was"----he paused, remembering---"Marcus Favonius. What can I do for you?"

This was the moment. Flavius was not one for fancy maneuvers or nuance. The only way this was going to work was for him to appeal to the regular army's natural dislike of the Praetorians. He took a deep breath.

"Marcus Favonius needs your help, sir. The Praetorians are after him, sir, not for anything he has done but because his family couldn't keep its nose out of politics. He has served the empire for 15 years, sir, and is just back from fighting on the Rhenus. It's not right, sir. I appeal to you as an honorable member of the army and a former comrade," said Flavius.

He had rehearsed the words on the way to the headquarters, and they came out in a rush.

Postumus stared at him for almost a full minute, then sighed. "Times are complex," he said quietly. "And you know the vigiles is not the army, and that the army has no jurisdiction in Rome."

"Yes, sir, I know that," answered Flavius, "but the warrant is not public and I don't even think it is official. Legate Quintus Pompeius still has the power to assign soldiers to other places, places a long way from Rome."

Postumus smiled thinly. "Have it all figured out, have you, optio," he said.

"No sir, I am flat over my head," replied Flavius. "I just don't know who to turn to but my comrades."

Flavius gave himself a pat for an artfully done line. It would appeal to the prefect both as a member of the army, and a former comrade.

Postumus stared at him. "Such an order could put more than the centurion and you in danger," he said.

"I know that sir, but there doesn't have to be record, does there?"

"And if you get caught?" asked Postumus.

"We will swear we forged the whole thing, sir. And since there won't be a record, that is plausible, don't you think?" said Flavius.

"What happens on the other end when you show up with the orders?" asked Postumus.

"I figure good centurions are in demand these days, what with the Franks, the Carpi, and the Goths pounding on the borders, sir, and that anyone would be happy to have someone like Marcus," he said, adding again, "sir."

"You and Marcus?" asked Postumus.

"Yes sir, and his signifer, sir," replied Flavius.

"Why not Marcus's whole extended family," said prefect, acidly.

"Sorry, sir. The man is a Greek who saved his life in Gaul. Brought down a German the size of a tree with a sling, neat as you could wish, sir," he replied.

Postumus considered for a moment. "Wait here," he said. "I promise nothing."

"Thank you, sir," replied Flavius.

Flavius stood at attention until Postumus left the room, and then started shifting from one foot to the other. Finally, he began pacing back and forth, glancing at the door. It seemed like hours before he heard footsteps coming toward the room. He quickly shifted to attention, saluting Postumus as he came in the door carrying a folded wooden tablet. After returning the salute he handed it to Flavius. "I fancy you will like the weather where we are sending you better than northern Gaul," Postumus said. "Report to the VII Legion in Tarraco. Luck be with you, optio."

Flavius saluted. "Thank you, sir, and thank the legate. We are forever in your debt."

"You are indeed, optio," replied Postumus. " I would move with dispatch if I were you. My greetings to Marcus."

Flavius saluted smartly and left the vigiles headquarters. For the first time since arriving in Rome he was feeling hopeful that they might actually pull this off. But first things first. Transportation was the next problem. Traveling by road was out. There were half a dozen guard posts from here to the port of Ostia, and Flavius knew better than to show these orders unless it was absolutely necessary. The orders were genuine enough, but they included the names of Marcus and himself. Demaratus was simply titled "signifer." Those names might jog some Praetorian sentry's memory. It would be best to slip out without having to show anyone anything, and hope the orders worked when they arrived in Tarraco.

The solution was the river, so he headed for the bridges on the west side of the city.

He had already decided that the Agrippa Bridge would be safest because it was isolated from the bridges that fed the city's center. Below the bridge were several small craft that moved people up and down the river. One boatman was working on a tiller and Flavius nodded to the man. The man stopped his work and nimbly jumped to the stone causeway beside the river, wiping his hands on a piece of leather.

Flavius quickly negotiated passage to Ostia, adding extra so the boatman could hire an ox team to pull his boat back up river to Rome after dropping them off.

From the Agrippa Bridge he headed south along the banks of the river, toward the Portus Aemila.

Gangs of slaves announced the river port. Most were carrying or hauling carts filled with barrels and amphorae of wine and oil, bundles of Egyptian cotton, and stone and marble for the city. Like most non-household slaves, they were closely guarded by soldiers. The slaves looked exhausted, thin and worn out. They were many.

Flavius presented himself at the port master's office and asked about ships heading west from Ostia. There were few, because it was late summer, and the winds would soon turn contrary. But there was a seagoing ship, the Isis, just finishing loading a cargo of lead and glass headed for Tarraco at next noon's tide.

"The ship's master is loading cargo right now," the port-master said, pointing to a long barge tied up in the river. Slaves were piling bundles and pigs of lead on board.

Flavius thanked him and headed for the barge where he found the captain seated under a small awing drinking wine and making notations on a small scroll. The man was short, broad, and not overly friendly.

"We don't have accommodations for passengers," the captain said. "My crew sleeps on deck."

Flavius smiled. "Beats swamps in northern Gaul," he said, assuring the captain they would be no trouble and paying the man a premium for the passage.

"Noon tomorrow," the captain told him. "The Isis ties at the south mole of the Harbor of Claudius. Don't be late. We sail when the tide is right."

Flavius promised him they would be on time and headed back to the Inn to talk with Demaratus.

The optio's decision to include Demaratus had been spur of the moment. The Greek was smart, and since their escape would be by sea, Demaratus's skills as a sailor might be useful. On the journey to Rome, Flavius also discovered that Demaratus spoke several languages. Flavius himself was not well educated and had no desire to go beyond what he needed to be an officer in the army. But unlike many in his station, he was not defensive about his own ignorance, nor contemptuous of learning. If they were going to survive the next couple of weeks, it would be by brains and guile, not strength. The Greek was smart. He would serve.

Flavius made his way back to their lodging to await Demaratus's return.

II

"Sir?"

Tribune Antonius Clodius looked up from his desk at his secretary, Aulus Nonius, standing at attention. The boy was slight, appearing even younger than his years. He was a smart lad from a good family, but he would never be a soldier. Of course, the problem with Rome these days, the tribune thought, was that the Empire had all too many soldiers and not nearly enough smart, young lads.

"Yes, Aulus?" he answered.

"They are here, sir," replied Aulus.

Antonius leaned back in his chair. "What do you make of them, secretary?"

Aulus looked startled by the question, which was not one a tribune of the Praetorian Guard would normally ask a being as lowly as a secretary. But Antonius Clodius asked disconcerting questions on a regular basis. Aulus considered what he was going to say, and then ventured, "They are not a pair I would like to meet after dark, sir"

Antonius grinned. At least the boy had a sense of humor and knowing the men of whom he was talking, a discerning mind. "Indeed, they are not, Aulus. Send them in, but I want to see you directly afterwards."

"Yes, sir," said Aulus and vanished through the office door to the outer waiting room. Moments later there was a knock.

"Come in," said the tribune, rising from his chair. Two men entered, saluted smartly and stood at attention. Antonius slowly looked the two of them over. He was familiar with the service records of Lucius Mallius and Sextus Aqullius, if you could call it "service."

Lucius was a great hulking beast with a scar on one cheek. The man was a sadistic bully, widely feared and hated in his cohort. In form, Sextus was his opposite: thin and rangy with eyes that shifted from Antonius, to the room, and back to Antonius. Both men had just been released from the Praetorian prison, Lucius for beating a member of his century almost to death, and Sextus for cheating at dice.

Antonius sighed. Had the times come to this? That a tribune of the Praetorian Guard would be employing these two scums of the earth? Well, times were what they were.

"Lucius Mallius and Sextus Aqullius," said the tribune, staring at the two of them. "You have been found guilty of crimes that merit either death or a life sentence to work in the marble quarries. Do you have anything to say for yourselves?"

Lucius blinked, trying to absorb the words. Add stupidity to the rest of the charges, thought Antonius. Then the hulking Praetorian began to protest, "The other fellow started it, sir, I was just defending myself. His contubernium mates lied, and..."

"Shut your mouth," snarled Sextus. "The tribune didn't ask us here to hear you whine."

"Why are you here, Sextus?" said Antonius quietly. Sextus might be a cheat, but he was not stupid, and this was not a job for a stupid person.

"Because you want us to do something, sir, and whatever it is, we are your men," Sextus replied.

Have I become so obvious in my old age, thought Antonius, or is the dishonorable period we are living through so all-consuming that even two thugs like these can see that their "talents" might be useful? He would take a long bath when this matter was over.

"There is a service you can perform for your legion and emperor that can wipe your record clean," said Antonius. "Do you wish to consider it?"

"We honor our legion and our emperor," replied Sextus. "We will carry out whatever service you order, sir."

That the thin legionnaire could utter the words "honor" without gagging at least suggested that the man had an iron constitution.

"You are not 'ordered' to do anything," replied Antonius. "I have a task that must be carried out quickly and quietly."

Lucius blinked again, not following.

"Certainly, sir," replied Sextus. "What is the nature of this task?"

The Tribune reached into a desk drawer and withdrew a small scroll. "There are two names and one unnamed person on this scroll. It is the emperor's wish they be eliminated."

"Yes, sir," said Sextus. "Is that a warrant?"

"It is not," replied Antonius. "It is a list. You will find the address if one of the men on it. This man is a centurion in the XXX Legion. The other name is his optio. The third person is the centurion's signifer, but I have no name for him. He is, however, a Greek."

"I don't like Greeks," rumbled Lucius.

"Quiet!" hissed Sextus, and Lucius retreated into a glowering sullenness.

"I think we can handle that, sir. How soon would you like this to happen?" asked Sextus.

"Tonight," replied the tribune. "And you will leave your uniforms here."

"What if we are caught?" put in Lucius, finally catching the gist of the conversation.

"That is not my problem, legionnaire," replied Antonius. "But I strongly urge you not to be caught. The consequences for you will be most distressing."

Sextus saluted. "Sir, you can count on us."

The tribune wondered whether counting on men like Lucius and Sextus would preserve the Empire or accelerate its demise. Well, he had his orders and now these two had theirs, and if the pillars of Rome trembled as a result, the Gods willed it, though in fact he didn't think the Gods cared a whit.

"Dismissed," said Antonius, which brought the two men to attention and sent them marching out of his office. He sat back down in his chair. Murder. And not murder of some conniving politician, but murder of two decorated soldiers who had spent their youth defending the borders of the Empire. A wave of depression swept over him.

There was a knock at the door.

"Come in, Aulus," he said.

The secretary entered and saluted. "You wanted to see me?" he asked.

Antonius considered the young man. He was an efficient secretary, bright, hardworking, and with that rare quality that makes such staff members indispensable—the ability to anticipate. But could he keep his mouth shut?

"The two men who just left my office?" said the tribune.

Aulus frowned and shook his head. "Two men, sir? What two men?"

Antonius gave him the ghost of a smile. Good lad. He would go far. The tribune shook his head, "Nothing, Aulus."

"Yes, sir. If there is nothing else, I will return to my work." He saluted and left.

When the door closed, Antonius rose, went to a small sideboard and poured himself a cup of wine. "And so is honor served," he said to himself, downing the cup in a single swallow.

III

The pounding had been going on for some time before it pulled Marcus back from his memories of northern Gaul.

They were here.

He was momentarily confused, reaching for his sword before he realized he had been holding it all the time. But the pounding cleared his head, and he rose from the chair to face the door. He would meet them on his terms, not theirs. He would smash into them; throw the squad off balance and take down as many as he could. He would then fall back and defend his door. He took a deep breath. Life was complex, but he was fond of it. He regretted leaving it. Gripping his sword, he grasped the handle of the right side door. Flinging it open, he threw himself at the men in the street.

He had expected a full squad, but there were only two and both were putting their hands up as if to surrender. At the last second, he turned his sword thrust aside, but unable to stop his momentum, he slammed into the man standing in front of the door, sending him sprawling onto the stone flagged street. The second man ducked behind a pillar.

"Centurion, it is Flavius and Demaratus," said the man on the ground, then added, incongruously, a formal salute: "Ave."

Marcus looked at them blankly, wondering for a moment if they were his assassins, immediately rejecting the idea.

"Flavius, what are you doing here, and come out from behind the pillar, Demaratus," he demanded.

Flavius climbed to his feet, started to speak, stopped, straightened his helmet and uniform and pounded his heart with his right fist. "Centurion Marcus Favonius Facilis. I have orders from Quintus Pompeius Falco, Legatus Augusti."

Demaratus stayed behind the pillar.

"Orders?" Marcus asked.

"Yes sir," said Flavius, and handed Marcus a thin, folded wooden tablet, sealed with red wax.

Marcus took it, looked at it for a long minute. He was having trouble shifting back into a world of orders and subordinates. "Orders," he repeated blankly.

He broke the seal and unfolded the tablet, skimming its contents, looking for the signature. Quintus Pompeius had been his commander in Britannia. At least it was not a summons that could only end in a dishonorable execution. He would fall on his sword long before he would answer an order like that.

"We are assigned to Hispania, Flavius and Demaratus," he said, "but it appears the Gods have other plans for us."

Demaratus was never certain what the Gods' plans were, except that they usually bode ill for those in their power. He had also observed that the Gods had a system: they favored big armies over small ones (they made an exception on occasion for the Greeks) and showered wealth on those who figured out how to earn it. The Gods helped those who helped themselves.

In a cursory way, the signifer believed in Zeus, and the others —in particular, Athena—but most of all he was a firm believer in realism, common sense, and self-preservation. A Roman would never stand behind a pillar, but there were a lot of Romans getting killed these days.

"There is a boat waiting for us near the Agrippa Bridge, centurion," said Flavius. "It will be a quicker trip than by horseback."

Marcus shot him a searching look. Marcus liked to believe that no one knew of his dislike for horses, when virtually everyone in his century knew that the Pilus Prior hated horses and would gladly march 20 miles a day to avoid mounting one. This quirk made him popular with the average trooper, who had to march the same 20 miles, albeit carrying 60 pounds of equipment, plus weapons, armor, and shield.

Flavius' face was expressionless, which Marcus suspected hid a good deal, but he let it slide.

The optio added, "There is a ship leaving for Tarraco on the morning tide, centurion. A ship will avoid . . .," here Flavius searched for words that would convey the need for both speed and stealth without letting his officer know that the three of them were frankly on the run, ". . . a long and tedious journey."

But there was no need for Flavius to be diplomatic. Marcus had long ago worked this out. A land journey would give the Praetorians or their agents a much greater opportunity to assassinate him. Marcus was no admirer of ships—they disagreed with his stomach—but if he wanted to live, he would have to take to the sea.

And he wanted to live.

Marcus reentered the house and quickly gathered a small bundle of clothes, and a purse filled with gold. He was tempted to take some scrolls and a few treasured things but resisted. Baggage would slow them down. Within less than half an hour they were headed for the Agrippa Bridge and the small boat that awaited them.

Demaratus, who had trailed behind the two men as they made their dash for the river, was not sure what he was doing clambering on board the small vessel headed for Ostia. Only a few hours before he was packing up his belongings and preparing to get out of Rome as quickly as possible. He bore Marcus no ill will. Indeed, he liked the genial centurion, and he enjoyed his new job as Marcus's signifer. The pay was higher, the food was better, and the work a good deal easier. But Marcus's family appeared to have made the wrong choices in politics. Of course, he had to admit, that was also dangerous in Athens, his home city.

Following his discussion with Flavius north of Rome, Demaratus had decided that a trip home, or even to Syria, might be a good idea and he would have been on his way but for the appearance of Flavius, just fresh from the docks, at his bedroom door. The optio caught him as he was rolling up a few belongings and stuffing them into small pack.

"You are making a mistake," said the optio.

To Demaratus, the essence of Rome was not the Palatine Hill, the massive architecture, or the huge aqueducts. It was men like Flavius.

The optio's face was broad and flat with a nose that at some time in the past may have been large, but had been broken so many times it was simply a smear in the center of his face. He was not particularly tall, but he had massive arms and legs and a chest that seemed to start under his chin and run down to just above his knees. Demaratus had seen Flavius flatten men twice his size. The optio could also drink more than the entire century. In short, he was what Greeks thought all Romans were: barbarians.

"Look, Flavius, I understand your loyalty to Marcus and Rome. You have served with the man for years. But I am just a signifer, and it really isn't my fight," said Demaratus, continuing to put the last items into his pack.

But Romans could surprise you and just when you thought you had them figured out, they did something unexpected.

"I don't give a rat's ass for Rome, and I have no intention of falling on my sword for anyone," Flavius said. "Our centurion is a winner, even when things look hopeless. I have seen him do it scores of time. Just when you think he is finished he pulls out a victory. I like you, Demaratus, and right now you are a marked man. Wherever you go, they will get you. Your best chance is with us."

Demaratus was unbalanced by Flavius's line of argument. He had expected "honor," "loyalty," and "courage," and instead he was getting something Greeks always paid attention to: the odds. It appealed to him.

"What's your plan?" said Demaratus.

"I've got orders that send us to Hispania. Lots of Greeks in

Hispania, Demaratus. All we have to do is catch a boat at Ostia that will take us to Tarraco," said Flavius.

Demaratus silently corrected Flavius—Iberia, not Hispania. Tarraco was not his favorite city, and, while grand, had none of the grace of the Greek trading port of Emporion. But Flavius was probably right. The Praetorians had a long reach, and if Demaratus left he would be alone in the fight.. He finally nodded. "What do we need to do?"

The next several hours had been a blur, and now they were boarding a small boat headed for Ostia.

As the small river craft slipped its moorings, Marcus re-read his orders. He was being assigned to the VII Legion Gemina Hispania Pia at Legio in the province's northwest. He searched his mind for what he knew about the VII Legion. Even though he considered himself a bit of a military historian, it was not much. The VII was an anomaly because it had spent virtually its entire existence in Hispania. It was the general rule to assign legions to areas far from the place it had been recruited. Yet the VII was composed almost entirely of native Hispanians.

The emperor Galba had formed the Legion back in 68—its nickname was the Galbiana—and the following year it had fought with great courage at Coemina, when Antonius Primus had defeated the Vitellian forces in the civil war.

The VII was so mauled in the fighting at Coemina that it was merged with another legion—hence the name "Gemina," or "twin"—and served shortly in Gaul and Pannonia. But it was quickly returned to Hispania, where once again it chose the winning side in the civil war that brought Septimius Severus to power in 197. While many of the great families of Hispania supported Clodius Albinus, the governor of Britannia, over Severus, the VII had stayed loyal to Severus, earning the title "Pia," or "faithful," when it was all over.

The VII Legion Gemina Hispania Pia had a knack for picking winners.

Marcus had not paid attention to the military situation in Hispania, although he knew there were restless tribes in the west and northwest, and raids from Mauretania Tingitana had recently plagued the south. He also knew that the provinces of Tarrocoensis in the east and Baetica in the south were rich, with powerful local families that played a key role in the politics of Rome. Emperors Hadrian and Trajan, among the greatest in the history of the Empire, were from Hispania.

Well, we will see what the Gods bring, he thought.

Marcus shifted his thoughts, feeling a certain shame about the way he had left Rome, and a good deal of apprehension about what was happening to his family. He finally put that aside. If he had stayed, he would be dead in a week. His four brothers and sister were survivors. They would figure out some way to avoid the ire of Philippus. In any case, there was nothing he could do for them anyhow.

He considered his optio in the bow of the small boat. Flavius had once again saved his life. He had done so on at least three other occasions, including when Marcus had been awarded the Corona Vallaris for "first over the ramparts" of a Welsh hill fort. He was first over the wall, and then found himself in the middle of a dozen bloody-minded Ordovices who would have done for him had not Flavius thrown himself into the middle of the

Celts. Flavius won a Corona Aurea for that. Marcus believed he should have been awarded the coveted Corona Civica for saving his life, but that was an award the army would not likely give to a second-in-command.

He opened the orders and gave them a more careful read. They looked perfectly correct unless someone questioned Quintus Pompeius's authority to make such an assignment. Quintus was a legate, but a legate of vigiles, hardly regular army. But the man had fought with honor in several different theaters, and his wealth and influence were on the ascendancy. If no one questioned the right of a vigile legate to reassign the three officers, the orders would stand up. It all depended on whom he reported to in Tarraco.

The presence of the Greek frankly surprised him. He had made Demaratus his signifer because the man had saved his life in northern Gaul. One did not look for loyalty in Greeks. Intelligence, guile, courage, yes, but always for a profit. Well, was that a whole lot different than Romans these days?

Flavius and Demaratus were a startling contrast. Flavius had the rough-hewn looks and gait of a Roman street tough. Demaratus was slight, lithe, with clear features and short, curly hair. Marcus imagined that he must do very well with women. What he did not look like was a legionnaire.

Marcus pulled the cloak around him, suddenly chilled by the uncertainty of the future.

Demaratus watched Marcus gather his cloak around him. Flavius said he was a winner, and the Greek had a grudging respect for the opinions of the street-wise optio. Anyone who could weather the slums of Rome, and 15 years in the Roman army, had to have a good feel for survival.

Marcus didn't particularly look like a winner, although Demaratus had difficulty with the way Romans looked in general. They were built wrong. Their faces were too round, their noses too prominent, their torsos absurdly long, and they had little, short, thick legs. A true-to-life statue of a Roman was simply incapable of looking elegant.

The centurion was of average height and pudgy, with a broken nose and soft, brown eyes, neither handsome nor ugly. If the man had character, it was the inside kind, and Demaratus would wait to make that judgement.

At Ostia, the river craft turned into the Trajan Canal that linked the Tiber to the inner Harbor of Trajan, the latter built with the booty of the Second Dacian War, and then to the outer Harbor of Claudius. The merchant vessel was tied up at the southern arm of the harbor.

By the time they reached the ship it was mid-morning, and they quickly transferred their belongings on board.

The merchant vessel shipped no oars, so it had to be towed out to the harbor's entrance by smaller boats until it could hoist its square mainsail. When the ship cleared the two embracing arms of the harbor, Demaratus finally relaxed. At sea, he was home.

IV

⧓

Sextus and Lucius were drinking in a small taverna a short distance from the Forum of Augustus. They had been drinking since they left the Praetorian headquarters in the late afternoon. Sextus nursed his wine, but Lucius drank down cup after cup.

"Enough," said Sextus. "This is not some fat merchant we are after. This Marcus is a centurion, and he might have his optio with him. Drunk you are useless to me."

"Then why are we sitting in this taverna instead of getting on with it?" slurred Lucius.

Lucius sober was an asset, Lucius drunk was an encumbrance, thought Sextus. He should have anticipated that the dumb ox would drink too much, but the two of them had needed a place to lie up until the night deepened. He had no intention of going up against this centurion, and maybe his optio, when they were awake and ready. But bringing Lucius to a tavern was clearly a bad idea.

"Because we need them to be asleep before we try this," whispered Sextus. "Come on, we are getting out of here."

"Wait, we haven't finished our wine," protested Lucius belligerently.

"Shall I tell you what they are going to do to us if we fail?" hissed Sextus. "They will ram a hot poker up your ass and burn off your cock—slowly. And that will be just the beginning."

Lucius sat back, a little more sober.

"Would they really do that, Sextus?" he asked.

"You have no idea what a Praetorian torturer can dream up, Lucius, so we are leaving, and you are going to sober up, right?" answered Sextus.

The huge Praetorian lumbered to his feet, nodding his agreement, and the two left the tavern and headed toward the Tiber bridges, Lucius staggering a bit as he followed Sextus.

Despite the darkness, the house, with its two odd looking pillars, was easy to pick out. Sextus and Lucius sat and watched it from a nearby fountain, but they had not seen anyone go in or out, and no light gleamed from under the door.

"They're asleep. Let's go kill 'em," whispered Lucius. He was considerably more sober than when he left the taverna, but his breath was still heavy with wine.

The big man's impatience irritated Sextus, but he had to admit there was no reason not to make their move. They were each armed with a gladis sword, a pugio dagger hidden under their capes. Sextus rose and led the way down and across the street to the front door. Tentatively, he pushed on the door, and it swung open.

The thin Praetorian quickly stepped back, sensing a trap,

but the door remained ajar, and there was no sound or motion from inside.

"Dumb bastards left the door open," whispered Lucius.

"Maybe. Maybe they are waiting inside. Let's take it careful," said Sextus. He slowly pushed the door open and stepped into the front hall. The house was silent, with not a glimmer of an oil lamp. The only light in the house came from the moonlight that streamed through the central atrium. "Something's not right," whispered Sextus.

Both men crouched, alert in the hall for several minutes. Finally, Sextus touched Lucius's arm and pointed toward rooms that led off the hallway. The two crept down the hall, quietly pushing open each door, but it was too dark to see. Sextus finally retreated to the front hall, searching until he found a lamp with a tallow candle. It took a few more minutes to locate a flint lighter.

With lamp in hand, they returned to their quest. Carefully at first, then with mounting frustration, they searched the house room by room.

"Looks like our birds have flown the coop," said Sextus, sliding his sword into its scabbard.

"They might be out," said Lucius.

"Did you see a uniform?" asked Sextus.

"No, but they could be wearing them," replied Lucius.

"Maybe. We wait until dawn," said Sextus.

"If they don't show, what do we do?" asked Lucius.

"We find out where they went and go after them," said Sextus.

"How do we do that?" asked Lucius.

"Isn't there a Titus Priscus in the First Cohort?" asked Lucius.

"I dunno," said Lucius.

Sextus considered his partner for a moment. It was likely that Lucius would forget his own name if someone didn't call roll each morning. Well, we work with what we have, he thought.

"I think we will tell the Tribune that he should talk to this optio," said Sextus

"Then what?" asked Lucius.

"Then we go hunting," answered Sextus.

V

The Isis was built wide—too wide, in Demaratus's professional opinion, more like a bucket than a ship—and she was none too well handled. The crew seemed disorganized in getting underway, and kept checking with the captain for orders rather than using their own initiative. He caught the captain looking in his direction. Demaratus had long ago discovered that while the Romans were dreadful sailors, they were inordinately sensitive about it and just having a Greek on board was enough to make the captain feel criticized. He ought to feel like that, thought Demaratus. The mainsail was a patchwork of fabrics which he couldn't imagine holding up in any kind of serious blow, and the two triangular sails above it looked like they were made out of castoff clothes. Ropes and lines littered the deck instead of being properly tied down.

His thoughts on the faults of Roman maritime skills were interrupted by a deep booming sound. Glancing back over his shoulder toward Ostia, he froze. A huge quinquereme, its banks of oars kept in cadence by a drum at the warship's stern, was just getting underway. Like all Roman warships, it was an ungainly, ugly craft, with none of the clean lines of a Greek trireme.

It sported a tower forward that would hold archers when the ship went into battle, and it had a great corvis tied up to its mast. The corvis, really nothing more than a broad plank with a spike at its end, had allowed the Romans to overwhelm the superior sailing skills of the Carthaginians in the first Punic War by simply turning every sea battle into a land battle. Drop the corvis on the enemy's deck and then board with armored legionnaires. It was the way the Romans typically solved all their problems: engineering and brute force. Of course, he had to admit, it worked.

The quinquereme was rapidly closing with the Isis, the warship's gleaming bronze ram pointed almost directly at them, its red oars glistening with sea spray. Demaratus saw that Flavius and Marcus had also stiffened. Had someone tipped off the Praetorians? Was the warship about to stop the Isis and put them under arrest? Demaratus eyed the slowly receding mole and figured that if they were boarded, he would slip overboard and swim for shore. He had no intention of fighting armored marines.

But the great ship kicked its rudders over to port and headed south, probably toward the naval base at Misenum. He noticed both Flavius and Marcus trying to appear unconcerned, just mildly interested in the sight of a navy ship. He caught the captain's eye on him, this time with a considered look in it. It was possible that the man was suddenly putting together several different threads: three officers traveling on a merchant ship; a hurried departure; the nervousness at the sight of a warship.

Add to that the political turmoil behind them and it wouldn't be difficult for anyone to add it up and figure out that the three were fugitives.

Demaratus gave the man a level stare and deliberately loosened his sagum cloak, exposing his short sword. The message was obvious: do something stupid and you won't be around to collect any rewards which might be out there. The captain looked away.

Marcus had caught the unspoken exchange between the captain and his signifer. He had had a moment of panic when he saw the warship looming up behind them and considered what he would do if the ship stopped them. His first instinct was to fight, but the marines would then likely kill everyone on board, including the captain and his crew. It was one thing to decide to go down fighting when it was just you, another when it jeopardized others. He was saved having to make the decision by the warship's course change, and he watched with relief as the great vessel swept across their wake and headed south.

When he turned his eyes inboard, he caught Demaratus in the act of freeing his sword from his cloak. His initial reaction was anger. If anyone on board the warship had been observing them, one of them reaching for a weapon was an immediate admission of guilt. But then he noticed that the Greek was not looking at the quinquereme, but the captain. Dematatus was telling the captain to mind his own business.

Marcus stifled a grin: he was being well looked after. Flavius had somehow gotten orders that put them a step ahead of the Praetorians, had arranged for the river craft and now this merchant ship. And here was his signifer warning the captain to watch his step. And I am supposed to be in command here, he thought.

Flavius had also relaxed and was pulling a hunk of cheese and some bread out of his pack. He raised his eyebrows and offered some to Marcus, but at that exact moment, the merchant ship slipped from the shelter of the outer harbor into the rollers of the Tyrrhenian Sea, and the centurion's stomach heaved. The image of the cheese and bread completed the circle of seasickness and with as much dignity as he could muster, he paced over to the downwind side of the ship and was violently sick to his stomach.

Flavius was careful not to look at the centurion. Marcus hated to appear undignified, but there was no way a person could maintain a sense of dignity while being seasick. Flavius understood that, but only in the abstract, since he never got sick himself, not even as a child.

He caught some tension between the Greek and the captain —the ship was small, so it was hard to miss any exchange—but figured that it didn't concern him and ignored it. Flavius's major worry was what would happen when the three arrived in Tarraco. The orders would cover them, but only if the authorities in Hispania didn't check with Rome. A request from Tarraco to Rome would take between two and three weeks, if ever, to get answer. As much as Flavius valued his own life and those of his companions, he had no illusions that any of them were particularly important or high up on some execution list. We are small fish, he thought, and we may slip the net.

But that would depend on Marcus. Thus far, the centurion had been uncharacteristically passive. Even his preparation for attacking the Praetorians was more an act of resignation than taking any initiative. He, Flavius, had gotten them out in one piece. (He reminded himself to make a proper sacrifice to Fortuna for granting his prayer.) But in Tarraco, Marcus would have to lead. The army would automatically look to the centurion, not his second in command, and certainly not a signifer.

That will happen or it won't, he thought, pushing it out of his mind and concentrating on the bread, cheese, and the darkening blue of the sea as the ship moved into deeper water.

Demaratus was doing his best to look calm, even though he was in a mild panic. The Isis (which he had dubbed "the tub") was heading due west, the route that would take it though the Straits of Bonifacio between the southern tip of Corsica and the north coast of Sardinia. Demaratus knew those waters and feared them, as any competent sailor would. At one point the channel was only seven miles wide, with a tangle of islands guarding the eastern entrance. If the wind was from the northwest, it could kick up wicked seas and fierce currents in the strait's shallow waters, which routinely smashed up ships and drowned crews. The passage was considered the most dangerous in Mare Internum.

Demaratus would have been concerned, even with a Greek crew; he was deeply nervous with a Roman one.

To forget his nervousness, he sought out Flavius. It was obvious that in his present condition Marcus would not appreciate company, nor was he certain how to go about initiating a casual conversation with a superior officer in any case. Flavius outranked him as well, but the two were co-conspirators.

The optio was sitting cross-legged on the deck, eating cheese and bread, which he offered Demaratus.

"Feeling right at home, are we?" asked Flavius.

"It is good to be at sea again," said Demaratus, omitting any mention of his reservations about whether they would ever see land again. "It is the journey's end I am not sure about."

Flavius was quiet, apparently wrestling with something. He is not sure either, thought Demaratus, which was hardly surprising. The next move will take skills and authority that the optio doesn't have, and this makes him nervous. He is not someone who tolerates feeling powerless very well, thought Demaratus.

"It will come all right in the end," mused Flavius, reaching for the cheese that Demaratus had taken from him. "When it's do or die, Marcus is at his best. He will see us through this."

Demaratus was not so sure. The centurion had let Flavius lead the way so far. But then, Flavius had known Marcus far longer than Demaratus had, and there was nothing much either Flavius or he could do at this point. Demaratus had long ago worked out the hierarchy of the Roman army and a signifer and an optio didn't count for much in the balance.

"So how come Greeks like the sea so much?" asked Flavius. "It seems to me they do rather well fighting on the land. That's how they beat up the Parthians, isn't it?"

Demaratus mentally replaced "Persians" for "Parthians," though in truth they were much the same.

"Not really," replied Demaratus. "It was Salamis which finished the great Xerxes."

"Salamis? What is Salamis? The Parthians got defeated at

Marathon and Plataea, after the Spartans softened them up at Thermopylae," said Flavius.

"You are well versed on the Greek wars, Flavius," said Demaratus, trying to keep the surprise out of his voice.

"Officers study battles, Demaratus. And those were big battles," answered Flavius.

How typical of the Romans, thought Demaratus, to rewrite history so it came out sounding like their own. The Romans always won on land, so the Greeks must have done the same. The Romans also tended to mix up the first and second Persian wars. Eleven years separated the Greek victory over Darius the Great at Marathon and the final accounting with Xerxes at Plataea.

It wasn't the mix-up that bothered Demaratus, however, but the reason the Romans ignored the great naval battle at Salamis, which had not only destroyed the combined Persian fleet, but also forced Xerxes to flee home. Plataea was won against a weakened enemy in flight. Salamis defeated the Persians at the height of their power.

The Romans ignored Salamis because it was a victory at sea and for the Greek underclass; poor, nameless rowers who out-thought and out- fought an enemy that had three times their number. Marathon! Everyone remembers Marathon because it was won by well-to-do, "decent" land-owning farmers, while Salamis was won by people like himself without money, land, or influence.

Of course, Demaratus had to admit, the Greeks weren't all that much better on the subject. Plato sniffed that Themistocles, the Greek commander at Salamis and Demaratus's hero, "had turned a nation of steadfast infantry into sailor rabble."

Demaratus decided to tease the optio a little. "Far-seeing Zeus grants to thrice-born Athena a wooden wall," he said.

Flavius squinted at him. "Would you mind explaining that little piece of Greek obscurantism to me?" he asked.

"It was the Oracle of Delphi's reply when the Greeks asked her how to defeat the Persians. The Spartans has already been defeated at Thermopylae. I suppose they did 'soften' the Persians up, but since the Spartans were all dead, who can say? In any case, the Persians marched through Attica and burned Athens. If they were 'soft' it wasn't obvious," replied Demaratus.

"So how does that explain the Oracle? Did the Greeks put up a wall?" asked Flavius.

"No," replied Demaratus, "but they rode in one."

Flavius narrowed his eyes again and said quietly, "An answer, signifer"—emphasizing the word "signifer."

Demaratus spread his arms to encompass the ship. "We are within walls of wood, optio."

Flavius frowned for a moment, looking like he was going to lose his temper, and then figured it out. "So ,Salamis was a naval battle?"

"Not 'a' naval battle, the naval battle, " responded Demaratus, "Far larger than anything you and the Carthaginians fought."

"Are you telling me a bunch of ships ramming each other was more important than Marathon?" Flavius asked.

Demaratus leaned forward, caught up in his own passion, forgetting for a moment that he was talking to a superior officer and a Roman at that. "The Persians lost 6,000 men at Marathon. They lost three times that many at Salamis, and when their fleet was destroyed, they had no way of supplying their army. It wasn't the rich and privileged that defeated the Persians, it was people like you and me, Flavius. Everyday people."

A sudden wall went up. "I am not poor and I am not 'everyday,' and I am not like you, signifer," said Flavius coldly. "I am optio behind a primus pilus centurion. And don't lecture me on war. I have forgotten more battles than you are ever likely to be in."

Demaratus recoiled, genuinely surprised by Flavius's transformation. The Greek had served most of his life on merchant vessels, where the line between officers and men was permeable, and where you could argue with a superior.

"Of course, sir, forgive me," said Demaratus stiffly. "If I have offended you, please accept my apologies."

He rose to go, but Flavius seized his arm. "Now look, Demaratus. In this army you get yelled at. It's just the way of the army. Don't take it personally, and don't go about sulking. You don't know a thing about me, and who I am is no one's business but my own. We clear?"

"Yes sir," said Demaratus, feeling angry and humiliated.

Flavius had surprised himself. He was not entirely sure why he had reacted the way he did, and normally he would not spend a lot of time examining his actions. But their situation was different. This wasn't just chewing out an underling. Right now, Marcus, Flavius and Demaratus were a century of three, and bad feelings among the three were potentially dangerous. At the same time, he had no idea how to repair it, or even if he wanted to. It was an unwarranted liberty on the Greek's part to assume that he and Flavius were the same. The Greeks had fought the Romans and the Romans had won. Greeks were smart, and he had nothing against them, but they weren't Romans. In the end they were no different than the millions of other people Rome had conquered.

He put it out of his mind. If he had been a little sharp, or even a little unfair, well, that's the way things are in the army and you just had to learn how to live with it. He snuffed the thinking part of him and watched the endless horizon of rollers, the slowly receding coastline, and the gradual turn of the day from afternoon to evening. He decided he liked boats.

Demaratus drifted forward, watching the spray break over the ship's high prow, rain bowing as it passed astern. He was deeply angry, angry with himself for allowing passion to let down his guard with a Roman, angry at Flavius for his arrogance, angry at the situation he now found himself in.

At the same time, he had learned not to let his initial reaction guide him. He felt dishonored, but dismissed the sentiment. The Roman was not dishonoring him, he was just treating him the way Romans—in particular, those in the army—treated everyone, including one another. His anger at Flavius was tempered by the fact that the optio had, by including him in the orders, probably saved his life. It was not the first time that his tongue got him into trouble. It was his anger at the division in Greek society between those who owned land and those who worked with their hands that had blinded him to the hierarchy in which he now found himself.

Thinking it through calmed him down, though he would not forget that wall.

Marcus struggled with his seasickness, staring fixedly at the horizon and trying not to look at the heaving deck. He had nothing left in his stomach, and the internal void helped clear his mind. He flinched from the idea that this would go on for six days, although his rational mind reminded him that he was unlikely to be this ill the whole time.

They were headed into a darkness much deeper than the slowly vanishing day. When he landed, he would go straight to the local garrison and hand in his orders. He would need to push without seeming suspiciously impatient. Thus far the weight had fallen on his optio. From now on it would be on Marcus. Three weeks from now they would be alive or dead depending what he did when they arrived in Tarraco.

Another wave of seasickness made Marcus consider that right now death would not be entirely unwelcome. Surprisingly, he still had something left in his stomach.

The winds were from the northeast and the merchant ship drove west for two days under clear skies and calm seas. Marcus had recovered enough by the second day to drink a little sour wine and water, and nibble at some bread. The captain announced that because the gods were clearly favoring them with fine weather and a wind on their quarter, the ship would bypass the port of Olbia at the north end of Sardinia, and push on through the straits.

Demaratus silently cursed the captain for his hubris. The gods rarely listened to prayers, he thought, but they never missed an opportunity to punish arrogance. "Foolish is the sailor who thinks he is in command," he said to himself, quoting, Aeschylus.

And sure enough, by midday the winds had shifted around to the northwest and began increasing in strength. This was the dreaded mistral that came off the Gulf of Leon, piling up water on the western end of the Straits of Bonifacio, creating powerful currents and dangerous seas. It was the wind sailors call "the widow maker."

Waves soon began breaking over the high bow and coming aboard, and crewmembers set to bailing. Flavius joined the bailers, as did Marcus, who looked white, drawn and unsteady. Demaratus joined them as well, but he really longed to give a hand with the sail or the tiller. Bailing was a job for landsmen, not sailors, particularly in a dangerous blow like this.

He moved aft where the captain was manning the tiller.

"I'm a sailor, sir. I can lend a hand with the rigging if you wish," Demaratus said, his voice rising to overcome the wind's pitch.

The captain hesitated—just what he needed in a bad sea, some Greek to criticize him—but his common sense won out.

"Take the starboard side and help take a reef in the sails," shouted the captain as the ship began pitching extravagantly in the heightening seas.

Demaratus worked his way to the windward side of the craft, where two sailors were attempting to reef the small, triangular sails above the mainsail. They were botching the job and one of them was entangled in the lines. He helped the man get loose and the three conferred briefly.

They decided to get the two triangle sails off and then to concentrate on the mainsail. The first took a few moments, but made little difference in the ship's behavior. The Isis was still leaping and plunging in the growing seas. The only thing to do was drop the mainsail lower on the mast, and then tie up the bottom of the sail to reduce the surface area exposed to the wind.

The men were sailors enough to recognize that the Greek knew his business. Greeks might be insufferable with their superior, know-it-all attitude about the sea, but they were handy when things got dicey, and both Romans were scared.

The mainsail bits balked, but Demaratus coordinated the work of the two crewmen and it eventually slid down a good ten feet. The three quickly tied up the bottom of the sail, and the ship's pitching and rolling immediately moderated.

The captain nodded his thanks, and the two crewmen staggered over to Demaratus to discuss whether they should further shorten sail. It was a dangerous moment. The ship was now in the mouth of the Strait, with islands to both side and currents ready to dash the Isis on the rocks and reefs that guarded them. Any major reduction in speed would give the currents the upper hand, and the Isis would be forced ashore.

On the other hand, the seas were growing higher and the wind was working itself up to a full gale. If the ship didn't reduce speed, it might put its bow into some slack wave and founder with all hands.

Not for the first time Demaratus cursed the Romans' naïve view of the gods. They believed the gods were beneficent, and if you said the right words and performed the right ceremony, everything would turn out fine. The Greeks knew better. The gods were petty and vindictive, and their major pleasure was reminding humanity of its mortality.

Demaratus worked himself aft again.

"Sir, I do not think the ship can withstand this storm on its present course. I suggest we set a sea anchor and ride it out," Demaratus yelled into the captain's ear.

He saw the captain hesitate. Setting an anchor to stern was not particularly difficult, but the ship would have to turn in these seas to present its stern to the wind. A moment of bad luck, a second of indecision, and they would all be dead.

He doesn't want to take the responsibility, thought Demaratus. He gave the captain an out.

"Sir, I have never set a sea anchor, just watched it done," said Demaratus. "But I have worked the tiller on other ships. I wouldn't be of much use either constructing the anchor or coordinating your crew, but I can steer the ship."

The captain shot him a searching look, but then nodded. "Watch out. The rudder balks when it turns to port," he said, and let Demaratus take the tiller. The captain staggered aft, calling the crew to help him assemble the sea anchor.

The tiller slammed into Demaratus, went slack, and attacked him again, like a thing alive. For a scary moment, the ship started to turn away from the wind, but Demaratus strained until the tiller caught hold and put the Isis's bow back into the teeth of the mistral.

Aft, the crew and the captain were pulling a spare spar onto the deck, fixing a cross tree to it, and wrapping the spars with an extra sail. Demaratus glanced nervously aloft at the main sail that he had dismissed so contemptuously back in Ostia, but patched or not, it was holding.

When the anchor was finished, the captain looked up. It was time.

The ship would have to be turned so its stern faced the wind.

The drag of the sea anchor would keep the ship's stern pointed into the wind, allowing them to ride out the gale. But turning the ship was enormously dangerous. If the Isis presented her side to the wind for more than a few moments, a sea would roll them over like a log and that would be the end of their story. Timing and judging the seas was the tricky part of this operation.

The captain pulled himself aft by the rigging lines and joined him at the tiller. "Once she begins to turn, she is quick in stays," shouted the captain, a statement that Demaratus found difficult to believe. But he had to assume the captain knew his own ship.

"I will handle the sails," the captain shouted over the scream of the mistral. Coordinating the tiller and sails would be crucial. The ship would have to show more sail to turn quickly, but if it showed too much, the winds would rip the mainsail to shreds in the middle of the turn and the waves would pound the Isis to pieces. If it didn't show enough sail, the craft would stall, presenting its broadside to the seas, with the same results.

Demaratus would have to look for a momentary lull in the waves that would give them enough time to complete the turn. He glanced forward where the captain and the crew were watching, noticing that everyone had their eyes on him, including Marcus, Flavius, and several crew members who were frantically bailing.

Demaratus needed to act soon. The ship was already feeling sluggish because the bailers could not keep up with the seas that were pouring in over the bow. Agnostic that he was, he said a short prayer to Athena, asking her to help him demonstrate the natural superiority of the Greeks to these Romans. That prayer just might work, he thought.

A huge wave broke over the bow, swamping the crew and running aft to swirl around his feet. But the sea also flattened just a bit in its wake. He signaled the captain and tugged the balky tiller to starboard. Slowly, but with gathering speed, the tub began to turn. The captain and two crew members hoisted the mainsail up about five feet, and the ship lay over as the wind caught the increased surface of the sail.

For a moment Demaratus thought it was too much sail, and that the force of the wind would bodily push them underwater. But in this case, the water in the hold that had made the ship sluggish at the beginning of the turn acted as a stabilizer and she came around. Out of the corner of his eye, Demaratus watched a huge wave approaching them, but the ship steadied onto its new course and the wave passed harmlessly under the stern.

The captain and crew lowered the mainsail again, and staggered aft with the sea anchor. Tying it securely to the aft rail, they hurled it overboard. Almost immediately the ship halted its lunges to port and starboard, with the waves passing under her stern rather than hammering the Isis's bow. The captain and crew returned to the mainmast and lowered it so just a scrap of sail showed, further moderating the movement of the ship.

The captain nodded him a salute, and a few crewmembers raised a cheer, which he waved away. More importantly, the captain headed back to spell him at the tiller and give him a rest.

The storm had pushed them backwards, out of the straits, so the ship now had some sea room on either side. They were headed back to Ostia, but the sea anchor would limit their eastward drift. Unless the wind blew for several days—almost unheard of at this time of year—they could now ride it out and then beat back toward Tarraco when the winds moderated.

Demaratus silently gave thanks to Athena and apologized to the tub. He decided she was much like her makers: awkward, but with surprising strengths. He worked himself forward where Marcus and Flavius were.

"Well done, signifer," said Marcus, using the formal title.

"Maybe I need to listen to this Salamis business," said Flavius with a grin.

Demaratus still felt the wall—after all, he had constructed some of it himself—but the comment helped to ease the tension between the two.

The Mistral blew for half a day while the crew and passengers of the Isis huddled against the bulwarks and bailed as much as they could. Sometime in the early dawn, the wind moderated and shifted around to the northeast. The sea anchor was dragged in and the mainsail hoisted a bit further up the mast. The seas were still worked up, but the wind was fair for the Straits, and the ship, battered and much the worse for wear, slowly made its passage through the dangerous waters. By mid-day the Isis was under full sail and making her way eastward in an efficient, if not graceful, manner.

Flavius again complemented Demaratus on his seamanship: "When you said cargo master, you might have said 'like Odysseus'," he said. "Who was that Greek who beat the Persians?"

"Themistocles," answered Demaratus.

"Right, well, like Themocles," replied Flavius.

Demaratus winced. Greek pronunciation tended to elude Latin speakers.

Marcus added that he would bring the Demaratus's actions to the notice of the authorities in Tarraco. Given the Roman army's low opinion of the sea and anything that floated on it, Demaratus couldn't see much coming of that.

For three more days the Isis drove steadily west, and Marcus gradually overcame his seasickness. In his mind it was replaced with a growing sense of tension about what awaited them in Tarraco. Early on the morning of the eighth day a crewman posted in the high stern called out "Land!" and the distant purple smear of Hispania rose on the horizon.

VI

Scipio Publius had constructed Tarraco to overawe. In the starkest way, it said: "This is the power and grandeur of Rome. Look upon its works, and tremble." A seaside amphitheater anchored the southern flank of the city's great harbor and Tarraco itself marched up the enclosing hills to an enormous temple at its apex.

The city, almost 500 years old, sat astride the strategic Via Augusta that led north to Massilia and Gaul, and then to Italia. One could ride a horse from Tarraco to Rome in a little over a week, not all that much more than a ship from Ostia would take.

It was the first Roman city in Hispania. Scipio and his brother, Gnaeus, had marched out of Tarraco to disaster against the Carthaginians. From it, Scipio's son had launched his attack on Hannibal's brother, Hasdrubal, and crushed him at Ilipa. Here, Julius Caesar outmaneuvered and defeated Pompey's forces in the civil war that ushered in the Augustines. If there was a hinge of history in Hispania, it was Tarraco.

Marcus watched the city expand across their horizon. He, Flavius and Demaratus had lined the bow, quietly examining their destination. The Greek had been to Tarraco half a dozen times, and he pointed out a few key buildings and sections of the city.

Marcus felt the tension underlying the conversation between the three as the Isis began working its way toward the long mole that enclosed the north section of the port. Whatever their future, its path lay ahead of them in that city.

Several hundred yards out from the mole, two small craft closed on the Isis. Many Roman cargo ships did not carry oars, so they needed help in docking at the wharves that extended into the harbor. The captain ordered the sails reefed, and the crew tossed lines to the two small boats. Slowly they began to pull the Isis toward a wharf just south of the mole.

"The first thing we do is find the baths," said the centurion. "I want full uniforms, including your paludamentum." Mentioning the formal cloak worn by officers underlined not only that he wanted his men to look properly attired, but that he was taking charge. "Signifer," he added, "you will wear your wolf skin."

Demaratus sighed audibly—even in the harbor he could feel the heat of the land—but answered, "Of course, sir."

The closer the Isis drew, the more frayed the grandeur became. The harbor and the docks were massive, and constructed of solid stone, some faced with granite, others with marble. But there was plenty of room to tie up, and the ship passed one large warehouse that looked deserted.

"Not very busy looking," commented Flavius.

"No," replied Demaratus. "Partly because the season is late, but also because much of the trade has moved north to Barcino."

"How come?" asked Flavius.

Demaratus shrugged. "Barcino is closer to Narbo and Gaul and many traders prefer its port. But then cities rise and cities fall, and the reasons are not always obvious."

"Greek philosophy?" snorted the optio.

"Just observation," Demaratus replied. "History is long and fickle. Athens was once the center of world. Look at it now."

"Athens lost a couple of wars. That's why we aren't all speaking Greek," Flavius responded.

Demaratus shrugged again. "Maybe." His anger with Flavius caused him to withdraw from really engaging in a conversation. Plus, you never knew what would set these Romans off. His silence had the added benefit of annoying Flavius, who was looking for a conversation to alleviate his anxiety. "Let him stew," thought Demaratus.

As the small boats drew the Isis up close to one of the long wharves, two slaves on the dock tossed hawsers to the ship's crew. The crew hauled on them, drawing the Isis alongside the quay. As soon as the ship was secured, the captain let go the tiller and strolled forward.

"Well, a bit of excitement, gentlemen, but all safe and snug now," the captain remarked with a smile.

"We are in your debt, Captain," said Marcus politely. The centurion handed the man a small leather bag that clinked with coins. "Please accept this for yourself and the crew on behalf of myself and my men."

"Thank you, sir, and may I wish you the best of luck in your new assignment," he replied.

Demaratus watched the man closely, and he caught a sidelong glance from the captain. Demaratus said nothing but the Greek's stare was level and not overly friendly.

"And my thanks to you, Signifer Demaratus," the captain said, extending his hand.

Demaratus took it briefly and nodded. "I do not trust this man," he thought.

The three gathered up their uniforms and meager baggage and headed toward the lower town, where Demaratus said there was a decent bath near the amphitheater. They passed an enormous structure that the Greek identified as the Praetorian Tower. The name caused them to glance at one another and then grin. They were feeling slightly giddy after the escape, and the grin had a certain co-conspirator sentiment to it.

"No Praetorians in the tower," Demaratus said. "It dates from when Tarraco had a legion stationed here. These days the only legion in Spain, as far as I know, is the VII at Legio."

The port and the buildings surrounding it were impressive but slightly tawdry. There were numerous shops, outdoor stalls, and people, but the crowds were thin, and the piles of goods modest.

Before reaching the baths, they stopped in a small taverna at a busy street corner. They had not had much food for the past week, and in Marcus's case, virtually none.

Marcus had his doubts about the establishment, which was smoky and none too clean, but Demaratus assured him the food was good. And it was. The olive oil was fresh, with a sharp edge that burned the roofs of their mouths. The bread was decent and there was plenty of it, and the goat cheese was outstanding, buttery, and pungent. The fish sauce was the best Marcus had ever eaten, and the wine, while a little thin and sweet, was decent. They polished it all off with sweet honey cakes.

Demaratus excused himself and disappeared for a few minutes. He returned with instructions on how to get to their destination. "The VII Legion has a small headquarters off the plaza near the Augustan Temple," he said. "I know the streets that will take us there."

Feeling full for the first time in a week, the three headed for the baths, and for the next two hours, soaked and scrubbed a week of grime and salt spray from their bodies. Marcus paid a small fee for all of them to have a shave and a haircut, and then they all spent a good half-hour making sure their uniforms were correct.

Marcus cast a critical eye on his two men.

Flavius looked every inch an optio. His chain mail, torques, and various awards were polished, as was his helmet with its distinctive black and white crest. Flavius favored the old-fashioned double belt, his sword on his left, officer style, and his pugio on the right. A six-foot hastile cane sporting a steel lion's head topped off his appearance. The lion's head was unusual, and the only bit of vanity Marcus had ever seen Flavius exhibit.

Demaratus may have been a Greek, but he looked the very picture of a Roman officer. His chain mail fit him like a glove ("If I tried that with my chain," thought Marcus, "it would look like I was carrying a cart wheel around my waist"). His sword belt was perfect, and his pugio had a distinctive mother-of-pearl handle. He was not carrying a signum, of course, because they were not yet assigned to a century, but he had hung the wolf skin around his shoulders and attached the head to his helmet. Marcus tugged the wolf head with its teeth and glass eyes a little higher up the helmet.

He turned to look at himself in a mirror. He had lost weight on the voyage, which made his chain mail sag a little more than usual. But the cloak hid some of the ill-fitting parts of his uniform. He had brought his vitis cane, part of a centurion's badge of office, but he always felt awkward with it. Normally he never carried the cane because he had long ago stopped striking his soldiers for infractions of the rules. As a result, the vitis felt foreign to him, and he had to remind himself not to keep shifting if from one hand to the other. But, overall, he had to admit he didn't look bad.

"Gentlemen" he said, motioning toward the tall, arched doors.

The baths had been warm and steamy, but outdoor Tarraco was like an oven. The heat, dry and intense, was a world away from the cloying mugginess of Rome.

As the three climbed the long hill toward the temple plaza, the town lost some of its frayed appearance. The houses here were well kept, the streets clean, and there were pots everywhere, filled with lavender and flowers that Marcus recognized. Others were unfamiliar, obviously local. A regiment of tall, severe Cyprus trees lined the top of the hill, and spaced along the main street were public fountains.

They drew some stares, which suggested that fully uniformed

officers were somewhat of a rarity in Tarraco. It was also possible that their outfits distinguished them from local army officers, and with politics being what they were in the Empire, three strange, formally dressed army officers would excite comment.

The plaza below the Augustan temple was enormous, dominated by a statue of Scipio Publius. The temple itself was impressive, with a long row of pillars on either side of the main entrance, and an ornate frieze, some of it covered with gold leafing.

Demaratus said the building housing the VII Legion was next to a temple of Ceres. The building was one of the smallest on the plaza with a single sentry at the door. He snapped to attention but did a poor job concealing his curiosity.

Marcus returned the salute and entered a square, pillared hall. Directly ahead of them at the far side of the hall were two finely carved, open double doors. Marcus, with his two officers dutifully behind him, led the way toward it. Inside the double doors was a tesserarius writing on a small tablet with a scroll of papyrus in front of him.

He was so engrossed it was several seconds before he felt their presence. Looking up with an annoyed expression he suddenly took in the three superior officers and their resplendent uniforms. He, himself, was dressed in a normal, everyday army tunic, without sword, helmet or armor.

He started, dropped his stylus, stared for a moment, then straightened up into a semblance of attention.

"Ave, centurion. Tesserarius Sextilius Germanus at your service. How can I help you," adding "sir" at the last moment.

"At ease, Tesserarius Sextilius Germanus. I am Pilus Prior

Centurion Marcus Favonius Facilis. This is Optio Flavius Priscus, and Signifer Demaratus. I would speak with your tribune," said Marcus.

"I am sorry, sir, Tribune Flavius Felix is in Gerunda gathering some recruits, and Legatus Titus Valens is in Legio with the VII Legion," said the tesserarius.

Marcus frowned, and the tesserarius quailed a bit. "Why is this man afraid of me?" thought Marcus, then quickly supplied the answer: the man assumed Marcus, Flavius and Demaratus were on an official mission from Rome and, during these unsettled times, such envoys generally meant trouble. For all the tesserarius knew, they had been sent to arrest his tribune and legate.

"Who is the centurion on duty?" asked Marcus.

"Antonius Crispus. He is hastatus posterior of the Tenth Cohort, sir. I will send for him," said the tesserarius. He signaled a junior librarius and told him to find the centurion.

They had hit their first obstacle. A junior centurion in a lower ranked cohort would be unlikely to make any decisions concerning assignments without first clearing it with his superior, either the tribune at Gerunda or at least the pilus prior of his cohort, which would mean they would cool their heels in Tarraco until someone with enough authority to make a decision arrived.

The tesserarius broke into his thoughts. "The tribune is due back in three days, sir. We have accommodations for you and your men, of course. I am sorry about this situation, but we are somewhat thin in personnel right now, and we were not expecting you."

Marcus nodded and waited patiently for the centurion to appear. It was several minutes and the tesserarius was clearly uncomfortable, shuffling things around on his desk, fidgeting with his stylus, and looking unhappy. Flavius and Demaratus stood like marble statues staring at the young officer, which only increased his discomfort.

When Antonius Crispus appeared, Sextilius Germanus was visibly relieved.

Antonius Crispus was a junior centurion, but he was hardly a young man. Probably almost a decade older than Marcus, he was broad and compact, with an open, unrefined face. He was likely someone who, through bravery and perseverance, had come up through the ranks to hold his present position. He looked some-what flustered by this appearance of three splendidly dressed Roman officers and not a little concerned about how they might make his life difficult.

Marcus decided to seize the initiative:

"Centurion Antonius Crispus. I am happy to make your acquaintance. This is my optio, Flavius Priscus and my signifer, Demaratus. I am Marcus Favonius Facilis, formerly Pilus Prior of the Second Cohort of the XXX Legion Ulpia Victrix. We have been reassigned to VII Legion Gemina Hispania Pia. It looks like we will be seeing a good deal of one another."

Antonius blinked, trying to readjust his initial wariness to the friendly centurion standing in front of him. He took in the torques, the awards and in particular the Corona Vallaris, and decided that the fancy uniforms concealed real soldiers. "Yes sir, I think we certainly will. We are short on experienced officers, sir, and we are spread from one end of Hispania to the other."

Marcus pulled his orders from an inner pocket of his cloak, but Antonius waved them aside. "Those are for tribunes, sir. I suggest you leave them with Sextilius here and he will give them to our tribune, Flavius Felix, when he returns from Gerunda. In the meantime, let me show you to quarters," he said.

He was about to usher the three out, when he remembered something. "Sir, what cohort were you assigned to?"

"The First Cohort," answered Marcus.

"Well, someone has their head on straight in Rome," said Antonius. "The First is under strength and we had a rather unfortunate business with a centurion which I will tell you about later. Sextilius," he said to the tesserarius," you had best put them on the rolls so they can draw food and equipment."

"Yes, sir," the tesserarius answered.

Marcus warmed to the older centurion. The man wasn't shy about making common sense decisions. They were past at least part of the first obstacle.

"XXX Legion," said Antonius, signaling the three to follow him, "you've been fighting Franks, have you?"

"We have indeed," answered Marcus, and the two fell into a technical discussion about the recent border wars in northern Gaul as they left the headquarters, crossed the plaza and headed for what passed as barracks. They were hardly that. The building was three stories, spacious and virtually deserted.

"Not many people about," said Antonius. "We only have a century of regular troops stationed in Tarraco, so there are only four or five officers here, plus some of the headquarter types like Sextilius. I think you will find the accommodations quite comfortable, sir."

"I am sure we will, Antonius, and more so when you start calling me 'Marcus' rather than sir," he answered. He said it with a smile and a friendly hand on the junior centurion's shoulder just in case the man took it as a rebuke.

He needn't have worried. Antonius grinned back at him. "Marcus it is. Sorry to be formal, but we are all a little uncertain about what is going on in Rome, so maybe we are a bit careful."

"Wise of you," Marcus replied. Marcus did rank Antonius, but the situation was delicate. Marcus and his men were, thanks to Antonius, "on the books," but they had not yet received an assignment, so technically they were "guests" of the VII. Guests did not lord it over their hosts. And while Marcus was a senior centurion, and first centurion of his old cohort at that, the status of officers was in part a function of their success in command. His awards helped, but no one really rated an officer until he had proven himself in the field. Marcus' and Flavius's awards were proof of their fighting credentials.

The rooms were indeed spacious and comfortable, and Antonius introduced the three to the few other officers in residence and showed them where to draw their bedding and equipment.

VII

Demaratus spread out his few belongings in his room and sought out Marcus and Flavius. He found the two engaged in deep conversation at the main dining table off the kitchen concerning the latest gossip on the politics of Rome with the centurion who had escorted them, Antonius.

The Greek listened to the conversation for a while, but it bored him, and he needed to buy some clothes. He returned to his room, took off his armor, but kept his cloak and pugio.

"Sir," he said to Marcus, "I am going to the market by the port. There are some items I need. Will you be needing me for anything?"

Marcus said no, and waved him away. Flavius did not even look up.

Demaratus left the barracks, acknowledging the sentry's salute with a nod. Heading back down the same way the three men had come up from the docks, he ran through a list of things he needed. His purse was thin, so need would have to take the place of desire. Most of all he required some comfortable clothes in this hot weather, and he knew of a clothing store near the Praetorian Tower owned by a Greek family he was casually acquainted with. They might give him a bargain, and considering his present finances, he could use one.

It was a relief to be free of the army (and Romans) for a bit, and he took his time walking down the long hill, looking into shops, and examining wares, and watching people. Tarraco had quite a different flavor than Rome. There were Romans, of course, and Greeks, but also people whose appearance he was unfamiliar with. A tall, attractive woman with blond-red hair and freckles passed him by. She wore a long, flowing dress with an ornate Celtic pin at the shoulder, and she gave him a bold look. Demaratus was used to women looking at him, and he smiled and bowed slightly. She smiled back, said something in slightly accented Latin, and swept by with a toss of her long hair. Demaratus grinned and decided he liked Tarraco. He would have pursued her were he not in a hurry to buy clothes, but he took the time to watch her turn down a side street and cross a small courtyard to a house. He noted the house.

The market was not very crowded and several stores were closed or deserted. "You are not long for this world, Tarraco," he thought, which bothered him not in the slightest. Hadn't Tarraco strangled Rhodes and Emporia? Now it was the city of Scipio's turn. He liked Barcino much better in any case.

He browsed some jewelry displays, where a ring sporting a carved garnet octopus caught his fancy, but the ring cost more than his combined purse.

After an hour of wandering through stores and sidewalk displays, he reached the clothing store he was seeking. It was cool and pleasant inside and as he came in, a man behind a small desk—Androdamas? He hoped his memory served him—greeted him.

"Demaratus, you have returned to Tarraco. Welcome," the man said with his hand extended.

"Greetings to you, Androdamas. You are well?"

The man shrugged. "Business is not great. I must send to Barcino for some of my supplies. It makes things more expensive. What ship do you come on?"

Demaratus was about to reply when two men barged into the store.

"Hey, Greek! We need some service," one of them said.

They were local vigiles, dressed in chain shirts and infantry helmets, and armed with short swords and old-fashioned hoplite spears. The speaker was broad with a body giving over to fat. His companion was taller, with a long, sallow face.

"Excuse me, Demaratus. I will be right back," said Androdamas, with a trace of impatience.

He threaded his way through racks and shelves to the front of the store. "Gentleman, I will be with you in a moment. I am helping another customer. Please feel free to look around," he said politely.

"You mean this is all for free?" grinned the fat one. "Fine with us." He reached over and took an expensive, well-cut cloak from a rack and slipped it on. "Pretty good deal, ain't it?" he said to his stone-faced companion.

"That cloak is 200 denarii, sir," said Androdamas.

"No, it ain't," said the tall vigiles, "you said it was free."

"Nothing in this store is free," said Androdamas, "but I am sure I can find you something for you that will not be so costly."

"Nothing is going to cost anything, Greek," snarled the fat one, and slammed the butt of his spear into Androdamas' chest, knocking the man back into shelves filled with cloaks and tunics, scattering some of them on the floor.

Demaratus stepped quietly between the Androdamas and the two men. "Put down your weapons," he said.

"So what's this, Julius? Another stinking Greek?" growled the fat vigiles.

Demaratus had thought this through. There was no sense arguing with the two men. Now that he was close, he could smell the wine on their breath. He would have to assert his authority, but without a uniform to back it up.

Almost before the man had finished the word "Greek," Demaratus used the flat of his hand to slam the side of the vigiles's helmet where the cheek piece came down from the crown. Demaratus was slight, but strong. Several people had made the mistake of underestimating his strength based on his size. The blow staggered the vigiles and sent him reeling into the door jamb.

"You address me as 'sir,'" said Demaratus.

The vigiles named Julius raised his spear.

"How is it you would like to die, vigiles? The penalty for disobeying a superior officer is either crucifixion or death by wild beasts in the arena," said Demaratus, adding thoughtfully "although I am not clear if you have a choice."

Demaratus ignored the spear pointed at his chest and addressed the now enraged vigiles recovering from his encounter with the doorframe. "Your name and rank?" he said.

"Just who do you ..." started the fat vigiles, but Julius was suddenly looking a little unsure of himself, and the point of his spear had begun to waver.

"I am Demaratus, signifer of the First Cohort of the VII Legion. I have just been sent here from Rome," he said, a semi-truth, but the two vigiles exchanged glances. "Now, your names and ranks?" he said impatiently.

The two vigliles—clearly neither of them was very bright—continued to stare at him.

Demaratus's voice took on what he hoped was a Flavius parade-ground growl. "Stand at attention when I address you, and if I don't get those names right now, I'll make sure you end up coming out of some particularly unpleasant animal's asshole!"

The two men suddenly concluded they were in trouble, although actually they weren't in much trouble at all. But they were too surprised or stupid to figure that out. No one got the death penalty for beating up a Greek. However, Demaratus was thoroughly enjoying himself.

The two men pulled themselves into a semblance of something that might be called "attention," although the fat vigiles' helmet was slightly askew.,

"Names?" repeated Demaratus, indicating to Androdamas that he would like a stylus and tablet. The man fetched him one from behind the small desk. Demaratus noticed a child—no, older than a child, but not yet a man, peeking out, wide eyed, from a room behind the desk.

The tall one stepped forward and announced, "Julius Faber," then hesitated, "we are just ordinary vigiles, sir. That's our rank."

Demaratus gave him a stony stare and turned to the man he

had struck. He could see the man struggling with anger and fear at the same time. "Good," thought Demaratus. "Romans should try to think two things at once. It will make them better people," though he held out no hope for these two drunken bullies.

The man steeled himself: "Cassius Rufus, sir."

Demaratus wrote down both names, and then, putting his arms behind him, slowly approached the two. "Stealing from citizens? This is what vigiles in Tarraco do? If you tried this in Rome your own century would beat you to death with clubs, or you would spend the rest of your days in a galley. I intend questioning other merchants in the area to see if you have tried this on them."

"We just had a bit too much wine, sir," Julius said. "We meant no harm. We were just having a bit of fun with a Greek." He mumbled the last word when he remembered whom he was talking too, and that it was Cassius' "stinking Greek" line that had gotten the two of them in trouble in the first place.

Demaratus pushed his face right up to Julius's chin (it was as high as he could reach) and said icily, "Do you want to have fun with me, vigiles?"

The man gulped. "No, sir. We are very sorry for saying or doing anything that offended you."

Demaratus was tempted to make the men apologize to Androdamas, but stopped himself. There was nothing to be gained from further humiliating these men, and it might rebound on Androdamas in the future. Instead, he stared at them for a full minute, while they sweated and fidgeted.

"Dismissed," he said with as much contempt as he could put into the word. "I will consider what to do with your names."

Both men saluted him and fled.

He turned to Androdamas, extracting himself from the cloaks and tunics, and asked if he was all right.

"I am fine, and much in your debt, sir," he answered.

Demaratus grinned at him. "So, when you thought I was a sailor it was 'Demaratus,' but now it is 'sir.' Demaratus will do just fine. Since when have Greeks thought soldiers were better than sailors?"

Androdamas grasped his hand. "What you did took a great deal of courage, Demaratus. Those vigiles could have killed you before you had a chance to identify yourself."

"In that case I would have insisted on a major reduction in your prices, Androdamas."

"You may have your choice of anything in the store, my friend," he replied.

"Oh, no need for that. With my purse as thin as it is, I will need some bargains in any case," said Demaratus, "And who is this lad? Come out from behind the desk, son."

Androdamas beamed a bit. "That is my son Telamon," he said, then calling to the boy, "Telamon, come meet my friend Demaratus."

The boy hesitated, then slipped a heavy knife into a drawer in the desk and came forward.

Demaratus laughed. "Well done, Telamon. You live up to your namesake. Though one hopes you never have a son as thickheaded as Ajax."

The boy smiled and shook Demaratus's hand. "That was wonderful, sir. Those two make trouble for everyone. I can't wait to tell my friends. Would you really feed them to the lions?"

"It would probably kill the lions," Demaratus grinned back at him.

The line got a laugh, although as much from the release of tension as in any acknowledgement of Demaratus's humor.

Demaratus spent an hour trying on various tunics and finally chose two with a slightly Greek cut. Androdamas refused to take any money, but Demaratus insisted. "Look, Androdamas, you said business is not good, and I am now an officer, not a poor sailor. My purse is thin only because I haven't drawn any pay yet. On top of which, all I did was my duty."

Androdamas arched his eyebrows a bit at that. "It is not my experience that the Roman army goes about protecting people against vigiles."

Demaratus shrugged. "The world is going in lots of different ways, my friend. Who knows what the gods have in store for us."

Androdamas put his hand on Demaratus's shoulder. "Wait. I have something for you. Since it is a gift, you cannot refuse it." He stepped into the back for a moment and returned with a wooden case. "This for you, my friend."

Demaratus took the box and laid it on the desk. Working its cover off, he found he was looking at a knife with a slightly curved blade and a bone handle, inset with red coral. It was lovely and Demaratus had never seen anything quite like it. He took it out and found it perfectly balanced. Testing its edge, he drew blood on his finger almost without touching it.

"Thank you, Androdamas. It is most unusual."

"It is special steel, Demaratus," said the shopkeeper, "made east of Syria."

"A Parthian blade?" asked Demaratus.

"Not Parthian," answered Androdamas. "It was made in a place called Damascus. It is said that no armor can resist it."

Demaratus found the blade flexible but with a feel of great strength. He knew better than to test its edge again. He thanked Androdamas again and gathered his purchases.

"You always have a place here, Demaratus. If there is any service we can perform for you, you have but to ask," said Androdamas.

"You have done more than enough with this blade, my friend," Demaratus said, but then hesitated.

"Yes?" asked the shopkeeper.

"Androdamas, there is something you could do for me. If you hear anyone asking questions about a centurion by the name of Marcus, or an optio named Flavius, or just three officers who have recently arrived in Tarraco, could you let me know? We are staying in the VII Legion barracks off of the temple plaza."

Androdamas said, " Of course," and then turned to Telamon. "Keep your ears open, son, but do not tell this story to anyone. Do you understand?"

"Yes, father," Telamon replied.

Demaratus thanked Androdamas again, and winked at Telamon. "If those two come back, just cut them up into pieces with that big knife, okay?

The boy grinned.

VIII

After two hours and a good-sized amphora of decent wine, Antonius and Marcus had run out of gossip. There was a moment of silence between them.

"What is this business with the centurion of the First Cohort?" Marcus finally asked.

Antonius immediately looked uncomfortable and glanced around him.

"Have you seen the Temple of Augustus?" he asked.

This must be delicate indeed, thought Marcus, because there was no one around but an occasional slave. Flavius had left an hour ago looking for the training field where troops were being drilled.

"No, this is my first trip to Tarraco. I would be in your debt if you would show me," Marcus replied.

The two strolled out of the barracks and headed across the temple plaza.

"Sorry for the secrecy, and sorry for the fact that I have to ask you something," said Antonius, looking distinctly uncomfortable.

"Go ahead," replied Marcus, "I have no secrets." How easy it has become for you to lie, he thought.

Antonius took a breath and asked him, "Are you a Christian?"

Marcus shook his head. "No, and I don't know much about them. They didn't have much of a presence in Gaul. Jews, aren't they?

Antonius threw his hands into the air. "Well, that is what I thought, but Jews have more common sense, and they don't make trouble. Well," he added, "at least not recently. These Christians are always making trouble."

Marcus frowned. "We aren't fighting Christians, are we? And what does this all have to do with the First Cohort?

"No, we aren't fighting them like we're fighting the Lusitanians, but that doesn't mean they aren't trouble, and they're making lots of trouble in the First Cohort."

Marcus didn't know enough to ask questions so he just waited for Antonius to go on. He knew there was growing tension between the Emperor and some Christian bishops, but he frankly hadn't paid it much attention and didn't know what the friction was all about.

"The princeps of the First Cohort is a Christian," said Antonius.

Marcus shrugged. "I had a centurion who worshipped an Egyptian goddess, and there was an optio in the Third Century who worshipped Baal, which he heard about from his brother who served against the Parthians."

"Oh, I don't care what people believe," said Antonius. "I have a signifer in Legio who lights incense to a beech tree."

"A beech tree?" said Marcus.

"Yeah, some sort of Celtic god. Its name is Fagus or something," said Antonius, as the two approached the steps leading up to the temple. "No, it's not what people believe, it is what they do. And some of these Christians have decided that they don't have to worship the emperors because their god is above everyone else's."

Marcus absorbed this for a moment. "Above the empire? That's an odd thing for a centurion in the Roman army to believe. What did he do to get in trouble?" asked Marcus.

"Wouldn't pay his yearly sacrifice and wouldn't take orders because he only accepts the authority of his god," said Antonius with a sidelong glance at Marcus.

"Well, that would do the job," said Marcus. "Was he arrested?"

"Yes, but not right off. A lot of people tried to convince him that the yearly sacrifice was just one of those things you did in the army, like drill or getting killed," said Antonius, with a sigh.

Marcus had a feeling Antonius was one of those "people," but didn't say anything. "Where are they now?" he asked.

"He was arrested in Corduba, but no one there felt they had the authority to do anything. I mean, religion is hard to deal with, right?" he asked Marcus.

"Hard to deal with indeed," Marcus agreed.

"So, they sent him to Carthago Nova and he is in jail awaiting a decision from Rome about what to do," said Antonius.

"That," mused Marcus, "will depend on what happens between

Phillip and Decius. Decius, I am told, is no admirer of Christians, particularly ones who challenge the Empire's religion."

They had entered the temple, but the two paid little attention to anything in it.

Antonius sighed again. "I don't wish him ill," he said, "but he had to know what would happen."

"Were there others involved?" asked Marcus.

"No, anyhow not any who went as far as he did," answered Antonius, "but refusal to follow orders is like a disease. It can spread. Once someone resists authority, it occurs to others that they might like to try it as well. The First and Second centuries were serving together at the time, so we scattered all the optios, signifers, and tesserariuses to other areas of the empire. It has left us pretty thin, and some of the locals who don't like us are noticing that we aren't exactly at full strength."

"I see what you meant by 'bad business,'" said Marcus.

"And you can see why I said that Rome had its head on straight," Antonius said. "A group of experienced officers with your records will help calm things down."

Marcus nodded, not trusting himself to expand on his earlier lie. There were some in Rome who probably would like to toss Marcus, Flavius and Demaratus into the same place as the centurion of the First Cohort.

Antonius laughed. "Well, I hope you enjoyed the temple, Marcus."

Marcus blinked. He had barely noticed the temple.

"Shall we keep talking and walk to the forum? You cannot notice it either," Antonius said with a grin.

"Lead the way," answered Marcus, and the two plunged into

a discussion of the First Cohort, how to reconstruct a century gone bad, and what the restiveness of the locals was all about.

Flavius had listened to Marcus and Antonius for a while, but he was restless. While both men tried to include him in the conversation, Flavius felt the chasm of rank, particularly when another centurion was around. He could converse normally with Marcus—well, sort of normally—but not when anyone else was around. In private, one could let down the barriers, but not in public.

A change of topics gave him an out. "Sir, if you don't mind, I would like to watch the VII's training techniques," he said.

Marcus could see that Flavius was uncomfortable in the conversation and readily agreed. In any case, training techniques were a proper thing for an optio to study.

"Sir," said Flavius to Antonius, "where might your Field of Mars be?"

"The Field of Mars is a good distance from the city, so they are training in the circus today. If you cross the plaza and take the street by the Ceres temple, it will take you right to the circus. The optio in charge is Domitius Celer," said Antonius.

"Thank you, sir," Flavius replied, waved at Marcus, and went out into the hot afternoon sun.

The circus was no more than a 15-minute walk. Long and narrow, it faced the sea on one side and what looked like an older forum. Flavius had caught sight of the newer forum from a distance, deciding that he would visit it before they left the city. If they left the city.

There was a single century training on the field, and Flavius could see it was a mixture of more experienced men and what appeared to be raw recruits. The former were lounging near a Scorpion artillery piece, while the latter stumbled and sweated their way through marching and maneuvering drills in full armor and equipment.

Flavius frowned at the loungers, but saw the reason: the optio was the only officer on the field, and he had his hands full with the new soldiers. There was no one to work with the more experienced soldiers.

Flavius strolled over toward the drill and watched. Domitius Celer was trying to get the troopers to break out of marching mode and fall into a fighting formation. It was an uphill battle. The men (really boys) turned the wrong way, bumping into one another. One line of a dozen men was too close to one another, and when one stumbled, the whole group went down like a row of dominos. The men lounging at the Scorpion laughed.

The laugh bothered him, not so much because it humiliated the recruits—the optio in charge was already elucidating on their parentage, or lack thereof—but because on a training field everyone must work.

The optio noticed him, saw the uniform that identified him as a fellow officer, and told the men to take a break. They gratefully leaned on their pila and shields.

"Domitius Celer, Third Century, Tenth Cohort, right now a vexilla to train this lot how to be soldiers," he said, extending his hand, adding, "hopeless."

"Flavius Priscus, lately of the XXX Legion Ulpia Victrix, now assigned to the First Cohort," answered Flavius, grasping the man's hand.

"Well, the First can use some experienced people, though I am not sure I would wish it on you," said Domitius, sliding his helmet back and wiping his forehead.

Flavius had begun to wonder himself what they were all getting themselves into. "Can you use a hand?" he asked

"Aye," said Domitius. "You could light a fire under that lot," he said, indicating the men lounging near the Scorpion.

"Would you mind a little pila practice?" asked Flavius.

"Fine by me," answered the optio. "But best not stand in front of them."

Flavius grinned and, hands behind his back, strolled over to the men. They gave him a wary look but came to attention. He looked them over, keeping a friendly smile on his face. Never let the enemy know what you're up to, he thought.

"Your optio tells me there isn't a more accurate lot of pila throwers in the empire. 'They can thread a needle,' he says," said Flavius, picking up a padded training breastplate. The men definitely had stopped smiling. "So, I would like a little demonstration."

He tied the straps of the breastplate to the Scorpion, and then motioned the men back. They trotted back about 25 feet.

"Twenty-five feet," Flavius said, with a wondering look on his face. "My grandmother can hit something at 25 feet, and she is ten years dead."

He motioned them back to effective pila range: 50 feet. A pilum could be thrown 100 feet, but not with any accuracy.

"Men, that there is a Frank, or maybe a Goth, though the smell is not quite right for a Goth," he said, raising a round of grins. "He is coming at you with a lot of his friends behind him.

You would rather not meet those friends, and the best way to do that is put a pilum right through the center of his chest. That makes the lads behind him think a bit, and once you got a Goth or a Frank thinking, then the battle's mostly won."

He motioned one of the men to step up to where he was standing. The man handed his shield to another and put his toe on the line.

"Fighting without a scutum, are we? Now that's a brave lad, though maybe a bit stupider than that Frank over there," said Flavius, pointing at the padded breastplate. "You fight with a shield, so you have to throw your pilum while you hold it."

"Yes sir," the man said, retrieving his shield, and looking nervous.

"What's your name, son?" asked Flavius.

"Fabius, sir," the man replied.

"Now we have a little game we play, Fabius," said Flavius. "You hit that man in the center of his chest and you don't do guard duty tonight. But if you miss him, you not only do guard duty, you trot around this circus twice." He paused for a moment. "Hit the Scorpion and you do it four times."

He smiled pleasantly, and motioned the man to throw.

Fabius drew his pilum back and hurled it. The spear came nowhere near either the breastplate or the ballista machine.

"Well, Fabius, you missed the Frank, and that's bad for you and your century. But you also missed the Scorpion. In fact, you barely hit Hispania." The remark raised a chuckle from the rest.

"You find it amusing, do you? " said Flavius coldly, turning to the others and adding a bit of parade ground rasp to his voice for the first time. "There a lot of people out there who would like to see the Roman army throw a pilum that way, so they can get about the business of killing and looting. You want to tell me what is funny about that?" he said, pointing to another soldier.

The man said nothing.

"When I ask you a question, soldier, you better answer it. If I get pissed at you, the Franks and Goths will seem like your mother's tit," said Flavius, his voice rising to full volume.

"Sir," the man said, standing rigidly at attention.

"Your name," roared Flavius.

"S-S-S-Sossius, s-s-sir," man replied, blanching.

Flavius abruptly dropped his voice to almost a whisper. Pointing at the breastplate, he said softly, "Frank."

Sossius stepped up and hurled. Flavius noted that he set his front left foot much more solidly than the first man did, and that he pivoted his right foot correctly. The pilum did not strike the center of the breastplate, but it pierced the section below the chest. The man looked pleased.

"Hold that pose," roared Flavius. The man froze, his right arm extended, his shield dropped slightly to his left. "Sossius has his feet right, and because he has his feet right, that there is a dead Frank, even though it will take him awhile to join his ancestors," Flavius pointed out. "That's good."

The man started to relax.

"Move when I tell you to move," shouted Flavius. The man assumed his frozen, mime-like position.

"But tell, me Sossius, what are you going to stop with your shield way down near the ground? Expecting a visit from Here-cura, are we? Figure she might come right out of the underworld and skewer you? No need to worry. Some friend of that Frank has already put a javelin right into your chest, and you better hope it doesn't hit a seam between your plates. Keep your shield up!" said Flavius.

Domitius had stopped the drilling and quietly led his men over to watch Flavius.

"You," said Flavius to another soldier, "give him your pilum. Okay, Sossius, let's try that again."

The poor soldier looked like he would rather be facing real Franks than performing before this strange optio.

The man gripped his shield, stepped forward and hurled his pilum. It just barely pierced the right side of the breastplate, but he kept his shield up. He turned to look at Flavius, expecting an avalanche of abuse.

"Not bad, son," said Flavius mildly. "You kept your shield up and I doubt that Frank is going to be a whole lot of use for a while."

The man's relief was palpable.

"Next," said Flavius.

For the next hour the men hurled their pila, while Flavius critiqued their footwork, their shield position, and their follow through. A trickle of men jogged around the circus because they had missed the target, but by the end of the exercise their accuracy had decidedly improved, and Flavius handed the experienced men off to Domitius for drill, while he explained the intricacies of the pilum to the novices.

"Pay attention to your pilum," Flavius instructed a semi-circle of sweating soldiers. "A pilum is your friend. It can knock an enemy's shield out of the fight. Once you get your pilum in their shield, they have to just toss it away, because you can't get one of these spears out, once it's in. That means your enemy fights you with nothing but hope" (the comment raised smiles), "and the Roman army always defeats hope."

Flavius ran his fingers up the long head of the pilum's point. "This point will bend when it strikes something. That means the fellow you throw it at can't throw it back," he explained, "Getting killed by your own spear makes a mess of your day." The joke brought a round of laughter.

"All right, now" said Flavius, "Let's see what you can do."

Few of the recruits hit the target, and several them couldn't throw much beyond 30 feet, but Flavius was patient with them, rather than abusive. "Set those feet! Pivot that leg! Don't hide behind your shield, aim!"

By the time the sun was beginning to settle in the hills west of the city, the recruits were getting the idea. Domitius called a halt to the training and sent them back to their barracks.

Flavius and Domitius walked slowly back to headquarters, talking training methods and tactics. Flavius explained that his centurion was experimenting with a century formation that was wide, rather than deep, with two or three lines of men, rather than four. Domitius grunted non-committedly.

They dropped off their equipment at the barracks and headed for the baths.

IX

❦

For the next two days Marcus took in the sights, while De-maratus—finally drawing some pay—disappeared into the city each morning. Flavius rose early and he and Domitius headed for the field of Mars to work with the recruits. The underlying tension of their situation made it impossible for any of them to relax, but none of them wanted to look anxious or nervous.

Marcus felt the most at loose ends, and he was not comfortable with it. One morning, as Domitius and Flavius were setting off to torment their charges, Domitius mentioned to Marcus that he might find it of interest to drop by his old commander's house, which was not far from the Temple Plaza.

"He fought the Parthians, sir. He has some grand stories, and no one much bothers with him these days. Parthia seems a long way off. But he was a fine centurion, sir," said Domitius.

Marcus, restless, decided to take Domitius's advice and visit a retired comrade. Domitius had written down the address, and Marcus finally tracked it down. It was a modest domus. After hesitating about knocking—did he really have nothing else to do? —he finally figured that at least he could let an old comrade tell war stories. He might someday find himself in the same position.

He knocked, but there was no response. He waited for a few minutes, then knocked again. When there was no still response, he started to turn away, but before he had completed the turn, an old man answered the door. He was slightly stooped, but his eyes were bright, and he moved briskly.

"Yes?" the man, said. Then took in Marcus's uniform. "Greetings, comrade," he said.

"And you as well, sir, " replied Marcus. "I did not mean to disturb you, but Domitius Celer suggested that I might drop in on you, and since I am new to Hispania, I hoped that you might have time to see me."

The man laughed. "Time? Time is my enemy these days. He lies in wait for me each morning and challenges me to fill his demands. There are times I would rather be facing the Parthians," he said. "You have come as a cohort in our most desperate hour to save us from working in our garden or re-arranging our spices. Please, come in. I am Valerius Tullius."

Marcus took to him right off, and after a short tour of Valerius's modest house, the two sat in the atrium and drank wine.

It turned out that Valerius was a storehouse of information on the politics of Hispania, as well as the VII Legion. And the politics of both were inordinately complex.

"I only know rumor about the situation with the First Cohort, Marcus, but I know you will be going into something of great delicacy," said Valerius. "I am an old man now, and the world I grew up in seems increasingly to be more myth than reality, but for what it is worth, the VII Legion is the oldest and most provincial legion in the Empire. You must insert yourself carefully."

Marcus sat silent for a time. "I hear you, comrade. And I will think on it."

Valerius poured another round of wine and sat back. "So, Marcus, have you ever fought cavalry?

"Not really, brother. The Franks had some, but cavalry is not effective against disciplined infantry," replied Marcus.

"Oh, yes, maybe in the middle of the Gaul forests mounted troops weren't too dangerous, but remember what happened to Crassius and Scipio," said Valerius.

Marcus nodded agreement, "but Scipio was a fool to divide his forces, and wasn't Crassius done in by mounted archers? I haven't heard that the natives here are much for the bow."

"No," said Valerius, "the native cavalry does not use the bow, but that doesn't mean it is not effective against infantry. The Lusitanians are great horsemen, comrade, and their charge is indeed a danger, even to the most disciplined infantry."

"How so?" asked Marcus.

Valerius sat back and was silent for a moment. "They pick their ground. They like a slope, and they charge down it. A wall of horsemen, shields to the front, lances to the fore, has great force, and if your men flinch, they are gone."

Marcus conjured up an image and found it disturbing. "What do you do, comrade?"

Valerius laughed. "First you have to take away your men's scutums."

"Their shields? Why should I want to take away their shields?" said Marcus.

"Oh, not permanently," replied Valerius, "and not during the battle."

Marcus was by this time looking not only confused but in the initial stages of suspecting that the retired centurion's mind had succumbed to old age.

"During training," explained Valerius, "you have to take their shields and hit them over the head with them. Then they just might be willing to accept a different way of doing things."

Marcus laughed. The innate conservativeness of the Roman Army was a standard joke among those who dared suggest that changed conditions might require different tactics.

"So, after I hit them over the head, what then?" asked Marcus.

And so, Valerius Tullius, centurion retired, introduced Marcus to the secret of fighting cavalry.

On the night of the third day, Marcus was trying to read an essay on morals by the Greek Stoic, Claudius Aelianus, but his mind kept drifting. He had read the same passage over several times before he finally put the scroll down and lay back on his couch. He was somewhat resentful of Demaratus (whom he suspected had found a female companion) and Flavius. Both had kept busy all day, while he wandered around like a lost spirit. He considered trying to sleep, but the heat and his restlessness made that impossible. He was just getting up from his couch when the young tesserarius, Sextilius Germanus, appeared at his door.

"Greetings, Centurion Marcus Favonius Facilis," he said, saluting.

"Greetings to you, Sextilius Germanus. What brings you here at this hour?" Marcus asked.

"I have a summons for you from my Tribune, Flavius Felix. He would like you to see him as soon as possible," answered Sextilius.

A tiny sliver of ice went down Marcus's spine. A summons in the middle of the night could be an arrest warrant. But would the Tribune know this quickly about their hasty departure from Rome, or that their orders were only semi-legitimate? Would he conjecture that something wasn't right about the whole matter and lock them up just to be on the safe side? Marcus could hardly refuse the summons, but he needed to think.

"I will be with you as soon as I put on my uniform," said Marcus.

"That won't be necessary, sir," said the tesserarius.

"It certainly will be necessary, tesserarius. One does not appear before his commanding officer in his night shirt," said Marcus, gathering his things together.

"Of course, sir," replied Sextilius, relaxing.

Well, that was a welcome sign. In fact, as Marcus began to add up the signs, they were mostly good. The middle of the night was bad (but tribunes loved to be arbitrary and quirky— they weren't much use for anything else). If this were an arrest, Sextilius should have arrived with a squad of soldiers (although Marcus had to admit it would be difficult to scrape up such a squad given the thinness of the garrison in Tarraco). In any case, he would have his sword. He would not submit to an arrest.

He was ready in a few minutes, then remembered Demaratus and Flavius. He was not sure the former was in the barracks, but he had said goodnight to Flavius. He would have to warn them. As he belted on his sword and picked up his vitis cane, he called to the night slave. "Go and tell my men that I am summoned to meet with the tribune," he said. The man bowed and left.

Sextilius said nothing (which, again, Marcus interpreted as a good sign) and stood aside as Marcus strode out the door. The heat had come off the night, and the two crossed the temple plaza in the cool of early morning. A quarter moon hung in the eastern sky; the stars dimmed by a screen of high clouds announcing the possibility of rain.

The two men entered the headquarters and headed for the room where Marcus had first encountered Sextilius. A man was seated at the same desk, the orders from Quintus Pompeius Falco opened, alongside what looked like a roster list. Marcus noted that there were no extra sentries in the room, and he relaxed. "How could this be an arrest?" he thought.

"Centurion Marcus Favonius Facilis, welcome," said the tribune. He was taller than Marcus, but not built quite so solidly. He wore a simple tunic and a wide, gold bracelet on his left wrist. His hair, cut short with slight bangs, had hints of gray, and there were outdoor lines around his eyes. He was handsome in a pedestrian way, a well-formed face with nothing terribly distinguishing about it.

"Sir," said Marcus saluting him.

"Please sit down, Marcus," said the tribune, waving him to a chair.

Marcus sat down stiffly, considering he had his sword belted on. The tribune ran his hands through his hair, shuffled the orders around and looked at Marcus with a strained look on his face.

"We have a problem, Marcus," said the tribune.

"Sir?" answered Marcus, stiff with alarm.

"It's your orders, Marcus," answered Flavius Felix.

"My orders?" replied Marcus, already beginning to think how he would get out of this. He was not overly concerned with himself, but he needed to warn the others and was worried that his simple statement to them that he had been summoned would not do the job.

"Yes, your orders, Marcus. You have been assigned to the First Cohort in Legio, and I have every intention of seeing that come to pass. The First Cohort needs all the help it can get. But I am going to ask you to delay going to Legio and taking up your command, " said the tribune.

Marcus said nothing for a moment. He had an initial spasm of relief, but he was also thoroughly sick of uncertainty, and this tribune was being opaque.

"And why is that, sir?" said Marcus, watching the tesserarius flinch at his tone. It had an edge to it, but Marcus was feeling irritated.

If the tribune resented his tone, he made no sign of it. "We have a situation with the Second Century of the First Cohort in Corduba," he said, "and I need an experienced centurion to take over that century. The two centuries have been in Mauretania Tingitana for the past six months, and they have just returned to Hispania. Both were badly mauled in fighting there, and they lost many of their officers. We are quite short of experienced commanders, and the centuries must march north to Legio. I would like you and your men to go south and join up with the Second Century."

Marcus relaxed, but was still puzzled. "Of course, sir. I would be honored to serve the Second Century, but I am surprised by the loss of so many officers." In fact, Marcus already knew why the Second Century did not have a centurion, but he wanted to hear the tribune's version of it.

The tribune looked slightly uncomfortable. "Well, some of the officers were lost in battle, some to disease, but we have also had some trouble in the ranks," he said.

"Trouble?" Marcus asked.

The tribune again passed his hands through his hair, slumped in his chair, and sighed. "Yes. It is more of this Christian business. The Second Century's centurion was arrested for refusing orders. I assume Antonius told you about the situation?"—Marcus nodded that he had —"and the men refused to march north until their centurion was released."

"Actually refused?" said Marcus.

"Well, in a way. They didn't come right out and refuse but they just sabotaged everything," said the tribune. "I am not sure what the details are because I have been in the north. What I do know is that there was a request from the pilus prior of the First Century for experienced officers." He added, "There is some unrest among the tribes in Lusitania and we are not comfortable with the centuries marching north without experienced officers."

"We can leave tonight if you like, tribune," said Marcus.

"Oh, no need to go off in the dark. Daybreak is fine. It will take you about nine days to reach Corduba. My tesserarius will give you your orders and travel money. We do not have many formal army accommodations for you to stop at each day like they have in Italia, so you will have to stay in inns," said the tribune.

"Yes, sir. We will gather our things and be off at first light. Is there anything else, sir," said Marcus.

"No. Luck be with you, centurion. We will meet again in Legio," he said, dismissing Marcus.

Well, thought Marcus as he left the headquarters and hurried toward the barracks, nothing is simple in this place, is it?

X

The sleek Liburna slid past the harbor moles in Tarraco and swung towards a long quay. The captain glanced at his two passengers. They were a motley pair, as surly as a couple of feral dogs. They had come aboard at Ostia with authorization he was not in a position to question and an attitude he had had to swallow. He doubted they were his equivalent in rank, but the orders they carried put him at their "disposal." He had initially tried to be friendly, but the two were puffed up with their importance and treated him like a deckhand. His only pleasure was that they got badly seasick when the Liburna encountered the tail end of a storm blowing its last gusts. Nothing like vomiting your guts out to take the edge off an attitude.

The two were huddling near the bow talking in low whispers. The captain wished he knew what this was all about, and then quickly corrected himself. The less he knew, the better. But it would be a relief to rid him of the two men.

As the ship closed on the quay, slaves on the shore gathered to catch the heavy ropes the crew threw to them to tie up the ship.

Reluctantly, he made his way forward. The two men stopped conferring as soon as he neared. What a pleasure it would have been to pitch them off in the middle of the passage.

"Gentlemen," said the captain. "Welcome to Tarraco. I am sure you will be about your business ashore."

The thin one called Sextus gave him a haughty look. "You will keep your ship here for our return, captain."

The captain reddened. "My orders were to convey you to Tarraco, gentlemen. This is Tarraco. There was nothing about a return passage, and this ship has work to do. You will disembark immediately or I will drop you over the side," he replied quietly.

"You can't talk to us that way," the big one—Lucius? —complained. "You are supposed to be at our disposal." The lout said the last word with a sneer.

The captain crooked a finger and half dozen crew members and marines dropped the ropes they were handling and came forward. "Do you want to see why I can talk to you any way I choose?" asked the captain in the same quiet tone. Neither of the men had endeared themselves to the rest of the ship, and the looks the crew were giving the two were black and dangerous.

"Now just a minute," started Lucius, but Sextus silenced him with an elbow. The thin man smiled at the captain. "Of course, we will disembark, Captain. And I am sure that our report on all your help will be well received in Rome. I wonder if you could point out a ship called the Isis to me."

The captain stared at him a long moment before reluctantly surveying the ships tied up at the quay. Finally, he pointed to a rounded tub of a vessel. "I believe that is the Isis."

"Then we will be out of your hair as soon as we gather our

gear, Captain," said Sextus with a thin smile. Lucius glowered, but said nothing.

Dangerous men, both, thought the captain, but the thin one was not as smart as he thought he was. At some point in the future, the gods would instruct him on that point. The captain nodded at the gathering of men at his back, and they parted to let Lucius and Sextus through to retrieve their equipment and depart over the plank that now anchored the Liburna to the quay.

"Why did you let that puffed up rooster talk to us that way?" grumbled Lucius as the two men made their way toward the Isis.

Sextus whirled on him. "Shut up, you fool. This job is off the books. Our warrant isn't a warrant; it's just a license to kill. If we get in trouble, those pigs in Rome will pretend they never heard of us, and then you can start thinking about that poker up your ass. We're only useful if our lords and masters think we can serve them. Annoy them and we're dead. Us getting into a fight with a captain of a Liburna might just annoy them. Shall I tell you about the poker again?"

Lucius mumbled something that Sextus ignored as he led the way to the ship the captain had said was the Isis.

The crew of the Isis, under the direction of a man whom Sextus took to be the captain, were storing jars of wine and fish sauce when the two Praetorians stepped on board.

The man gave them a hostile look. "Who are you and what's your business on my ship?" he said.

"Did you carry three army passengers on your voyage out from Ostia?" asked Sextus.

"What business is it of yours?" the captain said belligerently.

Sextus leaned into the captain's face and whispered: "My friend Lucius here likes to take out men's livers. Not quickly, mind you. And since he is not overly bright, he does so whenever I tell him. And because we are here on the business of the Empire, we can do so right here on the deck of your ship, and no one will intervene. So, would you like to answer my question?"

The man stiffened. "I am just a captain. I carry any passengers that pay. I don't have anything to do with..."

"Spare me your explanations," said, Sextus. "Did you carry three men? Was one a centurion, another an optio, and the third a Greek?"

The captain nodded. "Yes, and I knew they were up to something. They were sneaking around the whole time they were on board. They threatened me, so I had to take them. Otherwise, I would have alerted the proper authorities."

"And have you done so?" said Sextus.

"Well, I haven't had the time, but I intended..." stuttered the captain.

"Shove your intentions up your ass. Where did they go," said Lucius.

"I don't know. They just left," said the captain, visibly trembling.

Lucius grabbed the man by the throat and lifted him off the deck. The captain struggled to break the huge man's grip but failed, slowly turning blue.

"Let him go, Lucius," said Sextus. "They wouldn't have told a toad like this where they were headed anyhow." Lucius squeezed a little more, then dropped the captain, who crumpled to the deck.

"So, what now?" said Lucius once they were back on land.

"Let me think," said Sextus. He led his partner from the ship and down to the quay and stood looking at the city.

"Hey, you slimy little Greek, what are you staring at?" bellowed Lucius. The target of his anger was a young Greek boy who had been observing the shipboard scene and was now watching the two Praetorians. Lucius took a kick at the boy, but the latter dodged and ran off into a warehouse.

"According to the tribune, the three got orders to report to the VII Legion," said Sextus. He had been right. The optio they were after had a first cousin in the First Cohort, and the man had talked. The trail had led to the Vigiles. Sextus wasn't certain what happened after that—there was tension between the legate of the Vigiles and the Praetorians— but the tribune had made it clear that they were to avoid any official contact with the VII Legion.

"But we can't go talk to them," said Lucius.

"No," agreed Sextus. "Let's go get something to drink and a place to stay, and let me work this out."

"You think they are still here?" asked Lucius.

"I am not sure. We were only two days behind them. After we get something to drink, we will go look at some horses," said Sextus picking up his pack and slinging it over his shoulder.

"Horses?" said Lucius.

"If they have left Tarraco, they left on horses. We find the Army stables and chat up some of the handlers, and we will know whether they left or not," explained Sextus.

"You're smart," said Lucius.

"Not much to compare me to," muttered Sextus. If Lucius heard it, he didn't react.

XI

It was still dark when Marcus rose the next morning, but he found Flavius and Demaratus already awake and about, their equipment gathered near the front door. They both nodded greetings, and the three sat for a quick, impatient breakfast of bread, cheese, and olive oil. No one said it, but they were relieved to be free of Tarraco.

As they crossed the Temple Plaza headed for the stables near the circus, the sky opened. It had threatened rain late yesterday afternoon, but had perversely held off until the three were about to begin their journey south. The rain was uncomfortable, but it served to take the edge off the heat of the last week, and the three slogged silently through it, trying to avoid the larger puddles that gathered at uneven places on the plaza and in the streets.

It was only a short walk to the stables, but despite their cloaks the three were thoroughly damp by the time they arrived. Their humor was not improved by the fact that no one was up to help with the horses. As Flavius went off swearing and grumbling to roust the attendants out of bed, Marcus and Demaratus walked through the stalls, examining the horses.

They were a fine-looking lot. Everyone knew Hispania produced the best horses in the Empire, and there was a wide variety to choose from. Demaratus was already eyeing a white mare with a curiously small face. He was inspecting its teeth and running his hands over its withers and down its legs. Marcus, who couldn't tell a horse from a hedgehog—except he was rather fond of the latter—thought the white horse looked too delicate.

He passed a stall and then doubled back to look. The horse was large and black, although in the dim light of the stable lamps it was hard to tell much else about it. What attracted Marcus was that the horse was very still, doggedly chewing on something, uninterested in the world around it. Marcus liked this in a horse. The animal was also broad; in fact, quite fat. Marcus also liked a secure seat. It had long hair above its hoofs, so it looked a little as if it were wearing shaggy boots. When Marcus leaned in and petted it, the horse made no response.

This was the horse for him.

As he was stroking it, Flavius returned with two attendants who looked like they had gotten an earful from a very cranky optio.

"Found one, have you, sir?" asked Flavius, eyeing the great, placid beast with a certain distaste.

"Not much spirit in that one, sir," one of the attendants said. "He's been gelded. I have a swift little mare two stalls down."

Marcus shook his head. "No, this will be fine. He looks strong."

"Oh, he is that, sir," said the other attendant, " He'll walk you to Parthia if you like, but it will take a while."

"Saddle him, please," said Marcus, ending the conversation.

Flavius said he would like to look at the mare the attendant had first offered Marcus, and he and the first attendant went off to examine her. In the meantime, Demaratus had brought the white mare out of the stall and was walking it in a circle.

"She's quick, that one," said the attendant. "Tingus stock. She looks delicate but she can run down the wind."

"Fine," said Demaratus, "I will take her."

Flavius had returned leading a brown mare that paced and stepped a bit as it followed him. They added a packhorse to their little expedition, saddled up, and prepared to head out into the rain. "How far to the next station?" asked Marcus.

The attendant rubbed his face. "Well, it isn't like there are regular stations on the Via Augusta, sir. The next place to get horses would be Valentia, and that would be a good three-day ride. Where are you headed, sir?"

"Corduba," answered Marcus.

The attendant considered for a moment. "As I said, sir, it is three days to Valentia, and another good six days to Corduba from there. I would suggest not pushing the horses too much and keep them until you get to where you are going," he said, "that is, if you like them."

"Places to stay?" queried Marcus.

"I assume someone at headquarters told you that there are no army barracks until you get to Valentia, but there are some nice inns along the way. I will write out a list for you," the attendant said. "You might also think of staying at some villas on the way south."

Even though any house was obligated to shelter members

of the army, it would not be Marcus's first choice. The owners would ask for news of Rome, and that might lead to subjects the three men would rather not get into.

"Can we make Tortosa the first day?" asked Flavius.

"It's a long ride, but if it clears, you'll make it. You won't get in until late afternoon," said the attendant. "If you get to Tortosa today, I strongly recommend the Golden Porpoise. Good beds, good wine, and the best food in town."

Marcus smiled at him. "Thanks. Your name?"

"Julius Furius, sir, and this is my comrade, Julius Longinus," said the attendant, "We call ourselves 'the house of Julius,'" he said with a grin.

"Well, good health to your house and luck be with you," said Marcus, repeating an old prayer.

The three set off into a slackening drizzle, which began to lift after an hour. The clouds thinned except over the mountains to their west, and the sea was dappled with alternate patterns of gray and blue. The rain had called forth the perfumes of the countryside, and the air smelled strongly of rosemary, thyme, lavender, and damp, late summer grass. The land around them was largely flat, the mountains a good two hours ride from the sea. They passed orange orchards and numerous groves of olives. Interspersed with the neatly laid out fruit, nut, and olive trees were oaks.

The road was wide enough for them to ride side by side, but Marcus tended to lead, with the other two bringing up the rear with the packhorse. The silence was comradely, each deep in his own thoughts.

Marcus studied Flavius discreetly. Something had happened

between his two officers in the trip from Ostia to Tarraco. He had noticed a certain formal stiffness between the two since they had arrived in Hispania. He wondered what it was, but he knew better than to try to mediate among underlings. It never came out right. In any case, they weren't acting hostile to one another, merely "correct."

Flavius had enjoyed himself on the Tarraco training fields. His optio had spent most of his youth and adulthood in the embrace of army life, with all its ceremonies and schedules, and the last few weeks must have been disconcerting. Bellowing at recruits and passing on his enormous store of practical experience seemed to have taken his mind off of their uncertain future. Flavius looked relaxed and at peace.

"This is the life," Flavius thought to himself. The day had turned around from dark to light, which had to be an omen, he figured. Flavius was not deeply religious, but he believed in omens. When he was on the training field yesterday, a honeybee had landed on his arm. It just sat there for a bit, then moved on without stinging him. Everyone knew honeybees were good luck. He had also seen a great bird from a long way off. Flavius hadn't been able to identify it, but he convinced himself it was an eagle. Antonius also thought it might have been, but then Antonius could have been humoring him because he knew the three were starting off on a journey that had a strong element of uncertainty attached to it.

The thought brought him back from the cool, fall morning to what lay ahead of them. Men who wouldn't obey were something Flavius understood. He had been in the army too long not to know about mutiny. But men rebelled because they were ill-used, because they were besotted by greed, or because they were beaten and tired. They didn't rebel because they believed in a specific god. That made no sense. What kind of god would tell you to do that? Certainly not one that had your interests in mind.

Normally, uncertainty made him uncomfortable, but there was not a lot he could do about this specific uncertainty. That was his centurion's job, and while Flavius had no illusions that Marcus could solve all problems, he knew the man could handle this job. He was smart and the men warmed to him after a bit. The tricky part was negotiating the "bit."

He had watched Marcus take over when they got to Tarraco and maneuver them successfully out of the city and into an assignment, irrespective of how uncertain the situation they were going into was. Flavius decided he could relax; Marcus was in charge.

Flavius was amused that Marcus seemed so happy with his horse, though the great thing looked more like an ox than a horse.

He glanced at Demaratus, who was still a little distant. He now regretted his outburst, but what was done was done. He would think of ways to patch it up.

Marcus also watched Demaratus. He had to suppress a smile about the Greek's horse. Demaratus had found a kindred soul. It was a lovely creature, but skittish and lightly built. Marcus never thought of horses as being vain, but this horse seemed constantly aware of itself, much like her rider. But delicate looking or not, she could run. After the rain let up, Demaratus took his horse off the road and galloped it through a harvested field. Marcus could see that the animal was both fast and agile. She was too small for a fully armored man, but a light cavalry troop seated on horses like that would be virtually untouchable.

Demaratus looked his normal guarded self, but he also seemed relaxed. They had all eased up once they had cleared Tarraco. The Greek was constantly turning in his saddle and looked about him, and on occasion danced his horse ahead to examine something of interest.

Marcus looked down at his own horse. Its walk had an easy, phlegmatic feel to it, and the combination of its broad back and the tight grip of the four-horned saddle kept him comfortable and secure. At one point a partridge had burst from some bushes near the road, startling the other horses and causing Demaratus's mount to leap a good three or four feet sideways. His horse had ignored the bird and plodded on, either deep in thought or so stupid that it was incapable of being surprised.

He was growing fond of his horse.

Demaratus was falling in love with his horse. He had initially been attracted to her because she was different than any he had ever seen and her small head and hooves lent the horse a certain elegance. But when he took the animal into a fallow field alongside the road, the attraction turned into a deep and abiding affection. The attendant told him the horse could run, but he was unprepared for what happened when he put his heels into her flanks. She seemed to lift off the ground, not so much running on it as skimming the surface. The acceleration was so abrupt that he almost lost his balance, and by the time he recovered, the horse was racing across the field at a speed that brought tears to his eyes.

A low hedge rimmed the field's southern edge, and Demaratus panicked that the horse would hit it. He pulled on the reins to turn the horse, and the animal whipped itself around in a tight circle and raced off in the same direction they had come, with ittle loss of speed. Slowly he reined in the animal, talking to her. She responded perfectly. "I will name you "Aura," he said to the horse, slowing her to a lope and heading back toward the road.

The horse put Demaratus in a good mood. He had been brooding since the night before they left. He was no longer overly concerned with their situation. Marcus seemed to have matters under control. It was Coventina that was causing him distress. He had been taken with the tall, young woman he had seen on the street the day he had faced down the vigiles, and he returned the following morning to sit near a small fountain across from the street he had seen her turn into. He had marked the house she entered, but for all he knew she was a servant. He was certain she was not a slave, however, because she wore no ring, and her demeanor was altogether too bold.

To pass the time, he had brought a small velum book of Roman poetry with him which captured him after the first few poems, so much so that he didn't notice her come out of the house and into the street.

"And why would a Roman officer be reading instead of defending us from the barbarians," a nearby voice said.

He was so startled that he dropped the book, which she reached forward and retrieved. "Poetry? No wonder the Goths disturb our sleep," she said with a wry smile. She had an odd inflection in her Latin, as if it were not her first language.

She was wearing another long dress that was belted at the waist and held together at the shoulder with the same pin he had seen the previous day. The pin was silver, with a complex rune pattern. Her hair was waist length and filled with shifting colors: gold and brown, with highlights of red. Her eyes were wide and blue and her face framed by high cheekbones, dusted with freckles. She had a smallish nose that was just slightly turned up. The face was more interesting than it was attractive.

"The Roman soldier is mute?" she asked, this time showing a broader smile.

"I am not Roman," Demaratus stammered, "I'm Greek, " he said, feeling awkward and clumsy, two conditions he was unfamiliar with. "And poetry is humanity at its best," he added, feeling he made a good recovery.

She looked directly at him, (which was disconcerting. He was used to women being coy and flirtatious) and snorted. He had never heard a woman snort before, and, because he wasn't sure how she meant it, he went right back to feeling awkward and clumsy.

"Of course, you are a Greek. Do you think I could live in a port town and not know what a Greek looks like?" she said. "It was not your origins I was commenting on, but your uniform. Poetry and army officers are not often twinned."

Demaratus felt like he had set out for a pleasant day of sailing and had run into a heavy squall. "Well," he thought to himself, "either run for port or ride it out."

He performed a small bow. "In truth, my lady, I saw you on

my first day in Tarraco, and watched you turn into this street. I was struck by your beauty and fascinated by that unusual pin at your shoulder. I was hoping to catch a glimpse of you again, and so I have been waiting here all morning. The poetry passed the time." He said all this with what he hoped was his most engaging and disarming smile.

She put her hands on her hips and tilted her head back a little. "'My lady?' Well, you certainly are a Greek. But you don't expect me to believe all that nonsense about my pin, do you?"

"I admit it pales in your presence," he replied.

She laughed, shaking her head. "I'll bet you say that to all your women."

Demaratus realized too late that it was exactly the wrong thing to say to this disconcerting woman.

She leaned down to pick up two woven baskets at her feet. " You should sit in the Temple Plaza, Greek who dresses like a Roman. The daughters of wealthy merchants like to show their finery when they make sacrifices to Augustus. Most of them are empty headed, so you can fill their pretty little heads with poems and maybe even marry well."

Demaratus started to feel desperate. None of his charm was working, and he did not want this woman to just walk away, although she frightened him slightly. "Wait, please," he said. "Forgive me for sounding like those pretty Temple girls. I meant no disrespect. It is just that I have never met someone quite like you." He said it with a puzzled frown, a look that seemed to work.

"My people honor a quick mind and an agile tongue," she said, picking up the baskets but not turning to leave.

"You know the Greeks," he said, putting his palms in the air, "tongue-tied as a race and hardly a thought worth listening to."

This time her laugh was genuine.

He used the comment about her origins as an entrance: "Who are your people that can reduce Greeks to stammering inarticulation?" he asked.

She considered him for a moment. She had this unsettling way of looking directly at him, as if she were examining his thoughts. "I am Cantabri, from the north. My name is Coventina. And you?" she asked.

" My name is Demaratus. I am originally from Athens, although home is where I am," he answered.

She shifted the two baskets as if readying to go.

"And as I assume you are headed for the market, I offer myself as an ox," he said with a small bow. "I can make no claim to greater intelligence."

The grin she returned was friendly. "All right," she said, "if you behave."

Demaratus gave an almost perfect imitation of ox's low, which won the day. She tossed him one of the baskets and pretended to hit him with a make-believe driver's cane.

He had spent almost every waking moment he could with her. She was not a native of Tarraco, which explained her accent; Cantabrian was her native tongue. Her father had sent her to help care for her aunt who was stricken with a wasting disease. Her uncle was a gold and amber merchant; an amiable man who seemed so caught up in his wife's illness and his business that he paid little attention to his niece. Initially he looked a little uncomfortable with having a Roman officer around, but the

Greek deployed his charm and wit, and the man soon forgot all about him.

The more time he spent with Coventina, the more he was attracted to her. She was smart, funny, and competent at whatever she did. She also had looks that grew on him. What he initially thought was too tall, too thin, and horse-faced, now seemed majestic, slim, and strong featured. And whenever he forgot that she could read his thoughts, she set him straight with a particularly well-constructed dart of sarcasm. She could be devastatingly insightful, but she was never mean.

He asked her how she had come to be called Coventina, a question she met with uncharacteristic evasiveness. "Do you know much about bears?" she asked him. He admitted that he did not. Greece only had them in the north, and in any case, he explained it was not an animal that sailors often encountered. She was silent for a long time. "If we become better acquainted," she finally said, "I will tell you about bears some day." Until then, the subject was clearly off limits.

He did attempt to become "better acquainted," though when he tried to kiss her in the kitchen, she hit him with an eggplant.

In fact, the only time they had kissed was when he told her he was leaving for the south and would she mind if he wrote to her. "As long as it isn't poetry," she said with a grin. Then she put down a small tray she was carrying to her aunt, took him by the shoulders and kissed him full on the mouth.

He was so surprised he hardly responded. "Now go," she said. "I hate good-byes. If you feel like writing, write. I will answer." With that she picked up the tray and vanished.

"The woman is trouble," he thought, as he guided the horse

back to the road, but he felt a certain restlessness that he had never felt before.

The land they rode through was rich, and some of the villas were vast, bigger than anything Marcus had seen in Rome. For a while, the country was flat and rolling, the mountains to the west a distant smear. But the further they went south, the closer the mountains crowded up to the coast. There were few towns, which surprised Marcus. A similar stretch in Italia would be dotted with small to moderate sized villages. But the countryside here seemed to consist of citrus orchards and sprawling villas, with an occasional inn or cluster of houses. Traffic on the road was light and they made good time.

Marcus considered staying at an inn instead of trying to make Tortosa, but the miles rolled away and the early fall sun lingered in the sky, so he decided to push on. They ate on horse-back, passing cheese and bread back and forth between them, and taking long pulls from a wine bladder. The only time they stopped was to water and rest the horses at a small stream.

By late afternoon, the road had turned west, angling up the north side of a broad canyon. To the east, a vast delta of swampland and small farms marked the river Iberus's entrance into the sea. Clouds of birds indicated the winding course of the river. Ducks and geese mingled with sea birds, and there was an occasional cluster of large, pink birds that Marcus guessed were flamingos.

An enormous wedge of a mountain, its steep flanks covered with brush and an occasional oak tree, loomed over the road as it wound west toward Tortosa and the bridge that would get them across the Iberus. Not that there was much to the river at this time of year. A determined man could easily have forded it at the right place.

The three had made good time, and entered Tortosa with plenty of light. Marcus's horse might be placid and fat, but it was a powerful walker that never slacked its pace. By the end of the trip the other two horses were struggling to keep up with the stolid behemoth.

They crossed a well-built bridge and not far past it found an inn with a carved and gilded wooden porpoise hanging over its door. All three wearily dismounted and Marcus went inside to find the innkeeper. He emerged shortly and led the way around the back to a set of stables, where a young slave took their horses. "Bring our things in, and then rub down and feed our horses," Marcus said, tossing the boy a bronze coin. The boy looked surprised at the coin. He quickly slipped it into his tunic, and bowed.

Marcus felt like someone had been hitting his backside with a club, and he did his best not to bow his legs as he walked into the inn. He was also feeling that loss of balance which hours in the saddle give the inexperienced rider. On top of his exhaustion and pain, he was ravenously hungry. "The food here better be as good as Julius said it was," he muttered to the others.

The three sat, or rather fell, onto some benches around a table and Marcus signaled for food. A noticeably young slave woman appeared with an amphora of wine already opened and a cluster of cups in her arms. Normally Marcus would have frowned at the audacity of a slave deciding what wine they wanted but he was too tired to care and took the cup she filled from the amphora.

It was excellent; smooth, not too dry, with a flowery bouquet. He drained the cup in a single gulp, and noticed the others had done so as well.

After the second cup they began to relax, their color going from gray to pink. Well, not Demaratus. To Marcus's annoyance, he looked as fresh as he did when they left Tarraco almost 11 hours ago. "Good wine," the Greek said cheerily, which annoyed Marcus even more. He stopped himself from showing it, however, recognizing the innate unfairness of being angry with someone because they weren't as tired, sore, and hungry as you were. "You are getting old, Marcus," he thought.

The innkeeper, a stocky fellow who had the look of an army veteran, appeared at the table. "Welcome, gentlemen, I hope you find the wine to your liking? Comrades should have the best."

Flavius smiled up at him. "It is a fine wine. Where did you serve?"

"Oh, mostly here in Hispania with the VII Legion. I was with a vexilla in Mauritania for a bit, but mainly I served up around Legio. When I mustered out, I bought this place," he said. "Will you trust me on the menu tonight?"

Flavius grinned at him. "As long as it isn't cabbage, lentils and bacon."

The man laughed. "I tolerate no army fare under this roof, sir. I had quite enough of that."

"Then we put ourselves in your hands," said Marcus. "By the way, what is your name?"

"Appius Fulvius, sir, former princepus prior optio, Third Century, Second Cohort," he said with a small salute.

Marcus introduced himself and the two others, and the four

gossiped a few minutes about their destination. The innkeeper broke it off with, "But I am sure you are hungry, sirs, so first let's get some food in you."

No one disagreed.

The food was indeed good. There was grilled fish with three kinds of sauce, good bread and olive oil, and an enormous haunch of boar stuffed with dates and drizzled with honey sauce. They finished the first amphora of wine and started on a second. By the time honey cakes arrived for dessert Marcus was feeling almost human.

The innkeeper returned and sat down, and Marcus, Flavius and the man were soon deep into army talk.

Demaratus was perfectly willing to be a soldier but he found it excruciatingly boring to talk about. He nodded to Marcus and Flavius, complimented Appius on his fare, and said he was going outside to stretch his legs and get some air.

He pushed through the inn's door and out to the street near the bridge. There was a steady stream of traffic moving both north and south, and he watched it for a moment. He was just preparing to turn back to the inn when something tugged at his memory. A young boy on a mule, his face strained with exhaustion, was just coming off the bridge and passing the inn.

It was the boy from the clothing shop in Tarraco.

Demaratus wracked his brain for the name before it came to him: "Telamon," he called.

The boy pulled the mule to a halt and slid off its back as Demaratus walked forward and took the animal's bit in his hand.

"Sir, two men, they asked about you. They are looking for you," the boy said in a rush of words.

Demaratus glanced around. This was no place to have this conversation. "Let's get your mule to the stable and you can tell me all about it. You must be tired and hungry," he said, taking the boy by the hand and leading the mule with the other. Demaratus led them around back of the inn and handed the mule to the young slave. Then he took the boy to a corner of the yard, sat him on a small keg, and told him to tell his story.

Telamon took a moment to organize his thoughts, "I was down by the docks yesterday, helping my father pick up some cloth that had just come in. My father was in the warehouse and I was wandering along the docks looking at ships," he said. "I just happened to pass by three men talking. One was a sea captain, I think, and the other two were asking him questions. As I walked by, I heard the captain say your centurion's name, and some other name I never heard."

"Flavius?" Demaratus supplied.

"Yes," answered the boy, "or something like that. I didn't hear your name."

Demaratus thought for a moment, then said, "Go on."

The boy had ridden as far as the three men had on a much slower animal, and he was almost collapsing from exhaustion, but he took a breath and went on. "I tried to listen, but the big one saw me and gave me a kick. But I did see the captain pointing up toward the Temple Plaza."

"If we survive this," thought Demaratus to himself, "I will pay a call on that captain."

"What did they look like?" he asked.

"One is very big, sir, with a scar on his cheek. He was the one that tried to kick me. The other one was thin, but mean looking," the boy said.

"How were they dressed?"

Telamon thought for a moment. "I can't tell you exactly, but they had hoods on their cloaks."

"Were they soldiers?" said Demaratus.

"Oh no, sir. They were dressed just like everyone else," he answered.

The boy rubbed his legs and his face, and said, "So I ran right back and told my father. He immediately went to the barracks and asked for you, but they said you had left. He would have come himself but he can't ride. His back will not permit it. That is why he sent me."

Demaratus was confused. "Your father went to the barracks yesterday?" he asked.

"Yes," the boy answered.

Demaratus was quiet for a moment. "We had not left yet, had not even been given our orders. Why did they say we had left?" he said, as much to himself as to Telamon.

"My father said it was a young slave who told him," answered Telamon.

That could be it. The slave might have thought they had left, or was just being difficult, one of the small ways that slaves repaid masters for their bondage. Knowing then what he knew now would have saved this boy a long day's ride. On the other hand, it bought them some time.

"Telamon, you are a hero. We are all in your debt, my friend," said Demaratus.

The boy flushed pink from the praise.

"Let's get you some food and rest, comrade," said Demaratus, steering Telamon toward the inn. "Now when we get inside, son, don't say a word to anyone about this, all right?"

"Yes, sir," said the boy.

Demaratus found Marcus, Flavius, and Appius still deep in discussion, so he signaled the young slave and ordered food. He caught Flavius looking oddly at him. Demaratus discreetly signaled the optio to go to the stables. Flavius excused himself and walked through the inn's back door. Some of the boy's food had already arrived, which Telamon fell on like a wolf upon the fold. Demaratus told him he would be right back.

Slipping out through the back, he saw Flavius leaning his back against a stall with his arms crossed.

"Who's your little friend?" said Flavius. "And how did he find us?"

Demaratus decided to ignore the optio's suspicious tone. "The Praetorians are coming, Flavius. The lad in there is the son of a friend in Tarraco. He spotted them and then rode all day to tell us."

"How many?" Flavius asked shifting his tone to one of concern.

"The boy saw only two, and both were out of uniform," answered Demaratus.

"Out of uniform," said Flavius thoughtfully. "So maybe this is unofficial."

Demaratus nodded. "It would appear so, which might make our job easier."

"Job?" asked Flavius.

"We have to kill them," answered Demaratus. "In fact, I am going to have to kill them."

Flavius just stared at him. Finally, he said, "Aren't we moving a bit fast here? And why are you the one who is going to kill them?"

"Shall we wait until they take us, optio" Demaratus replied, "and isn't it obvious why I have to do it?"

"I hate guessing games, Demaratus. It isn't obvious to me," said Flavius, putting an edge in his voice, "so explain it, if you don't mind."

"These Praetorians are not going to arrest us and put us on trial, Flavius, they are going to kill us," said Demaratus. "If they were going to arrest us, they would have gone straight to headquarters. They didn't. They skulked about on the docks asking questions. This is almost certainly an 'unofficial' warrant by someone who doesn't like Marcus's family. Do you agree?"

Flavius hesitated, taking the argument in, then nodded. "Agreed."

"But they will pretend the arrest is legal, and once we give up our weapons, we leave for the underworld," continued Demaratus.

"Agreed," said Flavius again.

"We have to make these Praetorians disappear without any suspicion we had anything to do with it," said Demaratus. "If we fight them, it will be a public matter, and the authorities will have to investigate, and I think you will agree that a lot of questions about our orders and what we are doing here is not a good idea."

Flavius nodded agreement.

"If Marcus is involved in it, the likelihood is that this will be a public matter. Therefore, we need to keep him out of it, not just for Marcus, but for all of us."

Again, Flavius nodded, though he was looking increasingly puzzled. "All right," he said, "I see your argument, but why you?"

"Because you are his second in command, and if you are involved, Marcus will know. Can you say to Marcus, 'Excuse me, sir, while I vanish for a few days?' Of course not. The only person with any independence of movement here is me," said Demaratus.

Flavius was silent for a long time. "How are you going to kill two Praetorian assassins by yourself, Demaratus?" he finally asked.

"Let me work that out," Demaratus answered. "I have some ideas. Your job will be to give me twenty-four hours once we get to Saguntum."

Flavius sighed. "I guess you're right, but these guys...."

"They are Romans, Flavius," said Demaratus, still irritated over the incident on the ship. "That means they have one weakness: it never occurs to them they can be beaten. I won't defeat them; they'll defeat themselves."

Flavius pursed his lips, then grinned. "You like sticking it to Romans, don't you, Demaratus. Okay, we have two days to work out the details. I'll have thought of something by then." As they were walking back to the inn, he put his hand on Demaratus's shoulder and said, "But if you need me for the fight, you call on me, all right?"

Demaratus nodded: "Agreed."

The two went into the inn just as Marcus was rising and heading for bed. Demaratus introduced Telamon to the centurion and Flavius, and explained that the boy was there getting materials for his father. Telamon went along with the lie, and Demaratus arranged for the innkeeper to put a couch in his room for the boy.

XII

The four were up before dawn and Demaratus helped Telamon saddle his mule. He tied a bundle of bread and cheese to the saddle's back, and the two of them walked out to the bridge.

"Telamon, you have done us a great service, greater than you can imagine. You and your father must never tell anyone what happened here. It could put your entire family in great danger. Do you understand?"

"Yes, sir," answered Telamon, as he mounted.

"And when I return to Tarraco, Telamon, you and I will go out and find you the finest blade in Hispania, all right?"

Telamon glowed. "Yes, sir. I will look forward to that," he said. Then he leaned down and brushed Demaratus's shoulder. "Be careful, sir, they look like very dangerous men."

Demaratus smiled up at him. "Greeks are pretty dangerous too," he said with a wink.

The boy smiled, turned his mule and began the long ride back to Tarraco.

By this time Flavius and Marcus had loaded up and were

waiting for him. He quickly mounted Aura and the three trotted out of the stable and on to the Via Augusta.

South of Tortosa the countryside was wide, rolling, and rich with orchards and villas, the peaks once again receding to the west. But within a few hours the mountains began to press upon the riders again, so they were soon traversing a narrow strip, with the sea on one side and the hills on the other. It was another glorious fall day, clear and warm. When Marcus was deep in thought—which was often—Flavius and Demaratus would drop back and talk. By this time Flavius was in complete agreement, although concerned. At first, Demaratus was insulted by the concern, but it gradually dawned on him that Flavius was worried about him personally, and not because Flavius thought he was no match for two assassins. Of course, Demaratus was by no means convinced he was, but he kept that to himself.

Flavius had already figured out how to get the time that Demaratus would need. "I'll put a small pebble in your horse's hoof," he said—hurrying ahead with the plan when he saw Demaratus's look of horror that his precious animal might be harmed —"that won't hurt it, but will cause it to limp. I'll take a look and announce that the horse's hooves need work, and you tell us to go ahead and you will meet us. That sound okay?"

"As long as Aura is not damaged, fine," said Demaratus.

"Aura?" said Flavius. "What's that mean?"

"It is a wind that blows in the Gulf of Seronia. It helped defeat the Persians at Salamis," replied Demaratus.

"Oh," said Flavius, and then swallowed something he was going to say.

Demaratus suppressed a smile. "He is being careful about Greeks," he thought. "Good."

Flavius was silent for a moment, then asked, "How will we find them?"

"We have a description. What we need is luck," said Demaratus with a shrug.

The distance from Tortosa to Saguntum was almost twice the distance from Tarraco to Tortosa. They could have made it in two days, but Flavius and Demaratus decided that they did not want to get too far ahead of their pursuers. If they were going to confront the Praetorians, they needed to do so in a place like Saguntum which, according to Demaratus who had unloaded goods there, probably had more resident ghosts than people.

Marcus, however, wanted to step up the pace, so Flavius had to resort to the pebble in the hoof trick on his own horse, and then convince the centurion they were risking damage to their mounts. Marcus was very protective of his horse (even though Flavius was sure he could put a boulder in its massive foot and the fool animal would never even notice), so the argument worked. Flavius repaired his horse's hoof, but the entire party slowed down, and they spent two nights at inns on the road to Saguntum.

Late in the morning of their fourth day out from Tarraco, the three crossed a bridge over a small river and entered the city of Seguntum.

Though past its prime, its population drained by its southern neighbor, Valentia, Seguntum had a certain dramatic if aging grace about it. Built on the side of hill, with a dominating fortress on the ridgeline, the city was marked by a long, wide beach along its eastern edge, and the massive citadel at its crown. In between was a circus, a theater, and a graceful temple.

Demaratus had been to Seguntum twice and he pointed out the fort and the Temple of Diana. "It took Hannibal nine months to take that fort," Demaratus told Marcus and Flavius, "but he wouldn't touch the temple."

"Aye, this is where it all began," said Flavius. "When Hannibal took Seguntum, he started the Second Punic War. We had to come to the aid of our allies."

Demaratus grinned. "Since it was the only time Rome ever came to the aid of the Greeks, you don't suppose it was because they were looking for an excuse to fight the Carthaginians, do you?"

"Hannibal needed no excuse to fight Rome," said Marcus quietly.

Demaratus, recognizing this might be delicate ground, dropped the subject, although it irked him that the Romans always portrayed their wars of conquest as either Rome coming to the aid of some beleaguered ally, or as the victim of some attack. He had never heard a Roman say, "We went to war to capture slaves and steal everything those people have." Greeks were more honest about their avarice. Of course, he conceded, the Greeks were also a good deal less successful at stealing other people's things than the Romans.

On the way into Saguntum, Demaratus marked that there was only one bridge into the city, and that near it was a small taverna where he could sit and watch who crossed it.

They spent their first night in an inn near the beach, and in the morning, Demaratus took up his post at the taverna. It was tedious work, but he would have to do it alone. Flavius was busy with Marcus, refilling their supplies for the long haul over the mountains and down the Baetis Valley to Corduba. There were lots of towns in Baetica, unarguably the richest part of Hispania, but not until the travelers got into the upper sections of the Valley. Taking on supplies was not only prudent, it was required. Marcus said he wanted them all to leave in the early afternoon, but Flavius had already put his plan to keep Demaratus in Saguntum into motion.

At mid-morning, Demaratus got restless and wandered through the area close to the bridge. Several of the houses were deserted, with empty windows and weeds growing on their doorsteps. Others looked as if their owners had just left. One empty house had a table and chairs he could see through the partly opened front door in a room facing the street. Demaratus passed it by, then stopped, turned, and went back. He opened the door and walked in. The room was of moderate size. In it was a table, about six feet by three, surrounded by four chairs, one falling apart.

He suddenly had an idea. He quickly put the room in order and tossed the broken chair in the back room. He returned to the taverna and purchased an amphora of wine, several candles, and three cups and a plate from the puzzled owner. He added a loaf of bread, a wedge of cheese and a small pottery container of olives.

Returning to the house, he set the food, pottery, and wine on the table, along with a candle. He took a few other candles, put them in the back, and lit them. Then he closed the door to the back room and stood near the front door. He could see a faint glimmer of the candles through a crack near the handle and a shaft of dim light came from under the door.

Satisfied, he blew out the candles and carefully closed the front door.

Returning to his post at the taverna he noticed two horses tied up outside. He turned quickly and crossed the street with his face away from the taverna, then circled back and approached it from the rear. He couldn't go through the kitchen without provoking comment, so he approached a side window and carefully looked in. Two men were sitting at a table, waiting for their order. He could not see their faces clearly, but they fit the big and the thin body types that Telamon had described.

He waited until the big one turned to curse at the slave bringing them food. The man had a ragged scar running down one cheek.

Demaratus backed away and went directly to the inn by the beach. Marcus and Flavius were huddled around the horses, and Flavius was lifting Aura's hoof and shaking his head. "Oh, there you are, Demaratus, I'm afraid you've got a problem with your horse," said Flavius.

"Problem?" he answered, putting a concerned note in his voice.

"Aye, the mare's limping. We have to get someone to work on her hooves. They're a bit of a mess. Or else you need to go into Valentia and get a new horse," Flavius said.

Demaratus considered for a moment (they had carefully rehearsed this; since Marcus would not know a hoof from a hangnail, all they had to do was sound like they knew what they were talking about). "It doesn't make sense for me to exchange the horse. Getting her reshod or getting a new horse will still delay us until tonight or tomorrow," he said, shaking his head.

"I agree," sympathized Flavius, then seemed to have an idea. "Why don't we push on and you catch up? Even if you have to wait until tomorrow, we won't outpace this horse."

Marcus was not sure. "I am not comfortable breaking up our unit," he said, as if the three of them were a legion dividing its forces in the face of the enemy. He was not far off the mark, but only his subordinates knew that.

Flavius saved his best for last. "We could wait, sir, it is just that I hate to leave that situation in Corduba festering for even an extra half day. But, of course, we will do what you wish, sir."

"Oh, the man is good," thought Demaratus. He knew how anxious Marcus was to get to Corduba.

Marcus thought for a moment. "All right, then. Try to get on the road this evening if you can. If not, leave at first light."

"Yes, sir," answered Demaratus.

Demaratus helped the two get loaded and on their way, and then led the limping Aura back to the stable, where he quickly removed the stone.

His instinct was to return to the taverna immediately, but he mastered it. He loaded his gear on the back of Aura, and then, taking a roundabout route, walked the horse to a small, enclosed garden he had noticed near the deserted house. He put the horse in the garden, closed the gate and went to the house. The light was by now beginning to fade, so he lit the candles in the back room and the one on the front table. He cut the cheese into chunks and made the table look like someone had just finished a meal.

He drew his Damascus blade and slipped it into a small sheath he had made over the past two days. The sheath tied behind his right leg, so that the tunic hid it. Then he shifted his pugio so that it showed clearly. He opened the wine, took a long swig, gargled with it, then spit it out. He poured some onto his fingers and dribbled it on his tunic.

Carefully closing the door, he headed for the taverna. He had a moment of panic when he didn't see the horses, but then noticed that they had been moved around to the side. The Praetorians were still inside. "Let them be drunk," he thought.

He took a deep breath, rubbed his eyes until they were red, and pushed through the door. The main room had started to fill up, but the two Praetorians still sat at the corner table, talking. He had hoped to find them deep in their cups, but it was possible that Praetorian assassins were careful with alcohol.

His plan was subtle in conception, but needed to be bold in the execution.

He wove over to the table, put his hands firmly on it, and said, "Good evening, gentlemen," making sure they smelled his breath.

The two gave him a stone-dead look. The thin one said in a voice filled with contempt, "Something we can help you with, Greek?"

"Why no, my comrades—or should I say ex-comrades—but I think I can help you. For a cup of wine, of course," said Demaratus.

The big one with the scar reached out and grabbed him by

the throat. Demaratus felt like someone had put an iron collar on him. "Why don't I just break your neck, Greek? That would help everyone."

As he started to squeeze, the thin one put his hand on his arm. "Let him go, Lucius. Remember, they had a Greek with them."

Lucius slowly released his grip, and Demaratus gratefully gulped in a lungful of air.

"How can you help us, Greek?" asked the thin one.

"The word is you are looking for two men by the name of Marcus and Flavius, am I right?" asked Demaratus. "I served with them and I can deliver them to you. For a price."

"I thought you said a cup of wine would do," said the thin one with a smile that found no echo in his eyes.

"The cost of repairing my throat requires me to raise the price to 500 denarii," Demaratus said.

Lucius started to rise with a snarl, but the thin one cut him off. "Of course, if you can actually deliver them."

"Why are we negotiating with this piece of shit," growled Lucius, "let me take him 'round back, Sextus, and he'll be paying us 500 denarii just to get me to stop."

"Relax, Lucius. I am sure our friend here understands that people who cooperate with the Praetorians get their just rewards," said Sextus.

So, the dangerous one is Sextus, thought Demaratus.

"Ex-comrade?" queried Sextus.

"Yes, ex-comrade," said Demaratus, putting as much bitterness as he could into the phrase. "They tossed me out because I had an argument with that cursed centurion. They accused me of stealing!"

"A Greek steal?" said Sextus with mock concern." Why would they ever think that?"

"Well, that's what I told them," said Demaratus, slightly slurring his words and weaving a little.

"So, my friend, where are they?" asked Sextus.

"Not far from here. They are holed up in a deserted house because they are a bunch of cowards. I can take you there, but I want half the money first," said Demaratus.

Lucius started to rumble again, but Sextus silenced him. "Of course. Lucius, take our friend's arm and let us pay a visit to Marcus and Flavius."

Lucius gripped Demaratus's left arm, almost lifting him off the floor. The taverna owner started to protest that they had not paid their bill until Sextus turned and stared at him. The man stopped in mid-sentence and backed away.

"Lead on, Greek," said Sextus, quietly.

Demaratus noticed that both men were wearing leather jerkins. It wasn't armor, but it might turn a poorly aimed knife. He would need to keep it in mind.

The night was cool and the square near the bridge deserted.

"I want half the money first," said Demaratus, trying to sound sullen.

"When you take us to the house you get half. After we finish our business, you get the reward. Now that's fair, isn't it?" asked Sextus softly.

Demaratus let himself slump, and said, "All right," but wrenched his arm loose from Lucius, and put his hand to his pugio. "Tell him to keep his hands off of me," he said.

Lucius looked like he was going to charge, but Sextus intervened again. "Let him be, Lucius. Remember, he is a valued ally."

"Right," slurred Demaratus, "I'm an ally."

Both Praetorians glanced at one another and smiled.

He wove slightly (too much might make them suspicious) and headed for the house. As he approached it he had to admire his handiwork. A light flickered through the window and under the door. Demaratus pointed out the door. He suddenly felt a sword at his back.

"Now just hand me your pugio, Greek, and let's see you walk through that door first just in case you and your friends have a little party planned," whispered Sextus.

"But I won't have a dagger," protested Demaratus. "They'll kill me if they see me."

"Better you than us," rumbled Lucius.

Sextus pushed him toward the door, reached for the handle, and then quietly pushed him into the room. The candle guttered on the table where it looked as if someone had left a partially eaten meal. The light gleamed through the bottom of the second door, and Sextus nodded to Lucius and pointed to the door, shifting his concentration for a moment.

It was Sextus's first and last mistake.

Demaratus spun, driving his left hand down to deflect Sextus's sword and sliding the Damascus blade out of its hidden sheath. He drove the blade upward, aiming for the fifth rib, but he was slightly off balance and afraid the leather jerkin might deflect the thrust. But the knife treated cloth, leather, flesh, and bone as if they were smoke, and he felt the hilt slam into the Praetorian's chest.

The man tensed for a moment, then, dead, he collapsed heavily onto Demaratus before falling to the ground. The weight of his body threw Demaratus further off balance, so that he careened across the room, slamming against the table.

With a roar, Lucius charged.

Demaratus whipped around the table and kicked it upward into the Praetorian's face. It had about as much effect as if he thrown a piece of bread at the man. Demaratus saw the sword blade coming at him and he pivoted to his left to avoid it. The blade went past him, but then Lucius was on him, grabbing his knife arm with his left hand and slamming him against the wall.

The force of the blow stunned Demaratus, and Lucius pulled his right arm back to make the killing thrust. But Demaratus recovered, pushed away from the wall, and shot himself straight into the huge Praetorian, preventing the man from stabbing him with his sword. On the other hand, he was now locked in the Praetorian's arms, which allowed Lucius to slam him against the wall again. Demaratus felt like the dog that had the great misfortune to catch the bull.

Lucius pulled him back, and smashed him once more against the rough wall. Demaratus knew he could not absorb another blow like that. He lifted his left knee and drove it between Lucius's legs. The big man grimaced and faltered for a moment, just enough for Demaratus to turn the Damascus blade so that he could slide it across the top of Lucius's wrist. Any other knife would only have made a minor wound, but the fine edge on the Damascus blade cut deep, and Lucius grunted and pulled his hand back, while steadying his right hand for a sword thrust.

Again, Demaratus desperately embraced him, and the sword

once again missed him, sliding behind his back. Only this time his knife hand was free, and the Damascus blade went straight into the Praetorian's chest. It was not a heart stab like the one he delivered to Sextus, but he didn't dare pull it out and strike again. He had to marshal every bit of his strength just to hold on.

Lucius roared and slammed him against the wall, but with slightly less force this time than before. Demaratus desperately thrust the blade deeper, turning it as he did so. Lucius slammed him against the wall again. "Will the man never die?" thought Demaratus, on the point of blacking out.

Suddenly the big man shuddered, staggered, and collapsed on top of Demaratus. The Praetorian twitched for a few moments, then lay still.

For several minutes Demaratus could not move, could not even think. He felt crushed by the body on top of him, but he hadn't the strength to lift it. Slowly he began to work himself from under Lucius, until he could finally grab the table and pull himself clear. He lay there until he was suddenly panicked by the possibility that someone would walk by on the street outside and see the carnage.

He crawled to the door, shoved it shut and then sat with his back to it to catch his breath. Slowly the trembling of his body ceased, and the red mist that had fogged his vision right before Lucius finally succumbed to the Damascus blade began to lift. He carefully felt each of his limbs which, while bruised and painful, seemed intact. His left shoulder hurt and he touched it delicately. Something had gouged out a piece of flesh, but the shoulder moved, albeit painfully.

He rolled himself over to his hands and knees and, using the door handle, pulled himself erect.

He was stunned by the carnage. The walls were splattered with blood, and a great pool of it had formed in the middle of the room. Sextus and Lucius were both lying face down, which would not do. He leaned down and turned Sextus over. The man's face was a frozen mask of surprise. "Well, the world is a better place for your absence, you bastard," thought Demaratus.

He moved the body so its head was toward the door, then retrieved Lucius's sword and thrust it into the place where the Damascus knife had done its damage. He needed to make this look like the two men had quarreled and killed one another.

Lucius was a bigger problem. It took a long time just to turn the man's body over and he gave up trying to change its position. He found Sextus's sword and stabbed it into the gaping chest wound on the big Praetorian. He then retrieved his pugio.

He looked down at himself and flinched. He was covered with blood, virtually soaked in it. Well, he would deal with that soon enough.

First, he carefully went through the men's tunics until he found a small scroll. Unrolling it, he glanced at it. It was a description of him, Marcus and Flavius, although it simply referred to him as a "Greek," rather than by his name. He made sure there was nothing further to identify the three of them on either man, and then gathered up the plate, cups, candles, wine and food, stuffing them into a sack. No one must be able to connect him with the killing.

It was so dark outside that he stumbled on the step and almost sprawled in the street. Somehow, he made it to the small walled garden, where a quiet whicker from Aura almost made him weep with relief.

At first the horse shied away from him because the smell of the blood spooked her, but he calmed her down, loaded the household items on her, mounted, and trotted north toward the river.

XIII

Demaratus clung to his saddle as Aura left the road and picked her way down a steep slope to the small river that ran just north of Saguntum. The horse moved upstream with little urging, until Demaratus felt safe enough to dismount. He carefully tied the horse to a small bush and unloaded her. He removed the plate, the cups and the amphora from the sack, and smashed them with a rock, flinging the pieces into the river. Then, stripping off his tunic, he tore off one of the few pieces on the garment free of blood. He waded out until he found a spot where, lying down, the water would cover his body. Slowly and painfully, he lowered himself into the chill stream and lay back, letting the water wash over him.

He soaked for several minutes, then sat up painfully and began to methodically scrub his body with the small piece of cloth. The water was cold, but it felt good, and slowly he began to feel human again. Scrubbed, he climbed out of the river and retrieved his knife, which he also carefully washed. Finished, he sat for several minutes by a large boulder, letting some of the water stream off him. Finally, he rose, untied a fresh bundle of clothes—he regretted the destruction of one of the two tunics he had purchased from Androdamas in Tarraco—and laid them out.

Before putting them on, he made a bandage of his wash cloth and put it on his shoulder, which was scraped and oozing blood. Again, he took up his old tunic and searched for another piece without blood. It was hard to tell because even though his eyes had grown accustomed to the dark, the moon was not yet up and it was difficult to see. Finally, he was forced to find a secluded place and light one of the candles. He found a section of the tunic that only had a few drops of blood on it, and with his knife, cut a long strip of cloth.

He washed out the strip as best he could and then spent minutes painfully trying to secure the bandage.

When all was done, he dressed. He was hungry, despite the fight, but when he unwrapped the cheese and bread, he could not stomach it. He would do without.

He untied Aura, and slowly mounted, pointing the horse upstream and angling toward the ridge on his left. The horse followed the stream for a while and then headed into a copse of trees and onto a goat path winding upwards. He gave Aura her head and she picked her way up the long slope, finally breaching the ridgeline near a scatter of rocks and bushes.

He stopped her at the top and surveyed the countryside. A half-moon was just starting to climb over the mountains to the west, spilling a ghostly glow over the hills and valleys that marched off to the southwest. To the east he could make out the lights of Saguntum. Somewhere ahead lay the road to Corduba, although he was unsure where. He gently heeled the horse and she started down the long slope toward the next ridgeline.

For two hours he and Aura descended valleys and climbed hills, like a tiny boat on a gigantic, frozen seascape of waves and troughs. Finally, Demaratus caught a gleam of finished stone in the distance, and half an hour later, he and Aura scrambled up a steep gully and set off down the Via Augusta at a trot. A trot was the only pace that would keep him awake.

Flavius was worried and doing his best to conceal it, but it was difficult to hide his concern from Marcus. The centurion had a habit of disappearing into his own thoughts, but just when you thought he wasn't paying attention, it turned out he was.

"What's bothering you, Flavius? You've been distracted since we left Saguntum. Are you worried about Demaratus showing up?" asked Marcus.

The two had spent the night near a small stream, cooking their food over an open fire and rolling themselves in their cloaks to sleep. They had risen at first light and put together a simple meal of cheese, bread and olives. Still chewing on a piece of bread, Flavius had already begun to gather their gear and tie it on the horses.

"No, sir," Flavius lied. "I guess I am thinking about this business with the First Cohort."

Marcus gave him a long look that said he didn't quite believe him. "It is not like this is the first time we have commanded a troubled unit. What concerns you more about this one?"

Flavius was quiet a moment, and then said, quite truthfully, "This religion stuff makes me nervous. It's different than trying to win the men's loyalty or pull them up from doing something stupid. This is about what people believe, and you can't knock that out of their heads with forced marches or extra duty."

Marcus nodded. "I agree, but we haven't seen the shape of the battle field yet, so there is not much sense worrying about it now."

The two gathered up their cloaks and walked the road for a bit before mounting. It was a fine road, at least 16 feet wide, with well-dressed stone and efficient drains. They passed a marker indicating they had come 25 miles from Saguntum and had almost 300 to go before they reached Corduba. They were on the long leg of their journey south.

If Flavius had not been worrying about Demaratus he would have enjoyed the morning. The cloudless sky promised a hot day ahead, but for now it was cool with a slight breeze blowing down from the mountains. They were traversing a valley that gently climbed toward a tumble of some distant hills in front of them. According to the innkeeper in Saguntum, the Via Augusta skirted them, and then headed west-southwest and into the upper reaches of the Baetia River. Once they were through the gap in the mountains, they would just follow the river to the rich plains below.

But he was concerned. Part of him couldn't imagine Demaratus taking on two Praetorian thugs, although the Greek had a lot of surprises in him. He and Marcus would be fish food if Demaratus had not taken over during the storm. Still, Praetorians ... and then left the thought unfinished.

For three hours the two climbed up the valley, finally stopping at a small stream to water the horses and give them some barley. Flavius was fixing a feedbag on Marcus's horse, when the centurion said quietly, "Looks like we have company."

Flavius shaded his eyes against the sun and looked back down the road. A single rider was approaching a long way off, but there was no mistaking the horse's gate. "Demaratus for sure, sir," said Flavius, relief washing over him.

"Yes," said Marcus, and once again gave him a searching look. Flavius did his best to look innocent, even grumbling a little about how "Greeks were always late."

They let the horses eat and sat themselves down by the road to wait for Demaratus. As he drew close, Flavius noted the bandage. "Something must be wrong with his left shoulder," he thought.

By the time Demaratus drew up to them it was obvious something had happened to the man. He looked drawn and exhausted, and there were bruises on his face and a contusion over his left eye. Marcus frowned, "What happened to you, Demaratus?"

"Good morning, sir," he answered, and then shrugged and gave a weak smile. "Aura decided I was mistreating her, and tossed me into a stream bed."

"I'm sorry," said Marcus, "Are you badly injured?"

Flavius was certain that Demaratus's injuries had nothing to do with Aura, but it was a perfect cover story. If there was any tale that could take Marcus in, it was one involving a horse.

"No, I'm fine, sir. More embarrassed than hurt," said Demaratus. "I could use a little food, however. I planned to catch up to you earlier and only had a little bread with me."

Marcus and Flavius quickly unpacked the food, and they all sat as the Greek dug into some cheese, bread and wine.

"Any problems with the horse, besides it turning bad tempered on you?" asked Marcus.

Demaratus's answer was muffled by the food, but both figured out it was a "no," and then something about "fault," which was probably that he was to blame, not Aura. They gave him enough time to get some food in him, then mounted up and headed toward the mountains.

Demaratus volunteered to take the packhorse, and for a while Flavius and Marcus rode side-by-side, sometimes talking, other times taking in the countryside or retreating into their thoughts. Flavius eventually excused himself to relieve Demaratus, dropping back to move alongside the Greek.

"Are you really all right?" asked Flavius in a low voice.

Demaratus shrugged. "Well enough."

"What happened?" asked Flavius.

Demaratus was silent for a long time, then turned to look directly at Flavius. "They made a mistake," he said softly, handing over the packhorse's lead rope to him, and moving slightly ahead. It was a position the three held for most of the day.

The distance the three kept from one another gave Flavius an opportunity to think about their situation, which was not encouraging. If Demaratus—or any of them—were tied to the murders of the two Praetorians it would go badly for the trio. They wouldn't have the ease of a quick execution, or even a painful crucifixion. All of them would be a long time dying. Flavius was not overly afraid of death, but he had seen—and heard—men tortured to death. It could take days, with the torturers nursing their victims around each night so they could inflict another day of agony on them.

Two thoughts occurred to him: the business of the murders was by no means over, and under no circumstances could any of them be taken alive. If he had to, he would kill the other two with his own hands.

The road had first turned west, then southwest, bisecting a range of mountains to the north and south. Somewhere in the pass they crossed a divide, because the streams began to run southwest toward the great Oceanus Atlanticus rather than east toward the Mediterranium. They were at the high end of a valley where a number of small streams began to come together, steams that would eventually become the Baetis.

There were farmhouses and small villas, and they passed by mines, some deserted, some being worked by slaves. "Silver," Demaratus told them. "It is said that when the Phoenicians first came to Baetica the people there were using it for tools. The story is that the Phoenicians threw away the ballast from their ships and used silver instead, and that they even made anchors out of it."

"It was the life-blood of the Carthaginians, that's for sure," said Marcus. "Hispania is rumored to be a treasure house."

Demaratus nodded. "There is silver here, also near Carthago Nova, and on the far side of Corduba. There is gold in Baetica and cinnabar as well. And there is supposed to be gold from the grass roots down in Legio."

"A rich land," remarked Flavius.

Demaratus gave him a teasing smile: "Why else would the Romans be here?"

"Just following you Greeks, as I recall," Flavius answered mildly.

All three laughed. It was a good shot.

There was surprisingly little traffic on the road. Marcus thought that the current instability in Rome might be depressing trade and making people stay close to home, but Demaratus was of the opinion that it was a slack time of the year. The ports were concentrating on piling up supplies that would be essential for the winter and before the fall winds turned contrary. However, none of them were displeased by the seemingly deserted world they found themselves in.

Just as the shadows began to lengthen, they stopped and made camp at a quiet grove of trees near a steam with a small meadow for the horses. Demaratus was relieved to rest. He started to deal with feeding his horse, but Flavius waved him off. "Go soak those bruises in some cold water," Flavius told him, "I'll take care of the horses." Demaratus did indeed soak himself, and the chill waters helped not only to relieve his aches and pains, but energized him and gave him a voracious appetite.

The three sat wrapped in their cloaks around a small fire, eating, talking, and watching the stars begin to appear in the vast dome of the sky overhead.

It was the last night they spent camping. Within a few miles of their meadow camp, they began to encounter traffic, most of it local. But ox carts of ore were moving down the road toward cities in the Baetis flood plain, and occasional caravans of chained slaves were moving up toward the mines. Merchants and travelers began to appear in abundance.

They stayed a night in Montero Ordana, a village that lay

close up to the northern mountains, then moved on to a series of towns, each one bigger than the previous one. Their route took them through the history of Roman Hispania: Baecula, where Scipio defeated Hannibal's brother, Hasdrabel. Castulo, where Scipio's father and uncle were overwhelmed and destroyed by Carthaginian infantry and Numidian cavalry during the First Punic War. Statues and monuments marked the battlefields, engagements whose consequences still echoed throughout the Empire.

On the sixth day, they crossed a massive bridge into Corduba.

It was a city vibrant with life, so packed with commerce, wagons, and people that the three had difficulty picking their way through the crowded streets. This was a wealthy city, dotted with temples, public buildings, and rich looking houses. As Tarraco's star was descending, Corduba's was rising.

The legion camp was supposed to be on the northwest side of the city, although they got lost at one point and had to ask for directions. The camp was not large, because it had not been built to hold a legion, just a cohort or two. There was a sizable amphitheater west of the camp's ditch and ramparts. They passed through the south gateway with a wave from the two sentries on duty. The camp was almost identical to tens of thousands of other camps, from the border beyond Palmyra in the east to Britannia's River Tay in the north. Cohort barracks were to the left and right, and they could see a hospital near the east rampart. They considered stopping at the baths, but Marcus decided that it would be better to go straight to the Principia and give in their orders. They could worry about a bath later.

They dropped off their mounts at the stables just to the right of the Principia, instructing the attendants to reserve the horses for them in the future.

The two attendants looked at one another, and one asked, "The fat one, too?"

Marcus gave the man an icy look. "Yes," he said coldly.

"Where do you want your gear, sir?" the other attendant asked Marcus.

"We are assigned to the Second Century, First Cohort," answered Marcus.

"I'll see that your baggage is taken to the barracks, sir, and welcome to Corduba," the attendant said.

Marcus thanked him and the three went directly to the Principia, only stopping to look one another over and straighten various parts of their uniforms. Demaratus's contusion and visible bruises were quickly disappearing.

The sentry saluted them, and they presented themselves to the tesserarius at the desk inside the main entrance. He looked up, stood, and saluted them. "Aemilius Gratidius, sir. How can I serve you," he said.

Marcus returned the salute, introduced himself and his officers, and handed the man his orders. The tesserarius glanced at them, and said, "I will ask if Gnaeus Antonius, the Primus Pilus, will see you."

"No need, Aemilius," said a tall man who suddenly appeared from an inner room. "Gentlemen," he said, addressing the three, and waved them into the room.

He took the orders from the tesserarius and read them while the three men stood at attention.

Marcus covertly studied the man. He was close to six feet,

which was tall, though not overly so for the First Cohort, where the men were all required to be at least 5'8". He looked sick. His skin had a yellowish cast to it, and his uniform was too large for his gaunt frame, suggesting the man had lost a considerable amount of weight. His face was sunken, and there were dark rings around his eyes. He also had an ever-so-slight tremor in his left hand.

He looked up. "Have you had your baggage taken to your quarters?" he asked.

Marcus nodded, "Yes, sir."

"The First Cohort is presently training at the Field of Mars just beyond the camp," said Gnaeus. " I am unable to be with them because my presence is required here at headquarters. Centurion Marcus Favorius Facilis, your seniority makes you second in command. Get your armor on and join them. Tell your signifer to consult with my librarius. Dismissed."

The three stood frozen for a moment.

"It appears that speed is not one of your talents," said Gnaeus dryly.

The three quickly saluted him, turned and left the room. Flavius had a tight, angry look on his face, Marcus seemed thoughtful, Demaratus showed no emotion.

A young librarius was waiting in the hallway, summoned by the tesserarius. "Sir," he said to Demaratus, "Are you the Second Century's new signifer?"

Demaratus nodded that he was. "The records of the Century are in need of work, sir, " said the librarius, "If you will come with me."

The Greek nodded to Marcus and Flavius, subtly arched one eyebrow, and went off with the clerk.

The tesserarius, looking distinctly uncomfortable, asked them if there was anything they needed.

"A whole lot, Aemilius, but I doubt you could supply it," growled Flavius, and stalked out of the Principia.

Marcus took the sting out of the comment by shrugging at the officer and remarking that "It was a long ride from Tarraco."

Outside Flavius was fuming. "A fine welcome to a new command that was, sir. He'd have been more gracious with a herd of pigs."

Marcus put his hand on his shoulder. "The man doesn't look well, Flavius. And since when has politeness been a virtue in the Roman Army?"

"Sir, we are fellow officers," said Flavius, his voice still hot with outrage. "He isn't some tribune or legate, he's just a centurion, like you. If he wants to talk to an optio that way, well, it's stupid, but that's his business. But not you, sir. I wonder how many coronas he's won?"

Marcus had his arm around Flavius's shoulder by now and the two were walking to the First Cohort Barracks that were always right next to the Principia. "I don't know, Flavius, but let's not worry about it. We have a job to do, and looking at the Primus Pilus, we are going to have our hands full," he said. "And I don't recall that he is the first superior officer that has treated us rudely. Remember that tribune on the Rhenus?

Flavius sighed. "You're right, sir. But he was a tribune, Gnaeus is just a centurion."

"Just?" said Marcus with mock outrage, which got Flavius to smile and breached his bad temper.

"Right you are again, sir," said the optio. "We have work to do."

With considerable dismay, Demaratus surveyed the enormous pile of scrolls and ledgers on his desk. "Is this all?" he asked the librarius with a note of sarcasm.

"I am really sorry, sir. I know it's a mess. But the signifer stopped doing the books almost a year ago, and the Primus Pilus has been..." and let the comment die.

"What's your name?" Demaratus asked.

"Servius Livius, sir," the librarius answered.

"Well, Servius Livius, my name is Demaratus, and we have a lot of work to do. Why don't you get us some wine and let's begin," he said, smiling at the librarius. Demaratus could see no advantage to being short with the clerk, and every advantage to being friendly.

"Yes sir," said the librarius, with a touch of relief in his voice. "Shall I bring some bread and cheese with it?"

"You are an insightful and intelligent man, Servius," Demaratus said with a grin. "Bring a bowl of olive oil with it and I will nominate you for legate."

Servius grinned back, "Yes, sir," and disappeared.

Demaratus looked at the pile in front of him, sighed, and started to sort through it.

XIV

Marcus and Flavius stood at the edge of the training field watching the two centuries of the First Cohort go through their maneuvers. The centuries of the First Cohort were supposed to be twice the size of regular centuries, but instead of 160 men apiece, the units looked closer to 110.

"There might be a number of immunis," said Flavius, trying to account for the depleted size of the two centuries.

"Maybe," said Marcus. "Though even in a First Cohort there shouldn't be that many veterans excused from drill. How is the unit going to perform well in the field unless they are all drilling together?" He was silent a moment, then added, " I think I will check at the valetudinarium after we finish. Judging from the look of the Primus Pilus, there could be a lot of men in the hospital."

Both centuries were drilling under a single tesserarius, and the signifer was simply a legionnaire from the ranks. The tesserarius glanced over at Marcus and Flavius, then quickly called the men to attention, and strode over to the two men. He saluted, "Sir."

Both men saluted back, and Marcus introduced himself and Flavius, and asked his name.

"Manius Petreius, sir, tesserarius of the First Century, First Cohort and acting optio," he said.

Marcus smiled at him. "It doesn't look like acting; it looks like the real thing, Manius."

The man relaxed and grinned just a little. "Thank you, sir. Will you be taking over?"

"I am the senior centurion on the field today, but my command will be the Second Century. Since both centuries seem a little thin, why don't you continue as optio of the First and Flavius here will take the Second. I will act as centurion for both centuries," said Marcus. "I will introduce myself to the men."

"Yes, sir," said Manius. "Comrades! Fall into your centuries, four lines," he called out.

The men formed up, but slowly, and while the maneuver was not exactly sloppy, it was hardly polished. Marcus stood in front of both centuries and stared at them for a bit. The men looked back guardedly. "They don't know who I am, but they do know that they have lost many of their officers. I am an outsider, a usurper, sent here—as far as they know--by Rome," he reminded himself, "I am going to have to earn their loyalty."

He let them examine him. Some were watching his face, others were looking at his awards for valor, some stared at him with a mixture of resentment and resignation. "Those are the ones I will have to win," he thought.

"Comrades. I am Centurion Marcus Favonius Facilis, formally Pilus Prior of the Second Cohort, of the XXX Legion Ulpis Victrix." There was a slight stir. Marcus noted the reaction with interest, thinking to himself, "They expected a headquarters type, not someone who has been serving in the ranks at the front."

"My impression of Hispania," he continued, "is that it is a much nicer place than northern Gaul. However, if anyone here has an abiding love for rain, mud, cold, and bad-tempered locals, I will pull every string I can think of to get you assigned to my old legion."

The small joke sparked a round of quiet laughter. It also allowed him to smile at them.

"I know you have been through some hard fighting," he said, "and I honor you for that. I know that we will have some ahead of us. We need to be prepared, and drill is all about being prepared. My optio here, Flavius Priscus," he said, motioning toward Flavius, "and I have a few things we want to introduce over the next few days that will make us a better fighting force."

The "few things" got another stir.

"So, let's get to work," he said.

For the next two hours Marcus and Flavius worked the two centuries. The men started by taking up their weighted wicker shields and heavy staffs, and practiced attacking poles set in the ground. The afternoon was hot and the sweat poured off the men. After an hour of this, the officers broke them back up into two centuries and introduced the three-line formation. Marcus concentrated on coordinating the movement and timing of the three lines, while Flavius integrated the maneuvers with pila throwing.

The First Century caught on quicker, which was to be expected. Most of them were seasoned veterans with over a decade in the ranks. The Second Century was greener and tended to turn clumsy every time it tried something that was not standard drill.

The new formation and the closely coordinated spear throwing were new and interesting, and many of the men seemed to enjoy the break from routine. But there was an undercurrent, not of active resistance, but resignation. He didn't want resignation, he wanted enthusiasm.

It was just past mid-afternoon when he called it a day, and the men trooped back to their barracks.

As he watched them go, Flavius came up.

"What do you think, sir," he said quietly.

"They are not very happy, Flavius. So, we will have to make them happier," he replied.

Flavius looked at him: "Right. Got any ideas?"

Marcus smiled at his second in command. "Isn't that your job, optio?"

Flavius grinned. "I'll get right on it, sir. What's the plan for tomorrow?"

"More of the same," answered Marcus, "except for the javelins."

"Sir?" said Flavius quizzically.

"Javelins. Let's go see the armorer about javelins, shall we?" said Marcus.

"Are you thinking of maybe turning them into cavalry, sir?" Flavius asked, with a hint of exasperation.

"Not exactly, but I am thinking of cavalry, Flavius," said Marcus.

The armory was a combination blacksmith and general repair facility, with half a dozen men working on damaged armor, forging swords or pila, and casting lead pipes. The warmth of the day, combined with the heat from the forges, made the place feel like a baking oven. Everyone was dressed in leather aprons, so it was impossible to distinguish who was in charge. Marcus and Flavius waited patiently until someone noticed them.

"Sir?" inquired a burley, middle-age man. "Can I be of help?"

"Marcus Favonius, centurion in the First Cohort. This is my optio, Flavius Priscus."

"Julius Claudius, sirs, and welcome to Corduba," the man replied, wiping his hand and shaking theirs with a grip that could bend forged steel.

Even Flavius strained not to wince at the power in the man's hand. "Now, what can I do for you?"

"Two things, Julius," replied Marcus, his hand still tingling. "First, I would like to make sure the cohort's pila are weighted at their tips."

"Aye, we can do that. Looking for a little more penetration, are you sir?" asked Julius.

"Exactly," said Marcus, "and I want to be sure that we have at least two pila per man, plus two replacement tips."

"No problem there either, sir. We have plenty of extra pila points in store. I assume you want them all weighted?"

Marcus nodded.

"Do you have your own armorers to replace the pila points in the field, sir?" asked Julius.

"We do not," answered Marcus.

Julius rubbed his hand through his hair. "That is a bit of a problem, sir. We don't have many armorers to spare."

"How many can you let us have?" asked Flavius.

"Three, sir," the blacksmith replied.

"Well, we will have to make do with three, Julius, and hope that we don't need them," replied Marcus.

"And the second thing, sir?" asked Julius.

"How is your javelin supply?" asked Marcus.

Julius looked blankly at him. "Are you ordering for the cavalry, sir? The ala commander normally does that."

"No," answered Marcus, "this is for the cohort."

"Javelins for the cohort? What for?" asked Julius.

"To throw," put in Flavius.

"Yes, I got hold of that one right off," replied Julius with a little edge in his voice. "I was just wondering what you were going to throw them at. It makes a difference sir, because the point will be different depending on what your target is."

Marcus knew it was a bad idea to annoy armory craftsmen, even if they were junior rank, so he smoothed things over with an explanation: "Horses, Julius, not particularly the riders on them."

Julius frowned for a moment. "Do you want to kill them, sir, or just make them very uncomfortable?" he asked.

"What's the difference?" asked Marcus.

"If you want to kill them, sir, you will need a larger point and a couple of barbs at the end, although you sacrifice some of your distance because the javelins will be heavier," Julius said. "If you just want to discomfort them, all you need is a good sharp point." He added, "Both types of javelin, however, will still outrange your pila."

Marcus told him, " I am more interested in distance."

"Then we have lots of javelins for you, sir. We don't have

much in the way of cavalry these days in Corduba. Most of it is up north in Lusitania. So, we have a lot in storage. I'll get one," he said, and disappeared into the back of the shop, emerging a few moments later with a long javelin.

Marcus hefted it. It was less than half the weight of a pilum. He handed it over to Flavius who looked very doubtful about the whole endeavor.

"I'm not sure this will do much more than annoy cavalry, sir," said Flavius, balancing the javelin in his right hand.

Marcus was not going to debate his idea with Flavius in the armory. "These will do fine, Julius. Could you arrange to have 200 of them delivered to the training field tomorrow morning? I will also need extra javelins along with the pilas when we march north. Let's say four per man as well?"

"Yes, sir, 200 tomorrow morning. You want the weighted pilas then as well?" asked Julius.

"No, just the javelins. I want the pila by the time we march north," said Marcus.

"And would you know when that will be, sir?"

Marcus shrugged.

"Aye, no one is sure what is up these days. I will have the pila for you by day after tomorrow. Will that do, sir?" asked Julius.

"It will indeed, Julius, and my thanks to you for your patience," said Marcus.

It was unusual for a superior to thank an underling for patience and it clearly startled Julius, and, Marcus suspected, pleased him. He was certain the pila would be done on time.

Leaving the armory, he and Flavius headed for the hospital back inside the camp.

Marcus was annoyed at Flavius for challenging his idea in public, but he said nothing. The optio was a thousand times more important than the armorer, and if he could use a little charm to smooth things over with Julius, he could certainly do the same with Flavius.

"Flavius, we have to be tactically flexible, particularly here in Hispania where we're not fighting as a legion but as a cohort, maybe even as individual centuries," Marcus said. " We don't have the numbers to stop a full cavalry charge. The javelin was effective against the Parthians; it might work against the Lusitianians."

"But didn't the Parthians use bows? According to Antonius, the Lusitanians don't use bows, just lances," argued Flavius.

"Exactly," said Marcus, "they use the shock of a massed charge to break through a century's lines and scatter the coherence of the unit. Instead of fighting as a group, our men all end up fighting as individuals, and they don't do well that way."

"Yes, sir, I agree," said Flavius, "but what are these javelins going to do to stop that? They are too light to do much damage."

Marcus explained his idea: "The purpose is not so much to inflict damage, but to get the charge to flinch, maybe even tumble a few horses. The javelins let us do that before the charge comes into pilum range. When it does, I want those horses to be a little hesitant, charging a little slower. That way the pila will do maximum damage."

Flavius was silent a moment, then nodded grudging agreement. "It might just work, sir. It will certainly be a break in the training routine."

"I had that in mind as well, optio," said Marcus, at the last moment taking the sting out of his words.

The two had arrived at the valetudinarium, a large, airy building, with a long, central room, and smaller rooms off to the sides. It was adjacent to the baths, where both the men intended to spend several hours after the tour.

The hospital was fairly crowded, considering that the camp was only hosting two centuries at the time. Several dozen men lay on mats or sat around in circles, talking, and playing dice. Several of them saw Marcus and Flavius come in and stopped. Those standing stood at attention.

Marcus introduced himself and Flavius and told them to be as they were. A doctor had appeared out of one of the side rooms and introduced himself. "Timotheus, sir. A pleasure to meet you. Welcome to Corduba."

He was young for his post, but Greek, which probably explained why he was holding down a senior position at his age. Everyone knew Greeks made the best doctors. He called Marcus "sir," although technically a legion doctor was on a par with a centurion, albeit without the same power, pay, or prestige of a century commander. He was shorter than either Marcus or Flavius, with curly, dark hair and a small, well-trimmed beard. He was wearing a loose tunic and holding some old bandages in his hands.

"Thank you, Timotheus," said Marcus. "I wonder if we might have a moment with you?"

"Of course," the doctor replied, ushering them into one of the side rooms that clearly functioned as an office. One wall was taken up with square cubbies filled with scrolls, several of which were laid out on a table. The doctor pulled up three chairs and sat down.

"You have a lot of patients, doctor," said Marcus.

"Too many, sir. Mauritania was hard on the cohort. Besides wounds from the fighting, many of the men were stricken with fever. It killed some of them, others are in and out of the hospital. Many of them also have bowel problems that are difficult and stubborn to treat," said the doctor, stroking his small beard. "Even our Primus Pilus is not well, though he refuses to rest." He was silent a moment, then added, "And of course there is the arrest of the Second Century's centurion, which has hurt morale. When morale is low, men get sick and take longer to heal."

Marcus digested what the doctor said. He liked the fact that the man was clear and direct, not something he encountered often in doctors.

"I am not sure what our schedule is, Timotheus, but it is not unlikely that the cohort will leave for Legio within the week. Can you say how many of these men will be ready to march north?" asked Marcus.

Timotheus spread his hands. "Some will not be ready, some will, and then there is a group in the middle that I am uncertain about. Would you allow some of them to ride on supply carts?"

"I don't know if there will be supply carts, doctor. But we can certainly take extra mules and the men can ride them until they feel well enough to march," answered Marcus.

"That would be helpful," said Timotheus.

Marcus rose to go. "Would you prepare a list of the men you think will be able to travel north and give it to my signifer? His name is Demaratus, and he is presently in the Principia."

Timotheus arched his eyebrows at what Marcus assumed to be Demaratus's name.

"Yeah," said Flavius, also rising, "we're overrun with Greeks. I imagine you two will have lots to talk about." The tone was bantering and if Timotheus took offense, he didn't indicate it.

"Of course, sir. I will have the list by tonight," said Timotheus, seeing the two out.

Marcus and Flavius marched straight to the baths and for the next two hours tried to think of nothing but soaking and getting clean.

Two hours in the baths had succeeded in putting Marcus and Flavius in a good mood, and the two were setting up their room when Demaratus came in.

"Have fun with all those figures, Demaratus?" teased Flavius.

Demaratus didn't answer, but went straight to the center table and poured himself a cup of wine from the amphora the duty tesserarius had sent around. He downed it in a single gulp.

Flavius watched him for a moment. "That bad, huh?"

Demaratus looked up at Marcus. "It's a mess, sir, and the men are more than a month late on getting their stipendia."

Flavius whistled, "A month?"

"More like two, sir," said Demaratus.

Marcus shook his head. "That's no way to treat men who have just come back from war. What is the explanation?"

Demaratus ran his hands through his hair and rubbed his eyes. "The librarius says that with all the unrest in Rome everything is delayed, and hinted that the Primus Pilus has been too busy and ill to complain about the situation with any real vigor," answered Demaratus.

"Well, that explains part of the unhappiness out there on the drill ground," said Flavius.

Demaratus poured himself another cup of wine. "I suggested that we just take a loan from a local merchant, but Servius says Gnaeus doesn't want to make the VII Legion beholden to anyone."

"The men should not be held hostage to that point of view," said Marcus quietly. He put down some scrolls he was storing, put on his cloak. "I will have a word with Gnaeus," he said, and left.

Marcus strode into the Principia and asked the tesserarius, Aemilius, if the Primus Pilus was available.

"I'll see, sir," said the man and stepped into the inner room. After a moment he emerged and beckoned Marcus in.

Gnaeus was sitting on a round-back chair, scrolls and waxed tablets strewn on the table in front of him. "Yes?" he asked without looking up.

Marcus decided that the man was not simply sick, he was also rude. It was an irritating combination. "Sir, it has come to my notice that the men haven't received their pay."

Gnaeus looked up, sat back, and put his fingers together. "Observant, aren't we," he said.

"Hard to miss if you watch them drill, sir," Marcus retorted tartly.

"You have a sharp tongue, Marcus Favonius," replied Gnaeus.

Marcus considered his next comment. Gnaeus was his superior, but only just. The Primus Pilus was the senior centurion, but his power was more traditional than formal. A tribune or a legate could talk to a centurion any way he wanted to, but centurions were supposed to be respectful of each other.

"When it comes to the welfare of my men, Gnaeus," said Marcus, dropping the "sir", "I can be sharp indeed."

Marcus expected an explosion, but instead Genaeus rubbed his temples, and said mildly, "There is no money, Marcus, and probably won't be until we get to Legio."

"May I make a suggestion, Gnaeus?" Marcus asked.

"I'm not stopping you, centurion," responded Genaeus.

"I am sure I can arrange for a loan from a local merchant. Even if it isn't the full amount, it will raise the men's spirits," said Marcus.

Genaeus sighed. "You don't think I haven't thought of that? The problem is that any loan will encumber us with an obligation to whoever gives us the money, and that is a bad idea."

Marcus was silent for a moment. "If I can arrange for a loan that is obligation free, may I pursue it?"

Genaeus made a thin smile. "Have I been given a centurion or a magician?" he asked.

Marcus said nothing, just waited. Finally, Genaeus said, "If you can arrange that, fine. Don't bother me again with it," and turned back to his papers.

"Thank you, sir," said Marcus and left, furious at the high-handedness of the Primus Pilus, but satisfied that he had won the argument.

On his way out the duty tesserarius beckoned him over. "This came for you, sir," he said, handing Marcus a small scroll. Marcus looked at it blankly. It was a personal letter, but he didn't know anyone in Corduba. He untied the ribbon and quickly read it.

Even before he could absorb its contents, the tesserarius said, "It is an annual party given by the Dasumii family. It is always held the day before the fast of Ceres. Officers, centurion and above, are invited. Every powerful family and politician will be there."

Until that moment, Marcus had no idea how he was going to get a loan. He didn't know anyone in Corduba, and no one knew him. He tapped the scroll and smiled: the Gods work in mysterious ways, he thought.

XV

The two centuries were drawn up on the drill ground. Flavius and the young tesserarius, Manius Petreius, were putting them through their paces. The centuries advanced, wheeled, retreated, shifted from four lines deep to three, then back to four. Their moves were crisper than they were yesterday, but that was in part because the morning was cool and the men fresher.

Marcus had them practice the testudo, or "tortoise," where the men created a solid wall and roof of shields to protect the century from archers. The First Century did a credible job on the maneuver, the Second less so.

Following the formation drills, the men shifted to practicing hand-to-hand fighting with wooden swords. An hour of this was followed by a short break, and then practice with their pila. As the men were throwing their spears at bound grass targets, several mules appeared carrying bundles of javelins. The appearance of the cavalry weapons caused a stir.

"All right," Flavius shouted in his best drill field bellow, "put your pila over here by the mules, and take one of these javelins."

The men dutifully marched over, stuck their pila, point up, in the ground, and each was handed a javelin.

Marcus, Flavius, and Manius lined up the men three deep, and then Marcus addressed them. "Comrades. We are going to try something a little different today. We are not taking away your pilum, but we are adding a javelin. (There was an undercurrent of groaning—another thing to carry?) "You won't be carrying it" (a slight relaxing in the lines); "however, you will become proficient in using it (stir of confusion). This weapon will make a difference if we are ever up against cavalry. Watch."

Marcus had risen early, skipped breakfast, and spent almost an hour practicing with the unfamiliar javelin. He had probably thrown fewer than a dozen in his life. He soon found that the trick was to throw it with a high arc. Unlike the pilum, it did not have much penetrating power because it was so light, but if it were thrown in a steep, ballistic arc, by the time it struck the ground it had force and speed. The high arc would also allow the javelins to drop behind the cavalry's shields and fall among the horses and riders. The javelin would not penetrate heavy armor, but most cavalry was lightly armored. A horse could not maintain a full gallop for any distance if it and its rider were heavily armored. With luck and skill, the light spear would cause some damage to the horses and might even kill or wound several the horsemen.

He was used to the pilum, so he had to adjust his feet and remember to release the javelin when his arm was at the highest point above his shoulder. If the projectile was properly arched, it landed point first and stuck solidly in the ground. Marcus's hope was that any horse that struck an implanted javelin might shy away.

He explained about the arc to the men, then turned and hurled the javelin, making sure he kept his shield high and his body covered. Partly because of his morning practice, and partly because of luck, the javelin sailed over 150 feet and stuck firmly in the ground.

When he turned back to the men, he noticed that both Flavius and Manius looked suitably impressed. "When that javelin falls among those horses, they are going to be very unhappy," he told the men, raising a few smiles. "Unhappy horses don't always do what their riders want them to do, so your job is to make those horses as discontented as you can. Let's see what the First Century can do,"

He nodded to Flavius,

"All right," said Flavius. "When I say 'throw,' the first line throws, then the second line moves up. Each line awaits my orders. Got that?"

The first line nodded, and gripped their javelins. "Throw!" bellowed Flavius.

The results were mixed, but when they finished, Marcus pointed to the forest of javelins sticking in the ground. "Not many horses will want to come through that," he said.

For the next hour the men practiced throwing the javelin, and by the end, Marcus was satisfied that the light spear could cause considerable trouble. The next part he was not so sure of: throwing the javelin, retrieving their pila, and throwing the heavy spear.

They tried out various formations, but finally decided that

the first line would not be armed with javelins. The movement of throwing the javelin, then pulling the pilum out of the ground broke up the formation, with soldiers bumping into one another, catching their shields against the pila, and looking chaotic. A straight line of shields, pila at ready, intimidated an enemy, and trying to get the front line to do two things broke up the symmetry of the formation and the psychological impact a disciplined block of infantry imparts.

After praising the men and telling them they could sleep an extra hour the next morning, Marcus finally called it a day. The soldiers looked tired, but still had some spring in their walk, and the promise of an extra hour of sleep was well received.

For the next two days Marcus, Flavius and Manius worked on the timing and coordination of the two centuries and the mix of javelins and pila seemed to work out well. The two centuries were in the middle of practicing how to bend their flanks to prevent cavalry from sweeping around the unit and attacking from the rear, when Gnaeus, the Primus Pilus, showed up on the drill field.

He watched the two centuries for a bit, then motioned Marcus over.

"Sir," said Marcus, saluting the man.

Gnaeus's normally sour look had deepened. "Turning my men into cavalry, centurion?"

"No sir. Just giving them a way to deal with a mounted attack," Marcus replied.

"Well, I will not have the discipline of my infantry destroyed by some fool notion about horses. Horses are no threat to foot soldiers, and I won't have you putting that suggestion in their heads," Gnaeus almost hissed at him. The man was white faced, though whether from anger or illness, it was hard to tell.

Marcus stared at him for several seconds, and then replied in a tightly controlled voice. "It is not the horses I worry about, sir. It's the men on them. Crassus felt much as you do, and lost seven legions discovering that Parthians on horseback indeed posed a threat to infantry. It seems to me that Scipio made a very similar discovery not very far from here."

"Lusitanians are not Parthians or Numidians," replied Gnaeus, his voice rising with anger.

"I fancied much the same myself, sir," said Marcus. "And as you are finally on the field, you will, of course, make whatever decisions you wish about the First Century. I will continue my training with the Second."

Gnaeus was livid, but Marcus stood his ground. The Primus Pilus outranked him, but Marcus commanded the Second Century, not Gnaeus, and it was traditional to allow a centurion considerable leeway in matters of training and discipline if each century understood the basic formations and movements. Under normal circumstances, Gnaeus might have called in a tribune, or even the legate, to settle the matter, but there were no legates and tribunes in Corduba.

The two locked eyes for several seconds, but Marcus was not about to back down on something he thought might affect the fighting capabilities of his men.

"You do as you wish with your century's training, centurion," said Gnaeus, "but when we take the field, I command, and no century will go into battle armed with those foolish weapons. Do I make myself clear?"

Marcus nodded. "You do, sir. My men will practice with them and carry them on mules when we march north, but they are not to be armed with them in the case of a battle," he said. "Will there be anything else?"

It was close to insubordination, but Marcus had been in the army long enough to know how to skirt that edge without falling over.

Gnaeus did not answer, but instead motioned Manius over. Marcus turned, nodded to Flavius, who moved the Second Century further down the training field. As Marcus was joining them, he heard Gnaeus bitterly reproach his tesserarius and order the men to get rid of their javelins.

Flavius's face was expressionless when Marcus joined him with the Second Century.

"We will practice formations for a while, optio," said Marcus. He was tempted to continue with the javelin and pilum practice, but there was no sense being provocative. Flavius called the men to attention and began to take them through the grim ballet of war.

Flavius saw the falling out between Marcus and Gnaeus coming and wondered if Marcus had anticipated it too. Flavius had not been particularly enthusiastic about the javelins himself and had initially chalked them up to one of his centurion's quirky military experiments. Some of them worked quite well, others were simply harebrained. But as he watched the men begin to get the hang of the new weapon, he began to grudgingly admit that there might be something to it. In any case, the men enjoyed the break from routine and, given that this was not a happy unit to begin with, it was a clever idea for that reason alone.

But there was no way that the Primus Pilus would not resent a new centurion introducing a fresh training regime without first clearing it with him. Flavius assumed that Marcus had not done so because Gnaeus would have dismissed the idea, killing it before the centurion could test it. His commander was interesting that way. If he thought something was important, he would bend rules to make it happen, or just go ahead without asking anyone's permission. It was one of his more attractive characteristics, but it had gotten them in trouble on more than one occasion. It seemed he'd done so again.

If Marcus thought he was in trouble, he didn't show it. He was rapping out orders in a clear cadence, correcting the alignment of the century, and working on the men's timing. The soldiers were working well for him, probably because they held no love for the Primus Pilus, and anyone whom Gnaeus didn't approve of, they did. Everyone had seen the expression on Gnaeus's face and his obvious anger, even if they couldn't hear the words exchanged between the two centurions, and just as clear they could see that Marcus was not in the slightest bit intimidated by the head centurion. The men would learn that Marcus was not intimidated by much, thought Flavius—horses, the sea, and women excepted.

Marcus finally called it a day and sent the men back to their barracks. He and Flavius headed for the baths, keeping the conversation focused on purely professional matters.

XVI

Marcus stood before Flavius and Demaratus as they examined him critically. He was wearing his formal Paludamentum, which required him to drape it across his left arm like a civilian toga. He felt comfortable in a uniform, if for no other reason than it was a uniform over which he had no control. But this party would require him to demonstrate his taste in clothing, and he had none.

Demaratus had insisted that he needed a new tunic and dress caligas, and almost physically dragged him out to buy them. Marcus had fought the purchases, but finally gave in when Flavius deserted his standard and joined the Greek. Now he had to admit that the new boots and tunic did look nice, and he was even willing to concede that the cloak made him look—he searched for the word—respectable? He could not wear his harness with its awards, because civilians wouldn't know what they meant in any case, but his Paludamentum clasp was a circle of gold with tiny raised points, like a crown. Soldiers would recognize a Corona Vallaris.

Demaratus tugged Marcus's cloak a little and adjusted the shoulder pin and stood back. "What do you think, Flavius? Would you let the man borrow money from you?"

Flavius grinned. "Not a chance. He looks like he would cut your throat for a few coppers."

At this moment, Marcus deeply hated the two of them. They would never dare talk to him this way unless they knew he was utterly vulnerable, and Marcus in new clothes about to go to a fancy party was about as vulnerable as one could get. He glared at the two.

They grinned back. Then Demaratus turned serious. "Sir, I assume that this Greek doctor Timotheus will be there as well?"

Marcus shrugged. "I would think so. An army doctor is, in theory, the same as a centurion."

" Then I strongly suggest you speak with him on this matter of the loan," said Demaratus.

Marcus was puzzled. "Why would I talk to a doctor about who to get money from?"

"It is not his status as a doctor that I would consider useful in this situation, sir," answered Demaratus, "but the fact that he is Greek. We pay attention to matters of commerce and wealth."

It was a smart suggestion, and since he would be one of the few people at the party Marcus knew—he would avoid the Primus Pilus, although he hoped the man was too ill to attend— an attractive one.

The conversation was interrupted by a light knock at the door. Marcus opened it to confront a young slave dressed in a tunic considerably better made than his own. The boy made a low bow and then spoke:

"Centurion Marcus Favonius Facilis, Princeps of the First Cohort of the VII Legion Gemina Hispania Pia. My master Julius Dasumi bids me to escort you to his house."

Flavius and Demaratus exchanged glances but kept their faces expressionless. Marcus glowered at them and motioned the slave to lead the way.

Marcus emerged from the barracks to find a litter and four slave bearers ready to transport him to the party. He had no intention of riding on a litter and waved it off. "Lead on, boy."

Half an hour later he was not so sure passing up the litter had been such a good idea. The new boots were chafing at his heels, and even though it was now October, the late afternoon sun was hot, and his cloak made him sweat. He was also thirsty and growing increasingly cranky with himself for being too embarrassed and awkward to ride in a litter, and at this foolish party that forced him to dress up in this uncomfortable outfit. He was so wrapped up in feeling sorry for himself that he almost ran the young slave over. The boy had stopped in front of a sprawling villa and Marcus caromed into him, knocking them both off balance.

"Forgive me, sir," the slave quailed. "But this is the house of my master, Julius Dasumi." The boy was physically quaking and Marcus decided that Julius Dasumi was not a kind master, and if Marcus said something to him about the incident, the boy would be beaten.

Marcus smiled at the slave. "I would probably have walked to Gades if you hadn't stopped me. Thank you for your escort," he said.

The boy looked relieved.

Marcus stepped through two enormous, carved double doors into a columned portico. Beyond the portico was a vast atrium with a fountain consisting of several leaping bronze dolphins. Everything about the domus said its master possessed both power and wealth. The furniture was made of carved and polished exotic woods, and rich tapestries and brilliant frescos covered the walls. He had barely put his foot in the door when a slave offered him a tray of wineglasses. Not pottery cups, but real glass.

A crowd of close to a hundred people milled around the atrium, wandered through the rooms, or lounged on sofas and chairs. Some of them wore the purple-edged togas of the senatorial class, and virtually everyone looked better dressed than he was.

He stood there, glass in hand, feeling the outsider. A few people glanced his way when he came in, but went back to their conversations or eating. A great crowd of people surrounded an enormous table filled with dishes.

"Welcome, centurion Marcus Favonius," said a voice over his right shoulder. He turned to confront a man dressed in a rich toga. A slave to the man's right had just stepped back from saying something to him. Marcus realized the slave was a nomenclature, whose job it was to memorize names and remind his master of who people are.

"I am Julius Dasumi, Marcus, and this is my sister, Aelia," Dasumi said, "We are pleased that you have joined us."

The man was several inches shorter than Marcus. He was balding and had rings on his fingers, including one with a small walnut-sized ruby. His toga was of the finest linen, and he had an exquisite braided gold necklace around his neck. He offered his hand with a smile, but his eyes were hard as marbles and he examined Marcus as he might a bullock in the market or a slave on the auction block.

Aelia was as lovely as Julius was plain, and looked younger. She wore a stunning silk gown, pinned at the shoulder, and little jewelry. She doesn't need jewelry, thought Marcus. He took Julius's hand, and bowed to Aelia who gave him a steady look behind a ghost of a smile. Marcus felt awkward and out of place, and he stammered his way through the introductions and small talk.

His suffering was short. "You must eat something, Marcus, and make yourself at home. If you will excuse us, we have other guests to greet. I am sure we will have time to talk later," said Julius, dismissing him with a polite smile. Aelia arched her left eyebrow and seemed to wink at him as the two left, though Marcus might have imagined it.

In any case, he felt dismissed and out of place, and if he had any choice in the matter, he would have fled at the earliest possible moment. He immediately headed for a wall to blend into the furniture and draw as little attention to himself as he could. He didn't see Gnaeus, for which he thanked a pantheon of gods, or anyone else he knew. This had been a fool's errand and he cursed himself for thinking that anything would come of it.

"Marcus. Are you always so deep in thought?" said a friendly voice to his left. It was Timotheus, who broke off a conversation with two men to come across the room and take Marcus's hand. He felt a huge wave of relief, which he hoped didn't show.

The doctor dragged Marcus over and introduced him to the

two. One was the head of the local merchants' association, and the other was a private doctor. The merchant, Clodius Petreius was round and friendly, and the doctor, Petronius Equitius, was quiet and looked even younger than Timotheus.

They exchanged small talk, gossiping about the recent change of emperors in Rome. It was Marcus's first confirmation that Decius had come out on top in his battle with Philippus. He supressed the desire for more information, even though it directly affected himself and his family. Philippus had tried to kill him, but that didn't make Decius a friend. He steered the conversation away from the subject by asking questions about Corduba, and the recent unrest in Lusitania.

Clodius was unhappy about the latter situation. "Some of our traders have been attacked north of Emerita Augusta, and we have begun sending goods by sea. But the ports in the north and west are poor, and the roads are few. The distance adds expense and our profits are down." Then looking sharply at Marcus, he added, "We are hoping that the VII Legion will pacify the area and make the Via Plato to Legio safe again."

Normally, Marcus would never discuss military affairs with civilians, but the last comment opened an opportunity for him.

"We are headed north in the next few days, sir, and we will do our best. But," he added, shaking his head, "there are problems."

"Yes, we all know about this business with the centurion refusing orders," said Clodius," but isn't that why you are here from Rome?"

Marcus was impressed by the merchant's knowledge of the current crisis and surprised that he knew why he, Marcus, had been assigned to the First Cohort. There was no sense in divesting him of the illusion that Rome was so on top of matters in distant Hispania that it would send a special envoy, and every reason for Marcus to play up the "assigned from Rome" perception.

Marcus deliberately did not immediately respond but glanced around him before answering Clodius. "In part, yes. There are other matters" (a little mystery surrounding him might come in handy at some point), "but that is my main reason for being here," he said. "But there are some local problems that Rome was not aware of," he added with a frown.

"Local problems?" asked Clodius.

Marcus again looked around for effect, then lowered his voice. "Can we keep what I say here between us, gentlemen?"

"Of course," Clodius assured him, and the young doctor nodded assent. Timotheus was looking at him with a smile that only Marcus could have noticed.

Marcus shook his head. "The men were not paid their stipendia on Sept. 1."

Timotheus chimed in, "And it has had a bad effect on morale, particularly given all the uproar over this Christian business."

"Timotheus, why have you not said anything until now?" asked Clodius.

Marcus rode to the rescue: "The officers were asked to keep matters a secret until I arrived from Rome. You can understand that the last thing merchants in Corduba need is to think that the soldiers may not be dependable." He quickly added, "Of course they are absolutely dependable, but you know how rumors are."

Timotheus, looking grave, nodded.

Clodius pursed his lips in thought. "This is a scandal, really. Are you attempting to solve it?" he asked Marcus.

"It is difficult, Clodius, because I am a newcomer to Corduba. Normally the Primus Pilus would search out some key individuals in the city and ask for a loan, but the Primus Pilus"— Marcus coughed delicately— "has not been well, so the matter has fallen to me."

"Humph," said Clodius. "The Primus Pilus may indeed be ill, but even in good health he is a sour lemon of a man. I cannot imagine him asking for money, nor that anyone would give him any."

Marcus put on his "I-agree-but-can't-say-it-out-loud face" and looked troubled.

Clodius glanced sharply at him. "How much money are we talking about?"

"Thirty-six thousand denarri, which will pay half their stipendia. We officers, of course, will defer. It will be enough to hold the men until we reach Legio," answered Marcus.

Clodius smiled, patted him on the shoulder, and said, "I like a direct man who has the figures on his fingertips. I assume the army will be good for this?"

Marcus assured him it would.

"When would you need it?" the merchant asked.

Marcus spread his hands. "When could we get it?"

Clodius considered for a moment. "Tomorrow noon? " he asked.

Marcus was elated. That would give Demaratus time to distribute it at the end of drill. "Astounding, sir," he said to Clodius. "I simply don't know how to thank you, except to say that I will make sure the soldiers of the First Cohort will know of the support they have in Corduba. I must also say that I only wish our merchants in Rome were half as generous and half as efficient."

Clodius glowed a little and waved it aside. "When something is wrong, right it I say. You send your man around to my warehouse tomorrow and we will get this all solved."

Marcus felt a little guilty about the way he had manipulated the conversation, but Clodius seemed genuinely pleased that he had been able to help.

"Now, tell me about Gaul, Marcus. Gaul much concerns us these days," said Clodius, changing the subject. The question plunged Marcus into a discussion of the military and political situation on the Germanii border. Marcus tried to explain the new strategy of "strength in depth," and the advantages that it held over trying to hold the entire frontier area.

The merchant looked doubtful.

"It is not like the old days, Clodius," explained Marcus. "We no longer face individual tribes, but confederations of tribes, like the Franks, the Alamanni and the Goths. They can concentrate their forces and we simply don't have enough legions to cover the borders."

"But they ravage at will when they attack," argued the merchant, "We cannot do business or guarantee the safety of our goods."

Marcus admitted it was a problem, but pointed out that the solution was to fortify and reinforce the cities to prevent them from being overrun. "The barbarians do not have siege equipment, Clodius. They cannot take walled cities. While they are starving outside the walls, the legions will be concentrating to attack them. It has worked well, so well that the Franks have not made a major invasion in five years."

The merchant was not completely convinced, but thanked Marcus for explaining the new strategy to him. "It would help if the army would keep everyone informed," he grumbled.

"I agree," said Marcus, " and I will raise your complaint with the legate when we get to Legio."

Clodius finally broke off the discussion and excused himself. "I have some business to conduct, Marcus," he said with a wink, "It has been a pleasure. I am sure we will meet again. Remember, tomorrow at my warehouse. Timotheus knows the place."

Marcus shook his hand and watched as Clodius plunged into the crowd, shaking hands and patting people on the shoulder.

Timotheus sidled up to Marcus and said in a low voice," If you ever want to give up a career in the army for the theater, I have some contacts."

Marcus grinned. "You did rather well yourself, doctor."

Timotheus smiled, "All Greeks are actors, and the whole world is our *skene*."

"These are two men looking well pleased with themselves," said a voice over their shoulders.

Both men turned to find Aelia smiling at them.

"My lady," both men said, and Marcus gave her a wide smile. Marcus did not do wide smiles very often, particularly to women, who made him feel awkward, but he was feeling buoyed up from his recent victory, and he would have smiled that way had he turned to find himself face to face with the Medusa.

Aelia's standard enigmatic smile broadened. "My, we really are pleased with ourselves."

"We are indeed, Lady Aelia. I have discovered that the people of Corduba are among the most generous and gracious in the empire," said Marcus.

Aelia laughed—a charming laugh. "Have you been feeding him some of your potions, Timotheus?" she asked the doctor.

"Not I," said the Greek, "nor do I know of any that would elicit this state in a person."

Aelia lifted her elbow toward Marcus. "Being pleased with oneself is hard work, centurion, and hard work always stimulates the appetite. May I show you our table?"

Slipping his arm under hers, he said, "I would be delighted, my lady."

"I would be more so if you would stop being stuffy and call me by my name," she said, taking the sting out of the rebuke with a charming wrinkle of her nose. "While you eat, I will ply you with questions about Rome." Turning to Timotheus, she said, batting her eyes, "Doctor, I hope I am not being rude taking your comrade away, but a certain amount of rudeness is essential in the art of civility. Don't you agree?"

"Fully, my dear Aelia," said Timotheus with a grin.

As Aelia steered Marcus through the crowd, she explained that Timotheus was an old friend who had helped ease the pain of Julius's wife when she was dying. "It is perfectly acceptable to be rude to old friends," she said to Marcus, "especially if they know you are teasing."

Aelia was sophisticated, beautiful, and witty, everything he imagined he was not. It was only the lingering elation of his recent success with Clodius that stopped him from panicking in the presence of this refined upper-class woman.

On their way to the table, Aelia took two glasses of wine from a slave and handed him one. "To the new centurion of the VII Legion," she said. He touched her glass, thanked her, and downed the wine. It was wonderfully good and he suddenly wanted more. Normally Marcus was not much of a drinker, but the combination of the party, the business with the money, and this beautiful woman on his elbow raised a thirst in him.

She had already produced another glass for him and then cleared a space for the two of them at the food table.

The table itself was a good 25 feet long and probably six feet wide. There was not a square inch of it that wasn't festooned with dishes, plates and bowls, and the variety of food was over-whelming. He was bewildered by the choices, most of which he had never seen before. He poked vaguely at a round, fleshy thing that seemed filled with small balls.

"Sow's udder stuffed with sea urchins," said Aelia, shaking her head slightly. "It is an acquired taste."

"I have acquired too much in life as it is," said Marcus, adding "and this?" pointing to what looked like hardboiled eggs in a clear aspic. "Eggs and jellyfish," she explained.

Aelia leaned forward and took what looked like a tiny, furry sausage from a plate piled high with them. "You might like this, Marcus," she said with a smile. He looked closely at it. It was not only furry, it also had tiny ears. He looked at her puzzled. "Surely you have dined on dormice stuffed with pork and pine nuts," she said. "It is very popular." She was clearly teasing him.

Marcus picked up the little mouse with a look of distaste. "Many years ago, when I was a junior tesserarius in the north of Britiannia, the small fort I commanded was besieged by the locals. They couldn't get in, but we couldn't get out and we ran through our supplies," Marcus said. "We first ate all the sheep, goats and chickens, then the horses, and finally the mules."

Aelia looked aghast. "You ate horses before you ate mules?"

"Horses are pretty things to look at, Aelia," he answered, "but for an army, the mule is more useful. It carries our supplies, eats fewer oats than a horse, and has better stamina."

She looked slightly scandalized, though with Aelia it was hard to tell when she was teasing and when she was being serious.

"Anyway, we were finally reduced to catching rats in the storehouse and roasting them," Marcus continued, "and while we were hungry enough to think highly of them at the time, I made a pledge to never eat rats again. This," he said holding up the diminutive rodent, "is very much like a small rat. I think you would agree that the gods would frown on my breaking such a pledge."

Aelia laughed. "We mustn't provoke the gods, Marcus. What will you eat?"

By this time, the wine was beginning to make his head spin. He knew he had to get some food into him before he turned silly or sloppy in front of this worldly woman. He fastened his gaze on a haunch of something he suspected was deer, covered with onions, dates, raisins and honey. "This looks good," he said. Instantly a slave appeared, cut him a generous slice, and handed him a plate and knife.

"Would you like to try this, sir," the slave said, pointing to a pie. Marcus had never tasted anything in a pie he didn't like, so he nodded that he would. It turned out to be ham, cooked with figs, honey and bay. Both were delicious. He was wolfing them down when he remembered his manners.

"I am so sorry, I am afraid I have started to eat before you have even chosen a dish," he apologized to Aelia, "Army life does not make for good manners, I am afraid."

"Do not concern yourself, Marcus, I have already eaten. May I point out a few more dishes you might enjoy?" she asked.

He bowed his assent.

She pointed to two platters filled with what look like the biggest chickens in the world. He arched his eyebrows in a question, and she explained they were boiled ostrich with sweet sauce and flamingo cooked with dates. He asked the slave to cut him two small slices, which he found chewy and, except for the sauces, tasteless.

Aelia stopped in front of a platter filled with small birds. "Turtle doves boiled in their feathers," she said, then added, "Poor dears," while she stroked them.

It was a wry comment and Marcus laughed. He wondered if he did so too loudly. With the wine it was hard to tell. His appreciation of her humor was rewarded with a wide smile.

"But this, on the other hand, I insist you try," she said, pointing to some tiny pastries. She placed one in his mouth. It was delicious, but he wasn't sure exactly what it was. "Fricassee of roses," she explained.

He felt full and pleasantly drunk. He couldn't remember enjoying himself quite this much. "I cannot thank you enough, Aelia," he said. "I would probably still be staring at the food if you had not agreed to be my guide and sage, or worse, I would be eating pigs' udders or bringing down the wrath of the gods."

She put her fingers on his arm and gave him a smile that raised the hair on the back of his neck. "I am so glad I could be of help. Might you indulge me in a matter as repayment?" she asked.

"You have but to ask, Aelia," he said with a small bow.

"Good. I have something I would like to show you. Come," she said, slipping her arm into his and steering him toward a hallway at the far end of the atrium. The party was still going strong, so it took a while to negotiate the crowd, many of whom Aelia greeted or spoke with briefly.

They finally found themselves in a deserted part of the house. She led him to an ornately carved door and opened it for him. It led into a living room dotted with couches, tables, and chairs, and faced onto a small garden filled with flowers and herbs. She closed the door behind him, smiled at him, and led him to a cabinet. Opening it, she took out a helmet.

Holding it, she turned and presented it to him. "What can you tell me about this, Marcus?"

The helmet was bronze, covered with a green patina, and deeply pitted in places. It was curved to fit the contour of a head, with a small pedestal at the top. The front was dominated by a bell-shaped opening that allowed the wearer to see and speak. A long flange of bronze, inset with gold, was riveted into the area above the eyes and swept down to cover the wearer's nose. The combination of form and function was pleasing and menacing at the same time.

Marcus turned the helmet slowly in his hands, examining the inset gold and how the nose guard fastened to the helmet. He also ran his finger around the pedestal at the crown.

He looked up at her with a smile. "Where did you get it?"

"A merchant in Gades was in my debt and offered this in exchange. The debt was a trifle, and I admired the symmetry of this, so I accepted. All he told me was that it was Greek," she said.

"Yes and no," he said, running his finger around the helmet's edge. "Greek, yes, but no Greeks that we would know and none that probably called themselves Greek."

"You are being as opaque as an oracle," she said.

"I am sorry, Aelia," he said shaking his head, "it is just that I have never seen anything like this except on old Greek pottery."

He was silent a moment. "You know our myths, Aelia. Aeneas, fleeing from the fall of Troy, founded Rome."

"This is a Trojan helmet?" asked Aelia skeptically.

Marcus shook his head. "No, but it is like those worn by Aeneas's foes, the Achaeans, the people who became the Greeks. This is the oldest thing I have ever seen, although there are those who say the giant stone circles in Britannia are older."

He pointed to the small pedestal at the top of the helmet. "This was for a horsehair fringe, much like I wear on my helmet, but set so it swept from front to back. This," he said turning the helmet, "was a nose piece that would block a sword slash."

He lifted the helmet up and carefully slid it over his head. It was a little snug, but it fit. He stepped in front of a mirror and looked at himself. The image sent a small shiver down his spine. It was not as strong as a Roman helmet, and it restricted the wearer's view, but he found it a deeply intimidating artifact of war. His eyes stared out, deep from within the helmet, his lower face obscured by the nosepiece and the flared cheek guards. It was as if the ghost of some ancient warrior had suddenly manifested itself inside the helmet, surveying some ancient battlefield.

Almost unbidden, a line from Homer came to him, his voice echoing in the helmet: "I too shall lie in the dust when I am dead, but for now let me win noble renown."

He turned to find Aelia had taken a step back, her hand at her throat.

"I'm sorry," he said, "I did not mean to frighten you."

"You felt it also, didn't you, Marcus?" she said.

Slipping the helmet off he placed it on the chest. "Yes, but I don't know what the 'it' was," he said.

"Do you think it is haunted?" she asked.

Marcus considered the helmet. "No, not in the sense of a lemure. But it may have the power to conjure up memories from a past we have forgotten and speak to a future we cannot know. We are all haunted by that conundrum."

She seemed to relax, and putting her hand on his arm, she cocked her head at him. "You are an interesting man, centurion Marcus Favonius. You frighten me a little, and that is very attractive."

He smiled at her. "Since I have never been called frightening, interesting or attractive before, I am at a loss for words."

"Good," she replied with a slow smile.

They were interrupted by a sharp knock on the door, followed by another, more insistent.

Aelia pulled away and flashed an angry look in the direction of the door. She was in the middle of saying something when it opened and Julius Dasumi stepped into the room.

"Ah, here you are, sister," he said. "Your guests are asking after you." He nodded to Marcus.

Aelia quickly mastered her anger, although her narrowed eyes and thinned lips hinted at considerable internal outrage. "Have your parties become so dull that they flounder without me, dear brother?"

But her sarcasm just bounced off the man's aura of power and self-satisfaction. "Your absence makes the very heart of the world tremble, Aelia. Don't you agree, centurion?" he said, turning his cold smile on Marcus.

"My brother was not seeking an answer, Marcus," said Aelia. "You need not reply. This is just one of his business tactics."

Marcus had no intention of replying, although he would not have analyzed Julius's ploy as a business tactic. Striking at the weakest unit on the battlefield was a standard tactic for disrupting the enemy. It was just that Marcus was not sure who was the enemy: he or Aelia.

Aelia put both her hands on Marcus's arm. "We shall be along in a moment, brother. Be sure to close the door as you leave."

If Julius was insulted at the request that he act as a door slave, he gave no indication of it. He smiled, bowed, and left, carefully closing the door.

As the door closed, Aelia sighed, and looked up at him with a wan smile. "I am sorry to put you in the middle of a family dispute, Marcus."

Marcus smiled at her. "It came off a good deal more peaceful than disputes in my family. Please don't concern yourself with it."

"Well, I will concern myself with the fact that we did not get much time alone. Since I am sentenced to make idle chatter with my brother's business associates, will you at least share it with me? You might also find that knowing who is who in Corduba is useful," she said.

He patted her hand. "I would be honored."

Aelia put her index finger on his nose. "You are polite and honorable to a fault, Marcus. I will have to winnow some of that out of you," she said.

XVII

Aelia watched as Marcus strode off into the early morning streets. She was not certain what she was doing, standing outside to say goodbye to this man whom she barely knew. He was not a handsome man, and his charms were more obscure than obvious. She had noticed him only because he arrived disheveled and out of his element. This was hardly surprising. He was only a centurion, who had suddenly found himself in a house with the most powerful men in Corduba, if not Hispania. Reacting to her brother's cold dismissal of the man, she winked at him, which she saw surprised him. She liked that. Most men would not have shown they were surprised. Smooth he was not.

She noticed him talking with the merchants and that dear Timotheus, and whatever he was saying had them riveted. Discreetly, she slipped near the conversation and quickly figured out that Marcus and Timotheus were working Clodius Petreius for a loan and doing a brilliant job at it. The centurion's ethics may have been a little dodgy, but because the loan was not a personal matter, but involved paying his soldiers, his motives were honorable. Aelia liked people who stretched rules, so long as they were not themselves on the take. And when Marcus was so clearly pleased with his little coup, she wanted to pat him on the head and say, "Well done." That, of course, would not do. Aelia was direct, but not to the point of insulting people. Unless she wanted to.

He interested her, which is why she dragged him away from what was a boring party. She was interested in what her old helmet was, but it was more on impulse than anything else. But hearing him recite Homer, she suddenly decided she liked this man. She was about to initiate a much deeper discussion when her brother broke things up. But she liked the fact that Marcus was willing to be her companion for the rest of the night without making any assumptions. She smiled to herself. Unless she had taken the initiative to kiss his cheek, he would have left without even a hint of intimacy.

You are a silly and wrongheaded woman, Aelia said to herself, and you will never see this man again. Had the men of Hispania become so boring and predictable that someone like Marcus, a social inferior, attracted her?

She turned and drifted back to the house, where the slaves were already making the debris of the party vanish.

"You have perverse taste in men, my dear sister," said her brother Julius, sprawled on a couch. "Next you will take up with the butchers in the market."

Aelia considered her brother. There was a time when she had liked him, but that had begun to wane since their father died three years ago. Their father had divided his wealth equally between the two of them, an unheard-of liberty in the patriarchal

Roman Empire that had required an act of the Senate, but there it was. Julius might put on superior male airs, but she was just as wealthy as he, and certainly as smart, if not more so. This equality galled him and made him resentful, which was eroding whatever sibling affection she once had for him.

She ignored the comment and gave him a lazy smile. "Dear brother, you must do something about your parties. They make 'boring' seem like a compliment."

Julius reddened. He prided himself on his parties. "You should show a little dignity, Aelia. Rolling about with the low-born shames our family."

"Do you know, Julius," she said, tilting her head and narrowing her eyes to look at him, "you should not show your anger. You are not a particularly handsome man at your best, but anger makes you lumpy and actively unattractive. Good night, brother."

Julius said nothing, but his face darkened even more. The man is becoming very tiresome, thought Aelia, not for the first time wishing he would move to Gedes or even Tarraco.

As a slave helped her undress, she turned the centurion over in her mind. Well, if he writes, then we will cross that bridge, she told herself. Slipping onto her couch she was asleep almost immediately.

XVIII

Marcus watched the men of the Second Century dueling with wooden posts. Their weighted shields and heavy staffs were exhausting to wield in the mid-afternoon sun, but he kept them at it. There had been a slow trickle of men returning to duty, and they were soft and out of shape. Men who tired easily could make an entire unit vulnerable, and he was determined to make sure everyone was up for the long marches ahead.

He had a slight hangover from the night before. He was not much of a drinker, and several glasses of wine had done him in. He woke up thirsty and slightly queasy, and only the memory of Aelia saved him from descending into a foul mood.

He arrived back at the barracks only an hour before dawn and had, at the most, 45 minutes of sleep. Demaratus and Flavius were asleep when he got in, and he noticed they were keeping their voices down when the camp bell rang to announce the morning muster. He must look awful if the two of them held off kidding him about how late he had gotten in.

Aelia dragged him about the party, introducing him to

anyone of importance. Normally he would have felt awkward—his social skills were limited—but hers were so polished that the evening passed quickly. He initially had a suspicion she was trying to annoy her brother by keeping a lowly centurion by her side throughout the party, but he found that she steered him into conversation with other guests anxious for news from Gaul and Rome. It finally dawned on him that Corduba considered him an envoy of Rome and a bit of a mystery. Aelia was entertaining her guests with an insider who might have valuable information in a time of uncertainty and upheaval.

He wondered what she would think if she knew the real reason he was here in Hispania, and decided that she would consider it was perfectly grand that he was on the run. She kept him well supplied with wine, and changed the guests as soon as the conversation started to flag. It was one of the most enjoyable parties he had ever attended, but it ran late and he was anxious to get back to the barracks.

She urged him to take a litter, but he said he needed the cool morning air to clear his head and rid his body of the wine. She was sweet, accompanying him for a short distance in the street. She kissed him, telling him she expected to hear from him, and she was gone, leaving a lingering hint of rosewater and lilacs.

The long walk back to the camp cleared his head.

And so here he was, still feeling the ravages of rich food and good wine, and longing for a long bath.

He had sent Demaratus off with Timotheus to get the promised money from Clodius Petreius. Gnaeus had been too busy to see him after muster, so he wrote out the details of the loan. He was a little nervous that the Primus Pilus might think that the loan somehow "obligated" the VII to the Corduba merchants, so he was careful to explain that there had been no quid pro quo. He also said that he intended to distribute the half stipendia on the Field of Mars when training was finished.

That was more than six hours ago, and he had still not heard a word from Gnaeus. He couldn't decide if the man was just practicing his standard rudeness or was too ill to respond. But the uncertainty around the whole matter did nothing to alleviate his headache or his dark mood.

He signaled Flavius and Manius to call a break, and the men gratefully put down their staffs and wicker shields and gathered around the water buckets. Flavius drifted over.

"They're working better today, sir," the optio noted, wiping his brow clean of sweat.

Marcus nodded, but said nothing and immediately felt a pang of guilt. It wasn't Flavius's fault that he had overindulged in drink and food, but here he was taking out his bad temper on his second-in-command.

Flavius noted the mood and formally asked him what he wanted to do next. It gave Marcus an opportunity to make up for being such a sour presence.

"I would like to do some work with the javelins," Marcus said, "but the Primus Pilus is so pig-headed about them that I don't want to get Manius into any trouble by including the First Century. On the other hand, it doesn't feel right for the Second Century to work separately from the First."

Marcus knew that by bringing Flavius into his dilemma, he essentially was making the optio a co-commander. There was no better way to apologize to Flavius than to include him in a command decision.

Flavius brightened considerably. "We could work with the three lines and keep to the pilum," he suggested.

Marcus had come to the same conclusion, but he let himself consider it for a moment, as if it hadn't occurred to him. "Good idea, Flavius. Let's give them a few more moments rest."

For the next hour, the two centuries worked on formations and spear throwing. Virtually everyone, apart from a few of the men recently released from the valetudinarium, could hurl the six-foot pilum 50 feet.

Marcus was watching the Second Century advance in step, stop and throw their pila, when he caught sight of Demaratus and the young librarius, Servius Livius, leading a mule onto the field. Two saddlebags hung on either side of the animal, with a small table and campstool tied on top.

Just behind them were Gnaeus and Aemilius Gratidius, the tesserarius from headquarters. The latter looked unhappy.

"Now what is this all about?" Marcus wondered.

Demaratus halted the mule and began untying the table and stool, while Servius unhitched the two saddlebags.

"Sir, where do you want us to set up?" Demaratus asked him.

"I'll tell you where to set up, signifer," growled Gnaeus, finally catching up with the two men.

Demaratus was clearly startled. He had no idea that the Primus Pilus was behind him. He hesitated, looking at Marcus.

"I'm in command here, signifer. When I give a command, you had best follow it," snarled Gnaeus, catching Demaratus's glance toward Marcus.

"Of course, sir," answered Demaratus, "I just wasn't aware you had the time to join us today."

It was a reply that just edged on insubordination, but the Greek delivered it in such a respectful tone that Gnaeus would find it difficult to take offense. He did so, nonetheless.

"Who do you think arranged this whole matter, signifer?" replied Gnaeus, his voice rising so that both centuries could clearly hear what he was saying. "Do you think these good men could receive part of their stipendia without my authority? You are new to the VII Legion, otherwise you would know that the Primus Pilus looks after his men."

Demaratus flushed, his face bright with anger, but he said nothing. Servius, holding the saddlebags, froze. The headquarters tesserarius looked embarrassed.

Flavius appeared as if he were going to say something, but Marcus silenced him with a glance. Marcus was stunned by the Primus Pilus's comment. To demean an officer in front of his men was inexcusable. Marcus would have to act, but in a way that avoided a direct clash with Gnaeus. If this had occurred at headquarters, he would have challenged the man, but in front of the men that would be disastrous. At the same time, he had to support his officer or Demaratus would lose his credibility as a commander.

"The fault is not his, sir," Marcus said in as loud a voice as he could without making it seem obvious that he was publicly contradicting Gnaeus, "but mine. When you did not respond to my letter this morning explaining how the good merchants of Corduba had generously agreed to our proposal for a loan, I assumed more weighty matters had engaged you. It is good to have you here with us, sir."

It was a complex speech, to which Gnaeus did not know how to respond. Marcus was intervening between the Primus Pilus and Demaratus, but by referring to "our proposal," he was not directly contradicting Gnaeus's obvious attempt to take all the credit.

Before the Primus Pilus could recover, Marcus delivered a lie which he hoped would quench the expected explosion by Gnaeus: "Clodius Petreius, the preceptor of the Corduba Merchant Council and the man from whom my signifer picked up the money, is on his way here, sir. He is running a little late. Shall we wait for him?"

Gnaeus, still trying to sort out Marcus's first statement, suddenly found himself at a loss. Clodius's comment at the party, that the Primus Pilus was a "sour lemon," suggested that the two had tangled in the past. If Clodius showed up he would make it clear that Marcus had negotiated the entire loan, and Marcus suspected that Gnaeus would conclude that Clodius would enjoy discomforting the Primus Pilus. It would be Gnaeus, not Demaratus, who would then be held up to ridicule. The Primus Pilus could order his subordinates to be silent; he had no such powers over a man as powerful and wealthy as Clodius.

Marcus watched Gnaeus's face go through a series of emotions: outrage coupled with a sudden wariness. Once again it was obvious to Marcus that the Primus Pilus was not well. Finally, the man mastered his temper and replied, "The men have waited long enough, centurion. The stipendia should be distributed. We cannot wait on tardy civilians."

"Yes, sir," said Marcus, then turning to Flavius and Manius, ordered the officers to form their men in two century lines. Manius looked uncomfortable, Flavius like he was ready to cut the Primus Pilus's throat.

The men quickly formed two lines, jostling and joking with one another, in a fine humor. Demaratus, who always quickly mastered his emotions, set up the table and was opening the unit's payroll scroll, while Servius was pulling cloth bags filled with coins out of the saddlebags.

One by one, Demaratus called out the names of the men, while Servius counted out a pile of denarri. These days they were mostly bronze, with only a trace of silver. Inflation had taken a deep bite out of the average soldier's pay, so much so that many preferred to be paid in goods and services rather than money.

Gnaeus stood apart from his officers, occasionally glancing nervously back toward the camp. "He is expecting Clodius to appear and show him up in front of the troops," thought Marcus, suppressing a smile.

Flavius still had a look of thunder on his face, and when Gnaeus glanced his way, the optio locked eyes with him until the Primus Pilus looked away. Marcus would have to talk with Flavius. An open breach would undo all the excellent work they had done with the two centuries. When Flavius glanced his way, Marcus cocked an eyebrow and spread his hand in an indication that the optio should be careful. Flavius looked defiant for a moment, then nodded.

It occurred to Marcus that Demaratus was deliberately slowing the process down to annoy Gnaeus, which was fine with him. But he also worried that it might irritate the men. They seemed happy, however, and if they were impatient, they weren't showing it. As each of them received his stipendia, he returned to the ranks.

"Can't you move faster?" grumbled Gnaeus to Demaratus and Servius.

"The rolls have not been tended to for some time, sir," replied Demaratus. "This is the first opportunity we have had to get them fully straightened out. Do you have a suggestion how we might speed this up?"

Gnaeus glared at the Greek, but just said, "Hurry it along."

"Yes sir," responded Demaratus, and went on at the same pace. Marcus again suppressed a smile. Demaratus was repaying the Primus Pilus in his own coin.

When all the denarri were finally distributed—there were some left over for the men still in the hospital—Gnaeus strode to the front of the two centuries. "Comrades," he said, "the day after tomorrow we go home."

The announcement caused a considerable stir in the ranks, and then a cheer. It was clear the men were tired of being away from their base, where many of them had families. Marcus would have preferred that he had been given a little more notice, but he had long ago given up expecting any courtesy from Gnaeus. These next two days promised to be an organizing nightmare and the centuries were short on officers. He would have to appoint a tesserarius for the Second, and supplies and marching gear would have to be inspected.

"Dismissed," said Gnaeus, which brought Marcus out of his ruminations on all the things that needed to be accomplished in the next day and a half.

"Sir," he said to Gnaeus, "shouldn't we have an inspection tomorrow morning?"

The Primus Pilus gave him a hostile stare. "In the VII, the second in command takes care of details, centurion," he said. "You and your officers have much to learn." Gnaeus turned his back on Marcus and strode off toward camp.

The man was impossible, but there was simply no sense in arguing with him, particularly in front of the men. Marcus turned back to the ranks and announced that there would be a full marching inspection after roll call in the morning. There were groans because many had anticipated a night of drinking and carousing, but they dutifully fell into their centuries and marched off to the barracks.

Flavius drifted over and stood silently by Marcus. Demaratus joined them, as Servius was packing up the table and stool and loading the last coins on the mule. Nobody said anything for several moments.

Finally, Marcus said mildly, "Clodius never showed."

Demaratus grinned. The Greek knew that Clodius had not been invited, and that the enmity between the merchant and Gnaeus would prevent the latter ever checking with the former about whether Marcus had been telling the truth. Flavius had also figured out that the Clodius's business was just a ploy to outmaneuver the Primus Pilus, but the look on his face was still deeply angry.

"Demeaning a fellow officer in front of the men, taking credit for something he had nothing to do with," he whispered.

Demaratus shrugged. "By tonight the men will know who

secured their stipendia, and it is hard to feel demeaned by a man like Gnaeus."

"I tell you sir, I cannot abide that man," said Flavius.

Marcus let him cool off for a moment. "We have no choice but to abide him, Flavius. It is our duty," he answered, adding, "and we have much to do in the next day and a half."

He changed the subject to get his optio's mind off the Primus Pilus. "Flavius, we will need a tesserarius. Do you have any suggestions?"

Pulling the optio back to everyday problems worked. Flavius took a deep breath and considered for a while. "Sextus Aelius is a steady man, sir, and he has seen a good deal of fighting. He also is well thought of by the ranks," he answered.

"Isn't he the short stocky fellow?" asked Marcus.

"Right. Has a long scar on his sword arm. He is short for the First Cohort, but he is such a fighter that they made an exception to the height rules," Flavius replied.

"All right," said Marcus," send him to me before they all go off and get drunk.

Demaratus was quiet as the three headed back to the barracks and the baths. It had been an interesting day. He was not as outraged as Flavius and Marcus were over his treatment by the Primus Pilus because he knew the man was unpopular with the men. He had had a long talk with the doctor, Timotheus, as they headed off to secure the money from Clodius's warehouse near the Baetis.

The two men had started off wary of one another. To the Romans all Greeks were the same, while Greeks hardly considered themselves "Greek." Demaratus was from Athens, Timotheus from Corinth, both of whom had been at one another's throat for most their existence. Athenians considered Corinth to be little more than an open-air whorehouse, while Corinthians had a tough time thinking of Athenians as anything but arrogant imperialists.

But Athens and Corinth were a long way off, and a shared language and view of the Romans gradually thawed things out.

"Tell me about this centurion of yours," said Timotheus, "He seems an interesting man, and one who has struck up a"—he paused for a moment, then added— "friendship with the richest woman in Corduba, if not Iberia itself."

Demaratus cocked an eyebrow at the doctor. "That surprises me. Marcus has always seemed shy around women."

"Oh, I suspect Marcus had little to do with it all. When Aelia Dasumi decides she wants something, it is best to surrender before she lays siege. She takes no prisoners," replied Timotheus.

Demaratus laughed at the metaphor. When the Roman Army began a siege, everyone who did not immediately surrender was put to the sword or sold into slavery once the fortress or city fell.

"Well, he has depths which are not at first obvious, and he seems to me to be a good deal smarter than most Romans," said Demaratus.

Timotheus nodded. "Aelia is attracted to intelligence, but she is a quirky person. Since she has so much power and wealth, I think she is attracted by its opposite."

"Marcus is a pretty quirky person himself," said Demaratus. "Is this woman attractive?"

"'Attractive' doesn't quite describe her," replied the doctor. "She can make a room fall silent just by walking into it."

Demaratus shook his head. "The things I see in the man are things that men see. I am not sure what a woman would see in him."

Timotheus shrugged. "Who can figure women? Even horses make more sense."

The discussion about Marcus inevitably got around to the situation in the First Cohort, and the doctor was filled with gossip. From this, Demaratus discovered how unpopular the Primus Pilus was among the men, and the guarded approval they had of Marcus and Flavius.

"The men appreciate fighters, and they don't much like corporal punishment. It seems your centurion and optio can fight, and they haven't laid a hastile or a vitis on anyone."

"Marcus doesn't even carry a vitis," said Demaratus, "and Flavius is very protective of that lion's head on his hastile. No, they don't go in much for punishment. Marcus does have some odd ideas about how to run an army and how to fight battles. I suppose you have heard about the great javelin uproar?"

"It was a topic of conversation for days," said Timotheus. "The men are divided on how effective the javelins will be, but everyone enjoyed the clash between Marcus and Gnaeus. They were impressed that your centurion stood up to the Primus Pilus."

"He is not one to back down, though he generally avoids frontal assaults," said Demaratus, "He prefers to outthink and then flank his opponent. Much like the Athenians."

The doctor snorted. "I seem to recall it was the Spartans who figured how to outflank the Athenians, not the other way round," adding, "of course that was because they listened to their Corinthian allies."

They both laughed good-naturedly and continued a low-key banter interspersed with valuable gossip, all the way to the warehouse.

Flavius knew Marcus had changed the subject from Gnaeus to choosing a tesserarius so that he could get his temper under control. He had mastered it, but just. When Marcus walked ahead of them to the barracks, Flavius dropped back to have a word with Demaratus.

"I don't care if it is treason," Flavius said to the Greek, "it would be a pleasure to cut out that man's liver."

Demaratus said nothing for a moment, then simply commented, "One day he will make a mistake, Flavius. That kind always does. Then shall awful justice quench great excess, the son of pride."

Flavius whistled. "Nice line. If words were armies, the Greeks would rule the world."

Demaratus laughed. "Unfortunately, they are not, my friend."

Before going to the baths, Flavius went off to hunt up Sextus Aelius. He found the man with his contubernium playing dice and drinking wine. The men all stood to attention when he came into their barracks, but he waved them back to their games and drinking. He touched Sextus with his hastile and told him the centurion would like a word with him. The man immediately looked guilty—probably was, of something—as he straightened out his uniform and put on his helmet.

"We won't be long, no need for the rest of your equipment," Flavius told him. Sextus looked tense and came to attention.

Flavius suppressed a smile. He remembered when he was appointed tesserarius and was called before a centurion. He thought for certain he was going to be whipped for some transgression of the rules, as did everyone else in his contubernium. Flavius noted that the seven other men looked anxious.

The optio turned and Sextus followed him out and down the road in front of the barracks to the officers' quarters. He knocked at the door and Marcus told him to enter. He waved an unhappy looking Sextus in before him. Marcus was seated at a table removing his harness. Demaratus was nowhere around. He had probably gone off to the baths directly from the field.

Marcus stood when Sextus came in, and the man gave him a smart salute.

"At ease, Sextus," said Marcus. "My optio tells me you are one of the best soldiers in the century. Do you have anything to say in your defense?"Flavius grinned. Marcus's odd sense of humor could crop up in the strangest situations. Poor Sextus looked utterly confused.

"Uh, defense, sir?" he said.

Now Marcus was grinning at him. "If you are going to be an officer, Sextus, you need to be prepared for anything, even questions that make no sense."

"Sir?" asked Sextus.

"Put him out of his misery, sir," said Flavius to Marcus.

Marcus looked the confused man up and down. "The century needs a tesserarius, Sextus. Are you up to the job? An honest answer, now."

Sextus was silent for a long moment. "Yes sir, I would be honored to be a tesserarius in the Second Century. And yes sir, I think I can do the job."

"Well," said Flavius starting to take off his harness and chain armor, "we wouldn't have asked you if you couldn't." Turning to Marcus, he said, "I will make sure he is entered in the rolls. As for you, Sextus, turn in your plate armor and draw yourself some chain mail. You will be bunking with us from now on."

The man looked a little stunned until both Flavius and Marcus laughed and shook his hand. "You're an officer now, Sextus, so no more carousing and whoring about," said Flavius with mock sternness. "Now go get your gear, and join us in the baths."

XIX

Marcus had stripped to his tunic, but before heading for the baths, he and Flavius sat down and wrote out a list of things that needed to be accomplished in the next 36 hours.

"I will check with the armorer," said Marcus, "you be sure we have sufficient food and mules," adding, "find out how many of the men the doctor thinks will need horses for the first part of the trip."

"Yes, sir. I will get Sextus involved in this," said Flavius.

"Good idea," agreed Marcus. "Ask him to deal with the mules, and remind him we are taking extra pila and javelins."

In the middle of writing out the list, Marcus remembered Aelia. There was no way that he could squeeze in a visit. He would have to write a letter apologizing for leaving on such short notice, though how he would construct such a thing, he hadn't the foggiest idea.

But first things first, and the baths beckoned.

On the way to the baths, they ran across Manius looking harried. "Join us," said Marcus, but the First Century's tesserarius begged off.

"I have too much to organize right now," said Manius.

"What about your other officers?" asked Flavius.

"There are none, sir. The centurion has appointed me acting optio, but he says no one in the century is fit to be a signifer or a tesserarius," answered Manius.

"Honor to you, Manius," said Marcus formally, but then frowned. "But getting the century ready is a tall order for two men."

Manius said nothing.

"I take it the centurion is indisposed?" asked Flavius.

"Yes, sir," Manius answered.

"Well, first off you can stop calling me sir," said Flavius. "We're now the same. In fact," he grinned, "as you are optio of the First Century, and I am only optio of the Second, I suppose I should be calling you sir."

Manius smiled. "That won't be necessary, sir...I mean Flavius." He saluted Marcus and said, "Thank you for your congratulations, sir. You will excuse me; I have much work to do."

As Manius hurried off, Flavius and Marcus exchanged looks.

"Are you thinking what I am thinking, Flavius?" asked Marcus.

"If it is that we might lend him Sextus for the evening, then I think we are of the same mind," answered the optio.

"I'll talk with him in the baths," said Marcus.

Sextus, still heady from his promotion, was more than willing to lend a hand with the First Century. He cut short his bath, dressed, and went to look up Manius.

After the new tesserarius left, Marcus said, "Good choice, Flavius."

"Aye. He is a hardworking and responsible lad. He'll do.

Probably make a good centurion one of these days," answered Flavius. "But I have some concerns about this march north."

Marcus nodded. "We will have to be careful. I don't think Gnaeus is competent to command in the field."

"That could get tricky, sir," said Flavius.

Marcus said nothing.

The next few hours were exhausting, doubly so because while Gnaeus was too "indisposed" to do anything, he still managed to throw up one obstacle after another.

First, he objected to the extra mules for the javelins, relenting only after Marcus offered to pay for the mules himself. Then he refused to authorize extra mules for the men still in the hospital. "They can march," snarled Gnaeus "it will toughen them."

Marcus kept his temper about the extra mules for the weapons, but he lost it over the wounded and sick.

"We need every man we can get, Gnaeus," Marcus said, his voice rising. "The centuries are thin to begin with, and you are weakening us further. The doctor is only sending us men who will eventually be able to march. If it comes to fighting, we will need those men."

"Still afraid of those horsemen, Marcus?" sneered Gnaeus.

"Anyone who is not concerned for the welfare of his unit is a fool," Marcus shot back.

Gnaeus rose out of his chair. "Are you calling me a fool?" he almost screamed. Marcus could only imagine what the men in headquarters would be making of this clash.

Marcus's response was icy: "A commander who abandons his men is not only a fool, he has no honor."

Gnaeus's eyes bulged in their sockets and a vein in his forehead pulsed. "I could have you arrested for that remark," he shouted.

"You have no authority to arrest me, Gnaeus, and you know it. You command in the field, but here we are equals. My orders came from Tribune Flavius Felix, not from you," Marcus said quietly. "Put me on report if you wish and we will let the legate in Legio settle this matter. In the meantime, stay out of my way."

Gnaeus mastered his rage, then favored Marcus with a tight smile. "The legate, yes," he said, "we will indeed talk with the legate, Marcus. I am sure he will be deeply interested in these dispatches I am bearing."

A shiver ran down Marcus's back, but he controlled his facial expression and ignored the "dispatches" comment. "If there is nothing else, Primus Pilus, I have much work to do."

He put his helmet on, turned his back on Gnaeus, and strode out. He passed Aemilius, the headquarters tesserarius, who, white-faced, was actually wringing his hands.

Marcus strode out, a mixture of emotion. He was still angry at Gnaeus's mean-spirited obstructionism concerning the sick men. But he was also worried by the Primus Pilus's comment on the "dispatches." What could they say? If there were a warrant among them, Gnaeus would certainly have placed him, Demaratus, and Flavius under arrest. But if it were not a warrant, why would Gnaeus gloat about them?

Marcus made himself calm down. The dispatches might be nothing and, in any case, there was nothing that he could do about them. But he would not tell Flavius and Demaratus about them. There was no sense in raising their concerns about something that might just be an expression of Gnaeus's under-lying madness.

He suppressed his anxiety over the dispatches and turned to his dismissal of the Primus Pilus's threat to have him arrested over his remark about abandoning the men.

On this he felt he was on solid ground. A unit did not leave its men behind any more than it left its dead untended. And his orders put him, not Gnaeus, in command of the Second Century. He could not force Gnaeus to take the First Century's wounded and sick, but the Second Century would take care of its own.

He was returning from the armory when he got the news of how Gnaeus had struck back. Flavius met him before he got to the barracks.

"Sir," said Flavius, looking worried, "Gnaeus has taken two dozen men from the Second Century and replaced them with the wounded and sick from the hospital. He told me that if you were so concerned about the men, then you could nurse them back to health."

Marcus shook his head and laughed. "We can only hope the man shows such tenacity in the face of an enemy."

"We were short on men to begin with, sir. This could really hurt us," said Flavius.

"Or it could strengthen us, Flavius," replied Marcus. "Come, let's pay our new recruits a visit," he said with a wink.

"Yes, sir," answered Flavius with a touch of the long-suffering in his voice.

It was a short walk to the Valetudinarium. When Marcus and Flavius arrived, Timotheus was changing the dressings for some of the wounded. The men who could stand came to attention.

"I have just been informed that some of you will be joining the Second Century," Marcus said, "and I wanted to welcome you on behalf of my optio and myself. The good doctor here gave me a list of those who will need to ride until they can march with us. Since we won't have any cavalry, you will just have to constitute yourselves as a turmae of the Second Century," he said with a grin.

The idea of a bunch of wounded foot soldiers becoming the basic unit of a cavalry quingeniary drew a solid laugh from the men.

"It will be good to have you men from the Second Century back. And with the number of new recruits we have, you men from the First Century will all be appointed honorary optios," continued Marcus to another round of laughter.

Marcus grew serious for a moment. "We may see some fighting north of Emerita Augustus, comrades. That is only a little more than a week from now. If you can get yourself back into the line by then, we need you. But if you are in no shape to go, you will be hurting your unit if you come along. There is nothing to be ashamed of if you are wounded or sick. You came by those maladies honorably. For those who can make it, there will be an inspection tomorrow morning."

He saluted the men and he and Flavius left, only to have the doctor catch them just outside the door.

"That was just what they needed to hear, sir," said Timotheus. "I think you will have a little more than 30 men who will be able to go north with you."

"You see, Flavius," said Marcus, "we lost two dozen and got back over 30."

"I might add," said the doctor, "they will go with enthusiasm. Gnaeus has only come here to get medicine for himself. He has yet to say a word to the men. My only problem will be trying to keep those who can't make it north from insisting on going.

"Will you be accompanying us, doctor?" asked Marcus.

"Yes. I will leave an assistant here. My base is Legio as well," he answered.

"Good," said Marcus. "We may need you en route."

"I hope not," said the doctor.

"As do we all," said Flavius.

Marcus had been struggling with the letter to Aelia for over two hours, and so far, he had written nothing. Flavius, Demaratus, and Sextus had been in and out several times, all of them swallowing what they were going to say after taking one look at him. Their sudden truncating of complaints or questions helped improve his mood. He felt deeply incompetent trying to write what he was feeling, but somehow the fact that his officers were tiptoeing around him made him feel less vulnerable.

He finally got something down that sounded stilted and awkward when he read it aloud, but it would have to do. He had far too many things to accomplish in the next few hours to waste any more time on it. He was preparing to seal the folded-over letter, when he stopped, opened it, and added a short postscript: "I hope you will forgive my awkwardness in expressing what I feel, Aelia, and that this will not become a barrier between us."

He sealed it, quickly walked to headquarters, and handed it to Aemilius, who promised he would see that it was delivered tomorrow morning. As soon as he walked outside, he had second thoughts about his postscript, and almost went back to reclaim the letter and rewrite it. He even stopped and started to turn, when his new tesserarius, Sextus, appeared, saluted, and asked to speak with him. It seemed as if the Gods wanted that postscript to go to Aelia.

"Yes, Sextus," Marcus said, "What is the problem?"

Sextus looked uncomfortable. "Not exactly a problem, sir, but the Primus Pilus told me to mind my own business, and if I didn't have enough to do, I could clean out the heads."

Marcus smiled ruefully. Gnaeus was becoming unglued, which wouldn't have bothered him at all except that the man would soon be taking two centuries into the field against possible enemies. "Report to Flavius and...wait, locate Flavius and Demaratus and tell them we will have a staff meeting in half an hour."

Sextus hesitated a moment. "Should I clean out the heads, sir?"

"You take your orders from me, Sextus, not the Primus Pilus. Officers don't clean heads," Marcus said quietly. "Now go get the staff."

Sextus saluted and disappeared, leaving Marcus both bemused and troubled. He decided that he would do well to keep a running record of the Primus Pilus's actions in case this all really came down to formal charges when they reached Legio.

He was writing up the "clean the heads incident" when the three officers arrived back at their barracks. A quick report from each showed that everything was pretty much under control—Flavius needed Marcus's authority to get the stable to release the horses for the wounded—and on track for tomorrow. Marcus dealt with the stable hands, made himself popular by taking all the over-the-hill horseflesh off their hands, and went to bed.

The Second Century was strung out in a single line, 149 legionnaires. Almost 20 of these were the walking wounded from the valetudinarium, but by the time the century left Emerita Augusta, it just might be at full strength. Glancing over at the First Century drawn up 50 feet away, Marcus could see that his Second was larger.

Each of the men was in full uniform, which included armor, sword, pugio, two Pila, scutum, forked carrying stick, tool bag, wicker basket, kettle, bronze food box, stake, and dolabra entrenching tool. Marcus always marveled how he had ever managed to carry all that when he was in the ranks, reminding himself that that was a long time ago. And he also reminded himself that some members of the Second Century were older than he was.

Flavius was inspecting each soldier's tool bag, and woe to those who did not have a chain saw, a hook and a rope. He had them open their mess kits as well. They were supposed to have three days' rations in the kits, but the commissary had been tardy in supplying marching food, so Flavius growled a little at those who were short.

The men still had plenty to do before they left tomorrow morning, so he dismissed them once inspection was over. Gnaeus, however, was keeping the First Century on the field, and berating the men who were short a particular piece of equipment.

Well, the First Century was not his problem, and Marcus put it out of his mind. For the rest of the afternoon and early evening he and his officers were organizing the pack animals, gathering the javelins, extra pila, and doling out one mule per contubernium. The commissary finally came through with provisions, and each squad drew a week's rations of acetum, bacon, lentils, cheese, wheat, garlic, and onions, adding to it their own supplies of cabbages, parsnips, eggs, and early Fall pears and apples.

Many convalescents had moved out of the valetudinarium and back into the barracks, although few looked strong enough to carry 60 pounds of gear, plus their armor and weapons, and manage 20 miles in a day. Marcus, however, had a feeling that once they were on the march, the wounded would recover much more quickly.

He put his head into the almost deserted Valetudinarian to find the doctor packing his supplies of vinegar, turpentine, opium, henbane, and a vast array of hooks, forceps, needles, scalpels and the tapered wooden devices that were used to remove arrowheads.

"Is there anything you need, Timotheus?" he asked.

"No, my assistant and I will have everything packed, and we have already arranged for a mule. As you can see," said the doctor indicating the now largely empty hospital," I don't have much to do right now."

By the time everything was in place for the morning, everyone was exhausted. Marcus was dragging himself to the baths when Aemilius caught him.

"Sir, this came for you this afternoon," said the Tesserarius, saluting.

Marcus stared at the letter blankly before realizing that Aelia must have replied to his note. He was immediately self-conscious, mumbled a thanks to Aemilius, and tried to decide what to do. He was headed for the baths, but he didn't want to open the letter with others around because it might well be a curt dismissal. In fact, he didn't want to open the letter at all. Since Aemilius was still standing there, he decided to return to his barracks but open it before he arrived.

As he walked back, he used his thumb to break the wax seal. Taking a deep breath, he opened the folded letter; "Dearest Marcus," it read, "You are at your best when you are awkward. Go with care. Write me from Legio. Aelia."

He stared at it for a long moment. Was Aelia being sarcastic? Was she teasing him? Was she being sweet? He yearned to ask her or discuss it with someone, but he could not. He sighed and decided to take the letter on its face: she wanted him to write again and was kind about his awkwardness. He had doubts that his interpretation was the correct one, but the warm glow he got when he thought of the letter that way was so nice that he suppressed his inner demons. Stepping into the barracks, he slipped the note into his gear and headed back for the baths, happier than five minutes before.

The morning air was chill, the first real sign of approaching winter that Marcus had felt in Hispania. The two centuries were assembling in the Field of Mars, and the whole area spilled over with men, mules, horses, and baggage.

Even before the men awoke, the officers of both centuries had gathered for a sacrifice. A victimarii brought a lamb into the fort's Augustine shrine, cut its throat, and disemboweled the animal. While the officers looked on, a haruspices carefully examined the entrails. Marcus was not much for divination, and Demaratus looked like he was doing his best not to roll his eyes. Flavius and Sextus, however, concentrated on the actions of the haruspices, hanging on his every word.

After 20 minutes of examining the lamb's innards, the man proclaimed that the trip to Emerita Augusta would be uneventful, but then added, with a frown, "There is a cloud on the road to Norba."

Gnaeus snorted. "Maybe it is those horsemen that so plague the nightmares of Marcus. What say you, commander of the Second Century?"

Flavius stiffened with anger; Sextus looked pained; Demaratus looked amused; and Marcus merely shrugged, commenting mildly that it might not be such a good idea to make light of the gods before a journey. Judging by the looks of silent disapproval on the faces of the diviners, they agreed.

On the way out of the shrine, Gnaeus pulled him aside. "The First Century will lead," he said, quite unnecessarily, since the First Century always led. "You will hold the Second Century here until an important message that I am expecting from Gades arrives. It should only delay you a short time."

"Why are we holding up an entire century, Gnaeus?" asked Marcus. "You can have a horseman bring the message to us en route."

The Primus Pilus smiled unpleasantly at Marcus. "It is a very important message. I want a century to protect it."

"From whom?" asked an exasperated Marcus.

Gnaeus spread his hands. "Maybe your fierce horsemen, Marcus. In any case, you will await the message." He then added curtly, "You are dismissed."

By the time Marcus gathered his officers together he was boiling with anger. A delay would mean the men would march at the height of the day's heat, and would have to put in extra hours to catch up with the First Century. And of course, his century was saddled with the sick and wounded.

"Sir, this is not acceptable," said Flavius. "It will put an intolerable burden on the men."

"I believe that is what he has in mind," said Demaratus quietly.

Sextus said nothing, still not sure of himself as both the junior officer and the newest member of a group that had seen service together.

"We have no choice but to accept it, optio. You, Demaratus, and Sextus see to the men, and I will try to discover more about this 'important' message."

Marcus knew there was no sense in going to Gnaeus, but the tesserarius or the librarius at the principia might know something about it. Aemilius had been at the ceremony in the shrine, looking distinctly uncomfortable, but Servius the librarius had been absent. Since the Primus Pilus had left straight for the Field of Mars, Marcus would not run into him at headquarters.

Aemilius was not at his desk, but Marcus found him in the principia's small library. Asked about the "important message," the tesserarius told Marcus that it was the first he had heard of it. He also questioned its source. "Gades?" asked Aemilius. "Why from Gades? Both centuries spent very little time in Gades, and any important orders would most likely come from Cartago Nova or Valentia."

Aemilius sent for Servius, who arrived looking like he had come directly from his couch. The librarius also professed to know nothing about any message.

Marcus paced a bit. Gades as the origin of an important message made no sense. The VII Legion was controlled by the

Emperor, who directly ruled the provinces of Tarraconensis and Lusitania. In theory, the Senate controlled Baetica, although that myth had pretty much gone by the board in the last two decades. Any message directed at the VII Legion or any of its units would most likely come from one of the other two provinces.

He finally had both men write a brief note to the effect that they were both unaware of any message of importance due from Gades, tucked the notes into his pouch, and headed back to the Field of Mars. By the time he arrived the First Century had departed, although their trailing mule team was still getting underway. The men of the Second Century were sitting on their baggage, many of them playing dice.

"What did you find out, sir?" asked Flavius.

"No one has heard of any such orders, Flavius. We will wait two hours, and then leave, orders or no orders," he answered.

Marcus took out his scroll on Gnaeus, and noted down the whole incident, tucking the two notes from the headquarters officers into a small pouch where he kept the scroll.

For the next hour and a half, he paced back and forth, finally judging that he had had enough of this nonsense.

"Sextus," he said to the new officer, "Go to the principia and find out if any message from Gades has arrived. If it has not, tell the tesserarius that the Second Century is leaving, and he is to send the message on under armed escort as soon as it arrives."

"Armed escort, sir?" asked a puzzled Sextus.

"Yes, armed escort," Marcus said with a sigh. "Be sure you state that, and have the librarius write my orders out, with a copy for me."

Sextus went off looking thoroughly confused, and wondering whether being an officer was all it was cracked up to be.

Marcus called Flavius and Demaratus together, explained the situation, and told the optio to get the men up, loaded, and in marching formation. By the time the century was ready to move, Sextus had returned with a written copy of Marcus's orders, and the Second got underway, marching three abreast toward the Via Plato and the northern marches.

Flavius had encountered many officers in his day. There were those who delighted in cruelty towards their men, others who wanted nothing more than some quick service and an easy path to the Senate, and some who, through stupidity or blind arrogance, got their men killed. But he had never met a man like Gnaeus, who seemed possessed by a madness that was hard to explain. Marcus thought he was ill. He certainly was that, but Flavius found the man's enmity toward his commander inexplicable. In fact, Flavius didn't know anyone who disliked Marcus. True, some people were set on trying to kill him, but those weren't really "people," they were praetorians. Ever since they had arrived in Corduba, Gnaeus had been like a harpy, relentlessly seeking Marcus's humiliation.

He shook his head. Flavius had no illusions about fairness when it came to the Roman Army, but he expected orders to make sense. Gnaeus made no sense, and that worried Flavius. People who made no sense and had power were dangerous.

Marcus and Demaratus were up front leading the unit, and Flavius was at the rear, between the soldiers and the mule team. The mounted wounded and the doctor and his assistant trailed the rest. Each contubernium had designated one member to lead a mule, and throughout the day they would rotate soldiers back to the mule train. However, the century had not even cleared the northern part of Corduba when the column came to a halt.

Flavius trotted alongside of the now stationary century only to encounter a huge jam of ox carts, people, and even a few chariots. The crowd had spilled across the road from something that was going on just ahead.

He located the century's signum, under which he knew he would find Demaratus and Marcus. He found the two arguing with an ox cart driver.

Marcus was telling the man he would have to move, and the man was explaining that he couldn't move east of the road because it was swampy ground, and he couldn't move west because of the crowd.

Flavius arrived just as the three were starting another round of argument. "I'll go see what this crowd is all about, sir," he said.

Marcus, looking slightly harassed, told him, "The man says it's an execution, Flavius. See what you can do about moving it a bit further west."

Flavius tapped his hastile on the scutums of the three leading legionaries and indicated they should follow him. With them in tow, he plowed into the crowd.

There were so many people it was hard to see what was happening, and some in the crowd started to protest as the optio pushed himself to the front. But the three soldiers who followed him, with their shields and heavy spears, silenced the complaints.

Just as he was nearing what appeared to be the front rank

of spectators, a motion caught his eye. Suddenly two crosses were lifted above the crowd. On one was an older man, on the other, nearest to Flavius, a young woman. The blood from their hands and feet had already begun to run down their bodies and wind itself around the central posts. The man was silent, but the woman was sobbing something he could not quite make out.

"Here, here, move aside," said Flavius, "Army business."

The front rank of the crowd parted and the execution came into full view. A dozen vigiles were guarding an equal number of victims, all of them bound and seated next to the devices that would be their deaths. Flavius had never seen so many crucifixions at one time and he asked one of the vigiles what was going on.

"That slave there," said the vigile, pointing at the old man on the cross, "killed his master. So all the master's slaves are sentenced to death."

"Well, we've got a century that is bound for Emerita Augusta, and this execution has blocked the road, so will you move this lot a bit further in that direction?" said Flavius pointing west.

"I'll get my officer, sir," the vigile said and vanished into the back part of the crowd.

Flavius stood and fumed. Three vigiles were preparing to crucify another slave, a young girl. Not even a girl, really, but a child. She could not have been more than seven or eight years old. She was a pretty little thing, though her hair was tangled and matted, and streaks of tears cut lines down her filthy cheeks. She was making short choking noises as if she was trying to catch her breath, and she looked terrified.

Death and execution were an everyday affair in the empire,

but the crucifixion of this little girl tugged at something in Flavius. The vigiles were holding her down, preparing to drive the spikes into her palms, and one of them slapped her to shut her up. Her choking sobs changed into a high-pitched wail.

Flavius turned away and looked elsewhere. And then he could hear what the young woman was sobbing.

"Please sir, don't let her die like me. She is only a baby. Please, be merciful."

He shouldn't have glanced up, but he did. The young woman on the cross locked eyes with him, mouthing a prayer. "Kill her, quickly, please, sir." He looked down and turned away.

This wasn't an Army matter.

At this juncture a vigile officer—Flavius assumed he was an optio, although he would never use that term to describe a vigile—appeared. The man was dressed in a fancy uniform with a tunic of the finest linen.

"What's the problem, here," he demanded of Flavius. "I have orders to carry out these crucifixions close to the main road. They will serve as an example to all slaves," adding "Your century will have to wait. In any case, this is none of your business."

The man's timing was insufferably bad. Flavius had had several really awful days, and he was in no mood to let some dressed up martinet of a vigile use that tone of voice with him.

"Oh it isn't?" said Flavius softly.

Flavius drew his sword, grabbed the vigile officer by his tunic, and shoved him backwards. "Isn't my business?" he said a little louder. He found himself standing next to the child, now nailed to the cross still lying on the ground. He looked down at her. She was still whimpering, but she had focused on his face, her tiny chest heaving with great sobs of pain. Almost without thinking he put his sword to her breast and stabbed. Her small body arched for a moment, her eyes rolling back, and she was still.

The voice whispered above him: "Thank you, thank you, thank you...."

Recovering from his shove, the vigile optio blustered. "How dare you!" Turning to his men, he said, "Take that man under arrest."

Two of the vigiles started to step forward only to find themselves facing three legionaries, their pila leveled at their chests, and a look on their faces which suggested that there was nothing they would like better than for the vigiles to try to put their optio under arrest.

Flavius leaned down and closed the child's eyes. Then, stepping forward, he slowly and deliberately wiped his blade clean on the vigile optio's expensive tunic. "Death to the enemies of the Empire," he said softly.

The man recoiled, whether from the child's blood or the underlying violence in Flavius's quiet words was not clear.

"I want you 100 feet from here, or this century is going to demonstrate that crucifixion is not the only way to carry out an execution," he said loudly enough for the dozen vigiles to hear him. They glanced at one another and began dragging their prisoners and crosses in the direction that Flavius had indicated.

The crowd, making a wide detour around Flavius and his small squad of soldiers, followed them and the area began to clear.

Flavius turned to his soldiers. "Thanks, lads. I'll not forget this," he said.

"Our pleasure, sir," said one.

Flavius led the three back to the century which had already begun to clear a path through the Via Plata. The ox cart was moving off west of the road and the various wagons and chariots followed suit. Within a few minutes the Second resumed its march to Emerita Augusta.

XX

The Century finally cleared the tangle of people and carts near the execution site and pushed northwest out of Corduba across a broad, flat plain, toward a distant line of mountains. The day had turned hot, but the men were making good time. Marcus looked back over his shoulder at the column, not so much examining details as trying to judge the mood of the unit. Men were conversing quietly, occasionally laughing. They were headed home, and even though the Century faced at least three weeks of hard marching, the mood was light, almost gay.

The outskirts of the city gave way to rich villas and orchards, and field slaves looked up as the Century rolled by. At a small crossroads, two old men, with the look of veterans about them, sat in the shade drinking wine. Marcus saluted the two, who returned it, but remained sitting.

He stepped away from the head of line and went over to the patch of shade. "Greetings," he said politely.

"And greetings to you sir," said the shorter and stockier of the two men. "The Army's on the move today, isn't it? What's afoot?"

Marcus wiped his brow. "Just moving a part of the First Cohort back to Legio. Were you here to see the First Century come through?"

"We were here," said the other man, somewhat sourly Marcus thought.

"Not very comradely," said the first man. "Wouldn't tell us a thing. Pushing awful hard, they were."

Marcus looked down the road. The Century was passing him by, and several of the soldiers nodded greetings to the old men. One yelled out, "Now that's what I want to do when I muster out."

The old men seemed pleased that the soldiers recognized them as veterans.

"Friendly lot you got here, sir," said the second man, a tall fellow missing several fingers on his left hand.

"Good men," agreed Marcus. "How long ago did the First go by?"

The stocky man took a long pull on the wine bladder and handed it over to the other man. Wiping his mouth, he said, "Maybe three hours, sir. But that centurion was pushing them hard."

"He could do that, considering he was riding a horse," said the tall one. "Are centurions joining the cavalry these days, sir?"

Marcus smiled. The old veterans had earned the right to say whatever they pleased. "He took sick in Tingas," he explained.

"Aye. Probably sat on a stick and never got it out" said the tall one. "Must hurt to ride that horse."

Marcus chuckled, thanked the two men, and caught up with the head of the Century.

It was a long day, and some of the convalescents who had begun the day marching dropped back and mounted mules. But Marcus was surprised by the number who managed to stay on their feet hour after hour. He did stop for more rests than he would normally take. He wanted to keep the Century together, not strung out for a mile and a half down the road.

He dropped back to talk with the doctor, who seemed unworried about the men. "They are doing fine, given where many of them were just a few days ago, sir," Timotheus said. "Are we going to try and catch the First?"

"We'll see, " said Marcus, and moved up toward the front again. He passed Flavius who nodded to him, but seemed withdrawn and preoccupied. Marcus wondered what the problem was, but knew that Flavius could be moody. It was best to just leave him be if he was out of sorts.

As the centurion moved up past the marching soldiers, he noticed them watching him discreetly. "They are wondering if I am going to push them to catch up as well," he thought. He wished he knew the answer.

Flavius felt a little guilty ignoring Marcus, but he was still turning over the incident at the execution. Flavius had long ago developed a system that he found made his life easier: ignore things. He told himself that he never ignored really important things, but he just found things went smoother if he closed his eyes and pretended to be someplace else.

Occasionally it got you in trouble. He had a habit of doing it with women. He liked women, but they were complex and difficult and he decided that they were something he didn't want to understand or know about. Which meant he was still single and likely to remain that way. That never bothered him in the past, but over the last year he had begun to wonder what he would do when he completed his service. He still had ten years, so the issue was hardly pressing, but still and all, it passed through his mind on occasion.

Something about the execution was nagging at him. It was not the first time he had seen executions, and certainly not the first time he had seen slaves—and on occasion, a legionnaire—crucified. Indeed, he had seen worse. He watched a half dozen lions tear some criminals to pieces in the arena, which had bothered him. He had avoided the games and the arena since the execution.

But he had never seen a child formally executed. He had seen plenty of dead children. The Roman Army had a standard rule: resist and everyone dies. In general, Flavius agreed with it. It was hard, but it generally convinced the next group of people to lay down their arms. And that was good for everyone, right? The barbarians saved their lives by yielding, and even got some of the benefits of the empire. And no soldiers got killed. Everyone made out.

Slaves were just part of life. That's the way things were. If the Romans were strong enough to conquer you, then it made sense that you served them. If you fought back, you died. Sets an example. Isn't killing the little girl just like that?

His logic told him it was, but it still didn't seem right. Maybe this slavery business had some drawbacks he had never considered. Almost before the thought was formed, Flavius recoiled from it. That was not something he should be thinking about. By the Gods, he was turning into some kind of Greek with all this back and forth, and seeing both sides of an argument. He resolutely put the entire matter out of his head and concentrated on whether Marcus was going to push the Second Century to catch up with the First, or make camp in the next few hours.

It was a decision fraught with complexities and gave Flavius something real and comfortable to think about.

When the Century stopped for a break, Timotheus came up the column to report the progress of the convalescents to Marcus. His opinion was that they had about three more hours left in them before the march turned into a medical setback.

"Even riding in this heat is a trial," the doctor said. "They might do four hours, but they have already covered almost 12 miles. No complaints, but some of them are looking a bit strained."

Marcus nodded to him. "We may ask them to do four hours. I will stop then, even if we haven't caught up with the First Century," he said.

Timotheus saluted and went off to find Demaratus, who was sitting beneath the Century's sigum drinking water from a bladder. He handed it to the doctor, who took a long pull on it.

"Four more hours of this," Timotheus said. "Then we halt, First Century or no First Century."

Demaratus was silent for a moment. Then said, "It doesn't surprise me."

"Really?" asked Timotheus. "It gives the Primus Pilus something to put Marcus on report about. I thought you said the centurion avoided frontal assaults."

"He does," answered Demaratus, "but not if he thinks he can win. No legate with any sense is going to punish an officer for taking care of his men. Annoy too many soldiers and they are liable to stick a knife in you. Several emperors have been a little careless that way and ended up with short reigns."

"Well, I'm glad he made a decision not to try and catch that madman, Gnaeus," the doctor said, taking a final drink from the bladder and heading back toward the back of the column.

Demaratus pulled himself to his feet, straightened his uniform, and cast an unspoken question at Marcus. The centurion nodded, and Demaratus signaled Sextus to get the men up and in formation. The new tesserarius started shouting orders and the men gathered their gear and formed a column. A mule at the end of the line protested loudly, followed by a chorus of his comrades.

Within minutes the Century was headed north again, though the long miles and the hot sun had taken some of the high spirits out of the column. The conversation and laughter of the morning had given over to silent concentration on the task at hand.

The Century crossed a shallow river—most of Hispania's rivers at this time of year were little more than trickles—two hours after their last halt, and climbed a short rise on the other side. Cresting it, they found the First Century just to the right of the road.

At first, Marcus didn't know what he was looking at, because the Century was not in marching camp, but just sprawled out, almost two dozen tents scattered over an immense field of mustard.

Marcus halted the column and within a few moments Flavius joined him and Demaratus.

"Is that the First?" asked Flavius.

"It is unless someone has stolen their signum," answered Demaratus, pointing to the Century's standard set over a large tent.

"No ditch? No ramparts? No stakes? No intervallum? That's no camp, it's a...." and Flavius's voice trailed off in shock. Finally, he looked at Marcus. "What are we supposed to do, sir, join that sorry excuse for century?"

"It isn't the century's fault, Flavius. Keep the men here for the moment. I will go talk to Gnaeus," said Marcus.

He strode off the hill and down into the camp. There was no challenge because there were no sentries. The tents were neat enough and each contubernium was busy preparing a meal. The men who saw him saluted—he recognized several that Gnaeus had seized from the Second Century—but Marcus barely acknowledged them. Just before he reached the tent with the signum over it, Manius came out from it, his head down. If Marcus had not put out his hand, the new optio would have collided with him.

"Manius," said Marcus.

"Who? Oh, it's you sir," said Manius. He stopped, and saluted. He looked exhausted and harried. "Welcome. I hope your march was uneventful."

"Manius, why isn't the First Century in marching camp? asked Marcus.

"Because there is no need for a marching camp," said Gnaeus, pushing aside the tent flap. He looked white and drawn, and his left hand's tremor was more pronounced than Marcus had ever seen. "There are no enemies from here to the border of Gaul, unless we count your phantom horsemen."

"The Army does not halt for the night without building a marching camp, Gnaeus," replied Marcus. "You know the regulations. There has to be a ditch, and a rampart with stakes."

"Do you think to tell me my duty, sir?" replied Gnaeus. "Do you remember who is in command here? Put your Century to the left of the road and don't bother me with your fantasies."

Manius, standing next to him, was stone faced.

Marcus considered his reply. He was tempted to make a scene. By tradition and regulations, every Army unit in the field built a marching camp. Like everything the Romans did, its specifications were exact: a marching camp in Egypt was no different than a marching camp in northern Britannia: a ditch twelve feet wide and nine feet deep, ramparts four feet high, topped with stakes, an intervallum border of 20 feet between the tents and the ramparts, and four gates.

Camps were entirely a practical matter. If a unit were attacked, the ditch and ramparts would give it time to form up on the intervallum and march out one of the camp's four gates. The Roman army was a mobile army, one that used a combination of unit cohesion and maneuverability to destroy its foes. A marching camp enhanced all of those qualities. It also allowed for a minimum number of sentries, which meant that most the unit could rest and sleep.

Gnaeus knew all this, elsewise he could never have become an officer, let alone the Primus Pilus. Therefore, there was no sense in arguing the logic of why the Roman Army always built marching camps. Gnaeus's decision not to do so was either the product of his own illness or just plain perversity. Since he wasn't a doctor, Marcus could do nothing about the first, and because he was second-in-command, there was little he could do about the second.

The real question was: would the Second Century build a marching camp of its own?

The answer was complex.

If the Second went along with Gnaeus, it would place both units in danger, even if there were little threat of attack until they moved north of Emerita Augusta.

If the Second resisted and built its own marching camp, it would divide the cohort, which in the case of an attack would be equally as dangerous. All of this raced through Marcus's mind in a few brief seconds. "Yes sir," he said to Gnaeus. At this point in the march, he decided, disunity was a greater danger than Lusitanians.

Marcus strode back to the Second, still in formation at the top of the small rise.

"Optio," he said to Flavius, "we will camp the men north of the road. We have been ordered not to construct a marching camp. I would like to see the tesserarius."

Flavius's face went through a series of emotions, probably, Marcus decided, not very different than the sequence of emotions he had gone through in the conversation with Gnaeus: shock, followed by thoughtful consideration, then resignation.

"Yes, sir," Flavius said simply, and turned to begin directing the men. If Demaratus was thinking something it was not obvious, although it rarely was. The Greek was one of the more controlled people Marcus had ever encountered.

The century marched off the hill, then broke up and began laying out spaces for tents. The mules moved up and, one by one, peeled off to be tethered next to the animal's contubernium. The doctor and his assistant set their tent, and the two began examining some of the men who had ridden the first day.

Sextus arrived, doing his best to not look puzzled at this break from routine. "Sir, you called for me?"

"Yes, Sextus. We have been ordered not to build a marching camp, which will make your job a little more complex. Without a ditch and ramparts you will have to double the guard, and you will need to deploy some skirmishers," said Marcus. "Be sure to change them all every two hours."

"Skirmishers, sir?" asked Sextus, then caught himself. "Oh, yes. Sorry. I will get right on it, sir." He saluted and started calling out names.

"Good man," thought Marcus. Sextus had initially been confused, but then saw the need to have a screen of men placed farther out than standard sentries as an early warning device, just as skirmishers many times are deployed in front of a unit to probe and discover an enemy's intentions. Of course, it would mean that twice as many men would lack for sleep. But with only two-hour shifts spread across the entire Century, the men would still get sufficient rest for the march tomorrow.

Marcus saw Manius talking to the doctor, who gathered up some supplies and followed him back toward the First Century's camp. "So that is why we caught the First," thought Marcus. "Gnaeus is ill."

Marcus felt naked without the defenses of a marching camp, but now was not the time to make an issue of it. The crisis would come once they left Emerita Augusta.

He saw Flavius and Demaratus unloading their mule and headed over to lend a hand.

Flavius walked to the edge of the camp. Most of the men had finished eating and were putting away their cooking gear and getting ready for some rounds of dice before turning in for the night. Sextus had set the watch, which saluted Flavius as he went by. A thin screen of men was set out 600 feet from camp, the skirmishers that would give warning in case of an attack.

The optio has served 15 years in the army, and in all that time he had never slept in the field without the reassurance of a ditch and ramparts. If cavalry attacked the centuries, he was not convinced the skirmishers would be of much help. By the time they raised an alarm, the horsemen would be on them. On the other hand, it would give the men a sense of security, false as it might be.

And yet Flavius agreed with Marcus's decision not to make an issue of the marching camp. At this point the unity of the cohort outweighed sensible defensive measures. The two had talked while they were setting up the tent and Marcus had briefly out-lined his thinking. There probably wasn't another centurion in the army who would have bothered to explain his actions to an optio, which is why the man—as quirky and difficult as he could be—was a pleasure to serve with.

Flavius was just completing his circuit of the camp when the doctor crossed the road on his way back from the First Century.

Flavius raised an eyebrow: "Trouble?" he asked.

Timotheus had never had a real conversation with the optio, although he knew that Demaratus thought well of him, and that the optio and Marcus were close. But the instinctive reluctance to discuss a patient with someone else, coupled with the doctor's general wariness about getting too involved in the clash between the commanders of the two centuries, made him careful.

"Nothing new, optio. Gnaeus is still recovering from his bout with fever," Timotheus answered.

Flavius wanted to ask more, like "Is the man mad?" but he was not sure of the doctor's loyalties, so he merely nodded. Like two ships, unsure of each other's intentions, they kept a prudent distance and passed each other by.

By now the sky had gone from opaque blue to a dove gray in the west, and the first stars were winking on to the east. Some men had already rolled themselves into their cloaks while others tossed dice around small campfires.

Flavius returned to the officer's tent to find Demaratus reading by the firelight, and Marcus writing something in a small scroll. Marcus looked up and said, "You might have a word with Sextus, Flavius. This is his first night as a tesserarius, and he may think he has to stay up all night to watch over his sentries. I seem to recall doing something like that myself."

"And did anyone ever come and tell us to go to sleep, sir?" answered Flavius with a grin, then waived off Marcus's reply. "I'll see to it sir."

He headed back toward the north part of camp, the last place he had seen the tesserarius. He found Sextus just returning from a round of inspection with the skirmishers. "You need to get some sleep, Sextus. Sleepy officers make mistakes."

"Yes sir, but the centurion wants to change the guard every

two hours and I have to make sure the men get into position," answered Sextus.

"Choose senior men." said Flavius, "Tell them where to go, and have one man from each sentry group wake the next watch. Tell the men that this is all temporary and that you'll relieve them from sentry duty for a week when we get to Legio."

Sextus turned this over for a moment and then saw the logic in it. "Right, sir," he said, and headed back out to the most distant pickets.

"Good lad," thought Flavius. "He catches on quick, but he still wants to think about it. Might make a decent officer someday." He yawned hugely, and headed back to the tent. "Can't stay up all night, can you Flavius?" he thought.

In the morning, both centuries formed up, the First leading with a mounted Gnaeus at the head.

Watching from a distance, Flavius shook his head with disgust. Demaratus commented mildly that he thought the Primus Pilus might be out of uniform. When Flavius gave him a puzzled look, the Greek added, "No red cape."

Flavius chuckled. "Aye, he does act like he thinks he is a general. Maybe we should send him a laurel wreath."

"I was thinking more along the lines of hemlock," said Demaratus.

Flavius laughed out loud, drawing a disapproving look from Marcus who was just coming back from a short conference with Gnaeus and Manius. "I'm not sure what was in that scroll you were reading last night, Demaratus, but it put some vinegar in your blood this morning."

"Poetry always does that," the Greek said enigmatically.

"Everyone formed up, optio?" Marcus asked.

"Yes sir, all present and accounted for and ready to march," Flavius answered.

By this time the First was already underway. The Second would wait until there was a 50-foot gap between the two units, and then get underway itself. Behind both centuries was the combined mule train, plus the convalescents on horseback and the doctor.

For two days the cohort marched northwest, climbing out of the rich Baetis Valley and up over a pass on the third day. By then, most of the sick and wounded had recovered enough to join their contuberniums

The valley of the Anas was almost as rich as the Baetis Valley and the cohort made good time marching past orchards losing their summer leaves, and fields of wheat stubble. As in Baetica, the villas were enormous, some of them looking more like palaces than homes. Slaves were preparing the ground for a winter wheat crop, and carts carrying grapes and olives trundled down the Via Plata headed for the presses.

Once into the Anas, Gnaeus quartered the cohort at villas. He not only demanded shelter in barns and outbuildings for the men, but also insisted on quartering the officers in the main villa. Plus, he stripped the villas' smokehouses of hams and preserved meats, which made him immensely popular in the ranks, and immensely unpopular among the civilian population.

After the second night of what Flavius had come to call "sacking," the optio grumbled to Marcus that if Gnaeus kept this up, the local farmers would soon be joining forces with the Lusitanian cavalry to make common cause against the Roman Army.

"We'll be across the Anas tomorrow," said Marcus. "There are apparently some established camps west of Metellium. We should be back on our own resources then."

Late in the afternoon on the sixth day out from Corduba, the cohort crossed the Anas on a bridge just east of Metellium. The city was a grim looking place, set on a steep slope below a vast and sterile citadel.

"Not a place you would like to muster out in," Flavius said to Marcus as the cohort rested in a fallow field just north of the road.

"No," Marcus agreed.

"Lusitanians, Carthaginians, and Roman have fought over this ground," said Demaratus, handing a bladder of acetum to Sextus. "Sometimes against one another, sometimes among themselves. Metellium was a rock in a long and deep river of war."

"Greeks ever here?" asked Flavius.

"Some. They traded up the river from Esuris, but never set down roots. This place and Emerita are Roman from the foundations up," he answered.

"Is Emerita Augusta as ugly as this place?" asked Flavius.

"No, it's a lovely city," chimed in Sextus. "I've never been to Rome, but some say the forum at Emertia is every bit as good, and the Temple of Diana is the finest looking building I ever laid eyes on. Makes the Augustine temple in Tarraco look like a roadside shrine."

"Now, you wouldn't be from Emerita, would you?" asked Flavius with a grin.

"One of my ancestors was a founder. He was with the X Gemina, and wounded in the war with Carthage. The city was established to reward the veterans of the X and the VII Victrix," answered Sextus, a trifle defensively.

"I have never seen it," said Demaratus, "But I had a shipmate who said it was a fine city, though a trifle overbuilt."

"Unlike Athens?" put in Flavius.

"You have been to Athens?" asked Demaratus. "Why haven't you ever said anything about that?"

"Before I was assigned to Britannia, I was with the XIV Gemina Martia in Thrace. I saw it then. And I never said anything because it seemed a pretty small and provincial place to me," said Flavius with a grin.

"Athens was a great city when the Romans were gathering acorns, digging up roots, and living in mud huts," Demaratus bristled.

The three Romans laughed. "You're hard to get a rise out of, signifer," said Flavius, "but we know where the chink in your armor is now.'

Demaratus shook his head ruefully. "Who knew I would spend my days surrounded by barbarians."

The cohort pulled into a camp just a day's march out of Emerita Augusta. The camp was manned by a single contubernium of auxiliaries who kept it reasonably ready to host up to a full cohort. The reduced First had its choice of barracks, which were musty, but clean. The baths were primitive, but better than anything the cohort had seen in the last week.

By now all of the convalescents were back on their feet and marching in full gear. Marcus noted with pleasure that the Second Century was now larger than the first, but he doubted that Gnaeus would reclaim any of the First's soldiers because it would be an admittance that Marcus had been right to put them on mules for the first part of the trip.

Marcus's central worry now was what happened when the cohort left Emerita Augusta. He was not willing to move toward Norba without settling the issue of marching camps. He would rather avoid a direct confrontation with Gnaeus, but he wasn't willing to die in order to avoid an argument. He was reasonably certain that the legate would back him, because not building a proper camp each night was a scandal, but in the meantime he couldn't force Gnaeus to do something he didn't want to do. The man was a trial.

However, there was no sense wasting time worrying about it now. Some development in Emerita Augusta might alter things. He deposited his gear in the officer's barracks and headed for the baths.

XXI

Emerita Augusta was everything Sextus said it was, although the tesserarius pointed out that the proper way to enter the town was from the south, across the bridge that spanned the Anas. "If you enter the city from the south, you see it the way it was meant to be seen," Sextus said. "The forum and the Temple of Diana then lie to your right, and the great arch of Trajan to your left."

The two centuries had halted just east of the city to rest and make sure both units looked their best. Gear that had been carried by each soldier was loaded on the mules and the now riderless horses, so the men would march in unencumbered.

Sextus continued to talk about Emerita, and he was particularly proud about the bridge over the Anas. In the face of raised eyebrows and generally skeptical looks from the other officers, he stoutly maintained the southern span was more than a third of a mile long. "There isn't a more impressive city in the empire," he said, defensively.

"Well, given you've never been anywhere but Hispania and

Mauritania, Sextus, that is a pretty bold statement," said Flavius. "I think you should take a trip to Rome before you call a provincial capital the most impressive city in the empire," adding, "Looks a bit like Athens without the hill."

Demaratus smiled. "Ignore Latins, Sextus. They are easily threatened. It is a fine-looking city."

"Gentlemen," interjected Marcus, "While I do not wish to cut short your discussion of architecture and its relationship to power and beauty, might you help get us on the road again so that we actually experience this city?"

The three arose from the meadow where they were sitting and got the men into position. Sextus and Flavius walked slowly down the ranks in a quick inspection, tugging some of the men's equipment into place and generally seeing that the Century would present a respectable appearance when it marched through the town. The barracks were on the northwest side of Emerita Augusta, so the cohort would have to traverse the center of the city. It occurred to Marcus that that was exactly what Gnaeus had in mind when he chose the eastern approach to the city. Given the uncertainty about the situation north of the city, it was a smart idea. The cohort would have a calming effect on Emerita Augusta. Gnaeus was not stupid, just perverse.

The cohort marched past an enormous theater—Sextus bragged that it sat 6,000, drawing another round of kidding. The city was indeed lovely. Built on a broad, flat alluvial plain where two rivers converged, it was laid out in a precise grid, with wide streets and substantial houses. Two aqueducts swept in from the north. The city had the look of wealth.

The road into Emerita Augusta took the cohort past the

temple of Diana and the forum, and even Flavius admitted it was impressive. The cohort halted briefly to let cart traffic clear and the officers gathered at the front to look at the city around them.

Despite Flavius' teasing, Sextus soldiered on as their tour guide, pointing out that the forum's marble was imported, some of it from Italia. The man's obvious pride in his hometown eventually even silenced the optio, who admitted, "It would be a nice town to muster out in."

"That's what the men who built it thought also," said Sextus. "As you can see, it's laid out like a proper Army camp, sir. And when they built it, it was frontier out here."

"No walls," remarked Marcus.

"No, sir. They did that on purpose," said Sextus. "This was the westernmost city in Hispania, and the local tribes were still unconquered. But since the population was former soldiers, they figured they could defend their own. No walls made a point."

"They might need them in the future," Marcus said quietly.

The cohort was well received, with a large number of people coming out of shops or abandoning their wares to cheer the unit as it marched toward the barracks. Marcus noted the populace was well dressed, and the city had a scrubbed look to it. "Much like an Army camp," he thought.

A week on the road had tired the cohort, and it was a relief to get into proper barracks with proper baths. The men, the half stipendia burning a hole in their pouches, were impatient to drink some decent wine, sample the local population of prostitutes, and buy some extra food for the long march north.

Sextus was eager to show his fellow officers the city, and in the face of his earnest enthusiasm, Marcus, Flavius, and

Demaratus found themselves being dragged about the city to admire the forum, Trajan's arch, and to pace off the length of the bridge. It was indeed as long as Sextus claimed, although Flavius pointed out that it crossed an island in the middle of the Anas, so technically it was two bridges.

This set off a row, with Sextus leaning over the bridge and pointing out that it was all one structure, and Flavius claiming that the only thing that held the bridge up was the island, so the bridge really wasn't a big deal. Marcus and Demaratus smiled at one another. Sextus would have to learn that Flavius was as fierce about his hometown as the new tesserarius was about his, though the optio would never admit that it was simple provincialism that made him defend Rome.

After a long and exhausting day of playing tourist, Demaratus commented that instead of wasting time on the training fields getting the men in shape, they might just consider turning the Century over to Sextus for tours of the city. It drew a laugh, even from Sextus, as protective as he was about his beloved Emerita Augusta.

The baths soaked away all disputes.

The men had been given two days off to rest and carouse, so a restless Flavius found himself with nothing to do. Sextus was visiting family, and Demaratus had vanished into the city's market. Marcus was wrestling with headquarters over supplies for the coming march to Norba. So, Flavius wandered off, automatically finding himself headed toward the Field of Mars. There was a local Century of auxiliaries training, and some archers.

Flavius watched the auxiliaries for a while and then drifted over to the archers.

Flavius was not an admirer of archers, or rather, bows and arrows. The proper way to wage war, in his opinion, was to fight it out, man to man, with spears and swords. He found the idea of killing a man with an arrow distasteful, although it wasn't much different than killing a man with a spear. The bow had greater range, of course.

There were questions Flavius ignored, but never military ones. Why was he so disapproving of archers? He turned the thought over in his head. Well, one reason was obvious: they were auxiliaries. All slingers, archers, and, increasingly, cavalry, were auxiliaries. The Roman Army could not afford to assign valuable soldiers to anything but the infantry, the core of the empire's military forces.

He decided that the reason he didn't like archers is that they had it easy. They didn't have to carry a lot of armor, or shields and spears. Flavius was suspicious of doing things the easy way.

Because he disapproved of them, he had never paid a lot of attention to what archers did, so it was interesting to watch them.

There were twenty of them, which Flavius supposed was the basic unit for archers. They had set out large straw targets at various ranges that Flavius judged were about 100 and 200 feet apart, and were busy filling them with arrow shafts. The targets had a sheet of papyrus at their center, not much larger than a dinner plate. The targets were filled with shafts, and those that missed were almost all on the very edge of the targets. These archers were very good.

Flavius turned his attention to the archers themselves. They were not very big men, most of them slight. They looked vaguely like Greeks, but darker. He strolled over to someone who was obviously an officer, but who was also using a bow.

The man took in Flavius's uniform, put down his bow, and saluted.

Flavius returned the salute and introduced himself.

"Cleomenes, tesserarius of the Third Century of Cretan archers," the man said in response.

"Bit small for a Century, aren't you?" asked Flavius.

"Yes, sir. We would normally be sixty, but when we arrived at Carthago Nova after service in Numidia they broke us into three units. One was sent to Tarraco, and we were sent to Corduba. Last month we received orders to come to Emerita Augusta, but when we arrived, no one knew what to do with us," he answered. The man did not look overly happy about the situation.

"And you, sir? I don't recall seeing you here before today," Cleomenes said.

"Two centuries of the First Cohort are just passing through on our way to Legio," Flavius answered, and then had an idea. "Cleomenes, if you and your men have nothing to do, why not come north with us?"

The man looked doubtful. "What we would really like is to link up with the rest of our unit and go home to Crete," he said.

"Well, Legio is closer to Tarraco than Emerita, and you could at least get together with that lot," Flavius pointed out. "Even if you don't end up in Tarraco, you might get shipped out from a port like Brigantium."

"On the Oceanas Atlanticus in the late fall?" replied

Cleomenes, looking even more doubtful, "We could end up stuck in Legio."

Flavius shrugged. "It's the Army, tesserarius. We go where they tell us. But if you come to Legio at least you will be where someone has the authority to make a decision."

Cleomenes considered Flavius's comment. "That's a good point. We feel like a bunch of manes sitting around here. It's a pleasant city, but the men are a little bored. What do you suggest?"

It was Flavius's turn to consider the matter. He had been thinking through the coming week and the march to Norba, and he was convinced that Gnaeus was going to find some way to divide the two centuries. He had raised the possibility with Marcus who dismissed it with "The man is mad, but he is not crazy."

But Flavius concluded that the Primus Pilus needed to get to Legio first so he could poison the well before the Second Century arrived. Flavius was convinced that Gnaeus would manufacture some excuse, like he did in Corduba, to delay the Second Century. Flavius fervently hoped this was so because he knew that Marcus would disobey orders on the matter of marching camps and the cohort would then split wide open. Gnaeus might even try to arrest Marcus, which Marcus, Flavius, and Demaratus would resist.

But would the Second Century back them? Could it come to an actual fight between the two centuries? That would be a disaster of such proportions that Flavius immediately put the thought out of his mind.

Flavius was convinced that Gnaeus would lose in the end. He had watched Marcus writing things down on a scroll, and he was certain the Centurion was recording the mania of the Primus Pilus. It could all go wrong, of course, but Flavius felt the odds were on Marcus's side.

"Let me talk to my centurion, Cleomenes. And don't mention my proposal to anyone until you hear from me," said Flavius.

"Yes, sir. Not a word. I'll keep it between the two of us until we can talk again," answered Cleomenes.

Flavius headed back toward the barracks, turning over in his mind how he would raise the issue with Marcus. On these questions, Marcus had to be handled. Flavius was good at handling superior officers, although Marcus was smarter than most, so this would take some delicacy. An optio out recruiting auxiliaries on his own was not the way the chain of command normally worked in the Roman Army.

In the end, any schemes that Flavius might have needed were unnecessary. He arrived back at the barracks to find Marcus fuming over Gnaeus's latest maneuver, one that Flavius had accurately predicted, though not even he could have dreamed up what the Primus Pilus would do this time.

"We are to escort a party of merchants to Norba, Flavius," Marcus told him as he came though the barracks door. "That bastard has outdone himself. Not only will we be delayed, if we get into a fight, we will have to defend them as well as ourselves."

Demaratus and Sextus had still not returned, so Marcus felt a little freer to openly curse the Primus Pilus.

"It may not be such bad a thing, sir," mused Flavius. The optio thought it was an interesting reversal of the two men's response to Gnaeus's scheme to stick them with the wounded. Then it had been Flavius who had lost his temper and predicted disaster, and Marcus who saw it as an opportunity.

"Yes?" said Marcus with a trace of impatience.

"I think that Gnaeus is doing this so he can get to Legio before us, sir. He will try to make us look bad to the legate, but I don't think it will work. Once the commanders find out that the man didn't build marching camps, I think they will be careful about everything he says. Plus, it will avoid any possible conflict while we are in the field," Flavius explained.

Marcus nodded.

"I am also thinking that being nice to a bunch of merchants will put them in our debt, and merchants seem to have as much power in Hispania as the Army," Flavius continued.

Marcus was silent, listening.

"Given what you said that day the men got their stipendia, that merchant in Corduba"—Marcus supplied his name, "Clodius Petreius"— "is no friend of Gnaeus," Flavius said, then added what he thought would be the clincher: "And if we do get into trouble, we'll get a chance to try out those javelins."

Marcus gave him a long look. "You're getting better at handling superior officers, Flavius."

Flavius gave him a look of wounded innocence. "I'm just trying to be helpful, sir."

Marcus smiled. "If you get much better at this, you'll end up a legate one day."

"Tribune will do fine for me, sir. Just like retiring, only you get paid," Flavius answered.

Both men laughed, and were still laughing when Sextus walked in.

As Marcus filled him in (minus the observation on Gnaeus's paternal lineage and the comments concerning how to handle superior officers), the tesserarius's face grew long.

"Sir," said Sextus when Marcus had finished, "this could create real problems for us."

"Explain," said Flavius.

"The Lusitanian cavalry likes to charge head on, but if that doesn't work, they try to encircle you, sir," said Sextus. "A Century might handle that okay, but if we have to protect a convoy of merchants, it could stretch us pretty thin. If we had some cavalry, it would make a difference."

"The Ala II Flavia Hispanorum Romanorum has a quingeniary in Emerita," said Marcus, "but they can only release a turmae. The Primus Pilus has announced that the turmae will accompany the First Century," said Marcus.

"That doesn't make sense, sir," said Sextus. "If we are assigned to protect merchants, we should get the cavalry, not the First Century."

'The Ala II turmae will march with the First, day after tomorrow," said Marcus, his voice flat. "The matter is settled."

"Yes, sir," replied Sextus, looking unhappy.

"I have a thought, sir," said Flavius, seizing the opportunity.

"What would that be, optio?" asked Marcus.

"What about taking some archers along?" answered Flavius.

There was a moment of dead silence.

"Archers? Flavius Priscus, optio of the Second Century of the VII Gemina Hispania Pia is considering using archers?" said Marcus, his eyebrows rising almost to his hairline.

Flavius shrugged. "Well, we could use them to cover our

flanks, and their bows have more range than our javelins," he said, adding, "I met some today."

"The plot line thickens," remarked Marcus, just as Demaratus came in the door.

"I like plots," said the Greek. "What is this one about?"

"It would appear that our optio is enamored with archers," answered Marcus.

"Our optio should try women," said Demaratus, "Much more fun, although they can be expensive."

"And why is it that Greeks know everything, my dear signifer?" asked Flavius sarcastically.

"It is not a matter of the Greeks knowing everything," Demaratus said, leaving the line unfinished.

"Gentlemen, may we return to the matter at hand?" said Marcus. "Who are these archers, Flavius?"

"A piece of a Cretan Century that seems to have gotten itself stuck in Emerita Augusta," replied Flavius. "They are trying to link up with another unit of the Century that got sent to Tarraco."

"Cretans?" asked Demaratus. "When it comes to the bow, not even the Parthians can match them."

"The commander is a tesserarius named Cleomenes," said Flavius. "Sounds Greek, but he doesn't look like one."

"No, Cretans are not Greek," said Demaratus, "but he would have a Greek name." Then he smiled, adding, "although it is an odd choice."

"Why?" asked Sextus.

"Oh, by the Gods, here comes a lesson on the history of the Greeks," muttered Flavius.

Demaratus ignored him. "Cleomenes was a king of Sparta before the war with Persia. Not many people name their children after Spartans. They are not the most popular of the Greeks."

"There are Greeks that are popular?" asked Flavius.

"Enough," said Marcus, putting an edge in his tone to end the back and forth between his two senior officers. "How many men are we talking about, Flavius?"

"Twenty, sir," answered the optio.

Marcus thought for a moment. "They might be useful, indeed," he said. "I take it you had a discussion with this Cleomenes?" he said to Flavius.

"Yes, sir. Naturally I didn't promise anything," he said, adding, "They were awful good with those bows, sir."

"All, right, arrange a meeting with this Cleomenes for this evening. I want to have this settled before we all meet with the merchants tomorrow morning," said Marcus. "Sextus, be sure we have enough mules for the trip to Norba. Tell the stables to have the mules ready by day after tomorrow, although we may not leave until the day after that. Demaratus, find out how we put these archers on the rolls without notifying Gnaeus. Flavius, I want a reliable contubernium that we may have to keep in reserve to protect the merchants in case of trouble," said Marcus, "Let's get to work."

The group scattered.

Sextus left the ad hoc meeting feeling vaguely resentful. It wasn't that he was unhappy being an officer, although it was more work than he thought, or even being the junior. It was that he felt walled out. Granted, he was a newcomer and the three senior officers had served together, but it was more than that. On two occasions he had come into their barracks and seen the three go silent, then obviously change the subject. It was as if the three shared some secret.

They treated him well. Indeed, there were none of the rigid barriers that normally typified the relations among officers, like those of the First Century. They asked his opinion and listened to it. They assumed his competence, and yet were ready to be helpful, as Flavius was on the first night that he had been in charge of setting out sentries.

As he walked toward the stables, he turned the matter over in his mind. It was never clear to Sextus how the three officers had come to Corduba. The story was that Rome had sent them to replace the officers under arrest or scattered to other assignments outside of Hispania.

They were competent officers, certainly as competent as the ones they replaced. What didn't fit was that none of them had said a single word about the upheaval in the cohort that had brought them to Corduba in the first place. Sextus expected that all of the men would be forced to swear a sacramentum oath to obey the emperor and declare their allegiance to the state religion. But nothing like that had happened. If you came all the way from Rome to straighten out the mess in the First Cohort, wouldn't you at least lecture the men on the need for loyalty and the insidious nature of Christianity?

Unless, of course, that is not why they came. But if it wasn't for that, what was it for?

Sextus smiled to himself. He was still thinking like a soldier in the ranks, looking for hidden meaning in the actions of the

officers, relying on rumor and gossip. Given the general ignorance in which the ranks were kept, it was hardly surprising
that the men should have such an addiction: anticipating what
their officers were thinking was of paramount importance in
their lives.

He sighed and thought about his superiors. He generally
approved of them.

Marcus seemed reserved, as any good centurion should be,
but he could also be charming and friendly, and he had an odd
sense of humor that sometimes went over Sextus's head. The best
thing about the centurion was that he seemed to be unintimi-
dated by the Primus Pilus.

Flavius was an efficient optio, and he had the man to thank
for his job. But Flavius was unpredictable. Sextus had heard the
story about the vigiles and the execution, and it was hard to
fit what the optio did with the actions of a dutiful second-in-
command. Had Flavius deliberately provoked a confrontation
with the vigiles over a slave? Or was the optio just expressing his
frustration at the situation and punishing the arrogance of the
vigile optio? In any case, Sextus had never heard of anything like
what Flavius did that day.

Demaratus was not an easy one to figure either, though few
Greeks were. The signifer was quiet, but hardly timid. Sextus
had watched him skirt the very edge of insubordination with
the Primus Pilus the day they all got their stipendia. Demaratus
and Flavius seemed to have a long-running competition, which
was puzzling in and of itself. Seconds-in-command and signifers
normally did not banter with one another, but the two of them
were constantly poking at each other. Again, it was as if all three

were, on some level, equals, a concept that Sextus found difficult to grasp.

The new tesserarius arranged for the mules, being careful to request a half dozen more to carry the extra javelins and pila, and three extras for the archers.

"When are you leaving, sir?" asked the head groom.

"Have them ready the day after tomorrow, but we might not leave until the day after that," Sextus replied.

"Yes, sir. Hurry up and wait. That's the Army for you," said the groom.

Sextus headed for the baths. He didn't want to miss the meeting with the archer tesserarius.

Marcus looked out over the merchants gathered in the principia. There were about two dozen, wearing clothes that ranged from expensive to work-a-day. The camp tesserarius had put out wine and sweet cakes and the merchants were making short work of the refreshments. Marcus decided to give them a few more minutes, not only to eat, but also to let any latecomers straggle in. Civilians worked on their own timetables, and it wasn't the Army's.

The meeting had gone well with the officer of the Cretan archers. When Marcus laid out the problem of fighting cavalry, the tesserarius, Cleomenes, merely nodded. "Horses and riders are vulnerable, particularly if they aren't armored," the man noted. "Stick an arrow into a horse, and the animal and his rider are pretty much done for the day."

Marcus asked Sextus to talk a little about Lusitanian tactics, and the danger they posed to the merchants in the Century's rear. Again, the Cretan nodded. "We can keep the cavalry out of your rear," but added, "so long as we're talking about 30 or 40 horses. Much beyond that...." He shrugged and trailed off.

Marcus told him that the Century would release a contubernium to protect the merchants, which Cleomenes agreed would be a good idea. "Our vulnerability is that we don't wear armor, sir," the tesserarius said. "If the horsemen get in among us, we don't have much in the way of protection. Plus, a screen of infantry will slow the cavalry down and give us better shots."

Sextus played an important role in the meeting. The man knew Lusitanian tactics and had a number of suggestions about how the archers could harass the horsemen. "The Lusitanians don't have a formal military structure," he told Cleomenes, "but they do have battlefield leaders. Anyone with a torque is likely to be a commander of some sort."

Cleomenes nodded again. "We will target them," he said. "But it is my experience with cavalry that once a charge begins, commanders don't count for much. It is pretty much each horseman for himself."

"I agree," said Sextus, "but if a charge is broken, it's the commanders who can rally them."

"As I said, we will target them, but once the horses get within fifty yards, we have to concentrate on stopping those in the front ranks, not choosing targets among the officers," Cleomenes replied.

Marcus was satisfied with the back and forth. Cleomenes had come off as a solid, experienced and competent commander, and not for the first time Marcus had been impressed with his new tesserarius.

Someone dropping a cup brought him back to the present. A few more merchants had drifted in, and Marcus finally called the gathering to order.

"Good morning, gentlemen, I am Marcus Favonius, centurion of the Second Century of the First Cohort. We will be leaving Emerita Augusta tomorrow morning, and I would like you to be ready to leave shortly after dawn," he announced. "Questions?"

A torrent of sound assailed him, making it impossible to separate out individual inquiries. "Gentlemen, can we talk one at a time, and do you have a spokesman?" Marcus asked.

A short, stocky man stepped forward. "I am Tiberius Granius, a gold merchant. We have a number of questions," he said. "First, how many carts will we be allowed?"

Marcus shook his head: "None, mules and horses only." His response elicited a storm of protests.

"I am a linen merchant,"one man said, "I can't carry enough on horseback to make it worth my time." Others said they were pottery merchants and could not move their wares except on carts.

Marcus waved them to silence. "Gentlemen, we have a single Century and no cavalry. If we are attacked, we will have our hands full protecting you. Carts would make that impossible," adding, "They would also slow us down."

"Why are we not using cavalry?" asked Tiberius. "We have the Ala II right here in Emerita. Surely, they could spare us a turmae?"

"The Ala II has been ordered to remain in Emerita for the time being," answered Marcus. "The turmae it can spare left this morning with the First Century."

This news produced another storm of protests, which Marcus waited out. "I am sorry, but those are my orders," he explained, adding that the Second Century had managed to recruit some Cretan archers who would give the Century both firepower and tactical flexibility.

The merchants seemed unimpressed. "What are a bunch of archers going to do to stop a Lusitanian charge?" a tall, thin merchant asked.

"The Second Century will stop the charge," answered Marcus, and explained that the unit had been working on ways to deal with exactly what the merchant was worried about. "But Lusitanian cavalry is not armored, and archers are very effective against unprotected horsemen," Marcus added.

The mood of the merchants did not improve. "The authorities will hear about this," the linen merchant complained. Marcus was not sure if the man was talking about local authorities, who, in any case, would have no power in this matter, or VII's commander in Legio. He ignored the comment.

"Gentlemen, you are not required to hazard this trip with us," Marcus told the group. "But if you accompany us, you will have to accept the conditions I am setting, which includes a strong suggestion that you arm yourselves."

This comment unleashed another verbal storm from the merchants: "We aren't soldiers, we're traders"; "Why do we pay taxes if the Army can't protect us?" plus a variety of other complaints.

Marcus spread his hands. "I am sorry, but you must know that there is a certain amount of danger involved in this trip. It is only prudent that you come prepared."

The next point of contention was the number of mules.

"You can take three mules, maximum," said Marcus, eliciting a reaction that made the cart ban discussion seem civil.

It took almost two hours for Marcus to finally get agreement from them. He compromised on the number of mules—allowing four, not three—and agreed to start two hours after dawn. The merchants finally withdrew, still unhappy but feeling better after winning the point on the hour of departure and the mules. In fact, Marcus has always intended to allow four mules per merchant, but letting them win a point made it easier for them to accept his other conditions.

With the meeting over, the hard work preparing for tomorrow began, including arranging for a sacrifice. Marcus would have been happy to drop the whole thing, but Flavius asked about the details, and seemed distressed that Marcus had not made any arrangements.

"I heard an owl last night, sir, and I think we need to see what lies ahead for us," said Flavius. Marcus kept forgetting that while Flavius was logical and rational on almost everything, he had a streak of superstition in him.

The sacrifice was just one more thing to arrange on a long and exhausting list.

XXII

It was "the day of the owl," as Flavius would later say.

A thin drizzle started up early in the morning, so that by the time the century formed up, with its attendant train of mules and twenty merchants—some had had second thoughts about the trip and stayed in bed—everyone was damp. Flavius had placed the archers behind the century and in front of the doctor, his staff, and the merchants. The latter showed up late even with the departure extension that Marcus had granted them the previous day.

The merchants' spokesman, Tiberius Granius, sought out Marcus, who was dealing with a variety of last-minute glitches, to complain about the placement of the archers. "We need them to bring up the rear in case we are attacked," he said. "We have no protection."

Marcus patiently explained that in the advent of an attack, a contubernium of infantry would immediately fall back to cover the merchants, but that the archers were needed forward in order to harass any cavalry that might appear.

"But you said the archers would protect us," said Tiberius.

"And they will, but they will first help us break up any cavalry charge we might encounter," answered Marcus. "If we don't break the Lusitanian charge, protecting our rear will be irrelevant."

"That is not how it was presented yesterday," protested Tiberius.

"I said that this could be a dangerous trip," replied Marcus, putting an edge in his voice. "No one has to come with us. We will provide what protection we can. I am sorry, but a single century, even one our size, can only protect so much ground."

Tiberius went off grumbling, but Marcus noted that none of the merchants left for home. Profit was a powerful motivator, he thought.

By the time the whole party got underway, the drizzle had turned into a solid rain, and any part of the men or their equipment that wasn't wet before was soaked now. But the drains on the Via Plata were well built, so the road was clear of major puddles. In spite of the fact, they were headed toward home, there was no gossip or laughing in the ranks. The men had tucked themselves under their paenula cloaks and hoods, giving the century a faintly motley appearance.

For an hour the century and its retinue slogged through the heavy rain, but by mid-morning the rain had turned back to a drizzle and finally stopped altogether. Well before noon, the sun broke through and the clouds began breaking up. For another hour the column gently steamed as it marched along, until the warmth finally dried out most of the men.

No sooner had things begun looking up than Tiberius trotted up on a mule and asked when they were going to stop for lunch.

"We will rest in another hour, Tiberius," Marcus said, "but we do not eat until we camp for the night."

This produced another protest, which Marcus ended by telling Tiberius that if the merchants wanted an extended rest, they could do so anytime they wished and catch up with the century later.

The merchant left grumbling and fuming, and Demaratus smiled. "Nothing like the prospect of profit to get you going, and fear to keep you on your feet," he commented.

Marcus nodded agreement, but said nothing. He was too busy dreaming up curses to bring down on Gnaeus and mistrusted what he would say aloud.

The countryside around them was wilder and more deserted than anything they had gone through since the upper reaches of the Baetis River on their way from Saguntum to Corduba. It was a land of rolling hills interspersed with broad, flat meadows. The crowns of the hills tended to be heavily wooded, and there were times when the forests reached down to the road itself.

The century was making good time, and a little past noon Marcus signaled Demaratus to turn into a meadow at the foot of a long slope. The century swung off the road, followed by the archers and a somewhat bedraggled band of merchants. Flavius came forward, and Marcus told him that the century would rest for a half-hour in order to give the merchants a chance to eat something.

"But tell Tiberius no fires, optio, we haven't the time," he admonished Flavius.

"Right. This lot would settle in for the night if we let them," said Flavius and went off to tell Sextus the plan.

Marcus could see Tiberius arguing with Flavius, and saw him start forward toward the front of the column. He sighed. Next to merchants, mules were a pleasure. He was just steeling himself to deal with the man, when Demaratus said quietly, "Sir, there's a horseman coming."

Marcus turned to see what the signifer was talking about, and saw the lone horseman pounding down the hill directly in front of the century. The rider's body was flat to the horse's back, and even Marcus could see that there was something wrong with the animal. The rider was still a good three hundred yards from where the century was resting.

Demaratus squinted. "Is that a Lusitanian?" he asked.

Marcus took a long look, then turned back to the century. "Comrades! Form up! Three lines!"

There was a slight hesitation. The men were sprawled on the meadow, their weapons and shields mixed in with ration boxes and various personal bundles. Flavius and Sextus were making their way toward the front line.

"Optio," said Marcus, his voice controlled. This was not a time to exhibit excitement, which might be interpreted as panic. "We will shortly be under attack. Please align the century and arrange for the javelins to be sent forward. Bunch the merchants to our rear and put the contubernium in place to defend them. Send Cleomanes to me."

Flavius immediately turned, calling out orders and grabbing Sextus by the arm, pointing him in the direction of the century's mule train and the merchants. Marcus had time to note that Tiberius was nowhere to be seen. A small blessing.

The horseman was rapidly closing on the century. Marcus

noticed a long, red streak on the animal's left flank. The rider looked up and turned the horse toward the unit's signum. Marcus waited, noting out of the corner of his eye the century getting into position and Cleomanes pushing himself through the front line. He motioned the Cretan toward him, but lifted a hand to silence him, concentrating on the horseman.

The mounted man pushed himself erect. Marcus could now see that he was wounded, his left arm dangling loose from his shoulder. He was young, really no more than a boy, and his face was etched with a combination of exhaustion, pain and fear. But he pulled the stumbling horse, streaked with blood and sweat, to a halt a few yards from Marcus, even remembering to salute.

"Sir," the young man gasped, "Lusitanian cavalry behind me. Hundreds. They attacked us this morning. My Ala commander sent me to warn you."

Marcus waited a moment, then asked, "What is your name, soldier?"

The man looked confused for a moment then pulled himself together. "Cassius Cornelius, sir. Third Turmae, Ala II Flavia Hispanorum Romanorum," he answered.

Marcus suppressed a smile. Anyone who could remember a name as pompous and complex as that in the midst of a battle was made of good stuff.

"How far behind you, son?" asked Marcus.

The question was superfluous. Even as he asked it, Marcus saw horsemen crest the hill.

"They caught us by surprise," Cassius said.

Marcus kept his eye on the hilltop, which was rapidly filling with cavalry. "Well done, Cassius. Go to the rear. Have our doctor look at that arm."

"Sir, I would like to stay here in front," answered the horseman, sliding off his exhausted mount.

"Go to the rear, Cassius, and lend a hand guarding our flanks. We have a party of merchants with us, and we could use your help," said Marcus, adding quietly, "you have earned honor this day, comrade."

The man hesitated a moment, as if he was going to argue, but then took his horse and led it through the front line. A legionnaire patted him on the shoulder and said something that Marcus could not hear.

Cleomanes was waiting patiently.

"Tesserarius," Marcus said, "deploy your men behind the third line. When I lift my phylum straight up, open fire. Once the charge starts, concentrate on the front ranks. I want to bring some of those horses down."

The archer nodded and headed back to his men. He was a taciturn fellow, a characteristic that Demaratus said was a trait of Cretans in general.

The century was forming up into three lines. The men had cast their extra equipment to the rear, and spread themselves out three feet from one another. Marcus could see the javelins being distributed to the second and third lines. The men in the front line had sunk their extra pila next to them and the wall of shields—more than 150 feet long—looked solid, if a bit frazzled. In their rush to get into position some of the men had not removed their leather shield covers.

Many of the men were looking up the slope, their faces tense and anxious. The latter emotion surprised Marcus. Most of the men in the front line were veterans. Cavalry was intimidating, and battle was always a terrifying undertaking, but men rarely showed their emotions at this point in a fight.

"Sir," said Demaratus quietly, "Their shields...."

Marcus had deliberately avoided looking at the horsemen, because he wanted to show his men that the cavalry did not overly concern him. Now he looked back up the long slope and saw what had put fear in the men's faces. The first line of horsemen carried scutums from the First Century, and in the center of the wheeling mass of horses and men was the First Century's signum. The man bearing it rode a huge mottled gray, and the helmet of a legionnaire.

Marcus turned back to the century. "Comrades," he said, his voice raised but not overly so. He wanted the men to have to strain a little to listen. "Those horsemen up there think to terrify us by showing us our fallen comrades' shields. But those shields are too big to carry on a horse. They will blind themselves or their horses if they try to use them. Instead, they will come at us without shields and you will smite them. Our comrades from the First Century strike at our enemies from the very Elysian Fields themselves."

Once the shock of seeing the shields and everything it implied began to wear off, the men could see that a huge infantry scutum was a clumsy and awkward thing to wield from horseback. The tension remained, but some of the fear seemed to dissipate.

"Comrades," Marcus continued, "the man with the signum. He is mine. Anyone who puts a spear into him does double guard duty for the next month." It was a lame joke, but when tension is high, even bad humor works. A ripple of laughter spread through the Century.

But now it was time for the business at hand.

Marcus looked back up the hill where the horsemen were beginning to edge down the slope. He judged them to be about three hundred yards away. Searching the ground in front of the century, he located a small bush about seventy-five yards up the hill. When the horsemen reached that point, he would signal the archers to open fire.

He turned to pass the word for Flavius but found the man already at his side.

"I am going to have the archers open fire when the Lusitanians reach that bush," he said to the optio. "You should wait a single count and then have the second line throw their javelins. I will give the order to the front line to throw their pila."

Flavius nodded, then put his hand on Marcus's shoulder. "Be careful, sir," turned and vanished back through the front line.

Marcus turned back to the first line. "Comrades. Mark when I throw my pilum. Remember that your comrades behind you will throw their javelins first. Ignore them! Watch me. When I lift my arm to throw, pick out a target and bring him down. Hold onto your second pilum. We may need it to keep the horsemen at bay."

He waited a long moment, then added: "And comrades! The signifer and I would appreciate you stopping that charge before it gets to us. We would hate to take all the glory ourselves." This raised a genuine laugh, although Demaratus gave him a strained look.

He had gone over the drill dozens of times, but doing

something on the Field of Mars and on the field of battle were two very different things. Marcus worried that as soon as the front line saw the javelins, they would throw their pila, and most of the heavy spears would fall short.

At the last moment he had a stab of panic: would the century be overrun simply because what he was asking the men to do was too new and too complex? He repressed the feeling with a combination of discipline and fatalism: What happens will happen. There was nothing he could do about it at this point.

He turned back to face the hill. The horsemen had edged closer. They were now no more than two hundred yards away, although they were still milling around. Marcus suspected that the sight of the deployed century was giving some of them pause. The men on those horses were not trained and disciplined soldiers, but everyday Lusitanians. The man holding the First century's signum had his back to Marcus, and was shouting something to the men. Marcus suspected he was exhorting them in preparation for the charge.

Next to him, Demaratus had planted the signum into the ground and slipped his gladis out of its scabbard.

"So, did the Persians have good cavalry, Demaratus?" Marcus asked him as both stared up the long slope.

"Yes, sir, very good cavalry. We defeated them by avoiding it," he answered. "Greeks like to fight in narrow places, centurion, where horses cannot go."

"Well then, this is your opportunity to show us Romans that Greeks can fight anywhere," said Marcus with a grin.

Demaratus gave him a sideways glance. "It is a pedagogy I am willing to forego, centurion." Then added softly, "Good luck, sir."

"And to you, my friend," answered Marcus.

Marcus sensed the charge before he saw it. He could feel the ground begin vibrating from the mass of milling horses. Then the slope began to tremble as the horsemen began trotting toward the century, the gray stallion in the center, slightly ahead of the rest. The trot became a lope that almost instantly changed into a full gallop.

Marcus focused on the front line of horses. He judged there were maybe two hundred horsemen in the charge, with a similar size group still milling around at the hill's crest. He turned his eyes back to center of the charge, which was now rapidly approaching the small bush. He noticed with satisfaction that the Lusitanians had either abandoned the First Century's shields or were holding them by their sides.

When the charge was about ten feet from the bush, Marcus raised his pilum straight up, but saw no reaction by the horsemen. He wondered for a moment if the Cretans had missed his signal. Then a Lusitanian to the left of the leader reared back in his saddle and tumbled backwards over the horse, vanishing under the flood of horsemen that followed him. Several others followed him, and one horse went down, kicking and thrashing, tumbling two others behind it.

Marcus heard the javelins before he saw them, a soft whisper which quickly turned into a cloud of spears. Some struck the first row of horsemen—one drove straight into the chest of a shield-less man—but most fell among the packed cavalry behind the leaders.

The charge trembled. A whole group of horses stumbled, one leaping sideways, kicking and bucking in the midst of a full gallop. Gaps opened up in the charge, and Marcus could see horsemen pulling their mounts aside to avoid downed cavalry, which only caused collisions with horsemen alongside or behind them. The second wave of javelins accelerated the chaos, and the gaps grew wider and deeper.

Marcus drew back his arm, taking aim at the man on the gray. He waited just a moment so his men could see him, then threw his pilum. The spear missed the man, but it struck the gray just where the horse's neck entered its chest. The animal squealed, although the sound was almost lost amid the screaming of other horses, the blare of the cornilum, and the shouts of the Lusitanians.

Almost instantly a wave of pila followed his throw, and virtually the entire front line of horses went down, men pitching forward or backward over their mounts. The gray stumbled to its knees, driving the pilum so deep into its body that the spear disappeared. Its rider flew over the animal's head, the signum spinning backward into the mass of flailing hooves and thrashing bodies.

Some of the horsemen in the back of the charge managed to either maneuver through the pileup or vault their horses over the fallen vanguard, but another wave of pila from the second and third lines took most of them down. One small group of a half dozen fought their way through the front line of the Century, but the second line quickly surrounded and dispatched them.

Marcus had his sword in his hand—he had no memory of actually drawing it—and surveyed the battlefield. At least a third of the attackers had been unhorsed, killed, or wounded, and the ground in front of the century was a heaving mass of dying and dead horses, dead or stunned riders, many of them pinned to the ground by their mounts. The bulk of the horsemen were streaming back up the hill, although Marcus saw a group swing around the century's left flank. They were not enough to worry about, and he dismissed them. The archers and the rear contubernium could handle them.

The carnage was stunning, more because of the number of dead and wounded horses than the casualties inflicted on the Lusitanians. Marcus thought probably no more than about two dozen horsemen had been killed outright, but that at least double that were wounded or trapped in the enormous tangle of animal and human flesh.

If he ever got back to Tarraco, the first thing Marcus intended to do was to pay a visit to Valerius Tullius, the retired centurion who had suggested using the javelins as a way to break up a cavalry charge.

"Think they will try again, sir?" asked Demaratus at his shoulder.

Marcus had forgotten the man was even there, and it took him a moment to answer. "Not if we give those horsemen on the top of that hill something to do."

Demaratus gave him a puzzled look. "What did you have in mind, sir?"

"Watch," Marcus.

Turning back to the century, he found the men looked a good deal less tense than they had before, and the first line had already rearmed themselves with pila. He congratulated them. "Comrades! You have broken their first charge," emphasizing the word "first" because he did not want them to think this was over. It was greeted with broad grins and shouts.

He let them celebrate a few moments and then put his plan in place.

"Men, step back 20 paces. Keep in formation," he ordered.

Many of the soldiers gave him a blank look, glancing at one another. The drill was to advance and finish off the attackers, which is what Marcus wanted to avoid, because he was certain it would provoke another attack.

The men dutifully back paced, their shields in perfect order, each man's pilum at ready. When they had counted off twenty paces, they halted.

"Put your shields and pila at rest," Marcus ordered, which drew another round of puzzled looks. The Roman army did not go into parade rest in the face of an enemy, particularly one that had just attacked it.

Marcus turned back toward the hill, just in time to see a horse start to buck wildly from an arrow that had just struck it. He bellowed over his shoulder, "Archers! Cease fire!"

He searched the top of the hill for someone who looked like he might be in charge, finally spotting a man surrounded by about a dozen horsemen who seemed to be giving orders. He looked directly at the man for a long moment, then deliberately sheathed his sword. Walking forward, he retrieved a pilum that had fallen short, picked it up, turned it over, and drove the point into the ground. He then rested his shield against it and stepped back, never taking his eyes off the man and his retainers.

By this time, he had the attention of the horseman. He saw another group loping back up the hill from the century's left, so he assumed the flank attack had been beaten off. A few of the less badly wounded attackers had freed themselves from the tangle in front of him and were dragging themselves back up the slope.

"Signifer," Marcus said, "put up your sword and come with me."

He heard Demaratus slide his gladis back into its sheath, while mumbling something about the futility of trying to understand Romans.

Marcus headed for the spot where the gray had gone down. The horse's rider lay still in the grass in front of the now-dead animal. The man appeared to have broken his neck when he was thrown over the horse's head.

Demaratus had already figured out what Marcus was looking for and, stepping over the gray, he grasped the First Century's signum, which was partly pinned by a tan horse that still thrashed its head about. Both men grasped the head of the signum and pulled, slowly working it out from under the animal. When it finally came free, Marcus turned to the century and raised it up. A great cheer and a cornilum blast went up from the ranks.

He handed it to Demaratus, drew his pugio, and cut the throat of the fatally wounded horse. There was a man with his leg pinned next to the tan. He looked up at Marcus with fear. Marcus looked at him for a long moment, then saluted him, turned and returned to where his pilum and shield were.

Marcus turned his back on the century and fixed his gaze on the horseman. He and the group around him were debating something, and for several minutes nothing happened. Then the man broke loose from the group and picked his way down the slope to where one wounded man limped up the hill. Grasping the man by his arm, he swung the wounded horseman behind him.

Immediately, several dozen Lusitanians trotted down the slope and began retrieving their wounded. Many dismounted, either to put the wounded on their mounts or to help lever dead horses off of men. One man pulled a dead cavalryman with a javelin in the center of his chest from the pile, but hesitated, looking at Marcus. Marcus nodded, and the man dragged the corpse over to his horse, which shied away. He finally ended up throwing the dead man over his shoulder and carrying him up the hill.

"If you will pardon me for asking, sir, exactly what are you doing?" said the voice of Flavius over his right shoulder.

"He is filling those horses with dead and wounded Lusitanians, optio," answered Demaratus.

"And just as soon as you get appointed my centurion, signifer," growled Flavius, "I will ask you the same question. Until then I would appreciate you respecting the chain of command."

"Just trying to show initiative, sir," answered Demaratus with a smile.

"Gentlemen," said Marcus with a sigh, "I would rather emerge from this day with a minimal number of casualties among my officers." Turning to Flavius he asked him how the fight at the rear had gone.

"Fine, sir. That young horseman who brought us the warning showed us a pretty neat trick about keeping cavalry at a distance, and after the Cretans got back there and stuck several of them, they backed off and finally left," answered Flavius.

Glancing around to see that the three were alone, Marcus asked, "And Sextus?"

"Steady as a stone, sir. He recruited our two smithies and the merchants to help his contubernium keep the men supplied with javelins and pila, and did a fine job commanding the rear guard," said Flavius.

Marcus nodded. "Well, your timing on the javelins and pila was perfect, optio."

"My job, sir," answered Flavius simply. "Now this dead and wounded business?"

"Those are not professional soldiers up there, Flavius. They aren't trained to ignore death. Let them mingle with the dead and wounded and they will start thinking that maybe picking a fight with us isn't such a good idea," Marcus answered, "plus every horse carrying a wounded or dead man is a horse not carrying a Lusitanian cavalryman."

Flavius said nothing, which either meant he didn't agree with the tactic, or that he did but was angry with himself for not figuring it out.

By now most of the dead and wounded Lusitanians had been extracted from the massive pileup, and there was a stream of mounted and walking wounded moving up the slope, followed by men carrying the bodies of the slain.

"Our casualties?" asked Marcus.

"No deaths, sir. A few lads in the second line got lanced, but nothing serious," he answered, then added, "Oh, we have some thoroughly terrified and grateful merchants. Tiberius has turned quite pleasant on us, sir."

Marcus and Demaratus laughed.

"Maybe we can arrange to have the Lusitanians do this on a regular basis," suggested Flavius.

"I think our signifer would object, optio," said Marcus.

"You don't like cavalry, Demaratus?" asked Flavius.

"No," said the Greek, firmly.

Flavius grinned. Demaratus's discomfort with the charge had put him in a good mood.

The man Marcus has marked for a leader was back on the crest with his retinue. He wheeled his horse a few times, and then the horsemen disappeared from the crest.

Sextus soon joined the three.

"Well done, tesserarius," said Marcus. "You won honor in your first command."

Sextus flushed with pleasure. "Thank you, sir. The doctor said he would like a word with you when you get the chance, and Tiberius requested a meeting."

Marcus nodded. "Tell the doctor I will be along in a moment. And designate a contubernium to retrieve the First Cohort's shields and equipment from the enemy."

"Yes, sir," replied Sextus, turning back to the Century and calling out names. A few minutes later a squad of eight legionaries trotted up the slope and began picking through the tangle of horses and the few dead Lusitanians that had been left on the battlefield. Their main concern was collecting the spent pila. Most of the pila heads were bent, but shafts could be reused. The smithies would hammer new points on the spears when the century made camp. Soon a small pile of scutums, a scatter of helmets, and a substantial number of pila were collected.

Marcus walked through the front line and headed for the rear.

Demaratus had been afraid, so afraid that he had let his fear show. He had covered his fear with banter, but he was shocked at how intimidating the mass of horseman had been. He had never seen horses used in battle, except as scouts or to carry messages. The fighting in northern Gaul had been all infantry.

Like many Greeks, Demaratus prided himself on being a good rider, and felt comfortable around horses. But since he had spent much of his life at sea, he had never encountered a full-scale cavalry attack.

He was not clear exactly what Marcus was up to with his javelins, and he knew that Flavius had some doubts that the weapons would be effective.

"So, signifer, what do you think of our centurion now?" asked Flavius quietly.

"I think he is—what did you call him? A winner?" replied Demaratus.

"That he is," said Flavius.

"But you weren't convinced that this javelin business would work, were you?" asked Demaratus.

Flavius was silent for a long moment. "No, I'll admit I wasn't. And I am still not sure it would work against disciplined cavalry. But I have learned that our centurion sees lots of things we don't, and at a certain point you have to have faith that he knows what he is doing."

The comment surprised Demaratus, not because it was thoughtful—under the growls and rigidity, Flavius was as thoughtful a person as Marcus, maybe even more so—but because the optio was showing this side of him to a junior officer.

"Well, I have a good deal more faith now than I had a half hour ago," said Demaratus.

"The horses bothered you, didn't they?" asked Flavius, and then shook his head, adding, "they always bother me as well. It is not that they are really all that dangerous. A good, well-trained infantry unit is ten times as dangerous as cavalry, but there is something about a charge. It's grand and terrible at the same time."

Demaratus was even more surprised by Flavius openly admitting that he could feel fear. It was not only unlike Flavius; it was downright un-Roman. He felt some of the barrier that he had erected after the incident on the ship weaken. He gave Flavius a grin. "I thought being signifer was an easy job until I saw all that horseflesh bearing down on me."

"Yeah," said Flavius, "I wouldn't have your job out there all alone with the centurion." Then he grinned back. "I kind of like it back there," he said, using his thumb to indicate the rear.

They both laughed, and some of the long weeks of tension drained away.

XXIII

Making his way to the rear, Marcus encountered Cleomanes, who had gathered his men around him. He stopped and congratulated them on a job well done. "I am not sure we could have stopped the Lusitanians without you, and my optio says you were essential in driving off the attack on our flank and rear," Marcus told them.

The Cretans took it all in without much change of expression. The archers hardly acted like they had just been through a rather tense battle. Cleomanes's only comment was that the "young, wounded horseman" had been valuable in helping to stop the Lusitanians. In contrast, Marcus's men were grinning and celebrating their victory, and many of them had called out to him as he passed through their ranks.

Demaratus was right: the Cretans were controlled.

He found the doctor tending to Cassius, with three legionnaires waiting their turn to be treated. These must be the men who suffered lance wounds when the Lusitanians had broken through the front rank.

"How are you, men?" Marcus asked.

They responded in a chorus of "Fine, sir," "Not much of a wound," and similar sentiments. In truth, the wounds looked minor. One man, surrounded by his contubernium mates, had clearly lost a good deal of blood. The right side of his tunic was soaked with red, and the blood had run down his right leg, although it was already drying.

"Honor to you, men," said Marcus. "You can feel good about this day."

"Honor to you, sir," one of them replied. "You got our signum back."

"You were with the First, weren't you? asked Marcus.

"Yes, sir. Those were my comrades' shields," the man replied.

Marcus was quiet a moment. "We will find them," he said softly, placing his palm on the legionnaire's chest.

He turned to the doctor, who was wrapping Cassius's left arm. The young horseman already had a bandage wound around his lower chest.

"And honor to you, Cassius Cornelius. How is your wound?" asked Marcus.

"I can ride and fight," said the cavalryman, although Timotheus shook his head, no.

"I am sure you can, Cassius, but in these matters, we are ruled by the doctors," said Marcus.

"His arm will heal quickly, but the wound in his side will be aggravated by riding a horse, centurion," said the doctor, carefully tying off the bandage. "He must stay off horseback for at least a few days."

"Sir," protested Cassius, "You will need a mounted scout. I am the only cavalry you have."

"We have a long way to go, Cassius. We do indeed need you, but you will do us no good if you bleed to death in the process. When the doctor says you can ride, then you can get back on a horse," said Marcus. "Now, what was this trick of yours that my optio says helped save the day in our rear?" Marcus hoped changing the subject would divert the cavalryman.

"Yes, do tell us, Cassius," chimed in Timotheus. "All I heard was something about killing some mules."

In the face of both officers' interest, Cassius's protests died.

"I used fresh blood, sir," answered Cassius.

Marcus looked blank. "I hope not your own, Cassius."

The man grinned. "No, sir, not mine. There wouldn't be enough of it. I cut the throats of three mules, sir. The smell of the blood spooked the Lusitanian horses and they wouldn't come close. That gave the archers time to drive them off."

"Horses are afraid of blood?" asked Marcus.

Cassius looked slightly surprised, then quickly made his face expressionless. He was, after all, talking to a centurion.

"Uh, yes sir," he replied. "Horses are afraid of blood, particularly horse or mule blood. We have to train them not to bolt at the smell of it. These Lusitanians are fine horsemen, sir, but they aren't organized enough to really train their horses."

Marcus shook his head. "Well, it is a good thing we had you along, son." Turning back to the doctor, he said, "Timotheus, do your best to get this man back on a horse."

The remark seemed to please Cassius.

Marcus ended his visit with a few words of praise to the

contubernium that constituted the rear guard. The merchants were also gathered in a group with Tiberius waiting for a chance to talk with him but he had no energy for them. He told Tiberius that they needed to get the Century on the road and that they would have an opportunity to speak with each other after they made camp.

Tiberius looked like he was going to protest until Marcus mentioned the necessity of getting into a well-defended marching camp in better terrain. The merchant agreed that would be a splendid idea.

Within an hour, the Century was back on the road and headed toward Norba. Flavius and he had agreed that they would keep the day short and go into camp at the first good defensible terrain they could find. Both felt the pressure to push ahead and find the First Century, but the horsemen could return, and the last thing they wanted was an exhausted unit facing yet another charge. Marcus also wanted to make sure that the smiths had enough time to repair their pila.

A little less than three hours later they came across a broad, flat meadow with a stream at one corner.

Tired as the men were, there was no grumbling about constructing a proper marching camp with a ditch, ramparts, and stakes.

When the camp was built and the guard set, the four officers sat outside their tent drinking wine, too tired to eat a proper meal. It was largely a silent meal, except for Flavius's comment about the owl. Normally this would have set off an argument between Demaratus and Flavius, because Athenians were deeply respectful of owls, but in a measure of their mutual exhaustion, the remark passed without comment.

The next day, a light breeze from the north brought them the fate of the First Century.

The Second Century was two hours into its march when Marcus smelled the sweet, sickly odor of death. Demaratus looked over at him with an unspoken question.

"Halt the Century here, signifer," said Marcus. Flavius, who had also caught the smell, strode forward and joined them. For a long moment, no one spoke.

"Flavius, send for our young cavalryman," said Marcus.

"Aye, sir," replied Flavius, disappearing down the column. A few minutes later Cassius joined them, walking rather gingerly. His face was drawn and pale, whether from his wounds or what he knew to be out in front of the Century, it was hard to say.

"Are we close to where you were attacked, Cassius?" asked Marcus.

Cassius looked around him. "I am not sure, sir. I think so. We were not that far ahead of you, sir. The centurion had taken sick, and we only did half days. I must have ridden" ... he paused, thinking ..." about ten miles. My horse was wounded in the initial battle."

He paused, remembering. "They came at us out of the East, with the sun behind them, sir. Most the men were just getting out of their tents. Our turmae managed to mount, but what could thirty do against four hundred? I wanted to stay, sir, but my commander ordered me to go." Cassius closed his eyes, fighting back tears. "I should have stayed."

"If you had, we would have been dead as well, Cassius," said Demaratus.

The cavalryman nodded, but looked desperately unhappy.

Marcus considered what to do. "We will march the Century until we reach the battlefield. We will halt when we reach it and the optio and I will go forward. Sextus," who had just joined them, "set sentries out, and gather the bodies. Signifer, assign two men to help you collect the men's signaculums. We will need a record of who died here."

He handed his shield to Demaratus. "I will address the men," he said.

Marcus walked back under the stares of the Century until he was sure everyone could hear him. He ignored the merchants.

"Comrades, we are about to come upon those who have left us for the Elysian Fields," he said. "I am new to the First Cohort, but I feel their loss no less than you. We will treat our fallen with the honor and dignity they deserve."

He suspected that most the Century had already guessed what lay ahead. Their expressions ranged from distress to fury. It was the latter sentiment that concerned him. The rule in the Roman Army was simple: defeat was always avenged. But Marcus was of the opinion that retribution simply bred new rounds of stroke and counterstroke. He suspected that the Lusitanians' recent defeat by the Second Century would do more to keep the peace than any massive campaign of vengeance. He also hoped to build on his act of letting the Lusitanians recover their dead and wounded. War needed to have a purpose beyond revenge.

The Century pushed through a narrow place between two ridges and up a small hill. With each step, the odor grew stronger. Some of the men were gagging. The hilltop opened a vista to a wide meadow, with a long rise to the east.

At the foot of the slope lay the First Century.

Marcus called a halt. Without orders, the men dropped everything but their weapons and spread out over the ridgeline.

Even from this distance it was clear what had happened. The horsemen had swept down from the east and, shielded by the early morning sun, had overrun the camp. Some of the tents were still standing, though most were flattened and trampled. Partially clothed and naked bodies lay scattered everywhere, some in groups, and others by themselves.

"Sorry about the men, sir; they just broke ranks," said Flavius at his shoulder.

Marcus looked back and saw the Century spread out along the ridgeline. "Can you blame them?" he asked softly.

Marcus turned to Sextus. "Tesserarius, have the men gather their dolbras. Hold them here until Flavius and I signal you to come forward."

"Yes, sir," answered Sextus. "What shall I do with the civilians?"

"Tell them to keep their distance until the Army has taken care of its own, tesserarius," Marcus said. "Optio?"

Flavius, who looked grim, nodded, and both men strode down the hill into what remained of the camp. As they drew close, the smell was overpowering. The dead, who had lain in the sun for a day and a half, were beginning to swell with corruption, distorting men's bodies and faces. None of the soldiers that Marcus could see were dressed in anything but tunics. It was hard to tell if the naked men had been stripped after death, or if they were struck down before they could even throw on a tunic.

"Look at the wounds sir," said Flavius, "They hardly fought back at all."

Most of the men were lying on their faces, with lance wounds and sword cuts on their backs. Many were still entangled in their tents, and in some of the latter, lumps indicated the bodies of men who had never even gotten out of their bedrolls.

Near the center of the field, they came across Gnaeus. The man was lying on his back, a lance still lodged in the upper part of his chest. A great sword slash had opened one side of his face. He was clad in a tunic, and at his side was his gladis, one of the few weapons Marcus and Flavius had seen. It was clear that the Lusitanians had taken more than shields and the signum.

They both stared down at the man who had made their lives so difficult for the past two weeks.

"I hope he is at peace now," said Marcus.

Flavius was not so forgiving. "These soldiers are dead because of that man, sir."

Marcus said nothing, but picked his way through the carnage to the western edge of the camp. Here, a group of a dozen men had made a stand. Some were dressed in tunics, others in armor. They had managed to form a circle and, unlike most the other men, they fell fighting. Their weapons still lay scattered around them. In the middle lay the crumpled body of Manius Peterius, tesserarius of the First Century, his sword still clutched in his right hand.

"These men died with honor, Flavius," said Marcus.

"Aye. And the horsemen left them their weapons because of it," the optio replied, then added, "Manius was a fine officer, sir. This should not have been his end."

Marcus shrugged. "It may yet be the end of all of us, Flavius. At least they died fighting."

"These men never had a chance, sir. The bastard didn't even set out sentries," said Flavius, his voice cold with anger.

Marcus swept the field. His optio was right. There were no uniformed dead outside the perimeter of the camp. He shook his head. "A waste, my friend. A waste of good men."

"Some good men," growled Flavius.

The two men were silent for a moment. Marcus reached down and slipped the identifying signaculum off of Manius's neck and gently closed the man's swollen eyes. Straightening up, he nodded to Flavius.

"Right, sir. I'll get on it. We passed some woods back a piece. Shall I have some of the men cut trees for a funeral fire?" Flavius asked.

"Yes. And send some other men to that dry stream we crossed to gather stones for a cairn. The spirits of the dead surround us. Let us hope they are manes, not lemurs, but we should not tempt the fates. We need to do this right, Flavius, but we also need to be clear of this place by late afternoon if we can," said Marcus.

As Flavius went off, Marcus drifted back to where Gnaeus lay and discreetly surveyed the area around the dead commander. What would Gnaeus carry dispatches in? And where would he keep them? He opened the flattened tent, but there was nothing but a bedroll and some personal effects scattered and trampled. He made a slow circle of the area, but could find nothing that looked like dispatches.

Had the dispatches been taken because they were in some attractive saddlebag? Would some Lusitanian be puzzling over them at this moment? Would a duplicate copy have been sent through Tarraco? Or had Gnaeus, in his madness, imagined the whole thing? Marcus resigned himself to the fact that he wouldn't know until he got to Legio.

The grim task of gathering the bodies began. Some of the men who had formerly been with the First Century broke down when they discovered their contubernium mates. Others cursed the body of Gnaeus until Marcus put a stop to it. He noticed a group gathered around Manius, and how they gently picked him up and laid him down with the growing line of dead.

Out beyond the southern perimeter were a clot of bodies and a scatter of dead horses. Cassius stood in the middle of it, his head down, his hands in his face. Marcus assumed the cavalryman was standing in the middle of where the Ala II turmae made its stand. He started to move toward the young man, until he saw Sextus come over and put his arm around Cassius's shoulder. The two talked for a bit and then began to gather up the lead signaculums that would identify the dead.

Mules had begun to return, dragging tree trunks or loaded with river stones, and Flavius was directing the men on how to build a proper pyre. He built a separate fire to burn the tents and bits of equipment that dotted the battle scene. The Cretan archers and even the civilians had joined the labor, although the soldiers insisted that only they could handle their dead comrades.

By early afternoon, the huge pyre was built and the bodies and what few weapons remained were stacked on top of it. Marcus gave a eulogy, which said all the right things and mentioned none of the madness and stupidity that made the ceremony necessary in the first place. The cairn was built next to the pyre, which was then set on fire.

By the time the fire had burned itself down and the officers had made sure that the bodies were reduced to ashes, the shadows had begun to lengthen, and the silent Century and its train of merchants and mules resumed its march toward Norba, now less than a day away.

The Second Century went into camp only a few hours after it left the field of death. The men were exhausted, but they quickly and efficiently put together the marching camp. There was none of the banter that normally followed a long day's march, and Flavius noted that the men even chose to forego dice.

Flavius was returning from inspecting the ditch and ramparts when Demaratus fell in with him.

The two were silent for a moment. "Demaratus," said Flavius softly, "you once said something about 'pride' and 'awful justice,' do you remember?"

Demaratus nodded. "It was from the Iliad, Flavius."

The optio shook his head. "I loved the line at the time, but this justice is too awful."

"Pride punishes all who stand near it, my friend," said Demaratus. "There is no fairness in it. It is the justice of the Gods, not our justice."

"What's a smart man like you doing in the Roman Army?" asked Flavius.

"I like the company," Demaratus said with a slight smile.

"But not cavalry?" replied Flavius with a grin.

"Not cavalry," agreed Demaratus.

Demaratus looked at Flavius. "This does change things, Flavius," he said quietly.

"Aye, it does," the optio answered. "There will be no report from Gnaeus at Legio."

"And Marcus is acting Primus Pilus of the First Cohort," added Demaratus.

Flavius frowned. "Maybe, maybe not. We don't know what kind of reception we're going to get in Legio."

Demaratus shrugged. "How can it be anything but a hero's welcome? The Second Century defeated the men who destroyed the First Century. The books are balanced."

Flavius nodded. "I'm not sure about the balance thing, though I have a suspicion that Marcus has some sort of scheme afoot concerning that."

Demaratus arched an eyebrow.

"Letting those Lusitanians claim their dead and wounded, signifer," said Flavius, "you know that is not exactly standard policy on the battlefield."

Demaratus nodded. "No, that did surprise me a little. I assume he did it to get rid of the Lusitanians."

Flavius shook his head. "Marcus never has just one reason for doing something. That's what makes him so hard to second-guess, unless the subject is horses. I think he is up to something else."

Demaratus grinned at him. "And people say Greeks are convoluted."

"Oh, Greeks have nothing on us Romans when it comes to plots and schemes," answered Flavius with a certain complacency.

"I think Marcus has a plan for ending this Lusitanian revolt, and he started yesterday."

Demaratus looked at him blankly. "If I am so smart, why haven't I the slightest idea of what you're talking about?"

"Look at it logically, signifer," said Flavius (Demaratus flinched at the suggestion he might be "illogical"). "Marcus beats the Lusitanians, but lets them take their dead and wounded. You see, they owe him. The message is, 'Fight us and we will defeat you. But once it's over, then that's it.'"

Demaratus digested this for a bit. "You mean Marcus has no intention of retaliating against Lusitanian towns and villages?"

"We'll find out when we get to Narbo," answered Flavius, "but I would bet a stipendia that he will argue against revenge raids."

"Cassius is Lusitanian," mused Demaratus. "I wonder what he thinks of what Marcus did?"

"Well, the lad's a bit down right now," said Flavius, "but we should discuss it with him before he leaves us."

"There is another person we need to have a discussion with, " said Demaratus softly, "and without Marcus."

It was Flavius's turn to look blank.

"Sextus," said Demaratus.

"Sextus?" asked Flavius.

Demaratus nodded. "Flavius, we were assigned to the First Cohort around this whole Christianity business, and we have pretended that it doesn't exist. Remember, this was a century that almost mutinied over the issue."

"We were a little busy with other things," said Flavius, a bit defensively.

"I agree, but it's like being in the arena with a lion. Sooner or later, you pay attention to it or it eats you," answered Demaratus.

Flavius was silent for a long moment. "You're right, of course. I just don't much like this religion business. Training, marching and fighting is a lot simpler."

"I never thought I would agree with a statement like that, but I do," said Demaratus with a smile. "I suggest we wait until we are through Narbo and on the way to Legio. We will have almost two weeks to find the proper time."

"Agreed, brother," said Flavius, then turned himself back into an optio: "How successful were you in gathering the signaculum?" he asked, his voice easily slipping back into a superior officer's formal tone.

"We found only about a quarter of them," answered Demaratus, who always had difficulty rapidly shifting status.

Flavius nodded. "War trophies. It always happens when we lose the battlefield. Find much else?"

Demaratus shook his head. "No. A few coins, some letters, that's about it. The charge smashed up a lot of things, and the horsemen took everything that wasn't under or inside a tent."

Flavius nodded again. "Let's hope we have a better end, signifer."

The two had made a full circuit of the camp during their discussion, and headed back toward their tent; each was silent, caught up in his own thoughts.

The Century broke free of the hills that had flanked it since just north of Emerita, and rolled across a rich, flat plain toward a long, east-west ridge. The city of Norba Caesarina was lodged at its crest, spilling down its slope to a placid river running through its southern edge.

The Century had stopped two miles short of the town to make itself look proper. There was none of the lightheartedness with which the Century had approached Emerita, however. War and death had drained much of the spirit out of the men. But still and all, the Roman Army was the Roman Army, and when it marched into a city of any size, it looked its best.

"Not much of a city, is it?" Flavius remarked to Sextus.

"Not like Emerita or Corduba, sir, but then it is a city that has been abandoned and reclaimed many times, so I am told," answered the tesserarius.

"Really?" remarked Demaratus.

The three were slowly going down the line of march, checking that everything was proper. Flavius impatiently waived the merchants back from the main body of the Century. He had no intention of letting mere merchants march in with soldiers who had just fought a battle.

"Yes, sir," answered Sextus. "It was built on the ruins of an old hill fort when Rome first came here. But it was abandoned after Carthage fell. Then when Rome went to war with the Lusitanians it was rebuilt, but abandoned after the great massacre."

The two looked quizzically at him.

"The Lusitanians fought the Roman general Sulpicius Galba to a standstill, so he agreed to give them land and threw a big banquet for them," Sextus said. "When the Lusitanians came for the banquet, they were attacked. Those who were not butchered on the spot were sold into slavery."

"Well, no wonder those horsemen were in a bad temper," said Flavius. "When did this happen, Sextus?"

"Right before the third war with Carthage, sir," the tesserarius answered.

"Before the ... son, that was almost five hundred years ago! The Lusitanians are still in a snit about something that happened that long ago?" said Flavius incredulously.

"Yes sir," answered Sextus. "Lusitanians still sing songs about it."

"Maybe they could try singing less and forgetting more," said Flavius.

"Forgetfulness is a luxury of the victor," said a quiet voice behind the optio.

Flavius turned to find Cassius Cornelius. The young cavalryman had joined them.

Before Flavius could respond, Demaratus stepped in. "Well said, Cassius. How goes your wound?"

"It is fine, sir," Cassius answered. "I can ride again."

Flavius, however, would not be turned aside. "Are you telling me that those horsemen who attacked us did so because of something that happened five hundred years ago?"

Cassius shrugged (then flinched with the pain). "Yes and no, sir. The Lusitanians are unhappy because some of the big latifundia are encroaching on their lands to graze cattle, sheep and horses. That is what the revolt is over. But they also never forget the Great Massacre. It is just part of our myths."

"Our myths, Cassius?" asked Flavius.

"Yes, sir. I am a loyal citizen of the Empire," answered Cassius defensively. "But I am also a Lusitanian. I grew up hearing about the Great Massacre." He was silent a moment. "Those comrades I helped burn yesterday, they were Lusitanians also, sir."

"And they were fine men, Cassius," said Demaratus soothingly. "The optio and I are new to this land, and we are not always aware of how the past has molded it."

Demaratus watched Flavius wrestling with his initial anger, then taking control of himself. He was an interesting and sometimes quite admirable man, thought the Greek.

"What's this about the latifundia, Cassius? We've got big landowners in Rome, and they tend to want more than they have as well," said Flavius.

"The Lusitanians have always been horsemen, sir, without real towns or cities. Horses require lots of land for graze. We don't really have land that people own, everyone just uses it. So the latifundia claim that no one owns the land; hence they can take it. That was what sparked the whole thing off," said Cassius.

"Hmmm," commented Flavius. "It's never simple, is it? So how does it end?"

Cassius shook his head. "I don't know, sir. The Lusitanians don't have a single leader, so I don't know who you talk to. It is just a war that shouldn't have happened."

"One could say that about almost any war, Cassius," said Demaratus. "However, if we don't get this Century on the road, we might find ourselves in a war with our centurion," he said, pointing his shoulder toward Marcus, who had begun to throw impatient looks their way. "We will talk about this some more, Cassius. It interests me."

Cassius saluted, flinching in way that suggested he was not

quite as well as he claimed. Demaratus went toward the head of the column while Flavius headed for the rear.

And so, the Second Century of the VII Legion, with assorted auxiliaries and a body of scared and grateful merchants marched into the city of Norba Caesarina.

XXIV

It was the oddest collection of "soldiers" Marcus had ever laid eyes on, and he had no idea what he was going to do with them. But since it was his fault, he would have to think of something.

It had all started the day they reached Norba Caesarina. The city leaders were in a panic once they found out what happened to the First Century, and Marcus had been besieged by demands that the Second Century garrison the town. In spite of his explanations that Norba was in no danger from several hundred cavalry—particularly cavalry that had suffered a defeat—the quaestor and the aedile petitioned him to help fortify the town. Both douviri had gone north to Capera for a provincial council, so instead of the two senior magistrates, Marcus was forced to deal with the two town magistrates whose primary purpose was fixing roads and handing out contracts, mostly to friends and relatives for a hefty kickback.

Norba was in no danger from the Lusitanians. It was a city of more than 10,000 people, and the local vigiles could muster a full cohort of troops on their own. On top of the police force, a goodly number of Norba's residents were former legionaries, some of them freshly mustered out from VII Legion.

Marcus met with the veterans and between him and the former soldiers, had finally managed to convince the magistrates that they wouldn't be slaughtered in their beds.

In the midst of all this, Cassius Cornelius had cornered him in the local baths and asked permission to recruit some cavalry.

"We will need some kind of mounted force, sir, and I can lay my hands on enough residents to make up a turmae," Cassius pleaded to him as he was getting ready to enter the baths.

Marcus was distracted and exhausted or he might have questioned Cassius more. But he felt affection for the young man, so without thinking much about it he told Cassius to go ahead, but not to recruit from either the veterans or the vigiles.

Now he was much regretting his kindness.

Thirty men stood at attention before him, garbed in the strangest mixture of armor and uniforms he had ever seen. Most of them were young—very young—and were doing their best to look fierce. He would grant they looked earnest, but he was not sure whether an enemy would run or laugh.

Some, likely the sons of veterans, were clad in infantry armor, most of it too big for their wearers. Their heights and sizes ranged from tall to so short that Marcus at first took the man to be a child. One very heavy young man was wearing old-fashioned scale armor, which was missing pieces at various locations on the underlying mail. He looked for all the world like a huge spotted tuna in a school of mackerel.

Their weapons were a motley lot as well. Some were armed with short gladis swords, while others sported the long spatha blade favored by cavalry. One man, clad in mail and a type of helmet that Marcus had never seen before, was armed with an enormous broad sword, probably a war trophy from some bygone battle with the local Celts. Marcus summoned up an image of the man swinging the great thing and killing men on either side of him before lopping off his own horse's head.

Cassius, obviously proud of his scratch turmae, stood to one side looking like he had conjured up a legion of Spartans.

Flavius, who had joined Marcus, whispered, "Sir, what is this about?"

"Comrades," said Cassius in what was a fair imitation of an officer's parade ground rasp, "this is our centurion, Marcus Favonius Facilis, and our optio, Flavius Priscus."

The line of men stiffened, although they had all been standing rigidly at what they considered "attention."

Marcus, at a loss for words, acknowledged the salute with a nod, while Flavius, his face expressionless, glanced over at his centurion.

"Ahem," said Marcus, clearing his throat. "A fine-looking group of men, Cassius. Do they have mounts?" He was desperately hoping that they did not, because since the Century had only a few, the lack of horses would disband the unit then and there.

"Yes, sir," answered Cassius. "Each man has a horse, and we have a dozen extras as well."

"Wonderful," said Flavius, sounding like he meant the opposite. But Flavius also had a soft spot for the young cavalryman who had saved their lives and, not wanting to deflate him, brightened up his tone. "You did a fast job of recruiting, Cassius."

Cassius glowed. "Thank you, sir. Actually, it was easy. I made an announcement at taverns all over the city, and lots of people volunteered. I chose only the best."

Marcus decided that he didn't want to see the rejects.

Maybe he could scare them off.

"Men," he said, "I salute your courage. As you know, the turmae of the Ala II was destroyed by the Lusitanians, along with the entire First Century. Only Cassius here survived. When we leave the security of Norba we may find ourselves engaged with that same dangerous enemy."

But he detected not the slightest wavering in the ranks. If anything, they looked more eager. He sighed silently to himself. Well, we do need cavalry, so we will somehow have to make the best of this.

"Welcome to the Second Century of the VII Legion, comrades," he said as the men grinned and slapped one another on the back. "Dismissed."

The men looked confused for a moment, clearly not having the slightest idea what happened next. Flavius stepped in: "Quarter your horses with our mules, and our cavalryman will be with you in a moment to explain how to draw rations and equipment."

The group all gave a ragged salute and headed off to where their horses were gathered outside the barracks. As soon as they were out of earshot, Flavius turned to Cassius. "You think this lot is up to the job, Cassius?"

"Yes, sir. I know they look a little funny with all their different uniforms and armor, but they all know how to ride," he said a trace defensively.

"You will have to equip them as properly as you can," put in

Marcus. "That great broad sword will likely do us greater damage than it will the Lusitanians, and the infantry armor will have to go. And dig up some more spathas."

"Yes, sir, I will see to all that," answered Cassius.

Marcus smiled at the young man. "All right, Cassius. Do the best you can. I don't have the authority to appoint auxiliary officers, but since there is no one else to consult, I am making you acting turmae commander."

Cassius glowed still brighter. "Yes, sir. Thank you, sir. I will honor my appointment." He saluted and left.

There was a long moment of silence between Marcus and Flavius. Finally, Marcus said, "He caught me going into the baths."

"Yes, sir," answered Flavius. "He has initiative."

They both grinned at one another.

"Well, sir, look at it this way," reasoned Flavius. "If we come upon the Lusitanians they will be too busy laughing to fight," then added with a touch of wonder, "Did you see that big one with the fish scale armor?"

Changing the subject, Marcus asked about preparations for leaving, and for the next half-hour they went through their checklists. The Century had re-supplied at Norba, and the merchants had decided not to continue north in spite of the fact that they would have gotten more for their goods.

"That's good news," Marcus said about the merchants.

"Aye, we will move a lot faster, and it sounds like we need to make that council in Capera," said Flavius.

Marcus nodded.

Flavius hesitated a moment, then said, "Sir, what happened on the battlefield is already going around."

"As I recall, we defeated the Lusitanians," said Marcus in a neutral tone.

"Yes, sir, I know that. We also called a battlefield truce, sir, and some people are not very happy about it," said Flavius.

"Some people?" Marcus asked quietly.

"Not the men. They would march to Palmyra and back for you, sir. I mean the people in the town," answered Flavius.

Marcus nodded. He expected there would be a certain amount of controversy over his action. "Why are you raising this with me, optio?"

"A couple of those junior magistrates sent off a message to Capera, sir," said Flavius, "I thought you ought to know. I wanted to wring their necks, but..." he trailed off.

"I am glad you did not wring their necks, Flavius. That would make things even more complex," said Marcus.

"Yes, sir. That's why I didn't do it," Flavius answered.

But things got more complex anyway.

The benches in the curia were slowly filling up with council members, so to pass the time before the proceedings got underway, Demaratus and Timotheus examined the adjacent forum. It was mostly deserted, since all normal business had been suspended for the duration of the provincial council. As provincial forums went, it had a certain grandeur. A large arch served as the entrance to the forum, and the forum itself was flanked by Corinthian columns, its lentils covered with carved rosettes. The rectangular plaza was limestone, but the floor of the Imperial temple was fine marble.

Demaratus bent over, rubbing his hand over the polished temple floor.

"I did not know you were an admirer of marble," said Timotheus, casting a critical eye on the central cult statue.

"It is from Thessaly, doctor," answered Demaratus.

"How would you know that?" asked Timotheus.

"You forget I was a sailor. We carried marble on many occasions. Not to Iberia, but to Italia and even Britannia. We were returning from running wine and marble to London when our ship was wrecked near Burdigala," answered Demaratus, standing up and looking around him.

"Marble all looks the same to me," said Timotheus.

"As all sickness looks the same to me," answered Demaratus.

Timotheus smiled. "We know that which we know. Very Athenian, my friend."

They both studied the statue of Augustus with a critical eye.

"Roughly done," said Demaratus.

"Capera is even more a provincial town than Norba. One doesn't expect fine art in a place like this," Timotheus noted.

"Do you suppose they really think their emperors are divine?" asked Demaratus.

"They think everything is divine," answered Timotheus. "You know they have a goddess for door hinges?"

Demaratus stared at him blankly: "Door hinges?"

"Door hinges," answered the doctor. "Her name is Cardea, and every time I open a new clinic, I have to have an augur come in with his chicken."

Demaratus nodded. "I have seen an augur at work. Apparently, the way the chicken pecks tells the priest what the future will be. What happens if the omens are bad?"

"Pay enough and the omens are never bad," said Timotheus cynically.

Demaratus chuckled. "In many ways our masters are like children."

"Children that rule the world," said Timotheus quietly.

Demaratus nodded his head in agreement, and then changed the subject. "I have no concerns about today's council, doctor, because even if it condemns Marcus for his truce with the Lusitanians it has no power to do anything but complain. The provincial governor is not here, and he is the only civil authority that might cause trouble. Am I correct in that assumption?"

Timotheus took a while to answer. "You are correct that neither the council nor the magistrates have any power over the army. The VII swears allegiance to the emperor, not the civilian authorities, and in any case, the emperor has always directly ruled the provinces of Terraconisis and Lusitania," he said.

"Not Baetia?" asked Demaratus.

"No, Baetia was originally the Senate's province, but of course the emperor rules everything these days so wherever the army is, the army is the law," Timotheus answered.

"Will the sentiment of the council have an effect on the VII Legion's Legate, Titus Valens?" asked Demaratus.

"That is a more complex question," said the doctor slowly. "It will depend on what Titus thinks is in his interests. And it will also depend on what his tribunes say."

"Tell me more," said Demaratus.

"Our legate is a man who doesn't want trouble, and in

Hispania, civilians can be trouble. Remember, we are the only legion in the entire province, which tells you that civilian matters dominate the life of the peninsula," answered Timotheus. "If the civilians get up in arms about this, it could be bad for Marcus."

"There are a number of powerful merchants who are now in Marcus's debt," pointed out Demaratus.

"Yes, and that will work to his advantage. Many of them gave me letters to give to the Legate, and our commander will pay attention to some of those signatures," agreed Timotheus.

"What of the Tribunes?" asked Demaratus.

"They are different from one another," said the doctor. "Publius Felix is ambitious, but he thinks he is much cleverer than he is. Quintus Junius is old and worn out, but sensible. I suspect that Quintus will think the truce a splendid idea as it will allow him to get back to his books and his wine. Publius, however, may see an opportunity for advancement by denouncing Marcus and demanding war."

"Is there not a third tribune?" asked Demaratus.

"No, only two. Our third tribune was reassigned to Rome, and because of the recent turmoil no replacement has been appointed. Nor does the VII have a prefect. We are an old-fashioned legion and innovation in command structure is slow to take hold."

Demaratus digested this for a moment. "We met Publius in Tarraco," he said, "Does he maneuver to become legate of the VII?"

Timotheus laughed. "No. I said he was ambitious, remember? No one wants to be the legate of a legion whose major purpose in life is to try to get the locals to dig gold for Rome. Publius dreams of glory, and there is not much glory to be had in Hispania these days."

Demaratus frowned. "What do you mean about the locals and gold?"

"The area around Legio is rich in gold, but it is hard to get anyone to dig it," answered Timotheus. "In the old days the legions made war against the Arevaci, the Cantabri, or the Vettones and brought back lots of slaves. But who do you make war against in Hispania today? All of those tribes are now Roman citizens, even the Lusitanians. And, in any case, you could never catch enough of them to do the job."

The doctor chuckled. "Poor Titus is besieged not by mighty enemies whose defeat would bring him profit, but endless complaints from Rome about falling gold production. No, my friend, ambition does not lead one to become legate of the VII Legion, and there is little competition for the position."

Demaratus thought quietly to himself, "And yet this may work to our advantage."

XXV

Marcus wandered through the forum as the decurions filled up the benches in the curia. He stood looking at a monument to Turranius Rufus and his wife, who had paid for most of the stone plaza he was standing in. The council would be called to order shortly and he ran over what he wanted to say based on the discussion he had with one of Norba's magistrates the previous evening.

The douviri's name was Fabricius Tuscus, a retired centurion from Egypt's II Traiana Fortis Legion. They had spent the evening drinking wine, Marcus very little, the magistrate prodigiously.

The conversation, which began with the recent fight and then drifted into army gossip, finally worked itself around to the upcoming provincial council. After several cups of wine, the magistrate raised the issue that was most on Marcus's mind.

"There are many on the council who are concerned about this truce you have arranged with the Lusitanians," said Fabricius.

"No truce was 'arranged,' it was simply a tactic to keep the Lusitanians from launching another attack," said Marcus.

"There are some on the council, Arrius Granius in particular, who want to strip the Lusitanians of citizenship and wage war," said Fabricius, taking a deep drink from his cup. "He is a powerful and wealthy man, and the other decurions tend to listen to him. It can be expensive and dangerous to thwart him."

Marcus considered the magistrate. Fabricius Tuscus still had the hint of a powerful physique, though much of it had given way to a combination of weight and age. He had drunk a considerable amount of wine, but his speech was not in the slightest slurred, and his eyes were sharp and penetrating. Marcus decided that the old centurion was probably a formidable force in his own right.

Wording his comment carefully, he said, "I do not wish to thwart anyone, Fabricius, but only Emperor Decius can take away citizenship, certainly not a provincial council in Hispania." He paused, then added, "And while there is no excuse for revolt, I have heard that the Lusitanians may have some legitimate grievances."

"To what do you refer?" asked Fabricius.

"I was told that some big landowners in Norba and Capera have been grazing sheep, cattle, and horses on land traditionally held by the Lusitanians. The person who told me this claims that it was this seizure that led to the present uprising," answered Marcus.

Fabricius poured himself another cup of wine and refilled Marcus's. "That is not talk the decurions will want to hear tomorrow," he said. "They will want to know when the VII Legion will make an example of those who challenge the Empire."

"A few hundred horsemen are hardly a challenge to the Empire, Fabricius," Marcus replied.

"The 'few hundred horsemen' destroyed the most powerful unit in the VII Legion, Marcus. If that is not a challenge, what is?" the magistrate shot back.

"The First Century was overrun because its commander refused to build a marching camp. The First Century destroyed itself, Fabricius," replied Marcus.

Fabricius pursed his lips. "I had heard something like that," he said, "You know, Gnaeus Antonius used to be a fine commander, Marcus. Something must have happened to him in Mauritania."

"He was not well," said Marcus, not elaborating.

"But that is irrelevant. It is not an argument that will convince the council. It will demand war," said Fabricius. "They will say there is no excuse for revolt, and that an attack on the Roman army must be avenged."

"And in the wake of that revenge will come men like Arrius Granius who will then claim the lands that they now covet," said Marcus with a trace of bitterness.

The magistrate shrugged and drank some more wine. "That is the way of it, Marcus. Each of these decurions is worth 100,000 sesterces. It is only a quarter the price of becoming an equestrian and not close to the mountain of gold one needs to purchase a senatorship. But in Lusitania these lowly decurions are our equestrians and senators, and they will have their way."

Marcus leaned forward. "Not if a magistrate speaks up, Fabricius. I do not defend what happened to the First Century, but what about the rights of the Lusitanians, who are just as much citizens of Rome as are the decurions? A voice of reason in the council tomorrow might well find a way to settle this short of empty revenge."

"Revenge is never empty, centurion," said Fabricius. "It is fear that keeps the barbarians at bay."

Marcus shook his head. "We keep them at bay, but they no longer fear us, Fabricius. We can defeat them, but for how long? I stopped counting all the battles we 'won' in Northern Gaul, but for all our victories we are still fighting the same people we defeat year after year. The 'Pax Romana' is coming to an end, my friend."

He took a sip of wine. "As for revenge. You are right, it is not empty. It is a poison that raises up another generation to hate Rome. Do you know that the Lusitanians still talk about the 'great massacre,' an event almost 500 years old?"

"You seem to know a good deal about Lusitanian history," said Fabricius.

"My cavalry commander, Cassius Cornelius, is a Lusitanian," explained Marcus.

"You had best keep that a secret," said Fabricius quietly.

"The man saved the Second Century from destruction. If he had not, tomorrow's council may well have been presided over by the Lusitanians," said Marcus coldly.

"Calm down, sir. I am not your foe in this matter," said Fabricius, filling his cup again. "But I like being a magistrate, Marcus, and if I go against the sentiment of the decurions, they will turn me out at the next election. I will not advocate war, but neither will I oppose it. I will remain silent."

Marcus nodded. "I ask only that I get a fair hearing."

"I will see to that," said Fabricius. "I am the senior magistrate, so I will preside over the meeting. But I warn you, by tradition the richest decurions speak first, and it is among them that you will find the greatest sentiment for war and revenge."

"Well, we will see what happens, comrade," sighed Marcus.

Fabricius was silent, thinking. "Bring all your officers, Marcus," he finally said.

"Why? The battlefield truce was mine, not theirs. They had no choice but to carry it out. This is my responsibility," protested Marcus.

"You misread me, comrade. I will arrange for the council to bestow an award on you and your officers for your triumph over the Lusitanians and for saving the lives of the merchants," said Fabricius. "We will hold the ceremony at the beginning of the meeting. It might smooth your path or least soften some of your critics."

Marcus sat back and grinned at the old man. "Are you suggesting there is a relationship between decorations and politics?" he said with mock outrage.

"May the gods strike me dead if that is so," replied Fabricius complacently. "More wine?"

"Sir," said Flavius, breaking into Marcus's thoughts. "I believe the council is ready to begin."

It took Marcus a moment to shift from his memories of last night's conversation to his optio standing respectfully in front of him. He blinked at him, then said, "Yes, Flavius, thank you. Are the others here?"

"Yes sir," replied Flavius.

The officers were clustered near the entrance to the council.

Demaratus always looked like he had prepared for a formal

review, although once again his wolf skin was missing. It had first vanished on their way to Corduba, and its replacement went awry in Norba. It was clear his signifer disliked wearing the thing, and Marcus was on the verge of giving in to the Greek's resistance to the traditional uniform. Marcus was fond of wolves, and it seemed a bad idea to deplete their numbers just to get his third in command to look proper.

Flavius was always the same, though Marcus noted that he had recently polished his lion-head cane. Sextus stood at ease in his tesserarius uniform; his new officer was growing in confidence and fitting himself into the command structure. Young Cassius looked self-conscious in his officer's chain and short leather pants. Even the doctor was dressed in armor for the occasion, the only time Marcus had seen Timotheus in anything but his clinic garb or a dress tunic.

"Gentlemen," said Marcus, "we will be honored by the council for the recent battle. There is also likely to be a discussion that will examine our actions after the battle. I will speak for the Century, understood?"

The officers nodded. Even if they thought otherwise, an order was an order.

The group entered the curia and stood against a side wall. Fabricius, as presiding duoviri, sat on an elevated dais facing the door. He acknowledged their entrance with a nod. The decurions sat on benches facing the dais and all turned to look at the officers, some friendly, others guarded, at least a few coldly.

"Citizens," said Fabricius, "we are called here in provincial council to decide on matters that will strengthen and glorify the Empire." The opening line and the short speech that followed were pro-forma, like a prayer or a chant that no one paid attention to. People whispered to one another throughout. Some read. A few ate their breakfasts.

After the opening ceremony was done, Fabricius called the officers up to the dais and introduced them. He then gave a short speech on their recent battle in which the "Second Century's bravery and innovation won a great victory over the rebel Lusitanians and avenged their comrades in the First Century."

Marcus was surprised and gratified to hear Fabricius use the term "avenged" and, judging from the stir among the decurions, they had also made note of it. A heavy-set man in the front row leaned over to whisper something in the ear of a tall, gaunt, aristocratic-looking decurion next to him. The gaunt one nodded and flashed a quick, hostile look at Marcus. Marcus would bet a year's pay that the thin, haughty one was Arrius Granius.

When Fabricius had finished, he signaled to a slave who carried an ornate bronze box to the dais. In it were silver medals attached to red ribbons, and the magistrate proceeded to hang one of them around each of their necks. As "awards" the little medallions were not much to look at, and probably handed out for everything from making the town sewer work to successfully overseeing the local market. But Cassius was glowing at receiving the award and doing his best not to look as excited and thrilled as he was. The rest of them all looked properly solemn. Demaratus and Timotheus were obviously bored.

When the applause died down, the heavy man who had whispered to the tall decurion stood and signaled Fabricius that he wished to speak.

The magistrate frowned slightly, and addressed him. "Tiberius

Porcius, I must first ask the senior decurion, Arrius Granius, if he wishes to address the council."

The heavy man gave a small bow, and replied, "I have already inquired if the honorable Arrius Granius wished to speak, and he yields the floor to me."

Marcus watched the exchange narrowly. He had no doubt that this little bit of politeness between Arrius and Tiberius was planned out, but he was not sure why. He would have to be careful.

Fabricius signaled Tiberius to address the council.

Tiberius was heavy, but tall and broad. Marcus thought he must have been impressive in his prime. And while youth had yielded to age, he still carried himself with a certain elephantine grace. His toga was finely made and he wore a broad gold bracelet on his left arm, a mark of army service. Marcus noted that Arrius Granius wore no such bracelet and suddenly knew why the senior decurion had yielded the floor. He needed a veteran to lead the attack.

"Citizens, we are honored by the presence of these brave men," said Tiberius, addressing the council and taking in the officers with a sweep of his arm. The man's smile was broad and engaging, but it found little echo in his eyes. He soon replaced it with a sorrowful frown. "And yet I feel that it is my duty as a former soldier and officer to raise a question that is on the minds of many of us here."

He paused here, his staged reluctance perfectly timed.

"I would ask the honorable Marcus Favonius Facilis, centurion of the Second Century of the VII Legion Hispania, to explain why he has agreed to a truce with those who have revolted against the lawful authority of the Empire and our emperor Messius Quintus Decius?" Tiberius said.

He paused so long that Marcus stepped forward to answer, only to have Tiberius cut him off before he could begin. The timing was obvious: it put Marcus on the defensive and made Tiberius look like the authoritative voice at the council.

The initial skirmish had gone to the enemy.

Tiberius continued: "And not only did these rebels challenge the might of Rome, but foully murdered our friend and comrade, Gnaeus Antonius, Primus Pilus of the First Cohort, and all of his men."

There was a rumble from the council, which Tiberius allowed to subside before spreading his hands in puzzlement. "Are we to reward murderers and rebels with truces? Are we next to give them tribute?" he asked. "When I served with the V Macedonica we handed out no such rewards to our enemies. We crushed them on the battlefield, and razed their towns and crops. We did not ask that the Dacians love us, but that they fear us, and so they did."

There was an answering stir from the council, but Marcus noted that not everyone looked comfortable with Tiberius's speech. Several decurions frowned and crossed their arms. Arrius Granius stared intensely at the speaker.

Turning back to Marcus, Tiberius crossed his arms, leaned back dramatically and said, "I now ask Centurion Marcus Favonius why he has cast aside the traditions of the Roman army, traditions that have built the mightiest empire the world has known, and brought peace and prosperity to our lands?"

Marcus stopped himself from responding immediately. Two

could play this game and there was a long silence, long enough for Tiberius to begin to feel just the slightest bit awkward. But just as the man opened his mouth to continue, Marcus gave him a puzzled frown. "Truce?" he asked. "What is this truce you refer to, decurion?"

The use of "decurion" was correct, but slightly insulting, as Tiberius had used both Marcus's title and full name.

Tiberius flushed. "You know exactly what I refer to, centurion," he snapped.

Marcus put his hands behind him and casually strolled forward toward Tiberius. He stopped just in front of the man. Shaking his head again, he said, "I am puzzled by your term, decurion. I spoke with no one on the battlefield. The enemy withdrew following their defeat." Cocking his head slightly, he smiled at Tiberius. "If the enemy withdrawing from the battlefield is a 'truce,' then I can only pray to the gods that my life will be filled with them."

The remark drew a ripple of laughter.

Tiberius stood his ground. "You allowed the Lusitanians to save their wounded and to flee the battlefield with their forces intact," he said hotly, "If that is not a 'truce' I don't know what is."

Marcus allowed himself to look puzzled for a moment. "I am afraid I still don't..." he started to say, then caught himself. "Oh, you refer to our ploy to disarm the enemy."

"Ploy to..." began Tiberius, only to have the centurion talk right over him.

Turning to the seated council members, Marcus put his left hand on his sword pommel, and threw out his right arm. "Citizens! I only wish you could have been with us that day on the field of battle." Marcus was generally a quiet person, but he came from a family of politicians, and had sat in the great forum at Rome to listen to debates between the senators. He knew how to weave a tale.

Speaking in short sentences with dramatic pauses, he unfolded the story of the fight in the meadow: the lone horseman, the shock of seeing the First Century's shields, the thunder of the charge— "as if Bellona rode at their side"—the chaos, and the final triumphant moment when he and Demaratus—he paused to sweep his arm toward the signifer, who stepped forward and gave a little bow—reclaimed the signum of the First Century.

He stopped and there was silence. Then a great wave of applause broke out. Marcus noted that even Tiberius and Arrius grudging clapped their hands.

When the applause died down, Tiberius again tried to make his point. "The courage of Second Century did honor to the Empire, Centurion, but to allow these rebels against the august glory of the Emperor to take their dead and wounded from the field is a violation of everything...."

"I could see how one who was not there might think that," said Marcus, cutting him off again. Turning back to the council he put both hands on his hips and stared down at the floor, as if reconstructing a memory. "Battle is a complex business, fellow citizens," he said, looking up. "The army not only has to fight, it has to protect."

"It is well you ask this question," he continued. "Sometimes the logic of war and battle is many times hidden from civilians, but I, for one, believe that the more citizens know, the better they understand why we do the things we do to insure your protection."

He paused, then spread out his arms as if to embrace the council. "Here we were facing several hundred more horsemen." It was an exaggeration, but there was no one to contradict him.

Lowering his voice, so that the decurions had to lean forward and strain to hear, he continued. "We had no cavalry, a handful of archers, and a party of merchants to defend. And by now we knew the First Century had been overrun. My first thought was to Norba, to Capera. Were these cities besieged? How could we drive our enemies from the battlefield and keep this single century a fighting force to defend those cities?"

Marcus paused and leaned forward, as if waiting for an answer. Then putting his hand to his heart, he said, "And then the answer came to me in a way that I can only attribute to Augustus himself," he said. "A voice seemed to come from my heart," he said, dramatically thumping his chest. "It said, 'Battles are won not by strength alone, but strength and wisdom.'"

He dropped his head, and then looked up, shaking it as if puzzled. "What could it mean? How could we use wisdom to defeat our enemies? And then I understood, citizens. Augustus meant us to turn the weapons of the Lusitanians to our advantage. The cavalry, that a moment before had menaced our merchants and soldiers, now were burdened with dead and wounded soldiers, soldiers who had tasted the might of Rome, a message they would take back to their homes. "

He was silent a moment. "I was tempted to take credit for that wisdom," he said, placing his hand over his heart, "but I cannot claim for my own that which the gods bestow upon us."

Tiberius shot him a poisonous look and Arrius narrowed his eyes to slits. But the council again broke into applause, and there were shouts from the rear: "Well done, Marcus," "Praise be to divine Augustus," and other things he couldn't make out.

Tiberius, his fists clenched, his face taut, looked like he was about to say something when Arrius Granius silenced him with a look. The tall, thin decurion rose and signaled Fabricius that he wanted to speak.

So, thought Marcus, Tiberius was merely an auxiliary skirmisher sent forward to soften us up. Now comes the main attack.

Fabricius raised his arms to quiet the council. "The honorable Arrius Granius has asked to address us, citizens."

The decurions immediately quieted down. Those who were standing retook their seats.

Arrius waited until the chamber was silent. "Noble citizens," he said, "I am gratified that Centurion Marcus Favonius Facilis has clarified this matter of a 'truce' with our enemies, the Lusitanians. Our award to him and his officers does poor justice to the depth of courage and intelligence displayed by the Second Century."

The speech was delivered quietly, with a thin smile, and what Marcus's father would have called "dangerous eyes": cold and intense.

Marcus glanced at Tiberius who was sitting stiffly on his bench, staring straight ahead. Marcus had outmaneuvered Arrius's first assault, and the man had instantly abandoned his tactic of challenging what had happened on the battlefield. The shift made Tiberius look like a fool, but Arrius was not one who paid much mind to the damage he did to others around him, even to his allies.

"I would now like to hear the centurion's plan for subjugating the Lusitanians," said Arrius. "It is, I believe, incumbent upon us to punish those who would challenge the Empire and wantonly murder our courageous soldiers. What do you have in mind for driving these rebels from their lands and for teaching them a lesson they will not soon forget?"

Marcus had to admire the man. Suffering a reverse on one front, he had immediately shifted the focus from the battle to the aftermath, certain that Marcus had more in mind than a simple military tactic when he allowed the Lusitanians to take their dead and wounded. Marcus also suspected that Arrius was always more interested in what happened now than in what happened in the meadow. He would have to be very careful. Arrius was a far more dangerous foe than Tiberius.

"I have indeed been thinking about this matter, senior decurion Arrius Granius," answered Marcus. "And I believe that this body could be most helpful in resolving this situation."

"It will be resolved through blood and fire, centurion," said Arrius.

Marcus pursed his lips thoughtfully. "Yes, certainly that is one solution, decurion," he answered. "And while I am under strict orders to proceed to Legio, I am willing to spend a few days helping you to organize auxiliaries to pursue these rebels."

"We have a single cohort of auxiliaries, centurion," snapped Arrius. "This is a matter for the Army."

"For the 'Army,' decurion? The people of Rome are the Army, as the Army is the people of Rome," said Marcus. Turning away from Arrius to address the council, he said, "I am sure that there are many of you who yearn for the glory of battle, for the honor of victory. And if not for yourselves, then for your sons."

He hesitated a moment, as if considering, then added, "This will be expensive, of course, but far less so than quartering several cohorts of the VII Legion here in Capera and Norba."

"We pay our taxes, centurion. We pay them so we may live in peace. Keeping that peace, I believe, is your job," said Arrius.

Marcus smiled at him. "Citizen Arrius. Surely you understand that taxes in peace and taxes in war are different matters. If you want a war on the Lusitanians, then who will pay for this war? Is it not fair that those who ask the Army to wage war, and who will reap its benefits, should also shoulder some of the burden?"

The remark about taxes caused a stir among the decurions, as any talk of taxes normally did.

Arrius was in a rage now. "You mock the power of the Emperor with this talk of taxes and auxiliaries," he said, pointing a finger at Marcus.

"Mock the power of the Emperor?" said Marcus quietly. "Do you think I won the Corona Vallaris by mocking my Emperor? Do you think I wear these phalerae on my harness because I disdain the power of the Empire?"

Marcus let his voice rise with each word, until he was speaking loudly enough for everyone to hear him. "The empire is not only about power, senior decurion Arrius Granius. It is also about laws. I have heard that citizens of Rome have had their lands seized without payment or compensation. Have you heard this as well, senior decurion?"

"The Lusitanians are a race of traitors!" shouted Arrius. "They must be exterminated like any vermin that poison the land."

Marcus suppressed a smile. He knew his comment on taxes and sending the decurions' sons into battle would give the council pause, and he had hoped to maneuver Arrius into losing his temper. Both had succeeded and he could now play the calm voice of reason. The gods had delivered Arrius into his hands.

But as he ruefully commented to himself later on, the Gods have their own plans.

Cassius Cornelius, his face sharp with anger, his fists clenched, one on the pommel of his long spatha sword, strode forward, pointing his finger at Arrius. "Traitors? You call us traitors? The traitors are those who flaunt the laws of Rome and steal our lands."

"'Our lands'? 'Us'? It seems as if you harbor a Lusitanian snake to your bosom, centurion," hissed Arrius. "Maybe this snake can tell us how it was that the First Century was taken by surprise. Maybe it was not a surprise. Maybe it was treachery."

By now the council was on its feet and rapidly spinning out of control. Decurions were shouting at Cassius and Marcus, shouting at one another, shouting at Arrius, or demanding that Fabricius take control of the meeting.

Cassius and Arrius were face to face, the short cavalryman looking up at the much taller senior decurion. Tiberius made a move toward Cassius until Sextus stepped between the two and gave the decurion a challenging look. Tiberius stepped back.

Two large and hard-faced men that Marcus took for bodyguards rose to Arrius's right, one of them slipping his hand into his tunic. Marcus was about to intervene when he saw

Demaratus move quickly to intercept them. Both were twice the Greek's size but there was something about the signifer's look that made them stop.

"Citizens, citizens," cried Fabricius, trying to quell the uproar. "Sit and calm yourselves." He may as well have called upon a storm to cease its thunder and lightning.

Marcus was shocked and angry that Cassius has disobeyed orders to remain silent, although he felt a certain sympathy for the young Lusitanian. However, just when Marcus was seizing the high ground, Cassius's outburst had leveled the battlefield.

"Cassius Cornelius," shouted Marcus. "Silence!"

The power of his voice muted the crowd, but not Cassius, who continued as if Marcus had said nothing. "Citizens," he cried, pointing his finger at Arrius's face, "here is your traitor. It was Arrius Granius's illegal seizure of land that led to this war. It was Arrius Granius's attack on women and children that drove the Lusitanians to take up arms. And now he asks that you should give up your sons and your gold to feed his rapacity."

Flavius stepped forward to silence Cassius, but Marcus signaled him to let the cavalryman continue. Arrius might have wealth and power, but Marcus judged that he was not overly popular. He let Cassius continue. "We may yet regain the high ground," he thought to himself.

"How dare you..." began Arrius, but Cassius was aflame with passion, and rode roughshod over the senior decurion.

"There is no reason for a war. Good citizens of Rome, would you not defend your homes and your lands from seizure? Are not all citizens of Rome accorded the same rights and privileges?" said Cassius, ignoring Arrius and speaking directly to the council.

"I demand that this child be silenced!" cried Arrius, turning to Fabricius who had left the dais and was now trying to separate the protagonists.

Cassius pushed him away, threw off his helmet, and stripped off his chain shirt. The armor dropped at his feet with a clatter. The sound silenced the decurions who were arguing with one another or demanding order. Grabbing his tunic with both hands, he ripped it from his chest, exposing a long, red scar that traced itself from his breast to his waist. "Child? Is this the mark a child bears, decurions?"

Putting his hands forward, he turned them up at the wrist, spreading his fingers. "These are the hands that buried my comrades where the First Century fell. Like me, my comrades were Lusitanians, Lusitanians who died for Rome, who fell that you might live in peace and prosperity. Tell me, do your children use their hands to bury their playmates?"

The drama of the scar and the hands had riveted the council. There was not a sound in the great hall. Even Arrius was silent. All eyes were on the cavalryman.

Seeing an opportunity, both Marcus and Fabricius moved quickly to defuse the situation. "Decurions, we have much business and this is a matter for the Army. Please calm yourselves and be re-seated," said Fabricius, while Marcus took Cassius by the arm and pulled him back from the confrontation with Arrius. His passion spent, Cassius was looking apprehensive.

Flavius reached down, retrieved the cavalryman's chain shirt and helmet and handed them to him.

Arrius, Tiberius, and a small circle surrounding them were still standing, but most the decurions re-seated themselves, although the buzz of conversation continued.

Fabricius caught Marcus's eye and indicated the curia door with his head. Marcus nodded agreement and motioned to his five officers. "Time to leave," he said quietly. The six departed, Marcus holding firmly to Cassius's arm, as the senior magistrate was still struggling to bring the council back to order.

XXVI

Demaratus and Timotheus were the last officers out of the curia. Demaratus watched Marcus quietly tell Cassius that he expected to see him as soon as they reached their temporary headquarters. Looking both crestfallen and slightly defiant, Cassius nodded silently and followed in the centurion's wake.

"Interesting," said Timotheus quietly in Greek.

"Marcus is rarely boring," replied Demaratus.

"Do you believe that the spirit of Augustus advised him about what to do on the battlefield?" asked Timotheus.

Demaratus shrugged. "I have never known him to put much faith in the gods before, but figuring out Romans can be like divining the future by examining sheep livers. Whether he believes it or not, it was a timely intervention by divine Augustus."

"He does not seem the rhetorician, but he took over that meeting from Arrius Granius and split the council. His comment on taxes and their sons struck home, but he has made a dangerous enemy," said Timotheus.

"How dangerous?" asked Demaratus.

"Arrius is the wealthiest man in this part of Hispania, and he has close ties with the provincial governor in Tarraco and some senators in Rome. The governor is married to his niece," replied the doctor.

"Does he bear a grudge?" asked Demaratus.

"Do you know a Roman who doesn't?" said Timotheus. "In this they are much like us."

"How will this play in Legio?" asked Demaratus.

Timotheus was a long time in answering. "I am not sure," he finally said. "The governor will probably side with Arrius, but then again, neither the governor nor the Legate wants a war right now. Things are much too unsettled in Rome, and the province might indeed have to shoulder the cost. That is why Marcus's point on taxes worked as well as it did."

"Arrius's Senate allies might demand one," replied Demaratus.

"They might," said Timotheus, "but rumor is that the Goths have begun to cross the Danuvius in force. The Senate and the army will be looking north, not west, and as dramatic as the destruction of the First Century seems to us, it is a trifle in the balance of the Empire."

"So all this thunder and lightning may be little more than a summer squall?" asked Demaratus.

"I would not go that far," answered Timotheus. "Marcus will still have to convince Legate Titus Valens that the Second Century did the right thing, and he will have to fend off the enmity of Arrius. But watching him this morning makes me think he may pull it off."

The two had lagged far behind the other officers and were in no rush to catch up. They strolled along together, quietly taking in Capera's morning traffic. Finally, the doctor asked Demaratus if he knew what Marcus would do about Cassius's disobeying orders.

"I think not a great deal," said Demaratus. "Did you notice that while he ordered Cassius to be silent, he also allowed him to continue? The young man's insubordination served him well."

"As I said, my friend," mused Timotheus, "altogether an interesting morning."

Cassius stood rigidly in front of a stern looking Marcus. Flavius had gone off so the two officers could be alone. For several minutes Marcus said nothing, the silence causing the cavalryman to sweat and fidget.

"When I give you a direct order, Cassius Cornelius, I expect you to follow it," he said quietly.

"Sir, I..." replied Cassius.

"Silence!" thundered Marcus. "Your tongue has gotten us into enough trouble this morning."

Cassius stiffened even further.

"The chain of command exists for a reason, acting commander," said Marcus, his voice once again quiet. "I cannot have a man in my ranks who does not listen to orders. Most specifically, I cannot have an officer who disobeys orders. Such an officer not only endangers those who serve under him, he puts all of us in grave peril. Do you understand why that is so, Cassius?"

"Yes, sir. I would never disobey a command in the field," answered Cassius.

"You must never disobey an order, ever," snapped Marcus. "Do you think the business of war is just about what happens on the battlefield? War is as much about politics as it is about fighting, and I was fighting a war in that council today. You, my own officer, gave our enemies an opportunity. What you did was no different than if you had refused to carry out an order in battle."

Cassius blanched. "Yes, sir," he answered, "I see that now. I will, of course, resign my temporary commission."

Marcus let him fidget some more. "That is not an option for you, Cassius. You do not avoid the consequences of insubordination by resigning. You are in the Roman army until your term is up. It is also a coward's way out."

Cassius flinched at the word, but remained silent.

"You are not a coward, Cassius. You have demonstrated that in battle. But you will carry the burden of your disobedience until you regain my trust," he said sternly. Marcus did not want to break the young man. He had the making of good officer.

To soften the rebuke, he changed the subject.

"Cassius, you made a charge about Arrius Granius in the council today," said Marcus.

"I am very sorry about that, sir," answered Cassius.

"You mean it was untrue?" asked Marcus.

Cassius hesitated. "No sir, I am sure it is true. I just never should have spoken like I did."

"On that we are in agreement, acting commander," said Marcus dryly. "But on what basis did you charge that Arrius Granius was responsible for the crisis in which we find ourselves? Speak freely."

"Yes, sir," answered Cassius. He hesitated, gathering his thoughts before he spoke. "When we arrived in Capera I went to the house of my second cousin. He is a horse merchant and deals in cattle. He is also a decurion and was sitting in the back of the curia this morning."

"Go on," ordered Marcus.

"Aulus—that is his name, sir—told me that Arrius Granius had been seizing land to the west of here, claiming that it was land without owners," said Cassius.

"Is that true?" asked Marcus.

"No, sir. It is true that there is no single owner of the land, but that is because the Lusitanians own land in common. Each band of horsemen controls a piece of land, and on that land they graze horses, cattle, and some sheep. They also gather firewood and hunt, and a few sow crops," answered Cassius.

Marcus pursed his lips. "Hmmm. That is much like the Britons. So, what else did your cousin say?"

"Arrius Granius has many retainers and slaves, sir. He has almost a private army, and he sent them to chase off the Lusitanians so he could graze his cattle. When some of the Lusitanians objected, his men attacked and killed several of them. And then...." Cassius hesitated.

"And then?" Marcus prompted.

"Aulus said there was a Lusitanian camp nearby. Arrius's men attacked it and killed thirty people, mostly women and children because the men were out herding horses and cattle. When the men returned to the camp and saw what had happened, they swore a blood oath to avenge the attack, and called on their kin to join them," explained Cassius.

"And now Arrius expects the army to come in and clean up what he began," said Marcus as much to himself as to Cassius.

Cassius nodded. "Yes, sir. And there is talk among my people that they will raise up another Viriathus if this becomes a war."

"Viriathus?" asked Marcus.

"Yes, sir. Viriathus led the Lusitanians against Rome, and destroyed the Praetor Vetilius and his entire army. For eight years he fought Rome until Rome was finally forced to make peace. When the Romans broke the peace, he defeated them again," said Cassius.

"What happened to him?" asked Marcus.

"The Romans could never defeat him in battle, so they paid three of his friends to assassinate him," answered Cassius.

"And when did this all happen?" asked Marcus.

Cassius thought for a moment. "Almost three hundred years ago, sir," he finally answered.

"You Lusitanians have long memories," observed Marcus.

Cassius shrugged. "Most Romans know about the wars with Carthage, and that was longer ago," he said.

"I asked for information, not your views of Romans," snapped Marcus.

"Yes, sir," said Cassius. "My tongue does get in my way. I will apply myself to silencing it."

Marcus nodded. "You are dismissed, acting commander. I trust I will never have to have a discussion with you again concerning orders."

"No, sir. You will not," answered Cassius, saluting.

A few minutes after he left, Flavius entered, to find Marcus sitting thoughtfully.

"Did it go all right, sir?" asked Flavius.

"What? Oh, yes, you mean Cassius. He is a good officer, just young and impulsive," answered Marcus, somewhat distractedly.

Flavius nodded, waiting. "Is there something you want me to do, sir?" he finally asked.

Marcus stared at him for almost a minute (Flavius had learned to wait patiently with Marcus). "Yes, optio. Yes, there is. Cassius has a cousin here in town by the name of Aulus. Find him for me and bring him here."

"Aulus," answered Flavius. "Yes, sir. Will this afternoon be satisfactory?"

Marcus nodded distractedly and reached for a wax tablet and a stylus.

Flavius had planned to change into a tunic and do some shopping before his bath, but instead he saluted and left to look for Cassius. He found the man in the stables and asked him to produce his cousin for Marcus.

Cassius looked apprehensive at the request and mumbled something about getting his cousin in trouble.

"This isn't a meeting about trouble, lad," said Flavius. "I don't know what you two talked about in there, but if I had to guess why he wanted to see your cousin it had something to do with the council meeting this morning."

"Oh. Yes, of course," said Cassius relaxing a little. "I will make sure my cousin is there."

Flavius nodded. He wanted to know more, but didn't want to show a junior officer that a mighty optio was totally in the dark about what was going on. Leaving, he found Demaratus headed back to their lodgings with several packages in his hands.

Flavius filled him in on what he knew, which was not much.

Demaratus, in turn, told Flavius about his discussion with Timotheus.

They both digested each other's information. Finally, Flavius said, "I think Marcus is gathering a case to present to the Legate in Legio."

Demaratus nodded agreement. "That would be the best explanation for why he wants to meet with Cassius's cousin. I wonder what Marcus said to him about his outburst this morning?"

"Well, Cassius still had his head on his shoulders and his hide on his back, so a good chewing out was probably all he got. What he did was wrong, but the lad can talk, can't he?" asked Flavius.

"That he can. He rode right over Arrius Granius with those theatrics about his scar. It was a smart move. I had thought Cassius too young for such a maneuver," replied Demaratus.

"Marcus waved me off from stopping him," said Flavius.

"I noticed," said Demaratus. " I wonder if Arrius did." Then shifting the subject, he asked, "What is our timetable?"

"We leave at first light," replied Flavius.

"We have an unfinished task," said Demaratus quietly.

"Right. Sextus. We will be too busy today, but we should be able to find time before we get to Legio," said Flavius.

Demaratus hurriedly dropped off his packages. Marcus was writing something and barely noticed. Both officers went off to gather Sextus and Cassius to make the final arrangements about leaving at dawn.

XXVII

The Favonius family had gathered at Tiberius's house where, as the oldest, he was outlining the grim news that had brought them all together. Gathered in the atrium was a restless and pacing Mamercus, Julia, who continually dabbed her eyes and looked like she might burst into tears at any moment, and her husband, Lucius.

"We are marked," said Tiberius. "My sources tell me that Philippus has a list of over 200 names marked for assassination, and some, if not all, of us are on that list."

Julia gave a little gasp and clutched her throat. "My boys, my boys" she choked out in a whisper.

"I do not know if it includes the children. I am sending Sabina away to her aunt in Reate," said Tiberius. "I suggest you send Julius and Sergius with her."

"Have we heard anything from Marcus?" asked Julia.

"No," answered Tiberius. "My sources say he is no longer in Italia. The less we know of his whereabouts, the better."

"What makes you think the children will be safe in Reate?" asked Mamercus, his voice laden with anger.

"We do not know," said Tiberius, "but I doubt the Praetorians will venture that far while the situation in the north remains uncertain. If Philippus defeats Decius, then nowhere will be safe. But for now, I think they will strike only those close at hand."

"Then we should all flee," put in Lucius.

"Each family member should do as he thinks proper, but if we remain—albeit in hiding—then we will be ready to greet Decius when he arrives. It will look better if the family remains in Rome," said Tiberius.

"Already thinking of that Senate seat, Tiberius?" said Mamercus, with just the hint of a sneer.

"Yes, I am," replied Tiberius. "Fortune requires risk, Mamercus. If we stand as supporters of Decius against Philippus, the emperor will reward our loyalty."

Mamercus snorted. "A lot of good his rewards will do if we are dead."

Tiberius shrugged. "Do as you wish, Mamercus. I will remain in Rome and pray for a proper outcome to the fighting in the north."

Julia had begun to weep silently.

"Oh, I have no intention of fleeing Rome, Tiberius," said Mamercus, "but I will not skulk about in hiding. Philippus has no support among the herd, and even the Praetorians are careful when they enter the city. I intend to surround myself with citizens."

"Bravely said," replied Tiberius, "but you have neither wife nor children. Your life is your own. Julia and I have others to think about."

"I say we challenge this 'list.' I say we denounce it from the steps of the Senate and demand our rights as citizens. It will bring the herd to us and they will be our shield," answered Mamercus.

Tiberius sighed. "Brother, that will simply get us killed. If you defy the power of the Praetorians, they will have no choice but to act. Their power is fear. A challenge to that power strikes at their core. For myself, I think they will not actively carry out these assassinations until they see the outcome to the fighting in the north. But if you provoke them, they will have no choice. If we send off the children and go into hiding, I think we will be safe."

Julia nodded in mute agreement.

"Do as you wish, Tiberius. I intend to defy this so-called emperor and his Praetorian thugs. If you will not accompany me to the Senate steps, I will go alone," said Mamercus.

"No, no, you must not do that, brother," said Julia. "You will draw attention to the family, and they will kill us all."

"Sister, our protection is the people of Rome. If we try to hide, the Praetorians will hunt us down and kill us one by one. They will not dare to strike us in public," answered Mamercus. "And if they attack me, they will find that the Favonius are not sheep." Reaching under his cloak, he drew out a gladis sword.

Turning to Tiberius, Julia sobbed, "Stop him, brother. He will be the death of us all." Lucius rather ineffectually patted her shoulder.

"Go if you insist, Mamercus," said Tiberius. "You are the

master of your own fate. But spare us the theatrics. Save them for the mob."

Mamercus threw his cloak over his shoulder, the drape concealing the sword he had slipped back into his belt. He kissed Julia, who tried to cling to his arm, and nodded at Tiberius. Turning, he swept dramatically out of the house followed by two slaves.

"Tiberius, stop him!" cried Julia.

"It is alright, sister. Mamercus will do what he will do. Now you must make preparations for sending the boys away. Hurry," answered Tiberius.

"But he will be our deaths" said Julia with a wail. "Our deaths!"

"Lucius, take my sister and make haste," said Tiberius, addressing his sister's husband for the first time. It was a cowardly way of getting rid of her, but he had preparations of his own to make. As Lucius drew Julia away, he considered what Mamercus had said. He had always found his brother's penchant for the drama annoying, but, in this case, it might serve. And if he were to die, that too might serve.

Mamercus, clutching his cloak about him to conceal his sword, strode through the streets, headed for the Senate. He had already composed the speech he would make to raise up the city against the Praetorians and prepare the way for Decius's triumphant entry to the city. And he, Mamercus, would have set the spark that lit the conflagration. Tiberius yearned for a Senate seat. Let him take his place among the old men. Mamercus would sit next to the new emperor, who would owe him for delivering Rome.

Deep in thought, his head down, he was crossing near the Circus Maximus when someone called out his name. "Mamercus Favonius."

Mamercus turned and froze. The crowd on his left parted, revealing a tesserarius of the Praetorian Guard, backed by a contubernium of soldiers.

"You are Mamercus Favonius?" asked the tesserarius.

"Why is it the business of the Praetorian Guard to ask this question of a free citizen?" answered Mamercus in a voice loud enough to start attracting a crowd.

"My tribune wishes to speak with you, sir," replied the Tesserarius.

"A 'wish to speak' request requires a squad of soldiers?" said Mamercus. "If I wish to speak to a free citizen, I send him a polite note."

This raised a chuckle from the crowd that was beginning to gather.

"I have my orders, sir," said the tesserarius.

"They are not my orders, Praetorian. Tell your Tribune that I am on my way to the Senate, and that if he wishes to speak with me, he can find me there," said Mamercus in a voice aimed at the crowd. "Now, stand aside."

By now the crowd had grown to nearly a hundred people.

The tesserarius eyed the crowd. "I am ordered that you will accompany me, sir. In the name of the Empire, I require it.

"In the name of the Empire? Or in the name of the Arab?" shouted Mamercus. The jibe at Philippus raised a laugh, and a few in the crowd shouted, "Tell the Arab to go back to Mauretania," and even "Down with the Praetorians."

"Am I under arrest?" Mamercus asked the officer.

The tesserarius looked uncomfortable. "I have no warrant for you, sir, but I have my orders."

Turning to the crowd, Mamercus cried out, "Citizens! Is this what Rome has come to? That a man on his rightful business, a man on his way to the Senate, that speaks for the people of the Empire, should be taken away without even a warrant? Are we ruled by laws or by the sword?" Turning to the tesserarius he said calmly, "If I am under arrest, I demand to see my warrant and what I am charged with. If I am not, then be gone and bother me not."

The tesserarius looked grim. "I have my orders, sir." Turning to the squad of eight men, he motioned two of them forward. "Take him," he said.

The two men stepped forward, but Mamercus pushed them both away. "I warn you, Praetorian. I will not stand for this violation of the rights of a free citizen."

The officer drew his sword and put its point to Mamercus's breast. "You will come with me, sir."

With his left arm, Mamercus shoved the sword aside. Reaching across his body with his right hand, he drew the gladis out. The tesserarius stepped back, but one of the Guard drew his sword and stabbed at Mamercus. "Stop," cried out the tesserarius to the legionnaire, but Mamercus warded off the thrust, stepped inside the man's guard and drove his sword into the Praetorian's neck. A fountain of blood gushed out.

Pushing back the mortally wounded Praetorian, Mamercus stabbed at the tesserarius, wounding the man in his left arm. The officer struck back, driving his blade into Mamercus's chest. The other seven Praetorians immediately drew their swords and attacked the now staggering Mamercus. Badly wounded, he flailed at them, inflicting a minor cut on one of the men, before going down in a storm of swords.

The soldiers surrounded the body, which twitched and then fell still. "Alright, pick him up and bring him along," said the tesserarius. Two men leaned down to grab Mamercus under the arms, but a stone slammed one of them in the helmet, and he staggered back.

"Who did that," said the officer, turning on the crowd and leveling his sword at them. A rock hit him square in the chest, while another glanced off his shoulder.

"Leave him be, murderers" a man cried out from the back of the crowd. More rocks rained down on the soldiers, who dodged and twisted to avoid them. None of them had shields.

"Stand back," shouted the tesserarius, but the crowd had grown menacing and considerably larger. A large piece of paving stone struck one of the men on the leg, knocking him off his feet.

"Close up and retreat," shouted the tesserarius. "Take Antonius with you."

Two men reached down and grabbed the now dead legionnaire by the arms, dragging him backwards as the others held their swords at the ready, their faces to the crowd, and backed away. More stones followed, but no one wanted to fight the soldiers. Instead, the crowd surged around the body of Mamercus.

There were now close to 1,000 people milling around the Circus, and the Praetorians beat a hasty retreat to the jeers of the crowd.

Several men lifted up Mamercus and bore him away.

XXVIII

The Second Century departed Capera in the chill of a late fall morning, with the threat of rain moving in from the north. But even though the men faced ten more days of hard marching, they were anxious to leave the city behind, a sentiment Marcus and his officers shared. Home was in the offing, and like horses headed for their own stables, the men picked up their pace and the miles rolled away.

The country north of Capera is rolling hills dotted with enormous boulders. The land climbs from the plains toward higher mountains as the Via Plata slices to the northeast. It was unfamiliar geography to Marcus, Flavius, and Demaratus, so Sextus turned tourist guide again.

"These are called the 'Black Mountains,'" he said as the Century trudged toward a distant pass, and the description was, if anything, an understatement. The hilly terrain consisted mostly of enormous black and gray sheets of slate piled one on the other. The stone was the primary building material, so that it dominated not only the landscape, but the color of the towns as well.

Demaratus found it depressing, particularly since rain had begun to dog their progress. The palette of gray skies, black mountains, and gray towns at times made it difficult to discern the ground from the horizon.

For the first two days Flavius and Demaratus had been trying to find a few moments to corner Sextus, but the time never seemed right, or one or the other of them was engaged in duties that kept them apart.

The Century finally breached the last pass and found itself descending into Hispania's vast central plateau. After the confining geography of mountains and valleys, the two officers found the massive, seemingly endless expanse of grass and rolling hills vaguely disconcerting. It was as if they had been suddenly set adrift in an enormous inland ocean of rolling yellow hills crowned by oak trees. The mountains receded and then vanished, devoured by the vastness of the tableland.

Once they were free of the mountains, however, the opportunities for getting Sextus aside increased.

The Century had just finished a long day on the road and went into camp a half day out from Elmantica. Everyone was tired, but the prospect of good food, dry barracks and a decent bath had energized the men, and they threw up a marching camp in record time.

Sextus had just finished making sure his sentries were in place when Flavius and Demaratus intercepted him as he headed for the officers' tents.

"Comrade," said Flavius, "come walk with us." The comment was delivered as a friendly request.

Flavius and Demaratus led the way out of camp to a low knoll topped by a scatter of boulders and a great spreading oak. Even in late fall, the sun had a brassy fierceness to it that one avoided if possible.

The three stood under the shade of the great tree's bole and silently examined one another. Sextus looked uncertain, as well he should, having been called aside by two superior officers. "Sirs?" he asked somewhat tentatively.

Flavius took the lead. "During that dustup in the council, Sextus, one of those decurions talked about Gnaeus. Called him a fine officer. You remember that?"

"Yes, sir," replied Sextus.

"Gnaeus got a lot of good men killed back in that meadow, so I can't say as I would call him a fine officer," said Flavius, taking off his helmet and running his hand through his hair. "But it occurred to me that maybe there was a time he was. You don't normally get to be a primus pilus unless you are a pretty good soldier. Did something happen to him in Mauretania?"

Sextus was silent for a bit, gathering his thoughts. Flavius was doing his best to appear casual, but underneath the relaxed pose, he looked tense. Demaratus had not said a word, but he was examining Sextus intently.

"Something happened to all of us, sir," the tesserarius finally replied.

"Tell us about it," said Flavius quietly.

"Do you know what our orders were while we were in Mauretania, sir?" asked Sextus.

Flavius silently indicated "No."

"We went to reinforce the III Augustus, which had two cohorts in Tingus. Most of the Third was stationed in Numidia and near Carthage. Tribesmen from the mountains had taken to raiding the coast and had made the road between Tingus and Carthage dangerous. Our job was to help the III Legion defeat the tribesmen and reopen the road," said Sextus.

"What went wrong?" It was the first time Demaratus had spoken.

"Everything, sir. The III Augustus was more interested in what was going on in Rome than it was fighting tribesmen. The Legion wanted to remain concentrated in case something like a civil war broke out," answered Sextus, adding, "although I was just a soldier in the ranks then, and this is all second hand."

"Go on," said Flavius.

"The two cohorts in Tingus were understrength, and mostly green troops," continued Sextus. "Our two centuries ended up doing most the fighting, if you could call it that," said Sextus.

"You came back with many wounded," said Demaratus. "That sounds like there was a good deal of fighting."

"More came back sick than wounded, sir," said Sextus. "There was fighting, but it was like dueling with the wind. The tribesmen were all mounted, and the best horsemen I ever laid eyes on."

Demaratus nodded agreement. "Numidian cavalry very nearly destroyed Rome. Those who have fought it say not even the Parthians can match it."

"I don't know about Parthians, sir, but those Mauretanian horsemen make the Lusitanians look like foot soldiers. We could never catch them, and they struck at us whenever they pleased," said Sextus. "If we broke up into small units to chase them, they would ambush the units and be gone by the time reinforcements could get there."

"What about your own auxiliary cavalry?" asked Flavius.

"Useless, sir. They just didn't want to fight, not that I entirely blame them. That tribal cavalry was about as tough and mean as you could get," answered Sextus. "The fact our cavalry wouldn't fight was one of the reasons that Gnaeus was so down on cavalry, sir."

"So a lot of marching and small skirmishes was the way it was?" said Flavius.

"Yes, sir. But what brought the centuries down was the sickness," said Sextus.

"When we got to Corduba, a lot of you were still recovering," said Demaratus.

"And we buried a lot who never came home," said Sextus. "It seemed like everyone was sick in their bowels, or had that fever that runs hot and cold and makes you see things that aren't there."

"This is when Gnaeus got sick?" asked Flavius.

Sextus hesitated. "Not exactly, sir."

The optio frowned. "What do you mean by that? Did Gnaeus get sick after he got home?"

"No, sir," answered Sextus, "he got sick in Mauretania."

"Explain yourself, tesserarius," said Flavius.

Sextus was quiet for a long time, as if steeling himself. "That's when all this Christian business came up, sir," he finally said.

"Go on," said Demaratus quietly.

"There are lots of Christians in Mauretania, sir. They are very strong because they ended a drought," Sextus continued.

Both Flavius and Demaratus glanced at one another.

"What does a drought have to do with Gnaeus getting sick?" asked Flavius.

"Nothing, sir. It is just that Christians are magicians, and they can make things happen. They lay their hands on you and can make you get better. They have a way of driving evil spirits out of your body, the spirits that cause sickness," said Sextus. "This Jesus that the Christians worship was a powerful magician. He even made a dead person come to life, and he cured all kinds of diseases, even leprosy."

Demaratus smiled slightly. "Everyone claims their gods cure disease, Sextus."

"Yes, sir, I know, but the Christians say their god is more powerful than any of the others," replied Sextus. "And that is how the trouble started with our centurion."

Flavius nodded for him to continue.

Once again Sextus took a moment to gather himself. "So many of the men were sick that our centurion, Mamercus Rutilius, called in some Christian magicians. Gnaeus got angry and challenged Mamercus, said he was undermining divine Augustus."

Both Demaratus and Flavius looked puzzled. "I don't understand, Sextus," said Flavius. "So long as we give a stipendia to glorious Augustus, who or what we believe in is no one else's business but our own. Why would Gnaeus care?"

Sextus looked uncomfortable. "The Christian god doesn't tolerate other gods, sir. The Christians say there is only one god, and if you don't believe in him, the magic won't work. Gnaeus said that belief undermined the Empire."

"Well, he wasn't all crazy," said Demaratus quietly. "But what does this have to do with the primus pilus getting sick?"

"He got sick because the Christian god punished him for not believing," said Sextus.

"What?" asked Flavius incredulously.

"Yes, sir. Gnaeus challenged the Christian magicians. He said he would make a sacrifice to Augustus, Strenia, and Carna and make the men better. Instead, he got sick," said Sextus. "The magicians said this showed that the Christian god was more powerful than all the other gods, and that he punished those who did not believe in him."

"And did the Christian magicians cure the men?" asked Flavius.

"Those who believed, sir," answered Sextus.

"Wait a moment," said Flavius. "You mean everyone who said he believed in this Christian god got better? And those who didn't stayed sick?"

Sextus looked uncomfortable. "Everyone said they believed in the Christian god, sir, so they could get better."

"So, some people stayed sick?" said Flavius.

"Yes, sir," said Sextus.

"Then the Christian god didn't cure everyone, even if they believed in him, right?" Flavius asked.

"The magicians said that the ones who didn't get better just said they believed in the Christian god, but really didn't, so they weren't cured," said Sextus.

"And how did the magicians determine this, Sextus?" asked Flavius.

"Those who got better were sincere, those who didn't were not. That is what the Christians said," answered Sextus.

Demaratus chuckled. "Take the credit, accept none of the blame. With that philosophy I wonder why all doctors and emperors are not Christians?"

"And you believe this, tesserarius?" asked Flavius.

"I don't know, sir," answered Sextus. "I wanted the men to get better, but none of us wanted Gnaeus to get sick. It was the sickness and the curse that made him the way he was at the end. He wasn't like that before he got sick and the Christian god punished him. A lot of the men didn't like that."

"But Mamercus became a Christian?" said Demaratus.

"Yes, sir," answered Sextus. "But not all the men in the Second Century went along with that. It was just that when they arrested Mamercus the men were unhappy. He was a good officer and brave as they come."

"I am curious, Sextus," said Demaratus. "Are people Christians because their god cures sickness?"

"Not just because of that, sir," answered Sextus. "If you believe in the Christian god, you have everlasting life in a place called paradise."

Flavius looked blank. "You mean like the Elysian Fields?"

Demaratus answered. "No, not the same thing. Homer said that man had a soul and that it goes to the Elysian Fields if he dies in honorable combat, but no one knows what he meant. It is different than this Christian paradise. The Christians believe in life after death, like the Egyptians."

"Yes, sir, and only Christians can go there. A lot of the men find that pretty attractive," said Sextus. "What they don't like is that you can only believe in this one god."

"Well, Jews believe that. Aren't Christians just a kind of Jew?" Flavius asked Demaratus.

"They began as Jews, but they are very different now," answered Demaratus. "And unlike the Jews, they believe everyone should be a Christian."

Sextus nodded agreement. "They say everyone is the same. It doesn't matter if you are slave or free, rich or poor, everyone should be a Christian. They say if you don't believe, you will be punished, and if you do, you will be rewarded and have everlasting life."

Flavius gave him a considered look. "Do these Christians have any proof of this place called 'paradise'?" asked Flavius.

Sextus shrugged. "They say you have to believe."

"Neat answer," said Flavius cynically. "And they don't tolerate other gods?"

"No, sir. One of the Christian apostles—I forget which one—went to the temple of Artemis at Ephesus and prayed that his god would cast out the demon. And the alter of Artemis split in half," said Sextus.

"Did you see this?" asked Flavius.

"No, sir. I have never been out of Hispania except to go to Mauretania. It was what the Christians told us," answered Sextus.

By then the shadows had grown long in the short fall day, and a chill had begun to creep into the late afternoon.

"Well, that explains a few things about Gnaeus," said Flavius.

"Yes, sir," said Sextus, then hesitated, adding, "The Second Century is loyal, sir. There was never any danger of a mutiny. That was an exaggeration. The men were just sick, exhausted and frustrated, and arresting our centurion gave them a focus for their anger. They are good men, sir."

"We know that, Sextus," said Flavius. "We stood with them in the meadow. I never questioned the men, but we are new to the First Cohort and we need to know more about what happened in Mauretania. We appreciate your honesty in this whole matter."

"Of course, sir. We are fellow officers," answered Sextus. "Is there anything else, sir? If not, I want to make one more round before dinner."

"No, go right ahead," said Flavius with a wave. "We will see you at dinner."

Flavius and Demaratus stood, watching Sextus head for the nearest outpost.

"What's a demon?" said Flavius.

"I am not sure myself," answered Demaratus. "Some kind of monster. The Christians don't just believe in a paradise; they believe there is a place you go to be punished as well. I think these demons live there. They also believe demons enter people's body and cause sickness. The Christians lay their hands on people and drive the demons out."

Flavius gave him a long look. "You seem to know a lot about Christians. Do you believe this nonsense?"

"There are Christians in Greece, and some of their god's disciples were Greek, or so it is said," replied Demaratus. "Do I believe them about demons and paradise? I tend to believe what

I can see and feel, Flavius. I think we have one life to live. Does anything happen afterwards?" He shrugged.

"How can someone believe in this paradise stuff if they have never seen it?" asked Flavius.

"Have you ever seen divine Augustus? Or Fortuna? Yet we pray and sacrifice to both," said Demaratus.

Flavius shook his head. "That's different. We don't say if you don't believe in Augustus or Fortuna that some demon is going to get you."

"True," said Demaratus. "I find that part of their belief system distasteful. The Jews also believe their god is the one and true god, but they don't insist everyone else should believe that. In fact it is no simple task to become a Jew."

"Their one and true god didn't do the Jews much good," said Flavius brutally. "We scattered them to the four corners of the Empire."

Demaratus, still studying the departing Sextus, nodded. "And yet they still believe. In that sense these Christians are much like Jews."

"The more I hear about Christians, the more I think they are trouble," said Flavius.

Demaratus nodded. "You may be right in this matter, Flavius. I certainly know what I believe."

"And what would that be?" asked Flavius.

"That I am hungry," replied Demaratus with a grin.

"Then we should offer up a sacrifice to your belief," answered Flavius with a smile.

With the first moments of twilight settling over the land, the two men headed back to their tent.

Sextus kept turning the discussion with Demaratus and Flavius over in his mind. Their questions on what happened in Mauretania were understandable. They had apparently not been briefed in Tarraco or, more likely, Tarraco had no idea what had happened to the two centuries of the First Cohort when they went across the straits as vexilla.

But their ignorance about Christians puzzled him. They may, of course, have been playing dumb to see where Sextus's allegiances lay, but he did not think so.

This train of thought caused Sextus to circle back to the subject of who his officers were and why they were here. Nothing they said to him in the recent discussion gave him a clue, but Sextus had learned patience in the ranks. Information was like wine: the more it aged, the better it got.

XXIX

Aulus Nonius stood at attention while Praetorian Tribune Antonius Nonius skimmed the scroll in front of him. "Is this all you have?" he asked glancing up"

"Yes, sir. The messenger who brought the scroll knew nothing about its contents," answered the secretary.

The Tribune leaned back in his chair, tenting his hands over his chest. "Read it Aulus," he said.

The secretary retrieved the scroll and read it through, frowning by the end.

"What do you make of it?" asked Antonius.

"It would seem the two men had a falling out and killed each other. Apparently, they had spent the day drinking at a taverna. They were found with their weapons stuck in one another," he answered.

"Yes, so it would seem," said Antonius, "but what about the man they left the taverna with?"

"There is no mention of him after they left, sir. Do you think he killed our men?" replied Aulus.

"Maybe, or maybe he led our men into a trap," said Antonius.

The secretary shrugged. "They were both violent men, sir. I don't find it unlikely that they might have had a falling out."

"Possible, but the thin man dominated the big one. I can't imagine the lout challenging him," replied the Tribune,

"So, you think they were murdered, sir?" asked Aulus.

The Tribune was silent for a moment. "I don't know, but I am not about to let the deaths of two Praetorians pass by so quietly."

"They were not very good examples of Praetorians, sir," said the secretary.

"No, Aulus, they were not. Indeed, they were scum."

"Then what is the problem, sir?" asked Aulus.

The Tribune handed the scroll to the secretary. "They were our scum, Aulus, and the Praetorians take care of their own, even two men like these."

"So, what do we do?" asked Aulus.

"Nothing for now," replied Antonius. "The family of this centurion is marked for assassination, but they are in good favor with Decius. We do not know how that matter will come out."

"What should I do with this scroll, sir?" asked Aulus.

"File it, but we will keep it in our minds," said the Tribune. "Things may be different in the future."

"Yes, sir," said the secretary, taking up the scroll and leaving the office.

The Tribune rose and paced a little. This was the second time the Favonius family had wounded the Praetorians. He had no doubt but that his men in Hispania had been murdered. He had underestimated the centurion and his two officers. He cared not a whit for the two thugs. But this Hispania incident was now piled atop the recent debacle over the attempt to arrest the brother of one of the centurions. The Praetorians had now lost three men to this Favonius family, and that could not be allowed to stand. There was nothing to be done now, but Tribune Antonius Clodius was not about to forget or forgive this challenge to the Praetorian Guard.

XXX

Elmantica had the feel of a Roman city built over an earlier town. Like Emerita, the entrance to the town was over a long bridge spanning a river, and he city was centered around a forum and a theater, with temples crowning the rise at its center. But there was a vaguely un-Roman feel to the city's layout, some of it precise and Roman, the rest a meandering sprawl.

As there was no business going on during the Festival of Luna, a large crowd had turned out to greet the Century. The cover had been removed from the Mundus, releasing the spirits of the underworld to roam the world of the living. Until the ritual pit was covered again, people closed up shop to focus on both public and private rituals to appease the ancestors.

It was a solemn festival, and no business meant no taverns, so the Century would have to do with barracks food and wine. Normally the men would have considered it bad timing to arrive during Luna, but with less than a week to go before reaching Legio, virtually nothing could dampen their mood.

Almost as soon as they had arrived at the sprawling but somewhat rundown barracks at the north end of town, Sextus managed to corner Flavius and Demaratus so that he could lecture them about the history of Elmantica.

"You may have noticed that the city has a very different feel than Emerita," said Sextus pedantically.

Both Flavius and Demaratus nodded, doing their best not to look long suffering.

"It was the center of Celtic life in this area and dates back long before the wars with Carthage," Sextus lectured. "In fact, Hannibal himself besieged and took the city."

"Really?" responded Flavius in a voice that suggested Hannibal's conquest of the city was not foremost in his mind. But Sextus was tone deaf when it came to what he considered his duty to further the education of his fellow officers.

"Yes. It is said that he took three months to take the city," Sextus continued. "I can show you some of the Carthaginian ruins if you like, and point out how the older parts of the city still retain the imprint of the Celts."

Marcus saved them.

The centurion poked his head out of the officers' quarters and called for Flavius and Demaratus. "And Sextus, would you see that the animals get properly fed and watered?"

"Yes, sir," answered Sextus, saluting. As he turned to leave, he said to Flavius and Demaratus, "Maybe later I can give you a tour."

"Maybe," answered Flavius, muttering under his breath once Sextus had gotten out of earshot, "but not if I can avoid it."

Demaratus gave him a grin. "Sextus just wants us to know how important Hispania is. Someday I will take you to the parts of Greece you have never visited."

Flavius gave him a level stare. "I think maybe I will give up travel."

The two found Marcus at a small desk surrounded by piles of notes, wax tablets, and scrolls.

He waved them to chairs after they had saluted.

Marcus stared at the table for a while, as if gathering his thoughts, then looked up. "We will be in Legio in less than a week."

Neither Flavius nor Demaratus said anything since there was no reason to respond to the obvious.

Marcus pushed himself up from the table and began to pace. "We do not know what our reception will be, nor if what we left in Rome has followed us to Hispania."

Again, there was nothing to say, although both men were thinking that Rome had already followed them to Hispania. It had just not survived Segunto and an encounter with Demaratus.

"I want one thing clear: I ordered you to come to Hispania with me and, as my officers, you had no choice in the matter. What happened in Rome was my doing, not yours. Is that clear?" Marcus asked.

"We are all in this together, sir," replied Flavius. Demaratus nodded in agreement.

Marcus put his hands on the desk, and leaned toward the two men. "We are not in this together. I appreciate your loyalty and I honor our friendship, but it was my family that brought this on us, and it is my problem, not yours. If there is trouble when we get to Legio, you are not to support me, and you are to deny you had any knowledge of why I ordered you to come with me." He added, "This is a direct order, gentlemen."

"We will, of course, follow your orders, sir," answered Flavius, "but there is a problem in denying I had nothing to do with our coming to Hispania. I procured the orders through my cousin, sir, and either he or the prefect, Gaius Gallineus, may affirm that. I told Gaius that if we got caught we would say we made up the orders ourselves (this was the first time Flavius had mentioned this fact and both Marcus and Demaratus looked startled). The only one in the clear, sir, is Demaratus here," he said, indicating the signifer with his shoulder.

"What?" asked Marcus after a pause. "The orders are forged?"

"No, sir, not forged. The Legate signed them. The question is, did he have the power to do that?" replied Flavius with a shrug.

Marcus sat down, rubbing his temples.

"The way I look at it, sir, is we had no choice. I am just worried about what I promised Gaius," Flavius continued.

Demaratus looked thoughtful. "Would the new Emperor consider your family and the legate of the Vigiles an ally?"

Marcus looked up and nodded. "I believe so."

"So, the Praetorians may be careful how they proceed. Settling old scores may not be as important as settling new ones. On top of which, sir, your victory at the meadow means they cannot act in secret," continued the signifer. "At least in Hispania you have too high a profile for a secret assassination, and an arrest might be seen as an attack on a family allied to the new Emperor."

"That is all speculation, signifer," said Marcus.

"Yes, sir, I know that. But had Flavius not acted as he had, we would all likely be dead. Whether a legate of the Vigiles has the power to make such an assignment is an argument that is only relevant if the Praetorians want to pursue a hero connected with an influential family. My knowledge of the Praetorians suggests to me they will not do so."

"And Gaius?" asked Marcus.

"If they don't pursue it, we won't be asked. If we are, we tell the truth: we were fleeing a criminal disguised as an Emperor, and any efforts we took to avoid allowing the criminal Philippus to weaken the Roman army was justified, including forgery. It is the kind of battlefield ruse the Romans are famous for," answered Demaratus.

Flavius gave a low whistle. "Impressive, signifer."

Demaratus shrugged. "We Greeks invented rhetoric."

Marcus sighed. "Your logic is impeccable, Demaratus. But logic does not dictate what happens in life. Flavius saved us all, I agree, which is why I am giving you both the following order." Straightening up and shifting to a formal voice he said, "Flavius Priscus, optio of the Second Century, if we are asked about our orders, you will testify that I ordered you to manufacture those orders," said Marcus. "You will, of course, tell the authorities Demaratus was ignorant of the entire matter."

There was silence, until Marcus's odd sense of humor broke it. "If you like, optio, you can tell the authorities that Demaratus didn't know anything because I don't trust Greeks."

"Neither do Greeks," Demaratus deadpanned.

The three laughed.

Marcus got serious again. "I need you both to affirm my orders. Lately I seem to collect officers who think orders are just arguing points."

Flavius sighed. "Yes, sir. I will carry out that order."

"Demaratus?" said Marcus.

"Yes, sir," answered the Greek.

"All right," said Marcus. "Now, optio. Are we ready for to-morrow?"

"Yes, sir. First light," answered Flavius.

Dismissed, the two men left the room and headed for the baths.

"He knows something we do not," said Demaratus.

"Why do you say that?" asked Flavius.

Demaratus shrugged. "A hunch. I think there was something behind that speech, something he is not telling us. Maybe Gnaeus told him something in Corduba."

Flavius nodded. "You may be right. I have no intention of following that order."

"Nor I," said Demaratus.

Flavius put a restraining arm across Demaratus's chest. "This is truly not your fight, comrade. Neither Marcus nor I have to lie to put you in the clear. There is no reason for you to sacrifice yourself."

"If Marcus is taken in Legio, do you really think they will pat us on the back and send us off to the barracks?" said Demaratus. "The Praetorians I met in Segunto had orders to kill us all. This has nothing to do with truth or justice, Flavius. I am not going to follow orders because all it means is that I will be led to my execution quietly."

Flavius was silent for a bit. "You are right, of course. So we go down fighting. At least that way we preserve our honor."

Demaratus said nothing, which Flavius took for agreement. In fact, the Greek had decided that he would desert at the first sign of trouble and head for Tarraco. He liked Flavius and

Marcus, but he had no intention of dying for an empire that was not even his own.

The remainder of the march was eventless, but the closer the century got to Legio, the faster it stepped out. By the end, Marcus was having a difficult time staying at the front of the column.

There had been a short ceremony when the Second Century arrived and Marcus had formally handed over the signum of the First Century to the Legate, Titus Valens. The Legate had spoken warmly of the Second Century, but it was a pro forma, formulaic welcome, and gave no hint of any potential trouble for Marcus, Flavius, and Demaratus. As the century broke up to head for the baths, the Legate took Marcus aside for a moment.

"I want your report on my desk tomorrow morning, centurion. Will that be enough time to prepare it?" he asked.

"Yes, sir. I have been working on it as we marched, sir. I will send it first thing in the morning," replied Marcus.

Titus nodded, his face expressionless, and left. There was nothing in his attitude that indicated either hostility or friendliness. While Marcus worked on his report, Demaratus slipped out and found Timotheus unpacking supplies and putting his office at the valetudinarium in order.

"Greetings, Timotheus," Demaratus said in Greek.

"And to you, comrade. Are you ill?" asked the doctor.

"No. I just wanted to know what you were going to do with those letters from Corduba," answered Demaratus.

Timotheus smiled. "Already taken care of, Demaratus. As soon as I arrived, I sent them around to Titus, along with my report on the dead, wounded and injured. I wrote up my report when we were in Capera."

Demaratus said nothing. Then, finally, "Have you heard anything?"

Timotheus shook his head, "Nothing, which is not surprising. The loss of the First Century has been the only topic of discussion since I arrived. I do know that the battle in the meadow is well thought of."

Demaratus nodded. What he could not do was to ask the real question on his mind: were there any rumors about Marcus, Flavius, and himself?

He was too restless to return to the barracks, where he found Marcus's tension about his report impossible to be around. Instead, he wandered out the Via Praetoria to a taverna in the vicus, the settlement that had sprung up around the Legion's fort. He would wait until Marcus went to his afternoon meeting before slipping in and packing some clothes and equipment. He would make sure that Aura was saddled and ready.

Flavius wanted to be helpful, but he was too tense and nervous to sit still. He finally asked Marcus if he was needed, and the centurion, somewhat exasperatedly, waved him to go.

The optio made a direct line to the baths, checking out the lockers to see if there were any fellow optios in residence. Seeing three uniforms, he stripped and joined them.

He found the three men throwing dice in the steam room and introduced himself. They put aside their gambling and all four exchanged service records. It turned out one of the optios was first cousin of a man Flavius had served with in Britannia.

Service records turned to gossip and finally one man asked Flavius to describe the battle in the meadow.

Flavius was a good storyteller, and the three men were entranced by the drama of hurried deployment and the charge.

"Javelins?" an optio named Manlius Valeranus asked with a skeptical arch of his eyebrow.

Flavius shrugged and spread his hands. "My centurion has some odd ideas, but they work. We didn't lose a man."

"Hard to argue with that," said another.

"So, tell us a little about this centurion of yours," said Manlius, who being close to Flavius's age, was the senior of the three.

"He won a Corona Vallaris fighting the Ordovices," said Flavius. "He's a winner, and the men like him."

The three digested that for a moment, and then Manlius asked about the First Century.

Flavius was careful here, feeling his way with the three officers, not sure what they thought of Gnaeus. "Well, it looked like the Lusitianians caught them at dawn before most of them were out of their tents."

There was a long moment of silence. "How could cavalry get in among the tents?" asked Cassius Dentatus, the youngest of the optios.

"No marching camp," said Flavius.

"What?" said an incredulous Manlius.

"Aye," said Flavius, "and no sentries, not that they would have done much good against a cavalry charge."

The three optios glanced at one another, and then Cassius said, "Why weren't the two centuries together?"

"Gnaeus gave us a bunch of merchants to escort and always

kept a day ahead of us," answered Flavius. "We'd have ended up the same way if it hadn't been for that young cavalryman who warned us in the nick of time."

Manlius shook his head. "Gnaeus wasn't like that when he left for Mauretania. He was always a bit stiff with the men and a stickler for discipline, but he knew how to handle a unit in the field. Not building a marching camp," he said, letting the sentence trail off.

"A lot of good men gone," said Cassius quietly.

"Aye. We've all lost men, but not like that," said the third optio.

There was a long, comradely silence among the four men. Manlius finally said, "Well, welcome, Flavius. The VII can use some experience right now."

"What's with that Greek?" chimed in Cassius. "I am not sure I ever heard of a Greek signifer."

"He's a good man in a fight, comrades," said Flavius.

"Oh, I never faulted Greeks in a fight, but they can be a pain in the ass with their ways. Always thinking they are better," said the third optio, who Flavius had finally figured out was called Aemilius.

Flavius shrugged, then grinned. "Some of them are," a remark that raised a chuckle from the other optios. "Demaratus is Greek, all right, a sailor by profession. But he got us through a storm at sea, and he stood like Horatius at the bridge in the fight with the Lusitanians," adding, "and he is a good friend."

The last comment ended the discussion on Demaratus.

"So, who takes over as Primus Pilus now?" asked Aemilius.

There was a momentary freeze in the conversation, and Manlius shot the junior optio an angry look.

"Oh, it's okay, Manlius," said Flavius, catching the silent exchange, "I would be very interested in what you three think about the whole matter. It seems a kind of delicate business to me."

Manlius relaxed and pursed his lips. "Maybe not so delicate," he said. "You know much about the First Cohort?"

Flavius shook his head. "Only that the Corduba centuries had a rough time in Mauretania, and that there was some trouble with the centurion of the second."

"Well, the First Cohort has," Manlius paused thinking about how to put it, "a leadership problem" he finally added.

Flavius said nothing, waiting for an explanation.

"With Gnaeus dead, there are four centurions in the cohort, counting your Marcus," Manlius said, which was information Flavius already had: a first cohort always had double-sized centuries, but five instead of six.

"There is the Third Century in Barcino, and two here not counting your Second," Manlius continued. "Publius Fulvius commands the Third, but he is just marking time until he can get back to Rome. His father is a Senator and has plans for him. No loss when he goes."

"Aulus Junius is with the Fourth, and Cerficius Nonius is with the Fifth. Good soldiers, but just pups," said Manlius. "Both of them are from the south. One's from Corduba and the other Gades. Their families are big merchants and that's why they got whisked up the ranks so fast. For all that, they're both competent. But your Marcus is senior even if he is from another legion."

There was a long moment of silence, which Flavius broke

by changing the subject and asking about the tribunes. This shifted the conversation to standard gossip, and since optios were the source of most the gossip in the army, it was a long, leisurely bath.

XXXI

Marcus stood in the paved, colonnaded courtyard of the Legio Principia, with offices to his left and right. Behind the courtyard was the basilica where there would normally have been statues of the Emperor. It was empty now. Emperors came and went so fast these days it was hard for the stonemasons to keep up, Marcus thought cynically. He suspected that somewhere in the cellar, along with the Legion's treasury, was a statue of "Phillip the Arab." He assumed some local sculptor was hard at work on one of Decius to replace it.

He was in dress uniform, having been summoned this morning by the Legate. It was his first formal meeting with his commander and he was doing his best to mask his nervousness by examining the Principia. He could see the sacellum shrine screened off by stonework and carved panels of wood directly at the rear of the basilica where the VII Legion would keep its centuries' signa, busts of the imperial family—the sculptors must be hard at work on those as well—the vexilla flags, and the Legion's eagle.

"Sir?"

The headquarters tesserarius—what was his name? Spurius? Or something like that. Marcus pulled himself back from his thoughts to find the young officer standing respectfully in front of him.

"Sir, the Legate and the tribunes will see you now," said the man.

"Thank you," said Marcus, not trusting himself to use the man's name.

The tesserarius stepped aside and indicated an office with an open door.

Marcus took a moment to compose himself, made a quick self-examination to be sure his uniform was correct, and strode through the door.

The legate, Titus Valens, was seated behind a desk, his elbows resting on it, a scatter of reports and letters spread before him. Marcus noted his own report, and the letters he had brought from Capera on the Lusitanian uprising. There were other letters that he did not recognize. Seated on either side were the tribunes Publius Felix, whom he had met briefly in Tarraco, and Quintus Junius.

He studied them quickly. Publius Felix was as he remembered him from Tarraco—tall, handsome, and well-shaped—and he looked as if he was aware of all three attributes. He sat upright in his chair, his feet solidly on the floor, his hands on the chair arms. It was Publius who had sent Marcus, Flavius, and Demaratus to Corduba to take command of the Second Century. He did not look overly friendly.

Quintus was an older man, gone a bit to seed, with a fine

network of veins on his nose and cheeks. He was apparently a man who liked his wine and he sat relaxed in his chair, his legs crossed at the ankles. He gave Marcus a friendly nod.

The legate was as tall as Publius, but thinner. He had about him the look of gray—his hair, his eyes, even his skin. His expression was guarded, neither friendly nor hostile: watchful.

Marcus saluted and stood at attention.

"Centurion, please be seated," said Publius, indicating a chair the tesserarius had slipped behind Marcus. "Thank you, Spurius. That will be all. Please close the door when you leave," said the Legate. The tesserarius bowed and left, closing the door softly behind him.

"Centurion Marcus Favonius, we have been examining your report as well as some letters that were sent on your behalf, and we have a few questions for you," said Publius.

"Of course, sir," answered Marcus.

"What about this truce with the Lusitanians?" blurted out Publius. "Who authorized you to do that?"

"If you are the commanding officer in the middle of a battle, I thought your authority came from yourself, my dear Publius," put in Quintus mildly.

"I did not ask the question of you, tribune," snapped Publius.

"Well, then you got an answer gratis, so consider yourself ahead," replied Quintus smiling benignly at Publius.

"Gentlemen," said Titus in a long-suffering tone, "I will ask the questions here." Marcus suppressed a grin. It appeared as if he was not the only commander afflicted with feuding subordinates.

"Centurion, I would like to take you back to the period

before the battle with the Lusitanians, with an emphasis on the orders you received from Primus Pilus Gnaeus Antonius," said the Legate.

Marcus waited before replying, collecting his thoughts. The previous night he had rehearsed what he was going to say and had carefully organized his diary to back up his narrative. Starting with his arrival in Corduba, he took the three officers through the period before the two centuries left for Emerita Augusta, including the conflict with Gnaeus over the javelins and the wounded men. He also touched on the stipendia issue because he knew the VII Legion would have to make good on the loan.

"You say that the Primus Pilus removed men from the Second Century and replaced them with some of the wounded from the First, Centurion?" asked Quintus.

"That is a privilege of command," put in Publius.

"I was not aware that deserting one's comrades was ever a privilege," Quintus replied.

Titus shot an impatient look at his two bickering tribunes. "Did you take the wounded from the First Century with you?" he interjected.

"Yes, sir," answered Marcus.

"And how did they do?" Titus continued.

"All of them stood in the line against the Lusitanians, sir," he answered.

Publius had been leafing through some of the records that Marcus had given the Legate the day before. "Centurion, you say that when you left Corduba, the Primus Pilus ordered the centuries not to construct marching camps. Is this correct?"

"Yes, sir," answered Marcus.

"Did you protest this order, Centurion?" asked Publius.

"Yes, sir."

"Did you construct a marching camp for the Second Century?" continued Publius.

"No, sir, I did not."

"Can you explain why you did not?" asked Publius.

"In my opinion it would have created a dangerous and unacceptable breach among the commanding officers. I felt that, given the history of the two centuries, the risk of a division was greater than the risk of an attack," answered Marcus.

"Good answer," put in Quintus.

"I was not aware you were judging this matter," snapped Publius.

Quintus gave the tribune a level stare. "It was you who dispatched Marcus to Corduba with orders to quell a possible mutiny. Now you expect him to flaunt a division among the commanders? Anyone who has commanded in the field knows that internal division is more dangerous than 10,000 enemies."

"Publius is simply developing the facts, Quintus," said Titus, quietly taking control. Then he added, "Centurion, tell us what happened once you got to Emerita Augusta."

Marcus had watched the interchange with interest. Publius was playing the role of prosecutor, Quintus his defense attorney, with the Legate acting as the judge. It also appeared that Publius had not had much command experience, which was not unusual. Appointment to the position of tribune was as much a political plum as a reward for command prowess.

"Centurion?" prodded Titus.

Marcus had been so caught up in his analysis of the dynamic between the three men that he had quite forgotten to answer the question.

"Forgive me, sir. I was just refreshing my memory," he said. He told how he was ordered to delay his departure to accommodate the merchants and how he had recruited the Cretans as auxiliaries. He added that the latter had performed well and that he hoped that they would be sent on to join their comrades in Tarraco.

"We are considering the matter," said Titus, with a tone that suggested the Cretans were likely to see more of Legio than they wanted.

"Marcus," interjected Quintus—it was the first time any of the men had called him by his name—"did you build a marching camp once you had left Emerita?"

"Yes, sir. And since we were attacked before the first nightfall, the men were rather enthusiastic about it," he said.

The remark drew a laugh from Titus and Quintus, and even Publius cracked a ghostly smile.

"Now, about this truce..." Publius started to say.

"Excuse me, sir," said Quintus, interrupting, and turning to Publius, "I need to understand why the word 'truce' is being used here. Tell me, Marcus, did you have any conversations with the Lusitanians? Did anyone in your century have such a conversation?"

Marcus shook his head.

Turning to Publius, Quintus asked, "Then why do you insist on calling this a 'truce'? A truce involves an agreement between two or more parties. We who have commanded troops in the field would call your 'truce' a prudent tactical maneuver. Would not agree, sir?" directing his last comment at Titus.

"Tribune Quintus, this is a discussion with Centurion Marcus Favonius, not an argument between you and tribune Publius Felix," said the Legate, with an edge to his voice.

Marcus assumed the tension between the two tribunes was longstanding, and he suspected that whenever Quintus disagreed with Publius, the old tribune used his military service to bludgeon the other tribune.

"The VII Legion has lost its First Century, and you quibble about words as if this were a property court in Rome?" Publius shot back, ignoring the Legate's admonition to Quintus.

"I grieve for my comrades in the First Century, but it was not Marcus who brought them down, but that fool Gnaeus," countered Quintus, "If there is fault here, sir, we should not be looking at the man who engineered a victory over superior forces."

"Silence, both of you," roared Titus with surprising parade ground timbre.

Neither tribune looked particularly intimidated, but they both dutifully lapsed into silence.

"Centurion Marcus Favonius, I have no problem with the behavior of the Second Century during and after the battle with the Lusitanians. I think you were correct to be cautious. As you point out in your report, you had to assume the First Century had been destroyed, and that your responsibility was to protect the merchants and maintain the Second as a fighting force in case Norba was threatened," the Legate said.

"Nonetheless, you have left us with a difficult situation. We cannot simply ignore the attack on both centuries, let alone the destruction of the First," he continued.

"I agree sir. And it is doubly difficult when the army finds itself in the middle of a civilian matter," said Marcus.

Titus cocked an eyebrow at him. "Civilian?"

Marcus had carefully gone over in his mind what he was going to say. If he just shut his mouth, he had a feeling the hearing would go his way. But Marcus had a streak of perversity in him that his family and his officers were well aware of, and in this matter, he was sure the Lusitanians were in the right. He could not say that, of course, but he could suggest an alternative to igniting an endless cycle of revenge.

"Yes, sir. It may be that Lusitanian land was illegally seized by several wealthy landowners, and that a number of Roman citizens were killed in the process of that seizure," he said. "Armed men employed by one Arrius Granius apparently attacked a village and killed a number of women and children. I believe I included some letters on the matter in the material I sent you."

"I don't see what this has to do with the attack on our centuries," said Titus.

"In order to prevent a revenge raid on his villa, Arrius Granius told Lusitanians that two centuries of the VII Legion were marching to attack them. I included two documents attesting to this by leading citizens in Capera," Marcus continued.

"Are you suggesting that we should ignore this attack?" an incredulous Publius put in.

"Of course not, sir. The men who attacked our centuries should be brought to justice," answered Marcus, "but the matter has become tangled up with this charge that land has been illegally confiscated, and it has inflamed all of Lusitania. If it comes to war, it will likely be a long one and will require deploying the whole Legion."

"Centurion, I am well aware of what a war with the Lusitanians would involve," snapped Titus.

"Yes, sir, of course you are. I was merely thinking aloud to keep my train of thought. I apologize if I have misspoken. I was only going to suggest that there was a substantial vigile force in the area that could be reinforced with local auxiliaries if it came to a fight," Marcus added hastily. "If there were laws broken in the initial confiscations, and the magistrates acted with dispatch, it is possible that the attackers could be apprehended, and the law breakers brought to justice, without the situation breaking into full scale war."

It was an enormous mouthful and involved at least four or five interdependent courses of action. Marcus noted that Publius was frowning and looking lost, Quintus was nodding his head, and Titus was looking thoughtful. Marcus decided that Publius was not overly bright.

Finally, the Legate said, "Well, you do raise some interesting points, centurion. I will send a cavalry quingeniaery to Norba in the meantime and ask the provincial governor to meet with me. If the perpetrators are brought to justice, it will settle the matter. War, after all, is an expensive business."

"I really cannot accept that...." started Publius, to be quickly silenced by Titus.

"There are matters of policy here, tribune," said the Legate. "They are not matters to be discussed in this company."

The tribune subsided into "Yes, sir."

At this point the headquarters tesserarius slipped into the room and handed Titus a wax slate. The Legate looked down at it, frowned, and turned back to Marcus. "Centurion, would you excuse us for a few minutes? There is a matter the tribunes and I must discuss. Spurius will see you to a place where you can wait until we call you."

Marcus felt a cold spike in his chest. Was the tablet related to the "dispatches" that Gnaeus had spoken of in Corduba? Had a duplicate set come by way of Tarraco? Was he to be arrested and handed over to the Praetorians?

Marcus saluted and followed Spurius out of the office. The man did not seem particularly tense, and he gave Marcus a friendly smile, so an arrest seemed unlikely. But Marcus's mind was racing and the tension of the last several months came boiling to the surface. Should he leave? He could say he had to relieve himself and then warn the others. But if the note were nothing of consequence, his leaving would raise suspicions, which might cause the Legate and the tribunes to look into the details of his transfer. He felt paralyzed.

Some of the turmoil must have shown on his face because Spurious asked him if he was well, and if he would like a goblet of wine?

Marcus forced himself to relax and smile. "No, I am fine. I am not used to meeting with a legate and two tribunes at the same time."

"Hmmm. Well, that is likely to change," said Spurius, looking at him with a slightly amused expression.

"Now, what does that mean?" Marcus said to himself. Well, he would not allow himself to look nervous or awkward. "I have not had an opportunity to examine our shrine. You will find me there, tesserarius," he said.

"Yes, sir," answered Spurius. "I do not think they will be long."

Marcus made himself walk casually to the shrine and pretend to examine the Legion's Aquila, signa, and flags. He noted that the signum of the First Century was placed before the statue of Augustus, and he disciplined himself to appear interested. "What was taking them so long?" he asked himself.

He wondered if he had gone too far with his suggestion about how to deal with the Lusitanians. It was not healthy to give advice to senior officers, especially a Legate. But he also knew that a war would be little more than a forcible transfer of land from the many to a few, and he was wary of war whose sole goal was gold or greater wealth for a narrow class of Patricians. He understood this was dangerous thinking, but the last ten years had led him to the conclusion that each war was only a prelude to yet another war. There would be no glory in a war with the Lusitanians. Its victims would be citizens of the Empire, not the real danger to civilization that gathered and waited in the deep forests of Germania, the mountains beyond the Danube, or the windswept plains east of Cappadocia and Mesopotamia.

Titus Valens struck him as sensible, or at least as sensible as a Legate could be, given the multitude of masters and interests he served. There would be no honor in scattering villages of women and children, no triumphal march in Rome for bringing another land or people under the yoke of the Empire. It would be a dirty, exhausting war that would further drain the already depleted VII Legion, and one that might indeed raise up another Lusitanian hero to vex Rome. He could only hope the Legate was perceptive enough to see where a war would lead, and smart enough to take advantage of a way out.

After what seemed hours, but was probably only ten minutes or so, Spurius appeared at the entrance to the shrine and told him that the Legate and tribunes would see him now.

Marcus took a deep breath. Spurius escorted him to the door, opened it and stepped aside.

Well, he was not going to be arrested.

Titus and Quintus had broad smiles on their faces and even Publius had dropped his hostility for a neutral expression. All three were holding silver and gold chased wine goblets, and Quintus was handing one to him.

As soon as he took it, Titus raised his goblet. "To Marcus Favonius, Primus Pilus of the First Cohort of the VII Legion."

Marcus was prepared for anything but this, so he just stood there dumb. Quintus laughed out loud, joined by the other two men. "I hope you respond to adversity in the field quicker than you do to promotion, centurion," chuckled the older tribune. "You are supposed to join in this toast."

"Yes, of course sir. It is just that..." and trailed off, remembering, however, to join the toast and drink from the goblet.

"I believe the man is confused," said Publius. Although he smiled when he said it, it was not a friendly expression.

"And well he should be," said Quintus in a much friendly tone. "Not only promoted, but promoted to a cohort that no longer has a First Century."

Titus finally stepped in to explain. "We have decided to promote the Second Century. Since it is the unit that you led in battle, it is only right that it assumes the status of First

Century. One of your first jobs will be to rebuild the century that was lost."

"Thank you, sir. I am honored by your trust in me," replied Marcus, thinking the response came out sounding awkward and stilted. On the other hand, he was still feeling off balance.

"As Primus Pilus you will be expected to be a part of my staff," said Titus.

"Poor Marcus," said Quintus, taking a long pull on his wine goblet. "You probably thought being Primus Pilus meant money, power, and good food. And here you discover it means going to lots of meetings."

At this juncture Spurius put his head in the door, congratulated Marcus, and said "It will be a short while before everything is ready, sir."

Titus nodded. "Tell me when everything is in place."

The tesserarius saluted and vanished.

"It seems we need to wait a little more, Primus Pilus," said Titus.

Marcus was curious about what they were waiting for, but he was not about to let anyone know that it concerned him. Instead, he took another drink.

Quintus was already on his second goblet. Marcus noted that Publius just sipped at his wine and that Titus had not touched his after the initial toast. Marcus did not take a third pull on his goblet.

"So, now that you are part of our staff, Marcus," said Quintus, "you will have to share our headaches. Tell him about the Praetorian matter, Titus."

The Legate grimaced. "Bad business, that."

Marcus froze at the name "Praetorian," but tried to make himself look simply curious. He caught Publius looking narrowly at him. He would have to be careful around the tall tribune.

"Are there Praetorians in Hispania?" asked Marcus, trying to keep the tension out his voice.

"There were," said Quintus cryptically.

"Two Praetorians were found dead, and the civilian authorities are trying to say it is an army matter," said Titus.

"Dead here?" asked Marcus. He relaxed once he found out this had nothing to do with Rome.

"No," said Publius, still watching him closely. "In Saguntum. Both were murdered."

"We don't know that, Publius," said Quintus. "The two could have quarreled and killed one another." The older tribune turned to Marcus. "Each body apparently had the knife of the other man in him. And it appeared as if there was a terrible struggle."

"Why is this your concern, sir?" asked Marcus of Titus.

"Praetorians" shrugged the Legate. "The civil authorities don't want to touch it. I don't blame them. But neither do we."

"When did this happen, sir?" asked Marcus.

"No one knows exactly when it happened, but the bodies were found in a deserted house about a month and a half ago," answered Titus.

"Did you go to Corduba by way of Seguntum, Marcus? asked Publius quietly.

"Yes, sir, and we would have been there at about the same time," said Marcus, shaking his head. "But we heard nothing about this. Who would have killed Praetorians?"

"That list of suspects would include most citizens of the Empire," remarked Quintus.

"It is not a joking matter, tribune," said Publius stiffly.

"Who's joking? They were not in uniform; probably out to murder someone they didn't like. So they picked a fight with the wrong person. Either way, the Empire is better for their absence," said Quintus.

"It is treason to...." started Publius, only to be cut off by Quintus. "Shit! Those soft, overpaid goons haven't taken the field in decades. They make war by butchering old men, women and children. Apparently, they don't do all that well when they come across someone who can fight. I would like to have the men who did that under my command."

"Quintus," said Titus, "that is enough. Praetorians or not, we are all in the same army. I will not have that kind of talk in my legion."

"Yes, sir," said Quintus, but he hardly seemed chastised.

Just at that moment, Spurius put his head back in the door. "Sir, everything is ready."

Titus smiled at Marcus. "We can't have such a big promotion without a ceremony, can we, Primus Pilus? Plus, we have a little surprise for you," he said, gesturing toward the door. Marcus followed the tesserarius out the door, followed by the Legate and the tribunes. Spurius led him across the long anteroom, through the pillars to the enormous courtyard outside.

As soon as he emerged from the Principia there was a great cheer. Drawn up in front was the First Cohort, minus the century that was on detached service in Barcino. Almost 500 men were lined up in three centuries, centurions and signifiers standing at attention in front of each. Each century's cornilum let out a blast, and the men, led by the Second Century, cheered again.

Marcus blinked, genuinely surprised. He had no idea what to do, so he retreated into a salute. He noticed that Flavius had assumed the position of centurion in the front of the Second Century—now promoted to First Century—so that the symmetry of two officers in front of each century would be maintained.

Grasping Marcus's shoulder, Titus Valens stepped forward, flinging out his right arm. "Comrades of the VII Gemina Hispania Pia! We have a new Primus Pilus, Marcus Favonius, formally of the Legion XXX Ulpis Victrix."

This set off another round of cheers.

Titus turned to him, gave him a smile, and said, "I think the men would appreciate a few words." The statement was couched as a request, but "request" was not in a legate's vocabulary, nor could any junior officer afford to treat it as anything but an order.

But Marcus's mind was blank. He had no idea what to say, and his growing panic only made the situation worse. He gulped a few times and finally managed to mumble out some rather pedestrian generalities about honor and service and Empire. As speeches went, it was not exactly an oration by Cicero.

It had the virtue of being short, however, and when he brought it to a ragged end, there was another round of cheering that Marcus suspected had more to do with the briefness of his speech than with its content.

"And now we have a gift for you," said the Legate, signaling someone in the back of the assembled centuries. There was some commotion and then the centuries parted and Marcus beheld his "gift."

If nightmares took form, they would come into the world in the guise of the horse led forward by Spurius Annius and two grooms. The creature was enormous, probably 17 hands at the shoulders, and as black as the heart of a mine. It seemed less a horse than a piece of chiseled stone, all angles and sharp edges. Veins etched its chest and legs, and its great neck was bowed, as the two grooms struggled to keep the pacing giant under control.

With a sinking heart, Marcus watched as the beast approached. When it got within a few feet it suddenly raised its head and stared directly at him. If Marcus had nurtured any hope that he might co-exist with this creature, it vanished at that moment. The look the horse cast upon him was incendiary, as if to say: "For uncounted generations your race has yoked my race, human creature. Today we even the score!"

Marcus found himself being pushed forward, the reins placed in his hands, and somewhere down a long corridor someone seemed to be saying that it was the finest and fastest horse in Hispania, and that once he rode it, no other horse would ever satisfy him. Never had he felt such a deep longing and affection for his fat old gelding that dutifully brought him to Corduba and which resided in the same stables that had given birth to this monstrosity.

He looked around desperately for help. Flavius looked strained and anxious, while Demaratus was stone faced. "Bastard," thought Marcus. "I'll bet he is laughing in his wicked Greek heart."

Hands were pushing him to mount, though it was the last thing on earth he wanted to do. Given a choice between abandoning his promotion or riding this horse, he would have joined the ranks of the junior centurions in a moment. But he had no time to think. Hands were helping him up to the four-horn saddle, and then the officers and grooms cleared a space to let him maneuver the horse.

He felt like he was on top of a mountain. He had never sat on a horse this tall and his stomach contracted when he contemplated how far he would fall if it came to that. But the horse turned when he pulled the reins, and while it paced in a way that sent chills up Marcus's spine, it seemed well behaved. Maybe, thought Marcus, the Gods are being kind.

Fat chance, said the Gods.

The horse seemed to explode. One moment it was turning and pacing, the next it was in a full gallop, thundering off down the Via Principia, headed for the main gate of the fortress. Marcus clung desperately to the creature, hoping it would slow at the gate, or that the sentries would stop the animal. But the horse only increased its speed, brushing past the two sentries as if they were scenery.

The village surrounding the fort was only about a hundred yards deep, and the horse was through it in a flash, scattering chickens, dogs and children. Once clear of the town, it angled away from the road, heading for a wall that enclosed some pasture for the Legion's mules. As Marcus watched the wall loom up, he pulled frantically at the reins, trying to turn the animal. He pulled so hard that the creature's head turned around so it was looking directly at him. Since this had no effect on the animal's speed, and since Marcus decided that the only thing more dangerous than a horse approaching a stone wall at full gallop was a blind horse approaching a stone wall at full gallop, he loosened the reins.

The horse whipped its head around and, while Marcus did not think it possible, increased its speed. Just as Marcus was certain that the creature intended to smash the two of them into the wall, it made a great leap.

Everything up to this point happened faster than Marcus could keep track of. But the jump seemed to play out in slow motion. Marcus was aware of an odd phenomenon: somehow the world had become inverted, with the cloud-flecked blue sky below him, and the dry, mottled landscape above him. These seem to spin for a while, and then something green came up at him very, very fast.

XXXII

Epilogue

Marcus was trying to make himself comfortable at his desk, but failing. When he returned to his senses after being thrown from the horse, he found himself sitting in the middle of a bush, though "bush" might be stretching the point. It did have branches and even a scrubby patina of leaves, but for the most part the plant was composed of particularly malevolent thorns. In spite of Timotheus's best efforts, some of them still remained in his backside. The doctor said that a routine of baths would eventually work them out, but for now, he felt like he was sitting on needles.

In a sense, he was surprised he could feel the thorns at all, given that he had also stripped a good deal of skin from his legs, sprained his ankle, and smashed both elbows. The field around the bush was dotted with stones, and Flavius was of the opinion that his survival was nothing short of a sign from the Gods. Marcus was of the opinion that the Gods had spared him only so that they could torment him further.

The Legate had been very solicitous, and had even called for a chariot to take Marcus back to the fort, but Marcus had insisted on walking. He had no intention of getting close to another horse, even if it were yoked to a chariot. The only bright spot in the whole sorry affair was that no one had been there to see him thrown off the horse. At least he was saved that humiliation.

Pushing aside his infirmities, he considered the two un-opened letters on his desk. They had both arrived before Marcus had reached the Legio fort, but the headquarters tesserarius had forgotten about them until this morning. He apologized profusely for the oversight, saying the letters had gotten lost in all the excitement of the Second Century's arrival. Marcus had waved him off in a rather bad-tempered way, which actually had nothing to do with the forgetful tesserarius and everything to do with his physical condition and the authors of the letters.

One was written on a papyrus sheet folded over and sealed with red wax. There was no missing the seal: it was the Dasumii family crest, a wild boar on a field of crossed spears. He had written Aelia twice, once from Emerita Augusta, and once from Norba. The letters had been painfully difficult to construct, and he tore up innumerable attempts because, on reading them, he found them insufferably dull or much too stiff and formal. Only in the letter from Norba had some of his loneliness and un-certainty about the future crept into his words, and even then, he only added them as a postscript.

He was insecure about his relationship with Aelia. She

seemed attracted to him—only the Gods would know why—and her note to him in Corduba was friendly and sweet. But he had only spent an evening and part of a morning with her, and the two had exchanged a single kiss, and that one a mere peck on the cheek as he was setting out for camp. He had no reason to hope for anything but friendly acknowledgement of his letters. But his heart wanted more. He toyed with the seal, then pushed the letter aside.

The second letter was a scroll, unmarked and unsealed, simply tied with a string. But he had an intuition that it was from one of his brothers or his sister. He had no idea what it might contain: a warning that the Praetorians were still stalking him? A plea from some dungeon for help? A list of his executed siblings?

He stared at it. He found it interesting that he was more willing to open the scroll, with all its portents of death and destruction, than he was to unseal Aelia's letter. He took a deep breath, said a short prayer to Fortuna, and untied the scroll. Rolling it out he first glanced at the signature. It was from his sister, Julia.

"Dear Brother," read the salutation, "I pray this letter finds you in good health, and that you are well.

"Our dear brother Mamercus was assassinated by the Praetorians shortly after you left Rome. He was taken near the Circus Maximus in broad daylight, but he fought with such skill and bravery that he killed one of them and wounded two others. A crowd gathered and threw stones at the Praetorians and would not let them take his body. The crowd carried him to our parents' home and laid him out in the atrium. You, our warrior, would have been proud of him."

Marcus had never gotten along with Mamercus, but he found his eyes stinging at the news. He also felt a surge of pride; Mamercus had not gone alone to his death, and the people of Rome had seen his courage and honored him for it. Marcus also had a twinge of guilt. He, Marcus, had slunk out of the city like a whipped dog. He even had a spasm of resentment: Mamercus always overshadowed him in life; now he had done so in death.

He returned to the text.

"The rest of us are all well. There was so much anger at the murder of our dear brother, that even the Praetorians hesitated to openly attack or arrest us. And when the news came that the swine Philippus had fallen to our glorious Emperor Messius Quintus Decius, they dared not act against us."

Marcus shook his head. "Glorious"? It would appear his family had picked the winning side this time. He wondered how long it would last.

"Your former commander, Quintus Pompeius, raised up the vigiles against the Praetorians and besieged them in their camp so that they could not enter the city."

Marcus raised an eyebrow at Julia's description of the Praetorian Legion afraid to confront a bunch of police and firemen. Quintus Pompeius had probably made an arrangement with the Praetorian commander that both would wait until Decius and Philippus had decided the matter of who ruled the Empire.

"Our brother Tiberius says that Quintus Pompeius has been made a member of the Senate and is one of the Emperor's intimate advisors. Tiberius said that Quintus spoke highly of you and said that if you return from Hispania, you might expect to be appointed a tribune."

Marcus smiled. Julia had no idea what a "tribune" actually did, she only knew it had prestige and that was enough for her. He loved his sister, but she was a shallow creature whose eyes widened and curtsies deepened in the presence of power or wealth.

"We hope you will return to us, dear Marcus. Your family and your future await you. Lucius and the boys send their love. Your dearest and loving sister, Julia Aquillius."

He did miss his family, as difficult as they were. Julia's husband, Lucius, was even shallower than his sister, and a good deal stupider. However, his two nephews were stout lads, and they always sat with rapt attention while he told them tales of strange people and distant frontiers.

His brother Tiberius was obsessed with power, but his niece Sabina was a delightful thing. She would bring him wine and ply him with intelligent questions about the world outside of Rome. A wave of nostalgia momentarily engulfed him.

Almost without thinking he had taken up Aelia's letter and broken the wax seal. He hesitated for a moment before opening it, but whatever it held, it could hardly be more unsettling than the letter from his sister.

"Dear, Dear Marcus" it opened, which allowed him to exhale. "I pray you are well. We know all about your battle with the Lusitanians, and Tiberius Granius has regaled all of Corduba with your courage. He said that you single-handedly wrested our eagle from the hands of the Lusitanian general."

Marcus groaned. It was a century signum, not a legion Aquila, and if there was a Lusitanian "general" on the field, it was not the man who carried the signum into battle. In any case, the man was stone dead by the time Marcus "wrested" anything from him.

"We are deeply saddened by the deaths of all those brave men from the First Century. How hard it must have been for you to come upon them. My heart goes out to you."

It was a sensitive thing to say, and Marcus felt a deep surge of affection for Aelia. She had not allowed his victory to blind her to the ultimate tragedy of war.

The letter went on with news and gossip. The authorities in Tarraco were having a serious confrontation with the Christian Bishop of Carthage and no one knew what the outcome of it might be, and a report that pirates from Mauretania Tingitana had raided several towns south of Carthago Nova.

She signed it, "My warmest greetings, Aelia Dasumi," but then added a postscript: "Dear Marcus: I look forward to your letters, but I cherish your postscripts. Love, Aelia."

Marcus felt the tightness in his chest ease. He almost plunged into answering Aelia, but then glanced outside. The afternoon was waning and he was due at a small taverna outside the fort. Flavius had asked him and Demaratus to meet him for dinner. His optio had been very formal about the whole thing, and while the last thing Marcus wanted to do was limp his way into the village—his sprained ankle was still swollen and painful—he could not refuse.

Groaning painfully as he pulled himself to his feet, Marcus took his cloak from the peg near the door, wrapped himself in it, and headed toward the taverna. The mountains to the north were purple and black, already beginning to vanish into the late fall evening. A last glow of pink touched the west, scattered by a rank of thin clouds. The latter promised rain sometime tomorrow or the next day. But in the east the sky was clear, and the first bright stars had begun to appear. The cold was sharp and would grow sharper as the evening unfolded. He tucked himself further into his cloak and hunched his shoulders to better trap the warmth.

Demaratus sat on a low stone wall just outside the vicus and examined the letter he held. He had read it through several times, but he set himself to do it again. Not that it was very long. Coventina's letters were much like the tall, red-haired Celt: sparse, business-like, and no nonsense, but with a hint of depth that was not immediately obvious. Or was he fooling himself?

He had written her letters from Corduba, Emerita, and Norba, mindful of her last words to him: "no poetry." But language was precious to the Greeks. It defined them, it made them different, and using it properly gave one a pleasure that had no equal. Plus, writing Latin was not easy. Demaratus thought in both languages, as well as a few others, but he wrote in Greek. Switching languages to speak was easy. But shifting the language of prose was a good deal more complex than just using another alphabet. Some Greek words simply did not translate well, and he found himself struggling to get his meaning right.

Since he was not certain of Coventina's affections his letters were careful, trying to strike a balance between friendship and intimacy. He felt he had achieved the perfect mixture, one that would invite without risking rebuke.

Subtlety, it appeared, was wasted on Coventina.

"Dear Demaratus," she led off the letter, "you write like my uncle speaks: wonderful sounding words that obscure as much as they reveal. My uncle is a famous and much revered oracle among our people, but I never have the slightest idea what he is talking about. I suspect others do not either, but they will never admit to it. The only time he is clear is when he is drunk. Then he is much like everyone else. I enjoy your descriptions of places I have never seen, but just when you are about to win my attention, words—many, many words—get in the way, and words that seem to say two things at the same time: that you fancy me; that you think me a friend. I did not kiss you goodbye or ask that you write to me as a friend. I have many friends, and in any case, women are better at that task than men. If you desire me you must speak like a normal man, not in the riddles of oracles." She signed it, "Love, Coventina," and then added a postscript: "I miss you when I am in the kitchen. I have great patience, but not for empty words. Write."

Demaratus did not know whether to be elated or infuriated. She had brushed off his careful prose as it were an annoying burr. He was humiliated that she had seen right through his effort to attract her while defending himself.

He slipped off the wall, too agitated to sit, and paced back and forth. No woman had ever talked to him this way! Comparing his prose to the nonsense of a sooth sayer? The cursed woman was impossible!

But as he calmed down, he also had to admit she had caught his attention. Demaratus liked intelligence, and Coventina had seen through him as though he were a piece of glass. "Fancy her." Did he "fancy her"? And what did she mean by "great patience"? She made his head hurt, and with fewer words than anyone had ever accomplished that feat before. The more he thought about it, the more he missed the sea with its dangerous simplicity.

Demaratus glanced around, brought back from his thoughts of Coventina by the gradual waning of the light and the chill that was creeping out of the shadows and beginning to make him shiver. He walked back to the wall and retrieved his cloak, slipping the letter into an inside pocket. It was getting late and he was due at the taverna for dinner. He would have to sort through his feeling for Coventina tomorrow. Pulling his cloak tighter around him, he headed back into the village.

The Golden Boar was set just outside the main cluster of houses, shops, and small manufacturers that made up the vicus. Roofed with tiles, the two-story building was much like taverns all over the empire: white plaster over stone, and a red stripe running around the lower quarter of the building. The Golden Boar had a ground level turret that projected off the main room and could be screened off for privacy. It was in this alcove that Flavius had arranged for the dinner.

He arrived an hour early just to make sure the taverna keeper had followed his orders to the letter: fresh trout, a haunch of venison, several of the house's specialty side dishes, and the best wine he could come up with. He demanded the finest crockery and wine goblets the taverna had.

He made himself stop fussing with the table and stepped outside to get a breath of the cold, evening air. He had a plan. It had come to him following the meeting of the provincial council in Capera, and had evolved during the march north to Legio. He was still not entirely comfortable with it.

Flavius had always been a creature of Rome, although he had barely seen it in the last seven years. It was where his family was, where he had grown up, and its teeming markets and crowded streets were a tonic for him.

But he did not want to go home.

He was not sure why, only that the feeling was a powerful one. Flavius was not a self-reflective person, as he imagined Marcus and Demaratus to be, so he rarely questioned his feelings. There was something about Hispania that drew him, but he couldn't put that feeling into words.

He knew that part of it was the comradeship that he, Marcus, and Demaratus had found since they had fled Ostia. It was a companionship that he had never known before, and he was deeply afraid—although he would never admit to that feeling— it would break up. Flavius had wheedled information from the headquarters tesserarius that Marcus had received a personal letter from Rome, and it didn't take much to figure out that it was from someone in his family. Philippus was dead, and Philippus was the enemy of Marcus's family. That meant that it was very likely that Marcus could go home, or that the two of them would be reassigned to their old legion. There might even be a promotion in this for his centurion.

As Marcus's optio, Flavius would be expected to accompany him. Flavius dearly loved his centurion. He would die for him (almost did on occasion). But he did not want to leave this land of vast spaces and unexpected events and people. Flavius felt a great wave of depression, a foreign and unfamiliar state of mind.

He did not want to lose Demaratus either. He had come to genuinely like the Greek, and he and the signifer shared a secret that bound the two together. He had no illusions about Demaratus's loyalty. He had paid one of the stable hands to watch over the signifer's horse, and he knew that the Greek had arranged for Aura to be ready at a moment's notice. A little surreptitious searching had uncovered a small traveling bag tucked away in a nearby stall. Had it gone badly for Marcus in Legio, Demaratus would have been off.

Two months ago Demaratus's actions would have bothered him, but this evening they didn't. The Greek's sense of self-preservation didn't mean he wasn't a good officer and a friend. Just a Greek.

Flavius had not thought through what he would say at dinner, and every time he tried to work it out, he fell into a muddle. A crunch of gravel broke his train of thought, and Demaratus loomed out of the dusk.

"Welcome, comrade," said Flavius.

"Welcome to you, Flavius," answered Demaratus. "I see our centurion is arriving as well."

Flavius turned to see Marcus coming out of the fort's main gate, trying his best not to limp. The two men waited for him to work himself down the road, and the three exchanged greetings.

"Centurion, signifer, our table awaits us," said Flavius, opening the door and gesturing them in to the smoke, noise, and warmth of the taverna.

The evening began badly. Both Marcus and Demaratus were preoccupied with their own thoughts, and Flavius was tense. He compensated for the awkward silences by pointing out dishes, pouring wine and making small talk, not among one of the optio's greatest skills. But the wine eventually had an effect, and the three fell into a conversation.

Flavius related his conversation with the optios in the baths, which sobered them a little.

"So, he was a good officer driven to madness," said Demaratus.

"It would appear," added Flavius, "but that madness lost us many comrades."

Flavius turned to Demaratus. "You received a letter from Tarraco."

Demaratus started. "And how would you know that?"

"It is the job of an optio to know everything," replied Flavius complacently.

Marcus chuckled. "Just be glad he didn't read it, Demaratus. I hope it was good news?"

Demaratus shrugged. "It was from a woman I met in Tarraco. Good news? Frankly, sir, it is hard to tell."

"The one you wrote to while we were on the march?" said Flavius.

"Yes. Is there anything else in my personal life you would like to know?" said Demaratus exasperatedly.

"Oh, many things, but I can wait. Can't figure her? Well, what do you expect? I saw the name. She's a Celt. Flame and ice, sometimes at the same time, and no manners at all, right sir?" said Flavius.

Marcus grinned. "They can be trying."

"But steadfast if they like you," added Flavius.

Demaratus was dumbstruck. Flavius had almost exactly described the letter from Coventina. He had a stab of suspicion that the optio might indeed have read the letter, but dismissed it. If Flavius had read it, his face would have shown it. The optio was capable of maneuver, but not guile.

The conversation shifted to Marcus. Flavius and Demaratus were curious about what happened in the discussion with the tribunes and the legate. Normally such a question would never be asked by junior officers, but the experiences the three had shared broke down many of those barriers.

Marcus filled them in on the meeting, but not completely. He was no longer just a centurion. He was primus pilate, and an intimate of the commanders. No major decision would be made without his presence. The three had been so close all these months that he felt a stab of guilt for withholding some of what had occurred in the meeting. But higher command demanded different behavior.

They drank a round of toasts to Marcus's promotion.

"How are other things, sir?" asked Flavius in a voice he tried to keep casual, but which sounded staged to Demaratus.

Interesting, thought Demaratus, Flavius knows something. The signifer discreetly pushed himself back from the table and focused on observing the two Romans.

Marcus smiled, looking slightly uncomfortable. "Fine, Flavius, fine."

Flavius said nothing, which said a great deal. There was a long and growing uncomfortable silence between the two. Finally, Marcus broke it. "I heard from my family," he said.

Interesting, indeed, observed Demaratus. Flavius knew he had heard from his family and his silence forced Marcus into admitting it. Where this was going, he wasn't certain, but he was watching two Romans maneuver on the field of battle.

"I hope they are well?" asked Flavius, a concerned tone in his voice. Concerned, yes, but something else. The sentiment was slightly forced. Apparently, Marcus did not notice.

"Yes and no. The Praetorians murdered my brother Mamercus, but botched it. He killed one of them and cut up two others before he fell. A mob formed and drove off the Praetorians. The anger over the assassination apparently spared the rest of my family. And they are on good terms with Emperor Decius," said Marcus.

"Good on Mamercus," said Flavius, fiercely. "Took down three of the bastards, did he? By the Gods, I wish I had seen that."

"Our old commander, Quintus Pompeius, has been elevated to the Senate, and according to my brother Tiberius, he is close to the Emperor," said Marcus, adding, "Tiberius says there may be a promotion to tribune for me if I return."

"And no one would deserve it more, sir," said Flavius.

The compliment was forced, observed Demaratus, and while the optio smiled, the rest of him looked distressed. This was getting more interesting by the moment. If Marcus was appointed tribune, then Flavius was almost certain to be elevated to a centurion or else a cushy headquarters job. Why did he look so tense? Demaratus loved puzzles, and this was a puzzle.

"I am not sure about an appointment to tribune, Flavius. My brother Tiberius always sees what he wants to see, rather than what is. However, a return to Rome is likely to be lucrative," said Marcus.

"No, sir. I don't think it would be, sir," said Flavius.

The bald statement froze the conversation. Demaratus blinked in surprise. If this was a chess game, Flavius had just upended the board.

Marcus was clearly taken aback. As close as the three had become, it had not reached the equality of directly contradicting a superior officer. "No?" he asked stiffly.

"Yes, sir. Forgive me for talking out of turn, sir, but if we go back to Rome, we'll be right back to where we started from. How long is this Emperor going to last? A year? Three years? And when the new one comes in, are we going to be on the run again, or end up butchered in our own homes?"

The words poured out of Flavius. "In Rome every toga hides a knife, sir. Out here it isn't that way. Oh, sure, there are bad types everywhere you go, but you can beat them here. If that slimy bastard at Capera had been a Senator in Rome, we would have been entertaining the Coliseum crowds the next day. Instead, that young Lusitanian kicked his scrawny butt. I didn't understand what you were doing that day when we backed away from the Lusitanians in the meadow, sir. It wasn't just a tactic, was it? You didn't want a war, and you were right, sir. The Lusitanians were doing exactly what any of us would have done: fight for our land and families. In Rome, we are nobody. Here we can make a difference."

Flavius was panting with exertion. Demaratus was certain that the man had never given such a long speech in his life.

"I think we should stay right here, sir. I think we are needed," Flavius finished. Then to Demaratus's surprise he turned his gray eyes directly on him. "What do you intend to do, comrade?" he asked.

Demaratus had absented himself from this conversation early

on, an observer, not a participant. Flavius's sudden question had caught him unprepared, and his mind went blank. Demaratus liked to think of himself as someone driven by cold logic and studied rationality. That was the Greek way, indeed their special contribution to civilization. Well, besides architecture, mathematics, and most everything else that made life worth living.

The Romans were powerful, but chaotic, driven hither and yon by passion or fleeting belief. They could engineer an aqueduct but could not bridge a thought. Not so the Greeks, and most particularly not Demaratus. In truth, the Greeks had a streak of madness in them, but none would ever admit to it. Demaratus had impulsively decided to throw in his lot with Marcus and Flavius back in Rome, but over the past several months he had convinced himself that it was entirely logical and rational to head off into the unknown with two strangers who were being tracked by the Praetorian Guard.

And now here was Flavius staring directly at him and asking him what he intended to do.

He parried for time. "I will go where I am ordered, Optio," he replied.

"That is not what I asked you, comrade," Flavius said impatiently. "We all go where we are ordered to. We are not ordered in this matter. We choose. What do you choose?"

Impulse seized Demaratus again.

"I like this place, Flavius, misnamed as it is," he replied.

Flavius looked momentarily confused, then grinned. "Okay. If we stay you get to call it 'Iberia.' But you still haven't said why you want to stay. It is far from the sea, Greek."

Demaratus considered Flavius's question. "It is far from the sea, and that wounds me. But it is not yet set in its way, which appeals to the Greeks. We might yet salvage it for civilization."

His remark drew groans from both Marcus and Flavius. Then he added quietly, "And I like the company."

Flavius turned to Marcus. "Sir?"

Marcus reacted to the question by staring into the depths of his wine goblet, and slowly turning it with his hands. The silence seemed to go on for minutes, until he finally looked up.

"I shall miss my pillars," he said.

Flavius started laughing silently and then loud enough for other diners to look at the table. Demaratus joined in and all three laughed as much from relief and the release of tension as from Marcus's quirky sense of humor.

When the laughter died down, Flavius lifted his goblet. "To comradeship," he said, and the three touched goblets and drank. Marcus started to thank Flavius for the evening, but the optio was not finished, and Marcus stopped.

"Gentlemen," said Flavius, refilling everyone's wine. When he had their attention he raised his goblet. "To Hispania."

The other two lifted their goblets and touched Flavius's. "To Hispania," they echoed.

Glossary and Notes

Glossary:

Acetum. Sour wine, the standard drink of soldiers.

Acta Senatus. "Acts of the Senate," world's first newspaper.

Ala. Auxiliary cavalry unit, roughly the size of a infantry cohort.

Augurs. Priest that examined if an action had divine approval.

Caliga. Hobnailed boots worn by soldiers.

Century. Basic administrative and military unit of a legion.

Cohort. Basic tactical unit of the legion.

Centurion. Commander of a century.

Cornus. Roman war horn.

Contubernium. Smallest unit in a century.

*Curia.*Meeting place for municipal councils.

Dolabra. Infantry entrenching tool, a sort of pick-axe.

Decurion. Magistrate of a town or city.

Domus. House.

Garum. Fish sauce.

Gladius. Short stabbing sword of the Roman infantry.

Greaves. Armor to protect a centurion's shins.

Hastile. A steel headed staff carried by optios.

Immunis. Veteran soldiers released from normal duties.

Intervallum. Border inside of a fort or marching camp.

Latafundia. Landowner.

Legate. Commands a legion.

Lemures. Hostile ghosts.

Librarius. Junior clerk at army headquarters.
Manes. Spirits of the dead.
Muria. The best fish sauce from Hispania.
Noman. Family name.
Optio. Second in command of a century.
Paenula. Cloak with a hood.
Paludamentum. Formal cloak worn by officers.
Phalarae. Medallions worn on an officer's harness.
Pilum. Heavy spear of the Roman army (pl. pila).
Praetorians. Emperor's personal legion, the only legion allowed in Rome.
Prefect. Third in command of a legion.
Principia. Army headquarters.
Pugio. Short dagger.
Quaestor. Magistrate elected for one year.
Quingeniaery. Cavalry unit. It is composed of 16 turmae of 30 men each. Normally from 480 to 500 men.
Quinquereme. Heavy Roman warship. Its name means "five," the basic team of rowers. It had three banks of oars.
Sacramentum. Oath of loyalty to the Emperor.
Sagum. Cloak used by soldiers, fastened at the right shoulder.
Scutum. Shield of a legionnaire, a 4 ft by 2' 6" rectangle curved to deflect blows.
Signaculum. Lead identification tags, the Roman Army equivalent of dog tags.
Signifer. Officer who carries the century standard and oversees the unit's books and the men's pay.
Signum. Century's standard.
Spatha. Long sword used by Roman cavalry.
Stipenida. Soldier's pay, paid three times a year.
Strigil. Bronze or iron razor used to scrape the body after a bath.
Taberna. Tavern.
Tesserarius. Junior officer in a century, oversees assigning guard duty.
Testudo. "The Tortoise," an infantry maneuver that forms a wall and roof. of shields. It is effective for sieging towns and to protect against archers.
Torque. Award worn round the neck or attached to a harness.

Tribune. Senior staff officer in a legion.
Trireme. Warship of the ancient Greeks, also used as a light warship by the Romans. It means "three," referring to its three banks of oars, each rowed by a single rower.
Turmae. Basic cavalry unit, normally 30 men.
Valetudinarium. Hospital.
Vexilla. Detachment of troops operating away from their parent body.
Vigiles. Police and firemen in cities.
Vitis. A cane carried by centurions, as a mark of office and a punishment device.

The Structure of a Roman Legion

A Roman legion was designed to be a tactically flexible fighting force. To enhance that flexibility, it was divided into discrete units. In that way, a legion resembled a modern infantry division, which is divided into brigades, battalions, regiments, companies and squads. The legion's units could act independently of one another so that they could reinforce a unit that was in trouble, exploit a weakness in the enemy's line, or block an attempt to outflank the legion. Mobility was the essence of a legion's tactics and made it virtually invincible for almost 700 years. Modern armies owe much of their organizational structure to the Roman legion.

A legion was constructed as follows:

Contubernium: An eight-man squad, the smallest unit in a legion.
Century: Comprising 10 contuberniums. A century is normally 80 men, commanded by a centurion.
Cohort (regular): Composed of six centuries, approximately 480 men.
First Cohort: Composed of five centuries, but each century has 160 men. A First Cohort would be approximately 800 men.
Legion: Made up of 10 cohorts normally deployed in three lines. When Headquarters units, plus specialists, are included, a legion would be approximately 5,400 men.
Legate: Legion commander.
Tribune: Senior legion staff officer (normally three per legion).
Prefect (Praefectus castrorum): Third-in-command.

The Structure of a Century

The century was the smallest tactical unit in a legion. That is, it was the smallest unit capable of fighting on its own. It was closest to a modern infantry company, although smaller. In the case of a century from the first cohort, however, it was somewhat larger than a modern infantry company.

A century had four officers:

Centurion: Commander.

Optio: Second-in-command.

Signifer: Holds century standard during battle and keeps the unit's books.

Tesserarius: Junior officer, who also sets sentry duty and oversees camp construction.

Centurions, in order of seniority:

First Cohort
Primus Pilus
Princeps
Princeps Posterior
Hastatus
Hastatus Posterior
Hastatus Posterior
(The five centurions
of the First Cohort
make up the *Primi Ordines*,
a group of the most senior
centurions)

Regular Cohort
Pilus Prior
Pilus Posterior
Princeps Prior
Princeps Posterior
Hastatus

Place Names

Hispania Names/Modern names
Asturica Agusta/Astorga
Capera/Capera
Carthago Nova/Cartagena
Corduba/Cordoba
Barcino/Barcelona
Emerita Augusta/Merida
Elmantica/Salamanca
Baetica/Modern Andalusia
Emporiae/Ampurias
Gades/Cadiz
Gaul/France
Genua/Genoa
Gerunda/Gerona
Legio/Leon
Saguntum/Sagunto
Massilia/Marseilles
Mauretania Tingitana/Morocco
Norba/Caceres
Pisae/Pisa
Tarraco/Tarragona
Tortosa/Tortosa
Valentia/Valencia

Rivers and Seas

Anas River/Guadiana River
Baetis River/Guadalquiver River
Duris River/Duro River
Iberus River/Ebro River
Mare Tyrrhenum/Tyrrhernian Sea
Oceanus Atlanticus/Atlantic Ocean

Acknowledgments

This book could not have been written without the careful copy editing of Anne Bernstein, Betsy Wootten, John Isbister and Roz Spafford, as well as their critiques and suggestions. Danny Hallinan was the book's historical editor and Jack Radey gave valuable advice on the Roman Army and ancient warfare. I am deeply grateful to readers like Susan Watrous, Antonio Hallinan, Danny Beagle and Linda Williams who gave me practical suggestions on how to make the book better, plus invaluable encouragement. My thanks go to Ann Higgins for the cover design and to Caroline Jennings for interior formatting and final editing.

Conn M. Hallinan was a long-time columnist for Foreign Policy in Focus, "A Think Tank Without Walls," and an independent journalist. He holds a PhD in Anthropology from the University of California, Berkeley. For 23 years he oversaw the journalism program at the University of California at Santa Cruz, where he won the UCSC Alumni Association's Distinguished Teaching Award, as well as UCSC's Innovations in Teaching Award and its Excellence in Teaching Award. He also served as Provost at Kresge College of UCSC, retiring in 2004. He is a winner of a Project Censored "Real News Award," and lives in Berkeley, California. The Middle Empire books are his first works of fiction.

Preview of Book II: Mauretania

The ships moved ghost-like over the swell, silent, almost invisible. Their masts had been struck to the decks so that there would be no silhouette against the moonless sky, and the tholes, filled with cloth, dampened any sound of the oars. With the tide approaching flood, the raiders would have several hours before they would find themselves stranded with the ebb.

One of the eight ships edged forward, feeling its way toward the beach, where small combers advanced and retreated on the sloping sands. Beyond the dunes were the lights of a town, but the night was advanced, and most of the small villas were dark. Near the water's edge a light gleamed, disappeared, then gleamed again.

A large man in the prow of the first boat whispered to a companion, and the oars dipped into the water, driving the ship toward the beach. The other seven ships followed. The man wore a long robe with half armor. He carried a small, rounded shield and a long, slightly curved blade. As the ship nudged the beach he slipped over the side into waist-deep water and waded ashore.

Another man loomed out of the darkness.

"Are there soldiers?" the large man asked.

"Only half a century," the man on the beach answered.

"Has the gate been silenced?" asked the large man.

There was no response for a moment. Then the man on the beach said, "No. You will have to take the gate yourself."

"You have failed me," rebuked the large man.

"I am a merchant, not a soldier," the man on the beach said, his voice muted but sharp with anger. "I said there were slaves to be taken, and rich looting as well. It is not my job to provide them to you on a platter. You have more than enough men to take this town."

The large man glanced to either side of him. Men were pouring off the ships and gathering in a ragged crowd just below the crest of the dunes. They had been instructed to remain silent, and for the most part they were, though there was an occasional "clank" as a shield collided with a breastplate or a helmet.

Another man, small and lithe, appeared at his elbow.

"Go with your archers and take the main gate. This man here will show you where it is. I will send soldiers with you to take it. Make sure no one escapes to give a warning. Hold the gate until I call for you," the large man said. "Now go!"

But the lithe man remained standing at his shoulder.

"The loot will be divided equally," said the large man. "You and your men will not be the poorer for this. After me, you will have the pick of the first five slaves."

The lithe man nodded and vanished.

By now all the men were ashore and the tension was building. The large man strode up the beach and plunged into their midst. They gathered around him and he waited until there was absolute silence.

"Hear me, brothers," he said. "This is a town filled with rich Romans and their slaves. There are only a handful of soldiers. But we must strike quickly. Take young women and children.

Kill the men and the old. They are of no use to us. The women and children are more valuable. And take only what you can carry. Everything will be divided equally when we return home, so don't get greedy. Pay attention to the sky! When it turns gray, head back to the ships. We wait for no one. Go!"

The mass of men turned and trotted toward the small resort town,

The slaver raid will plunge Marcus, Flavius, Demaratus, Sextus, and Cassius into a foreign expedition to Mauretania Tingitana, returning to a land the VII Legion Gemania Hispania Pia has reason to dread. The First Cohort will find itself fighting not only slave raiders and desert marauders, but also a powerful governor and imperial intrigue.

www.ingramcontent.com/pod-product-compliance
Lightning Source LLC
Chambersburg PA
CBHW062107290726
48975CB00001B/139